SALMON COTTAGE

BOOK ONE IN THE KINGDOM SERIES

LEO HOFFORD

PIDGIN PRESS

Pidgin Press Ltd

First Published 2022

ISBN

To
JOSP

ABOUT THE AUTHOR

Writer, gardener, advocate, duck father, padel player, odd job man. Married with three children. Living in the royal Kingdom of Fife.

1

UNFORTUNATE NEWS

Tullis, Fife 1903

I n the gloom of Mr Finnie's emporium, Calum Wilson looked at the red underwear and rolled his eyes. He heard a snigger from the back somewhere, soon followed by another, then a heavy snort from the fat boy by the window.

"Somethin' funny, Joe?" Calum said. He'd seen Joe and Tom when he entered the shop.

"Green eyes?" said Joe. "From recollection anyway. Just wonderin'. Red underwear? I'm debatin' to myself, is that the right combination?"

"Mmm?" He moved towards Joe. "No' sure I care what you're debatin'. Christ!" He gazed at Joe. "You're still just a bag of bones, man?" He poked his shoulder. "Is it the worms again?"

"Calum, come on," said Joe. "Let's no' be rude. I'm just passin' the time of day." He turned to Tom who was never far from Joe's side. He licked his cigarette paper, having rolled the tobacco tighter than he meant. He lit the slim wodge of tobacco that spilled coils from its end. It ignited, growling red as he sucked. Next to him, Tom breathed open-mouthed with a heavy, rasping sound.

"You need to stop blowin' aw that smoke on him," said Calum. "He's no' soundin' that good."

"A bird's been talking in my ear, Calum."

"Was the bird a tit?"

Joe released a light plume of smoke from between his thin lips. It drifted and hung like gauze at the lapels of Calum's jacket.

"That stuff's bad for you."

"It keeps me calm," said Joe. "Controls my anger."

Tom leaned back against the wall and let out a further rasp.

"I've nae time to hear about your problems, Joe. But what's wrong with the pie-eater? He's breathin' like he's gonnie die."

"Had an accident," said Joe. "Made him appreciate the sensation."

"The sensation of what?"

"The sensation of breathin'."

Calum smiled. "Funny you should say that, Joe. Last man to breathe like that was humpin' your mother." The fat boy began to rise. "Now, what is it you're so keen to tell me?" He looked around. "Your mam's name?" Mr Finnie frowned, stepping to one side to study the shine on his black shoes, as if shine could be measured.

"Nothin' much to say really," said Joe. "Just rumours, gossip and stuff, I suppose."

Calum studied the scar over Tom's mouth, across his throat, the two ends joining together like broken wire. Mr

Finnie stood pale as bed sheets on a line. He took a hand-kerchief from his pocket and dabbed his forehead like an act of surrender. He put a finger and thumb on either side of his moustache and smoothed it like a seal's pelt.

"Your wee friend doesnae get any prettier, does he?" He studied Tom. "Personality issues too, would you no' say?"

Calum moved back to the counter. He selected a second pair – green with black lace piping. "Is that all ye got?" He inspected the gusset with an unblinking eye, like a man who knew his hosiery. Mr Finnie showed the palms of his white hands.

Joe felt drawn to the same spot. "Why are you lookin' at that?"

"So easy to forgot you're just a baby, Joe. No' had a girl-friend yet, I'll bet. No' been there, have ye? No' a clue. I can tell by the soft fuzz on yer skinny erse."

"I've had ma fair share," said Joe.

"Male and female interaction, hey? All that stuff." Calum combed thumb and fingers through his steely beard. "A very special business, Joe. I'll tell you aboot it, when yev found yer knob."

There was a moment's silence. "I'm no' thinkin' you need to worry too much about they knickers, Calum."

"Why's that then?"

"I think we all know what special needs Mrs Wilson has just now," said Joe. "They special *physical* needs."

"What?"

"May just be gettin' taken care of."

Calum stepped closer. "What're you on about?" he shouted.

"Mind your anger, as they say." He drew on his cigarette and eased out a cloud between his teeth. Not great teeth, he would admit. His mam never invested much in infant oral hygiene.

"Do elaborate, Joe," he said. "Misunderstandings can get fuckin' awkward." Calum's own teeth were no' that white either.

"I thought you knew what I was on aboot."

"Enlighten me."

"Well, put simply," said Joe. "It's Logan. Sean Logan. Did you no' have an inklin'?"

"*Sean* Logan?" said Calum. "Yer aff yer chump."

"That's what I heard," said Joe.

"And ma wife? Is that what yer sayin'?"

"Indeed."

"Forgive me fer lookin' sae fuckin' skeptical but I do that when I see a fuckin' pig flying' across my vision."

"The thing is Tom here – "

"The fuckin' pie-eater, right? Who cannie breath right? He'd ken skeptical when it shat in his pie."

"Be that as it may, Tom saw it." He looked at Tom. "Straight up, clear fuckin' view." He looked back at Calum. "Erse tae toe. Is that no' right Tom? Fuckin' top and tail and plenty bits in between." Tom blushed and nodded.

"Dinnae be a dope! Logan's still in school!"

"Oh, I wouldnae say that," said Joe. "He's a right big bugger noo."

"Aye," rasped Tom. "Fuckin' strong with it. Well muscled, like!"

"Aye, you're right there Tom. The bits that fuckin' count!"

Calum pulled up the collar on his coat. He realised he was still holding the second pair of panties. Black piping or no', he threw them on the counter, next to the perfume that looked like water oot the crapper. "Nae ma fuckin' size," he said, as he left the store.

2

SALMON COTTAGE (1)

I t was a good number of days later. The sky was full of misery and rain. A relentless downpour stood stubbornly above them as they squatted low beneath the cloak of darkness, behind the old hawthorn hedge that weaved a leafless slice along the edge of a potato field.

No' that heavy kind of rain that peppers you like the jaws off a wave of Loch Tay midgies. This was rain that drowned a man in a billion tiny droplets, soaking every inch as it landed, pounding the earth as it dripped from the canopy of trees around them. It seemed to land and trickle down the back of the neck like one of they bucket showers we used to have outside the back door, where all the energy God can fuckin' muster is twelve inches of gravity. Everything they touched was wet and every leaf and blade of grass only served to make them wetter as they brushed past the foliage towards the house. But, of course, the rain was just the froth at the top of the pot.

Mebbe it was a good plan to wait until now, with darkness to hide their movements. But a good plan wouldn't clog your boots with shite before you've had time to sharpen your pencil. The sky had swelled into a heavy, black sheet and the rain washed through. It was not the easiest thing to know where to put your feet in this field. There were more ruts to get through than a goat in the breeding season.

Tom was thinking they should have taken the roadway up and round to Salmon Cottage. It would have been a sight easier and who was going to see them? This guy, Calum, was a bird brain. If he called him Joe's darling one more time, he would put his fist in somewhere soft. You had to ask, thought Tom, who the fuck was going to hear them either, in all this bloody wind? More chance of catching the minister with a bible on his head, having a wank. Aye, the roadway was the sensible option in this manoeuvre. Instead of which they were creeping up a potato field in a fuckin' blackout with rain in their boots and three inches of shite stuck to their soles. Tom could feel his stomach rumble because he had not eaten since three greasy breakfast sausages. The rain mixed with his spit and dribbled lightly from the corner of his mouth. He could hear Joe not far away, moving more lightly across the mud. He wondered why they were there at all, but he always followed Joe. Then he remembered.

They reached the top of the field. They could just make out the old cattle pen, the long barn and another outbuilding and a coop for the hens. They sensed the sea to their left and heard the occasional, distant wave rumble against the shore. Tom cast his mind back to the last chicken he ate. It felt like sometime in the late sixteenth century. There was an old stable at one end of the barn where any horses might be feeding. Any cows or sheep would be out in the field. All was quiet, just the sound of the fuckin' rain coming down on their heads, the gusting wind through the trees and the small river, the Bombo Burn, flowing higher and faster than usual at the far end of the field.

Calum took the Spencer rifle off his shoulder, pulled down the lever on the underside of the stock and released a new rimfire cartridge into the chamber. He looked at Tom and Joe who had registered the movement, then the sound. They were thinking for the first time that they may be expected to kill a man here. Simultaneously, they took a cap and ball revolver from their pockets and cocked the hammers, their thumbs slippery on the metal. Tom pointed the barrel straight at Calum who pushed his arm away with a combination of irritation and anxiety.

"Fuck's sake," gasped Calum at Tom, rolling his eyes.

"Fuck's sake what?" said Tom.

"Fuck's sake, dinnae point the bloody gun in ma face."

"Leave Tom alone," said Joe. "He's no' used to fuckin' guns."

"Fuckin' am so!" said Tom.

"Aye, alright," said Calum. "Just dinnae fuckin' point the bugger at me."

They climbed the wooden gate, making very little sound, but it was a high one, designed to keep people out. It was awkward to swing your leg over and still hold a cocked gun in your free hand. Beyond the gate, they made their way across the short stretch of stone ground between them and the house, treading as softly as was possible to silence the noise beneath their boots.

Calum followed the length of the building and looked in at the far window, but could see nothing through the drape. Joe felt the water in his boots and cursed the new blister on his heel where the leather had chaffed the skin. Tom breathed heavily against the quiet that engulfed him and his growing fear. The wind whipped at them in the darkness.

Calum went to the nearest window, stood on his toes and peered in. There was a similar drape across the opening but through the crack at the top he could see the back of a woman. Calum allowed himself a smile. She would be the old woman, the one Joe told him about. He knew she lived here with Logan. He reckoned he had no argument with her or the daughter. He remembered how his dad used to shout at women but in the end he was just a shoutey shite and nobody took much notice of him. It was Logan he was after. Mind you, women could be dealt with. That was the way it was. Most of them had a bark louder than their bite.

He peered through the window again. He'd expected Logan too. Had he taken that for granted? Fuck, this rain had washed away his brain. He'd been told that Logan stayed on the farm mostly, so he expected him to be there.

"If he's no' here," said Calum. "We'll no' hang around." He could see the terrified whites of their eyes staring back at him. "Fer fuck's sake. Dinnae shoot anyone unless I tell ye too." The woman would tell him where he was. They'd show her the guns; that would loosen her tongue. The three men went from the window along the mud border, up on the porch to the main door. Joe raised his boot as if he was Jesse James and wished to kick the sheriff's lardy arse. Calum stopped him with a light hand on the front of his shoulder and then gestured. Joe felt the door handle in his wet hand, squeezed the cold metal and turned. The door eased open and they entered Salmon Cottage.

THE REICHER

Lizzie was stirring a pot of stew. On the antique side of fresh and it did not look exactly like a stew. She was at the kitchen, to one side of the oak-beamed room in which the three men were now standing. Calum glanced at the petulant flicker of the fire, smoking through a pile of wet coal or peat, spitting and cracking, spewing puffs of black smoke against the steel grate. Yet the room was warm and in a way it was welcoming. Calum thought he could smell cooking. Wasn't that the smell? The happy smell he thought he deserved. He thought it was a stew but this rain had drowned his brain and upset his sense of smell. His eyes took in the whole room. There was no sign of Logan. He put his muddied finger to his lips or what seemed the likely repository of his lips, since all three had heavy wet hats on their heads and damp, cotton bags over their faces.

Tom glanced nervously around the room and saw little but walls and a clean floor. He breathed heavily against the cotton. He did not like this cloth over his face; it constricted his breathing and didn't feel natural. He wanted to eat the food in that pot over there. He wanted to scratch the scar on his chin that had a habit of itching when he got nervous. And he was nervous alright. He was the closest he'd come to shitting his pants since he ate that mutton chop against his mum's advice three weeks ago. In any event, this whiskered worm, Calum, was paying for the pleasure. But was he paying enough? He said they would kill whoever was here and he seemed like he meant it. His chin was giving him real gip now. He fancied a cheese sandwich and a glass of beer. He wondered why you had to waste time fuckin' about here getting a red face under the disguise.

The three of them moved quietly towards the hub of the kitchen where Lizzie was stirring the stew - or was it soup? She then stepped over to the sink to scrape burnt jam off a pan with a small knife. She was humming a tune, out of tune.

Joe was a man created by God with a pointed nose, and it angled its way through the material over his face, emerging on the surface like a round spot. Come to think of it, everything about Joe was pointed or lined or edged. He could have been okay looking in some sense but everything about him was creased into grey lines and folds. The only soft part of him at this juncture, was his nose as it emerged through the mask, dressing up as a soft boil.

Calum was not looking at Tom, but moved on ahead and looked towards the woman; he was satisfied that she was alone and had not been alerted of their approach. He signaled to Joe with his finger, first pointing at him and then jabbing towards the woman. Joe swallowed as if he had a hard pea the size of a wagon wheel caught in his dry throat. He stepped very slowly forward but had taken only a few ginger steps when he heard the squelch of water in his boots. Lizzie heard it too, for she spun around, immediately holding the knife out in front of her. She was no' humming any more and her eyes were wide as a full moon. She edged around the table, taking small steps backwards towards the far wall. She said nothing, but waved the knife about in a hypnotic, circular motion. Maybe she would have them all in a trance and eating onions. The men came fully into the room and stood pointing their guns at her. Calum lowered his rifle so that it was aimed at her feet. He raised the palm of his hand.

He coughed politely. "Where is he?" he said, his voice reassuringly calm and low. She failed to respond to Calum's enquiry and he repeated the question a little louder, as if presbycusis was an occupational risk. She stared back at them, the knife still raised and Calum stepped towards her. "Look. We're no' here to hurt ye."

"What do ye want?"

"To speak to Sean." Lizzie said nothing, but her arm shook as she held the knife steady.

"What aboot?"

"That's no' something for you to worry about," said Calum. "Just need to know where I can find him."

"He's no' here," she said.

"I'm no' sure I'm believin' ye."

"I dinnae ken where he is."

"Come on. I've no' come up here for that."

"I dinnae ken where he's gone."

"So you say," said Calum.

"I dinnae ken you either."

"That'll be the disguise," he said.

"I'll tell you again, he's no' here. He's gone on a trip."

"Where?" She was slow to answer. "Come on now," he said. "You want me to beat it out of ye?"

"I dinnae think ye want to do that," said a voice. "Wrang decision."

The voice came from behind them and all three turned to look. "Whoa!" They stopped their uniform movement in its tracks. "Dinnae turn aroond. No' unless you want a bullet in each of your stupid heids." A small woman had emerged from the doorway opening onto the pantry to one side of the kitchen. In two hands, she was holding a magnificent four-barrelled Reicher gun made in Munich at a place called Uterhaching.

4

A PRIVATE MATTER

I'd fuckin' tellt her before I left that the Reicher was a gun fit for a comedian. I told her to take me seriously and not waste her crochet time on such an old Bavarian circus trick as this. Yes, of course, you could fire it just once and release all four barrels simultaneously. Dandy, I said. If you were very accurate you might kill four people. On the other hand, if you had nae luck or skill at such things you'd kill naebody other than yourself. At the very least you might give yerself a nasty bruise on the bridge of your nose, from the recoil most like, and probably break a finger on the trigger guard into the bargain. You might even have the barrel insignia printed on your forehead for the rest of your natural life. Or it might blow up in your face, invert your two front teeth and burn the skin off your nasal cavity. If that's what yer after, I said, then be my guest and amuse yourself till all the breath has left your body.

"It's no' a real gun!" I said to her. Several times. "Amusement value only," I repeated. "Highly original for those wi' a sense of humour and aboot as good at self-preservation as a needle in yer eyeball." I implored her to take the Webley instead. Smaller, more effective, so much easier to handle. Quite the pretty thing, the Webley, and quite deadly if the idea was a little quiet sport of the breath-stopping kind. I told her she could fire the Webley with just the one hand and darn socks with the other and even then she might hit the bloody target.

"Enough of the profanities," she said. "I'm no' plannin' to use it at all," she said. "I'm seein' it as very much a position of last resort."

"Gettin' dead is the last resort," I said. "But the Webley, come on, you can keep that up your bloody sleeve."

"Naw," she said. "I'll take ma chances with this beastie." She picked up the Reicher, looking for the trigger like it was a buried coconut in the Kalahari Desert. "This will do fine," she said, when she had her finger on the metal guard.

Now, as she stood there, holding the Reicher into her shoulder, its four barrels aimed at the trio human target, it did cross her mind that the Webley might have been an easier proposition. Still, she put the thought out of her head. "Now, I dinnae pretend to be Johny Crackshot here but I'm willin' to bet all the gold in your back teeth that from here, in this small room with this gun of German design and Austrian manufacture, or so I'm reliably told, I'm willing to bet I can sink a bullet into at least one of your thick heads, if I have to." She paused. "If you're thinkin' you've got faster legs than I've got bullets, go right ahead. Make a dash for the door an' I'll do ma level best to blow yer heid into the fireplace." Nobody leaked so much as an ounce of breath or a sideburn hair in her direction. "Good," she said. "Now, I've also to observe the legal nicety that yous are in ma hoose and I dinnae recall invitin' you."

"We dinnae mean you any harm, Mrs," said Calum.

"What d'ya mean? Did you no' hear me? You're in ma hoose."

"We're lookin' for somebody."

"Is that right? Well, yev found someone an' all."

"Dinnae make things worse," he said. "I was explaining to the girl..."

"Explain to me then. And before you do that, mebbe start by droppin' the guns on the floor." Not one of them moved. "Take yer time," she said. "But make it this century, hey?" She paused. "Come on, now. Do this right nice, and careful as you go because we don't want any misunderstandings, do we? We're no' wantin' people getting shot and dyin' in the streets, then complainin' about it later. You with the whiskers can start off," she said.

Calum lowered his gun. "How do you ken I've got whiskers?"

"I can see them," she said. "I've got the power of bleedin' vision. Pokin' oot the side of that bag on your heid, like big weeds roond a thistle." He hesitated and then, bending his knees, he dropped the Spencer rifle to the floor and it made a clatter as it landed. Joe and Tom took their cue, leaned down and put their revolvers on the floor in front of their feet.

"Now then," she said. "This is doin' my nerves no good at all." She looked at Calum. "I'm no' expectin' three beauty specimens, but I want to see yer faces noo." She shifted slightly and moved her legs an inch or two further apart, as if she were securing her position to fire the Reicher by pushing the soles of her feet into soft mud. "Now, let's take aff oor hats, shall we? Nae need to be formal just because there are ladies present. It's no' bloody Sunday either. And let's do the face bags tae."

The three men raised their wet hats and dropped them

on the table. Tom and Joe pulled off their face bags. The tip of Joe's nose was contoured by the hole in the bag. A second or two later, Calum followed and removed his. "Ah-ha," she said. "So now we ken who is who. As if we didnae ken already."

"I didnae come here to cause you any bother," said Calum.

"That's no' my impression."

"My business is with Sean."

"What's yer business with Sean?"

"We've a score to settle. A private matter and no' one to be shared with you," he said. Marion moved her finger on the trigger. "I've a notion to kill him," said Calum. "But if I cannae kill him I'm happy to break his legs and leave it at that."

"Well, it may have been a private matter. It's no' a private matter any mair," Marion said. "You just entered ma hoose, wavin' guns aboot. This is not civilized behaviour where I com frae. A long bloody way from actin' polite." She did not take her eyes off him. "What is it that Sean's done that makes you think yer entitled to barge in here an' break his legs?"

He breathed in and exhaled. "I may as well tell you then," he said. "Irrespective of what you decide to do with that daft piece you're holdin'." He frowned. "The problem for young Sean is that he took up with ma wife." He turned his head fully towards her. "There's a price you pay when you do such things. Every man knows that."

"I see," she said. "A man tips his cap at Mrs Wilson and you go after him with guns and hired help from the deadly duo?"

"It wisnae caps that were bein' tipped," he said.

"Even so," said Marion.

"He has to pay for the dishonour."

"Why do you no' speak to her aboot it?"

"I already did," he said. "She noo understands ma point of view."

"In that case, what're ye doin' here, frightenin' the hell out of me and ma daughter?"

"He insulted her. Me an' all. Ma wife has learnt her lesson. Sean needs a lesson tae."

"Oh aye. And that's where you start breakin' pins an' shootin' folk?"

"The etiquette has to be followed. He needs to learn to respect the property of others."

"It'll no' do him much good if he's deid."

"He shouldnae have disrespected."

"I should shoot you noo," she said. "Dare say that would get your respect?"

"With that?" he said, indicating the Reicher. "It'll probably blow your ain head aff yer shoulders before any bullet comes near mine."

She held the gun more firmly and bit her lip. "Gamble if you like," she said. "Be my guest: take a risk noo." He stood there looking down the four barrels of the Reicher. He considered that the woman was mad enough to fire that thing. "Or you could leave whilst yer still alive, an think yersels bloody lucky I've got ma saints' cap an' cassock on the day." He looked at her, thought the better of it, then reached carefully over to the table and picked up his hat. He placed it firmly on his head. "Sensible decision," she said. "An' take the terrible twins with ye."

"I need that gun," said Joe.

Marion hesitated. "Lizzie, tak oot the bullets."

Lizzie leaned under the table, took each gun in turn and emptied the chamber, pocketing the contents. She walked round the table and picked Calum's rifle off the floor and emptied the bullets. Marion waved the Reicher at Joe and Tom. "Get oot!" Calum took his rifle from Lizzie and walked to the door. He gave her a final look. "Tell your nephew I wis sorry to have missed him." He opened the door. "I'll make sure to check he's hame next time." He moved half out the door. "Look here, mrs. He insulted me. That always pisses me aff. Tell him that frae me." He touched his whiskers. "We're both civilized, we know that that's just no' right. We have to behave like human beings, would you no' agree?" He smiled at her. Her hand tightened on the breech. He slipped through the door and was gone. The other two scuttled sideways, like crabs on a changing tide, facing into the room, following quickly behind and out the open door.

When Marion looked out of the window, she saw the shapes of the three men already melt together in the wet, dreary darkness towards the lane, beyond the gate. She slammed the door shut hard and slid the metal bolt, top and bottom. She looked at Lizzie and Lizzie looked back at her. "Christ," she said. "I fergot the bleedin' bullets fer this thing."

"Jesus," said Lizzie. "I'd rather you hadnae told me that."

5

SEAN'S RETURN

The royal kingdom of Fife. Three sides water and shaped like the head and shoulders of a Highland Terrier with the Isle of May puffed out like the dug was chasing a fleck of silver spit. Fife, where the smell of wet, brown forest soil hangs in the air, testifying to its love affair with farming and what comes off the earth. Connected by land and sea, by fish and fowl, one can look on any map and see the tick-like villages along its neck – Methil, Buckhaven, Wemyss. Beneath the snout, snug below the windpipe, you might find Dysart, a place of no interest beyond the pleasure of leaving it, but take the road north as I myself had done, step out of Fife in all its rolling, earthy, stony beauty, and you will fall upon Montrose, nestled on the eastern seaboard. Further west by the old roman road and you reach Buckstone, a place that had featured in my more recent activities and about which I will no doubt tell you a painful amount more.

So much for the fuckin' geography. Time to reveal myself. I'm the Sean Logan that the erse with the bushy beard is set upon expunging from these rolling hills. Round about the same time, I was riding home in a dead man's cart, dried blood under my nails and the stink of whale oil on my coat. On this occasion, as I departed south, I had no cause to meditate on the feathery delights of the Montrose wading bird, hosteled in its mud lagoon. I was headed for Tullis, my village, nestling some way across the River Tay, still a good distance to the south, deep in the eastern heart of Fife. Even this far north, spring was approaching early with strong flecks of pink and white blossom on the trees and the green growth was marking out space in the hedgerows.

As I drove the cart towards Tullis my tongue was dry and the events of the night weighed heavily upon me. I was bruised, battered, ribs had been mebbe cracked and broken and I smelled of smoke and a substance drawn from the head of a sperm whale. What I had considered important, those lifetime stooges, what I had always thought required to be addressed, had been confronted. Yet, here I was, in its aftermath, broken and sore and I had to confess, feeling only a little better for it. Would all that come later? That was what I was wondering. Where was the happy glow that should follow all that retribution? The heat had gone out of me and there was little left but coldness within and a slow, dancing breeze that whispered like a prickly reminder across my skin. I was the avenger, the Archangel Gabriel in a fuckin' tammie and showing a lot of attitude. I had worked the list of guilty candidates and completed my task. Yet, where was the pleasure that morning from all the carnage I had caused?

When I arrived at Salmon Cottage that day, I could perhaps be forgiven for an abject failure to keep my gun beside me. Of course, I knew where my rifle actually *was*. It was neatly holstered, hanging to the right hand side of the saddle on my horse, Master Henry. In normal circumstances, being a young man of considerable fitness and agility, I could access my rifle pretty quickly. There was a knack to it and it was a skill I had perfected. I could have my Enfield out of the saddle and in my hand, firing at a chosen target, in less time than it took a man to blow the snot from his nose. But, sadly, today was *snot* the day. My rifle hung from my saddle like church bells strung beyond my reach.

Earlier that morning, when I reached Tullis after a long ride, the sun was up but had given way to a grey and over-bearing sky. I had brought the cart down between the ash trees, brushing shoulders against the early buds of small spear-shaped leaves with their toothy edges. I chose not to look to my right, that gap in the trees and the broken stones that marked the track. I knew full well what lay up there. My memory was good of an old path that framed the border of a grazing field and on it went to the place that was hers. The thought of her up there gave me warmth in the coolness of the morning. I longed for her now right enough. I longed to stop and take the golden path but I missed the chance and the cart kept rolling forward. Her green eyes came to mind like they were there to torment me. She had said that from the house you could see the Logan farm or at the very least you might spot the fire smoke. It was Salmon Cottage she was speaking of. She said that if the air was damp you could taste the peat on the tip of your tongue, you could smell it when you breathed.

Sometimes, with all the tree growth, it was hard to see the smoke going anywhere. It was not so easy to see beyond your own fields, filled with grass, a smattering of crops, potato shoots, banks of trees and scattered weeds. I certainly had no memory of being able to see Tullis from her house, let alone having sight of the Logan farm. However, memory is an unreliable friend and I dare say I had my mind on the

smell of her skin more than on what trace of Logan smoke
still lingered in the air. Memory is the witness in a blindfold.
If I shoot a man, do I ever remember the terror in his eyes?
A horrible thought you might say, but think about it. Is my
memory not coloured by the circumstances in which I shot
him? It won't be his death I remember, surely? It will be my
memory of his death that I may have inadequately remembered. The truth may be obvious but it's never more than
one man's version of the same story. I'd never swear by it,
that's for sure.

Having emerged from the trees, the track became wider
as I manoeuvred the cart along the edge of the village. My
horse, the grand old Master Henry, was tied to the back
fender; a striking, characterful, chestnut, and yet he seemed
reluctant, hesitant, perhaps tired by the journey, wishing it
was over. We entered the main street of Tullis. I took in its
understated buildings, houses mainly, some wood, some
stone and earth, some held up with cow shit or hen goo.
Three homes on the one side and four on the other, some
more dead boxes parked just behind, some thatched and
mossed over, damp on the outside walls and no doubt
running water on the inside. The road through Tullis ran on
to the east across a square and more houses. The square
may have been a small common green, but it was early in
the day and nobody stood on it now. We rode on towards
that patch of green, more brown than green, more circle
than square, feeling the regular, stiffening breeze blow
across the rough path to the side, as it did most months of
the year. I knew, without looking, where the old church was
hidden, almost overwhelmed by the success of its cemetery,
but I doubted that too much had changed there in the short
time I'd been away. Mr Finnie's post office store was three
hundred yards further along; nothin' much good ever went

in there. The church had a heavy door and a tower to one side, like a large, upward pointing finger. The rusted, metal bell and the chipped, stone cross were obvious clues that this was God's home, the bodies stacked like plates to one side of the door and underground. There had always been a gold-painted fish on the roof. St Peter's fish? I don't know and I'm no' that bothered. There was a shop or two with the occasional swinging sign that offered supplies and services: *Cobblers* and *Victuals*. Mr Fawcett's hardware shop was tucked in along at the end. I'd have news for him. Mr Hamilton's house too, the big one behind, boasting a clutch of oil paintings of all God's animals and a small cellar of drinking wine.

There were people about now. A head with wet hair shining, the smell of damp cloth, three Belted Galloway cows herded along the street by a youth who looked at me like I was dressed back to front. The rough road stretching on, past a grey-skinned house and other sober homes and rusted sheds, leading to a fork in the road: the left took you to the sea where I knew from bitter experience that the water was sincerely as cold as the brow of my dead mother. To the right, you were on the road to Cupar, then Stirling and the stairway to the Trossachs. The better roads, with their raised spines, ready to drain off the early spots of rain, undulating like skins of coiled rope, trailing down to the boats that ferried passengers across the Firth.

I pushed on through the village, turned to the left and followed the track that would take me to Salmon Cottage, the repository of the Logan family fortune. I had no idea what I would find there. This side of Tullis you could almost smell the sea air and you could hear the yap of the gulls as they pivoted overhead. The narrower path out to the farm was bordered on each side by a brown and green hawthorn hedge, occasional rocks of varying size creating a wall and the odd rowan tree lazing its trunk, snakelike against the stone. I stopped the cart and touched the moss-topped wall. The old woman by my side stared at my hand vacantly; she had spoken no more words than the stone beneath my fingers. I could see the chipped pieces along the floor of the track, and I remembered all too well the sweat I put into laying that surface. I felt like spitting on it, but maintained my good manners, resisted the desire. The sky looked less threatening now, a lighter, whiter sheet, broken by the occasional tease of blue sky. There was a growing suggestion, in case anyone missed it, that we should not lose heart, that we could slap the cord of our tawny breeks, for spring was really fuckin' comin', make no mistake.

As I turned the last bend, I raised my head and took in the view. I picked out the old farm, Salmon Cottage, that housed all my broken memories. A part of me wondered if I would find it burnt to the ground, but that was me buffing a gloomy sheen to my character, the cup always dry, never close to full even when it was brimming over. I twisted round on the hard bench and I could see that the gate off the field that led to the cattle pen lay wide open, yawning its muddy lip towards the descending hills and the distant volcanic island of Inchkeith. I cast my eyes to the south, the old view, the sweep of my childhood. I could see the rough path cut through the side of a pasture field, its borders pitted with earth scoops, the work of moles or brown hares. Beyond the track, across the grey canopy of treetops, I could sense the water's edge and I could see the Firth, its shores jagged with rocky spurs, then a yellow sand, blown in a dust and a heap towards the piling dunes. I could see the golden green of the marram grass, stringy and dry, its roots in creeping, bindweed tourniquets, above which broad, aquamarine straws rose like knives and slumped. Stiff, sycamore, leafless saplings spiked the surface and there were patches of yellow-flowering, poisonous ragwort, tucked along the lower edges.

I smiled at the thought, but there was not much to laugh at. I remembered a boy pressing on down to swim in the sea one day in May, the blue-brown water, the tide spuming up the beach as high as late spring would allow, the wave tops spitting spray beneath the rising wind. To one side lay the Bombo Burn, a stream of water relentlessly whispering, meandering in small swirls and slurps along a tight ditch, edges forever crumbling, down by the hawthorn hedge, the polka dot, red, bird-berries alive in summer, and another light path cut with horses' hooves through the crust of winters gone and cattle tracks too, leading again to the shore.

This was Fife and everything led to and from the water. Carving east, it flowed by the length of the pitted, stone, wall with its round, black coping and broken filling. I had mended that fuckin' wall. More than once. More back-breaking work, it was a wonder I could walk. I looked on past the closed, wooden gate where the plough and other farmyard tackle would always lean rust-bound against the whinstone gable. Going beyond, the green field with its anonymous sheep's wool tagged on the wooden fence and tacked again by the prickly thistles.

I turned again to look over at Salmon Cottage. I dismounted from the cart, stepped forward several paces and attempted to throw up the metal latch. The latch was stiff and unyielding, its surface pitted by time and weather. With two hands and some persuasion it shifted and I was then able to open the wooden gate onto the yard. I remembered now those old roof joists that made the gate, how I cut them up, sized and treated them, then fitted the pieces together, to create a gate that had swung open without a squeak or a squeal, without anything to remind me of the day my mother died. I thought I heard some hens from round the side of the house. I looked up at the rusted iron fish on the roof gable, still twisting in the breeze like it had been hooked but was fucked if it was throwing in the towel.

Aunt Marion and Lizzie appeared on the doorstep, waving their arms at me, Lizzie stepping out from the shadows, just two paces ahead of her mother. I waved back. Suddenly they stopped in their tracks and at that exact point I heard that sharp click. You kind of know what it is when you hear it. It was a noise I'd heard before; a sound like a heavy key turning in a stiff lock. There were two further clicks, neither of which lessened my concern. Three clicks was making it all too fuckin' obvious. It could only mean that I had three guns pointed at my head. I knew that the rifle hanging off Master Henry's saddle may as well have been on a tea plantation in China for all the good it would do me. I, Sean Logan, dedicated avenger for all that was rotten in my world, was rooted to the earth like a biblical tree, hard by the gate to my yard, six to eight feet from my grand old horse, Master Henry, closer then to my certain death than I had ever been.

6

HORATIO'S RETURN

23 Years Earlier

I t was barely autumn, round about 1880, when my father, Horatio Logan, had begun his long walk home after the second Afghan war was over. He followed a route that took in northern Iran, Turkey and Bulgaria, before entering Romania, passing through the Slovak Republic and a plethora of other principalities. Then, on into Germany. It was more than a stroll to the shops to fetch a ham, but when all is said and done, don't we all come back to where we started out from? It was the close of the Afghan war and he was none too sure if they'd won or lost or squeaked a draw. He only knew that he'd had plenty - and plenty was enough.

It was the tribal chiefs and warlords who looked to have taken most of the spoils. It was no' the first time in human history that we'd been made to look like meat filling at a vegetarian picnic. He'd been an infantryman, part of the

British force under Major General Roberts in the attack on Ayub Khan. He swung his sword and discharged his powder with worthy virtuosity, killing some who strayed too close and injuring some who didn't, particularly at Kandahar where the Ayub Khan had finally been put back in his box.

My father was not apparently inclined to reminisce over all that useless blood. Not for him, lists of well-deserved vengeance or hits to settle scores. He'd seen death amongst those he knew. He'd drunk spirits with those who never saw the bottom of their cups. War had a rotten stink about it. Aunt Marion said he told her that the sight of a leg cut from a body left him pretty unmoved but the smell of it - that was a different matter. Not just the smell of death or infection; not just the rations that grew woolly with mould. It was the place itself, the warm fug, the dust, the dry wind, the decay of people in an alien environment.

He survived with his life still his own. He had avoided capture. Not everyone was so lucky; some he knew within his own regiment had been taken and expeditiously killed. Some had been mutilated - before and after death. He knew what the Afghans could do if the opportunity presented. Witness the bad dreams that left him drenched. Dreams about prisoners staked to the ground, a plug in his mouth to gag the swallow, and the Pathan women squatted above, peeing until the poor sod drowned in urine.

Horatio started home with thick, leather soles on his military boots, comfortable at the toes with snug heels. Open top sandals were not a sensible option. Proper calfskin boots had always been important to him: in war, you had to look after your feet. Without your feet you're going nowhere. He was not totally destitute. He had semi-precious stones in his pocket – a small quantity of amber, a green garnet tsavorite, two pink stones, a colourless goshenite and a lump of aquamarine. In Glasgow they would have called him a gem dealer. He also had some rough gold that he kept wrapped in a soft, pigskin bladder sewn into his inside pocket. He had a knife in his shirt, sheathed in embroidered leather against his chest. Armed with good boots, a knife and various minerals, with breath in his body and blood in his veins, he had all he needed for a quiet ramble through Western Asia.

Of course, the Afghan war never did properly conclude. Nobody said, right boys, grab your bivvies, first ship to Glasgow if you please; and step on that tailwind! The war surged like the rising tide and then seeped away again; forward and back through the years, before and after, like a horse endlessly spooked by its own shadow. They're probably still pullin' faces at each other now. He drank an extra cup of the local tea that morning, then headed up the goat paths that trailed across the hills to the west, steered himself into Iran and began the journey home.

In Mashhad he was bitten on the penis by a tik-tik fly. Penis is close enough, but it was believed to be a hairless patch on the underside of the gonad, or so Aunt Marion said. There was an understandably *brief* entry in his journal about it. Everyone knows, there are twenty-three species of tik-tik fly, each one of them recognised as fucking useless. Respect for the bee, the slug, the wood louse and the butterfly – I'll give you that in bucket loads by a handpicked, horse-driven cart. But the tik-tik fly? I sense the urge to pee all over it. Which is probably what my father was doing when it bit him. I read somewhere in Mr Shifner's school library that they kill up to three hundred thousand people worldwide every year. Serious numbers but precision is hard to come by. In fact, it may be more. I might say that was just the *tik* of the iceberg. I will, however, add that for a bug with a twenty-one day life cycle its kill-rate makes Ghengis Khan look like a pansy flower in a hairpiece.

Tik-tik flies do not normally leave the Kalahari desert, so it was no doubt something of a surprise for my father, Horatio Logan, to find one attached to the underside of his gonad in this part of Iran. Consequently, he lay in a Pashtun woman's hut, on a camp bed made of green tree and thick, dry leaves. He fully expected to die and maybe she thought she might inherit the pigskin bladder full of gold, not to mention those other gems he kept in the leather pouch. Sadly for her, the brown paste she spooned down his neck did not kill him and nor did the tik-tik fly.

My father hallucinated for more than a week. He thought that he was going to make use of that hole she had already dug for him. He knew he was sick and in his more lucid moments he realised seeing Fife or Salmon Cottage ever again was dissipating like the haar that pushed in from the sea and laid a shroud across that distant place. Yet, he turned the corner on the twelfth day and thereafter commenced a slow recovery. He still looked a lot like a bag of skin on a clothes hanger. He gave the old Pashtun lady half of what was in his leather pouch and, to his surprise, she waved her hands at him as if she had no need for his minerals. She was probably quietly annoyed by the success of her medical care. He took no notice and gave her half the gold as well. He had some more tea, spooning the dregs into his mouth, gathered up his things and headed out into the bright, unyielding light of northern Iran for the first time in seventeen days.

For reasons unknown to me and unexplained in his journal, my father Horatio took a diversion through a latrine in the ground known as Romania – a country of two principalities that had only properly existed for twenty years. The streets were dangerous and full of heavily-armed soldiers from the Turkish-Russian war, bands of thugs who were free with the use of their guns, fueled by white spirit, not unlike vodka.

It was in Romania that he came upon Tatiana, a woman with tanned skin, black hair, heavy jewellery, braids, in her mid to late twenties. The details are sketchy. The story of their love match sets him in a good light, but he wrote it down himself, so stock up on the salt before we start. He heard shouts coming from a house on the outskirts of a small town. I cannae tell you its exact name. I once tried to find it on a map, but there were many possibilities and most ended in *asov* or *ara*, so they all sounded feasible enough. My father's curiosity led him to investigate the noise to see what was happening. Not a good move. But then again, had he kept walking I would have no tale to tell and the world would have been a quieter place without my interventions. I may have been someone else, ignorant of what else might have been and none of what happened would have happened. Other things might have happened instead. These are the tricks life plays on us.

When he approached the house he came upon two men holding this woman by the arms; she was extremely agitated by her predicament, struggling to escape. Some of her clothing was torn - or so I imagine, without being prurient or salacious. There was pushing and shoving and she was doing all she could to shake herself free. The hard men with the guns wore Romanian army uniforms that were filthy and stained with grease or maybe it was fire ash or tar. You never knew what hole these guys came out from. Was it gun oil she could smell off the back of one man's tunic? A third man in a Russian army coat shouted at the woman in a language Horatio could not follow. He was not inviting her home to meet the parents. He hurled his hand against her face. There was an old man cowering by the wall, clutching an old woman in black clothing. In vain, they sought to silence the screams through the cloth they held to their mouths.

My father yelled at them to take their hands away, like he was policing a spat outside a pub in the east end of Glasgow. "Step away, young man! Desist from these unmanly practices!" In the circumstances, it seems a modest, reasonable request – but totally absurd. They turned their heads towards him as if he were mad or had grown wings oot his nose. The two men holding the woman threw her to the ground and swore. Then they stood up straight and swore at him. Two of them reached for the swords that hung from their waists. Beheading was popular in Romania but it's never really caught on in Fife. At the same moment, the Russian officer pulled a pistol from the leather holster on his hip. All this happened in less time than it takes a tik-tik fly to bite a man's penis, but already Horatio had raised his Snider-Enfield and fired off three quick shots. Each of the men fell to the ground and within approximately seven and a half seconds not one of them was still breathing. They were dead as the brick in my front wall, each with a blink of red drilled through the forehead.

It was a strange and impetuous thing to fix upon this woman and put his life at risk, all for someone he did not know. Yet, instinct had come to play an important role in his life. Instinct had drawn him into Romania, this broken principality, to this remote, lawless village, far from the capital. Instinct had drawn him to this half-derelict house where the young woman was the subject of this assault. My father lived by what his guts told him and what felt right and proper. Even the day he started walking home had been a day driven by instinct – why else would a man embark on such a journey across Afghanistan and Iran without even taking leave of the commanding officer? He followed his guts and shot these men and that was all there was to it. And it had been fine shooting too and, for God's sake, let's just remember the slaughter was not entirely undeserved.

Yet the woman, it seemed, was driven by instinct too. She followed him out of Romania, deciding with very little deliberation that she would leave everything she had behind her, including the impotent old man with thin lips and white stubble on his chin and the sobbing mother who'd now removed the cloth from the moustache around her mouth. Whatever instinct told her, she said farewell to the old folk and followed Horatio away from the town, bobbing along behind him, layered by skins of clothing to keep off the day's heat and the night's cold.

Over the days that followed, he grew to know Tatiana better and he surprised himself: he would look back to see whether she was still there and if he could see her, it lifted him. Small details at first, larger ones became apparent later. He scrutinised the deep pockets of her eyes, ringed in black charcoal as they were, and perhaps he would know they'd seen too much. The eyes almost spoke, something that was accentuated by the way she hid the rest of her face and concealed her hair. She wore a silver-threaded shawl across her head. You could be fooled into thinking she was a religious type, although Horatio doubted that. He never saw her pray. He never saw her on her knees at all. This was modern Romania after all. Up close you could smell her perfume that, by all accounts, was marginally overpowering. My father liked the perfume, he had no issue with that.

They spoke little or much on the journey, I don't know, but she attached herself to him and gradually got herself directly into his company. What do you think? Probably started boiling water for his tea, then moved on to cooking small plates of food and other domestic duties. I've not got a clue, but over time they grew closer, exchanged occasional words or expressions or a movement of the hand to indicate he was no' too disgruntled with her presence there. Mebbe shared some of their experiences, no' all at once but growing in boldness. They spoke in broken English, I imagine; or bad French and tortured Spanish, but they used the movement of hands and expression to signal to each other when their linguistic talents fell short. Without the need for deep discussion, mebbe she understood him. She understood too what war could do to you.

When the walk was finally over, having carved a route up as far as Tilbury, along the Thames estuary, they took a boat up the east coast to Scotland, landing at Leith, just north of Edinburgh and then, oddly, endured the worst, most turbulent part of the voyage: a short ferry ride through an easterly storm, over the water to Burntisland in Fife. It was cold when they arrived, a long way from the heat, dust and flies of Afghanistan. The hedgerows still carried the stubborn snow that would not melt. They took a horse trap to Tullis to complete a journey that had taken four months and nineteen days.

7

MASTER HAM

Tatiana became Horatio's wife. Plainly it was a role that was unfamiliar to her: she cut an enigmatic figure around Salmon Cottage. She was from a different culture and she had those unusual alien character-istics that had a knack for ruffling local feathers. My Aunt Marion said Tatiana had a habit of clicking her fingers when she wished to make a point. She wiped her nose with the open palm of her hand. She put her fork to the right of the plate and held it in a grip as if she might stab your face and drag it through the gravy. She ate all types of nuts. She would sell her soul for a hazelnut. She threw salt *across* her shoulder rather than *over* her shoulder. She wore a plain, glass bead on her ankle. She coloured her hair, its long, shiny coils betraying some trace of henna. She spoke very little but what she said was crucified by her Romanian accent. She was an orthodox Christian. She recognized the resurrection of Jesus. She had a blue crucifix tattooed on her shoulder. She understood my father and she could read his thoughts before he opened his mouth. He was in love with her but there was not much that the people of Tullis could ever find to like. Even her name excited animosity. She never understood why they did not like her.

"They dinnae ken you," said my father.

"Yes?"

"But they fear you." She made a face at him. "That's different. When you do that with yer eyebrow. Very, very frightenin'."

My grandfather lived with them. His wife, my grandmother, was dead now from tuberculosis - a slow death of blood-tinged sputum, night sweats and plummeting weight loss. My grandfather had a square head that was more or less toothless, had warts on his yellowed fingers and a long, hooked nose that protruded from a position too close to his eyes. To my grandfather's credit, even at his advanced age he clung to a good head of dull, grey hair. He made the most of this asset, for I am told he caked the thatch in duck fat and carried a pocket comb for dragging lines through its syrupy surface. A small man, he was kept in a lumpy bed recess just under five feet long, positioned at one end of the kitchen. When he became noisy or unruly, a heavy curtain could be drawn across him. Words came to him readily and audibly, even from behind a drape. He had a mouth shaped like a dark slit and when he spoke it reminded of a window snapping open and shut. He did not shave his beard more than once per week. He too was suspicious of his son's Romanian wife and he rarely spoke directly to her. When he did speak to her she stood puzzled and uncomprehending – her accent and his dentistry thwarted conversation. The three of them rubbed along together but Tatiana and my grandfather shared little love for each other.

Well, I've wasted a lot of time telling you about my grandfather. Some people don't amount to much – and he excelled in that department. He expired on the back of a pickle and ham lunch less than a year after Horatio and Tatiana returned from the Afghan war. Pickle and ham and compromised dentures can be cataclysmic to an octogenarian. He choked to death when he failed to cut the sandwich pickle to a readily edible size. Tatiana knew she was not to blame, even if she had provided the pickle and ham and had hidden the knife.

After his death, Horatio and Tatiana lived a quiet existence for the most part, the two of them together and largely inseparable. They worked hard on the farm – there's always a lot to do, as I know all too well. Busy with cattle, sheep, hens, potatoes, spinach, and asparagus; not to mention scabby mouth and cheesy gland and all the rest of the country shite that makes up farming. In general, the two of them stayed away from the village and as time went by any desire for social contact diminished. They became like islands in their own river.

With hindsight, it may be understood that the cruel events that followed were fuelled by precisely that lack of interaction between them and the villagers. Of course, people can try to be islands but not many succeed. I said that to Aunt Marion once.

"Some people say we're all individuals, and we're aw entitled to act in any way that accords with our principles."

"Baloney," said Aunt Marion. "Swim against the tide and you run a fat chance of drownin'."

"Can people no' choose how they live their lives?"

"People withdraw, fine. They pull away and button their tongues, but what's the rest of folk to make o' it?"

"Nothing to do with them," I said.

"They tak it personally. It's an insult!"

"I can't see that."

"And a sight more provocative than a few loose words."

"If they're wantin' to go aboot their business, keep themselves to themselves, come on, tell me why no'?"

"Cos people want to know whit's goin' on. They want to ken what they're doin' buried away up there."

What the hell, that was the route they chose. Their treasured isolation encouraged stories, rumours and fanciful nonsense. They were bowing before Cailleach, a one-eyed witch with bad teeth and foot-rot. Next moment they were dancin' jigs by a smoky fire behind the house. They got foreign diseases, some people said. And they've invented a few of their own, I shouldnae wonder. No doubt, put them into their blood and brown eggs for the breakfast.

"Ate rice for the carbohydrate and sheep testicles for the protein." That's what Aunt Marion reported. "And ate gobby berries from the wood. Even put ragwort poison in the trees to kill the birds." Dead Sanderling were said to have been hung from the wooden fence that abutted the track at Salmon Cottage, swinging in the breeze, a string of beaky corpses.

"What did she look like?" I asked Aunt Marion once.

"She was a great beauty. She had dark, flashin' eyes. Her pupils were black as coal and wide as tunnels. She wore a purple shawl."

"That's where I get ma good looks from?"

"Others called her an evil, tea-faced, witch, so take your pick."

Men from the village heard the stories, mulled them over like they were pulling fleas from a dog's fur and nodded their heads like they were no' that surprised to see so many. They all resented the isolation that the Logans imposed upon themselves. They resented the isolation the Logans imposed upon them. The situation created a mistrust that, one day, bloomed into hatred.

The local people perceived my mother as a threat - although nobody could explain exactly what she threatened them with or what they had to be afraid of.

"Always goin' on aboot her clothes, her look."

"Well, she stood out, did she no'?"

"Dark pencil roond her eyes. Got to say it wasnae a look you see a lot roond here. I heard someone once say, they'd seen her in Tullis, one of the rare occasions, and she had a chain on one ankle, made from silver balls and blue glass. As if that was her, a witch, nae further discussion required."

"As I say, she was different."

"She was that," said Aunt Marion.

I'm told there was a general feeling they wanted to send her home. Romania. After all that effin walkin' to get here. Resentment, anger, even fury at her and the place she had taken amongst them were never sufficient cause to lead to the events that followed. As in war, it took a small spat over nothing to move the crisis to the next level.

Sixteen head of cattle died for no obvious reason at the wet end of Hograt field, where the grass dipped into a large trough. There was a southwesterly wind prevalent at the time - not uncommon off the coast here - and it left a bad smell hangin' over the village.

Some said: "Is that no' the rain that did for those coos?"

Another said: "That field's a bleedin' bog!"

Another said: "The poor beasts musta drooned."

Nobody had the wit to notice that the farmer was a dozy drunk, too scared of the great outdoors to mind his cattle without a whisky fortifier. Others got it into their heads that Christ, it was Logan and that weird, black-eyed woman; they were the ones who'd brought all this upon them. Foreigners!

Some said: "These people with fancy foreign ways!"

Another said: "Well look here, someone's to blame. Things like this just dinnae *happen.*"

Another said: "Aye, someone's at it. Someone's gonnie take the blame for this shite."

Next, the broccoli crop wilted and slumped lower than a pig's belly, oozing a foul-stenching fungus. This and the many other disasters seemed to be turning Tullis on its head. Could she - by which is meant the Romanian lady - could she be responsible?

"You're right enough," they said as one. "Everything changed when she came."

"You're no' kiddin!"

Next, Mrs Hodgart at Smithston Farm lost twenty-seven Scots Greys, some top Bantams and a prize sow called Master Ham. Bang, gone, in just one night. The coop awash with blood and feathers, the sty the colour of beetroot soup. People crying out for illumination, whilst the chickens only wanted their heads. Everyone, from churchmen to cobblers, wanted an answer and they were prepared to look in some strange places.

"We'll need an enquiry into this," said Mrs Hodgart, red faced as the floor of her coop. "Maister Ham's deid," she wailed. "And all the hens are gone tae! Can you believe it aboot Maister Ham? The two hind legs and half the belly absolutely departed."

Legless and chopless. Would a fox eat twenty-seven chicken heads? Took nothing but the shoulders up. Very picky. Then, the constable from Cupar found seven toads, each staked to the ground with a thick bamboo cane. The local sleuths said the bamboo had all the hallmarks of Romanian manufacture.

When the hay in one of the old barns close to Tullis combusted, burning to ash not just the winter feed but the building with it, the time for a reckoning had arrived. There had to be more to it all than the whimsicality of God and the arbitrary weave of nature, far more than too much rain, hungry foxes and headless Bantams. It was clear that toads did not have the skill to stake themselves to the ground; the hind legs and belly of a sow would not, of their own accord, mysteriously part company from the trunk.

"There's someone to blame," said one.

"There's a right stink!" said another. "And it's no' a smell you get from roond here!"

8

BLACK CLOUDS

This was the reckoning. A Galloway cow lay dead by the shoreline where the Bombo Burn spread its flow past Salmon Cottage and eased out towards the waiting sea. She was just one dead cow amongst seven, but together they gave off a putrid stench that would take the skin off your nostrils. Still, nobody was that inclined to move them.

"I mind it well," said Aunt Marion. "When all that gas inside the guts gets leakin' out, oh my God! The stink of flatulence, you would no' believe!"

"Did it no' dissipate? It can no' have just hung aroond forever?" I said.

"They'd had a lot of warm weather for the time of year. Your dad said the stench just never seemed to clear. And of course, it was that close to here at the farm that everybody was sayin' it must be the Logans."

"Did they no' shift the bodies?"

"They did. Eventually. They had to get enough men together to move them but by that time they were rotted. They were like French cheese."

"Aye?"

"Aye. Every time they pulled on them, the legs came away like they were tearin' bread." Aunt Marion shifted in her seat. "I seen strong farmers empty their stomachs at the side of the field."

All this reinforced the view that Romanian magic was at work somewhere here. They couldnae blame God. Where's the satisfaction in that? They couldnae blame nature. That would have been like blowing warm breath up a penguin's *orificium venti*. People discussed these issues up against the falling dykes, behind their bedroom doors, under the sticky boughs of sycamore leaves, above the mole holes that were all over, coning the open fields and behind the udders of milking cattle. Some daft bastard even said that the Logan church attendance had been *very* poor recently. Well, let me tell you, it has remained singularly unimpressive to this day.

It was clear enough, there was a clamour for some unarticulated act of revenge. As far as they goons were concerned, something had to be done to put things right. That's what polluted their minds. All too quickly, events happened that set in train a string of consequences. All of it would lead me to this place I'm at today. This need to set the record straight, to have my ounce of flesh or something like it; to do whatever would silence my detractors. These were the voices inside my head: a small choir becoming louder.

9

THE ORPHAN

8 years later

I t's no part of my business to keep secrets here. That may be a wrong strategy given that I'm telling a story that does not always cover me in a cosy fleece of good intent and brotherly love. Then again, I tell my story and leave others to judge the guilt in all that I've done.

Aunt Marion raised me, along with her own daughter, Lizzie. I plodded merrily through my early years, submissive to their devotions and directions. It was they who dressed me in clothes cut from an old, crushed, embroidered, velvet curtain stumbled upon in my father's Afghan journeybag. I had no objection: heat from any source was welcome. Furthermore, there's nae doubting I presented a dashing appearance dressed in my brown drape, if just a little weirdly Pashtun for conservative Fife. It lasted a long while too, being cut from a large spread and making more than one outfit. Whilst I may have believed I was a fine figure to behold round about the Tullis medina, nevertheless I appreciate that my skin at that time was thicker than a pig's hide and I was mostly insensitive to the sniggers that snorted around me.

Not only was I a light orgasm of brushed velvet elegance in a fecal shade of golden brown, Aunt Marion and Lizzie saw to it that my brain got its share of stimulation; between them they decided that I was to have a proper school education. They pushed and prodded at the burgh authorities to take me in. Once those in charge had relented - as they were obliged to do thanks to the Education (Scotland) Act of 1873 - I quickly learned to read a book, hold a pen, add, subtract and make the occasional long division. To be honest, it was no' easy for Aunt Marion to take me down to the Tullis Board school to enrol me. It was a place with crumbled lime-plaster walls, the flaked paint floating to the stone floor, a surface that echoed back at my feet like a final reprimand. It had a tall, black, whinstone chimney and a solid, studded, oak front door that threatened to close forever behind me.

I was initially oblivious to those who pinched their noses in my company. Fair to say, memories of those things that had occurred and the ripples that had broken the water in all directions were still not far from people's minds. They didn't talk too much about it, but they knew what had passed at Salmon Cottage and the horrors that had been sown there.

As for school, it's got to be said, I had no time for my fellow students (and they had as much for me), but nevertheless I took a deep, enduring shine to the education I was offered. It drew me in like heat off a warm fire. I'm not modest enough to hide my achievements here: I was without doubt the top pupil amongst a trailer full of agricultural goons. Without wishing to shine the spit on my own genius, I was the deserving author of my good fortune. When others put their jotters away, I sat rooted to my seat, until Mr Shifner, a super stern schoolmaster in a dark tweed jacket, chaffed elbow leathers and black worsted trousers, tugged at his sideburns and said: "Logan, have you no' got a home to go to?"

The thing was this: I *wanted* to finish my work before I left. I don't know where this came from, this desire to know things, but there's no doubt I had it in buckets and spades. I had a simple, curiosity about the way things worked. My mind seemed always full of dull questions to which I sought dazzling answers.

Such exquisite curiosities smouldered like hot ash in the fire basket of my child's mind. As a distraction, I buried my head in a book about a girl called Alice who fell down a rabbit hole only to come face to face with a warren of anthropomorphic beasties. That story I found strangely chilling and I read it to the end. Fractions, multiplication, syntax, grammar, even the construction of the Latin gerundive sentence, held no fear for me. I was never afraid of facts, figures or anything else that came out of a book. I was dedicated to Mr Shifner's library which I spent the best part of five years stealing from.

All this maybe could explain to some small degree why I grew up with no friends. Friends were poor cohabitants of my curious world. Jesus God, it never occurred to me that they might be a necessary part of the human condition. It goes without saying, I'm no' looking for anyone to feel sorry for me; I was quite happy with the friendless nature of my situation. I shed no tears over havin' had no friends. To my understanding, it was perfectly natural and I would not have had it any other way. The friends I had were on the pages of the book I was reading; they were amongst the integers that formed part of the equation I was intent on solving.

Nevertheless, I was aware of a gap in my life created by the ghosts of two souls who would ever be strangers to me. Aunt Marion said, I should take my mind elsewhere, I could never know my parents now.

"I know," I said. "I know fine they're gone."

Yet, whilst they had no physical presence I still had the feeling they were in and around me, pushing and pulling and directing my decisions and thoughts. Of course, in truth, I was just a boy but sometimes I sensed I was acting a story in which I had been given the part of a fully-grown man. I stood apart with my shiny, dark hair, the smallest hook to my nose, my crushed velvet, Afghan clothing and my open, sometimes impertinent, demeanour. I carried in my heart a huge hole, a deep yearning for the mother I had never known and the father I could never have, filling me like hunger. It welled up inside and choked me. It was like a stone in my undersized shoe. It may explain why I rarely smiled and had an old man's frown. No amount of perusing the thin pages of my father's journal assuaged the regret, the heavy heart engendered by their absence.

I may as well confess one final curiosity about me: I did not speak. I could not speak. I'd never spoken a bloody word. I was, as my classmates endlessly pointed out, *just a dumb, fuckin' mute.*

10

THE MUTE

W e share the same ignorance as to why I was, in the Fife parlance, a *dumb fuckin' mute*. Was this connected to the dreadful events at Salmon Cottage on the night before my birth? I cannot tell you. Ask Hippocrates, ask the writers of the *Corpus*. Psychoanalyse our old friend Freud; free associate until your baws drop off. I do not profess to have any ready answer as to why I should have been born dumb. Like a cardplayer with only half a hand, I will say in my defence that I knew pretty early on that something awful happened at the farm the night before I was born and I've spent most of my life reassembling the pieces, creating multiple lists of those I held responsible. I had a sense of the connection between the moment I became the celebrated mute and the violence of my mother's mutilation, within a heartbeat of where I lay inside her. Her violation was mine too.

Whatever the reasons for it, I was always anxious around people. The biped was a curiosity that made me distinctly nervous. As a young boy, I always had a problem making and maintaining eye contact. Of course, when it came to the gruesome detail, the blood and guts of what occurred, Aunt Marion was not the kind of person to keep these things back.

"Better to know, than no' to know," she said. "Better to be ready to make an adjustment." She did not hold back. I might just as well have been there, Rubens-like, painting an oil canvas of the family slaughter. A *Massacre of the Innocents (Tullis, Fife)*. I could have had Lizzie do me a tapestry, if she could sew without smearing blood on the thread. Then again, blood on the thread might have added authenticity. I could visualise a tattoo on a shoulder or an arm, but where that memory came from I could never tell you. Was it my mother and her shoulder tattoo? The blue crucifix? Was it one of her assailants? Was it a memory at all?

"Memory has a habit of fallin' between stools."

Right enough, but the memory came from somewhere. Aunt Marion had no scruples about painting a portrait in rich colour of my father's bone-handled fish-knife; the wan that he was no' afraid to use. She would tell me these things when I was in my crib, when I was just a mute toddler.

"Get oot the hearth!" she'd yell as I ate lumps from the rope-handled peat bucket, before I could even walk. She told me the story of that night repeatedly – or at least what she knew of it and the snippets she thought I could digest. She had a way of gesticulating with a flat, vertical hand, a whole twisting right arm and a straight finger with an arthritic knuckle that made me know too well how my father filleted that man with the Afghan fish knife.

But, hold on now. When I was still five, Lizzie was reporting that I was a complete failure, that I was showin' no signs of adopting speech as a communication method. "Will he ever talk?" she kept asking. "Five," she said. "And no' a word." She would poke me with a sharp finger in the hope that pain might cause me to break the silence and make a potent sound.

"Mebbe he's nothin' to say." Aunt Marion countered. "We could all learn a lesson from that."

"Five years," said Lizzie. The water came out the top of her cup because she was intent on swirling it around the rim. Before it spilt, she said: "He should be talkin' by now."

"He may no' want tae."

"It's no' natural," she said. "Mebbe he's on the wrang food."

Aunt Marion looked up. "There's nothin' wrang with my food!"

"I never said there was. Yer missin' ma point."

"What is yer point when it's at hame?"

"He's got a tongue in his head, so why's he no' usin' it?"

"Because nobody said he had tae."

"Like a monk." She paused to look at me. "A very silent monk." She touched me on the chin and tried to force a finger between my teeth. "Have you looked in his mooth?" she said.

"Why?"

"Blockage mebbe?"

"That wouldnae stop him talkin'," said Aunt Marion. "Might stop him breathing."

"Mind," Lizzie said. "He's readin' now. So no' completely stupid. Did you see him read?"

"It's hard to tell."

"Think he understood what he was readin' too."

"I'm glad to hear it. Alert the school governors."

"Well..."

"You read a book recently yourself?" she asked.

"If he can read, why can he no' speak?" Lizzie leaned back on her chair, tipping the front legs off the ground. "He's got teeth after all."

"Teeth, hands, legs, feet. Aye, Lizzie, he's got the lot. He just cannae talk aboot it." Aunt Marion looked at her daughter. "I wouldnae do that if I were you."

"Do what?"

"Tip back on the chair." As she spoke, the chair slipped out from under Lizzie, spilling her on the floor. "I was gonnie say, but you beat me to it."

Lizzie uprighted the chair and sat down again, rubbing the side of her leg. "All I'm sayin' is, proper sounds and all that. Ye ken whit I'm sayin': speech."

"There's more to life than bletherin'."

"I wouldnae ken aboot that."

Lizzie looked at her hands. She appeared a simple girl but she knew her own mind. True, she was clumsy. Clearly, she had not attended a finishing school for ladies. She was honest as the day was long. "I ken yer nothin' much if you cannie talk," she said.

I could hear them over the top of me, like a strong draught blowing through the gaps around the kitchen door. I knew what they were saying but that awoke no desire on my part to share the medium of language with them. I was happy to move my lips and bash my fledgling molars together but could I make a noise? I suppose I liked the way they talked about me. After all, I could understand most of what they said.

It was not specifically that I did not want to talk; it was just that I lacked the inclination to articulate words and interact with those around me. There was nothing within that compelled me to talk, nothing that worked like a vocal trigger. I had no motivation. There were good reasons why a clever boy would keep things clammed up. In a sense I was like my father: both our worlds were surrounded by walls: his from stone true enough, but mine were no less impregnable for being invisible. The effect of not speaking is that everything stayed in that small cell, somewhere inside me. I had conversations, of course, just like any other boy, but they were interactions that took place inside my head and it was I who controlled them. The four walls of my skull became an alternative space inhabited by people who spoke and acted in any way demanded of them - by me. Inside the bone of my head there was a place that I could inhabit whenever it suited. I soaked up the life around me and peopled my brain from what I gleaned. It was a place where my mother and father could infuse, breathe, sleep and share a conversation. My mother could smile and eat an apple from that old orchard on the green slope to the other side of Tullis. Or she would hold her bottom lip. She could hug me close to her and my father could put his soldier-farmer hand on my skinny shoulder. I would feel the tips of his fingers through my cotton shirt. In my head I even had a bedroom with bookshelves. I had a silk Afghan rug on the floor, its pink and burgundy petals swirling around the aqua-blue, like thick-skinned flowers on water. I could look out the sloping window of my bedroom. When I was older I could see Ben Mercer, his spine yawning its pink, bloody lips to either side. I could see a man picking gunshot from a big cavity in his leaky gut. I could sometimes see out of the hole in his back if he stood against the light and puffed up his chest. This was the man I later knew as Mad Bob. In my silent world, I could lock the door without lifting a finger or a foot. That's the good thing about a bedroom and general living accommodation inside your head. That's the reward for being close enough to see the pain in their eyes, touching their fear and feeling their breath against my cheek. None of it was real in the accepted sense, but to me it was more vivid than life or death or the coals of a hot fire.

11

SILENCE

At the beginning, when I was young, people in Tullis would occasionally speak to me and they would expect me to answer them. "Morning, young Logan," they'd say. "What, nae voice the day, Sean? Even though the sun's shinin'? Even when the blossom's on the hawthorn?"

I thought, what right do they have to expect that? I had no inclination to answer, but I'm no' sure if I could physically articulate the words anyway. I'm certain that often enough, even if I could have spoken I would not have breathed a whisper. After all, the real conversations were goin' on inside my head. It's hardly surprising that they looked at me as if I was two legs short of a pit pony. As if, because I had no tongue, I must have no pulse and certainly nae brain inside my head, as if all the cerebrospinal fluid had flooded down the ventricles and swamped chloroform on my ability to think or talk. They might even have thought I was contaminating them with some of my mother's Romanian magic.

There were occasions when, as a young boy, I was sent

down to the village and at such times, I was forced to confront others with my inability to speak. Once I went to pick up some steel nails and wire wool from Mr Fawcett's shop, a mecca for cooking pots, wood glue, hammers and other useless hardware. It was a shop with nothing in it that ever amused me, but it had a rusty, tin roof and I loved being there when it rained because of the thunderous noise, like a thousand steel tacks banging against your skull. On this particular occasion it was not raining at all, so I had nae interest whatsoever in being in Mr Fawcett's shop other than to fetch half a dozen masonry nails and the wire wool. I was waiting for Mr Fawcett to put them in a bag for me, one that I had brought for just this purpose, when I was approached by an old lady (she seemed old to me) in a big, flat, crinoline hat containing two goose feathers and a floppy bow. She had on a canary yellow dress with a lace collar bucketing up her neck like a heavy pipe. The toes of her shiny, black shoes peered out beneath the hem. She looked like someone had rearranged a parrot and put inappropriate boots on it. She held a white lace handkerchief and she patted me on the head with the palm of her hand. There were liver freckles on her fingers and the skin was dry and withered.

I suppose I must have looked at her as if she had kicked me in the testicles. My startled reaction to being manhandled may have betrayed that I took offence at her pattin' ma head without a formal invitation. She'd no' the faintest clue about what I was thinking and was too steeped in her own decay to make an enquiry. She did not know I had a head that contained the other world, where I had a bedroom with bookshelves and occasional parents.

"What's your name?" she said, as if it were the key to a locked door. "Where's your school? Can you read?" I looked away. "You will have read the *New England Primer*? A fabulous book full of useful phrases. *A dog will bite a thief at night.* Have you heard of that one?"

If my head could have gone round three hundred and sixty degrees it would have done so twenty times.

"*The idle fool is whipped at school.* Have you heard that one?" She asked about my awkward velvet clothing. "I find the colour vulgar," she said. She turned to Mr Fawcett. "Who is the boy's mother and father? Where, who and what are they?" Mr Fawcett mumbled that I was a boy without the gift of a mother. That didn't put her off. She continued to offload a series of further enquiries. She saw me as a curious challenge to her perception of what was normal.

"He looks like a stray dog," she said. "A stray dog that should be re-kenneled." As I say, I had never before seen this odd bird in all my life, so I stared back at her with eyes that rose above the saucer hat, its feathers and floppy bow, but made no contact with anything larger than a fly on the window.

"Where is your talkative nature child?" she persisted, an edginess nesting in her voice. "I have asked you many questions, and yet you will not answer. What is it with you? Everybody's got something to say, isn't that right, Mr Fawcett?"

"Certainly," said Mr Fawcett. "A point well made."

"Even a Persian bird sings in April."

I looked at her and she looked at me. We connected in a solidarity of silent enmity. I wanted to take the pencil from behind Mr Fawcett's ear and spear each of her eyeballs.

"It's very irritating when you get nothing from a child," she said finally, as I wallowed in my ocular fantasy. "It's very irritating to me that when civil words are addressed to one such as you, you're not concerned to respond with anything more than vacant stares." I looked at her blankly. "You seem to be an annoying little boy, but it may not be all your fault." She bent down, her face closer to mine that I would have wished. "Believe me, there's nothing to be gained in life by staring and squinting and eating air." She smiled with thin lips that sealed her mouth like two skinny threads. "After all, you're not a fish."

"As I say, madam. I'm afraid the boy doesn't have the gift of speech," said Mr Fawcett.

"Surely that is nonsense," she answered. "All boys speak. Even the stupid ones speak." She looked down. "Come now. The ignorance of it is inexcusable. Don't worry if it makes no sense. Just move your jaw and adjust your lips. Like so." At which point she demonstrated her skill at moving jaw and lips, teeth and tongue in order to produce speech. "Let's-hear-you!" she instructed.

I continued to stare at the yellowing whites of her wrinkled eyes. The bags beneath sagged like they were full of coins. I stood motionless as a stone pillar.

"Infuriating," she said eventually. "Quite infuriating." Once more, she bent her face towards me but was met by a distance, deep and impenetrable as an earthquake fissure. She looked away from me and up once more at Mr Fawcett, who was wiping his damp palms against a green apron. He raised both eyebrows and both hands simultaneously, as if joined by a common string.

"He disnae speak," echoed Mr Fawcett, smiling dutifully. He had teeth that I had not seen before. "Never has done, I'm told, and that's the truth."

"I suppose that's a relief," she said. "That there are medical reasons behind this disappointing phenomenon. I'm so glad it's not just me he gawps at."

I took my bag of nails and wire wool and left Mr Fawcett's shop, my chin set firm against my chest, and not a second too soon or I might have laid a clenched fist on her. As it was, there were bloody half moons surfacing on the white pads below my thumbs. I did not know who she was. I had no reason to know that many years later I would point a gun at her and pull the trigger.

Having no voice in the classroom only served to spread distance between me and the other children. At first they would observe the crackling eccentricity. Then they would pick on it, like children do, until it bled a little. They chanted *dumb fuckin' mute!* at me like I was deaf not dumb. They did their best to tease me out of my threatening tranquility. I could have been a Zulu speaking Swahili or some other Bantu tongue and they would have been all smiles. Just like the old lady with the eyeballs and the lace neck bucket in Mr Fawcett's shop, silence to them felt like a defence they had no means to understand and were powerless to undermine.

Silence is a weapon and these boys never came close to drawing the voice out of me. As time went on, their endless jibes, like tiny broken fires, sparked and petered out. They abandoned the torture they sought to inflict and they left me alone. I suppose they thought where was the pleasure in a tormented beetle having the temerity to ignore you. They forgot about me, like I was a bee sting they once suffered; I was nothing more than a burst of apitoxin that they were now well and truly over. Like all the others, they talked over and around me, as if I was grey mist, invisible, vaporous or not even there at all. I was a disappeared child, a faint shadow woven into the faded lines of a drab watercolour. They could speak about anything and never think that I had ears on my head. If they noticed the ears at all, to them their purpose was no more than elaborate decoration on a strange bone. They were unable to acknowledge that those translucent tissue flaps were proper listening devices, connected to the billions of neurons in a cerebral cortex. A conduit from the outside world. They drew in the life and tempo of the other existence and fed the complex sponge inside my head; they made the presence in there one that I could bear.

12

THE SNIDER-ENFIELD

9 years later

I t was just a matter of time before I started using guns. My father had no gun cupboard, nae happy hook at the jail to hang his Snider-Enfield rifle from and nobody had thought to remove it from the house. The man I came to know as Mad Bob maybe remembered this firearm better than anybody. Every time he used the toilet would be a seismic jolt to his memory. I knew it was there in my father's room, on top of the old, oak wardrobe that smelled faintly of cheesy cloth and leather boots.

It took me a while to get it down off the top ledge and have a good look. I waited until Aunt Marion and Lizzie were out of the house. In I went, stood on a farm chair from the kitchen table and felt the dusty top of the wardrobe underneath my fingers. l gripped the cold barrel and slid it slowly over my hand. I took it down, the silence all around me, like a choirboy showing reverence to the crucifix at the altar. The chair was shoogly and made the rifle slip in my hand before I recovered my balance. I was pleased to discover that this was a decent gun, with a long barrel and a sleek, shiny, rosewood grip. I put my finger against the trigger, felt the cold metal against my skin, aimed at the black raven on the wall beyond the window and pulled the trigger, mouthing an explosion as I did. In my head - that is my dumb, fuckin' head - I saw a small Afghan assailant take the imaginary bullet and flop softly against the wall. When I looked again I saw there was no Afghan - and no raven for that matter.

I read a book about rifles that I found in the Modern Warfare section of Mr Shifner's library. Mr Shifner had always encouraged my reading (largely as a means to discourage my intrusions on his personal time) and slowly I had come to enjoy the free use of his books. Still, my sense was that he derived some small pleasure from a pupil who did not see an open book as an invitation to run for the hills. He was not used to any of his charges taking such an obvious interest. I suppose the one thing he liked was that, as a mute, I sat in total silence. He was happy enough to see me in there, on my leper's island, foraging quietly for knowledge amongst the books like a pig hunting truffles. For me, I didn't really think about the morality, but it was a logical next step to start stealing those books.

The first book I stole was called the *Nuttall Encyclopoedia* and it was reasonably informative to a boy with an interest in guns and small explosions and the release of inflammable oils and gases at high temperature. By way of background to the more scientific aspects of the book, it even told me the story of Jacob Snider, the American inventor, buried at Kensal Green Cemetery in London, who gave birth to the Snider-Enfield rifle, a gun that had gone from

firing three rounds per minute with the muzzle-loader to
ten rounds per minute with the breech-loader. At a single
stroke, he changed the world, allowing users to take ten lives
per minute instead of a paltry three.

My father had been particular with the cartridges too,
keeping a plentiful stock on the shelf at the back of the
wardrobe, wrapped in grease paper. Along with the rifle,
there were fourteen packets of what they called a "Boxer"
which was a new type of metal cartridge. All you had to do
with the Snider-Enfield was cock the hammer, yank the
breech block lever and fire. Boom! Say your prayers! A
deadly shot through the heart, my Afghan friend!

Thereafter, the Snider-Enfield and I spent plenty of time
together on target practice, usually at the beach. You could
have a lot of fun shooting at bottles and apples. When
apples were out of season and the bottles were all finished, I
had to improvise. I tacked a piece of paper to a tree. On one
occasion, I found a dead basking shark washed up on the
shoreline. I took some lime wash and painted a target on the
shark's belly. I held a cloth to my nose because the smell was
bad. I wrote the word "Mad Bob" slap bang in the middle of
the target. There were maggots already leaping in the
shark's gut and they moved a thousand tiny wriggles as I
jabbed on the paint. I stepped back, looking at my handi-
work. I walked away a good distance along the beach and
lay down against the Marram grass. I prepared myself and
got my breathing just so. Then I must have filled the shark
with twenty-five or thirty bullets, each one getting closer to
the centre. Clearly, it was not much fun for the maggots but,
having pulled back a further distance from the target, I
could even get a hit at five hundred yards. There were times
when I got lucky at a thousand yards, and that is a very long
way to travel to hit the shit out of a maggot. Most were safe

at that distance. The shark looked like egg nog by the time I finished, but I was pleased. The Snider-Enfield had proved it was a good gun and I was a competent shot. I was in good company too, having read that Kipling was fond of the Snider:

A Snider squibbed in the jungle -
Somebody laughed and fled,
And the men of the First Shikaris
Picked up their Subaltern dead,
With a big blue mark in his forehead
And the back blown out of his head.

13

THE SCHOOLYARD

1 month later

There are defining moments in every life, whether your journey is that of an ant, a leather army boot, a drunk sea captain or a hot shave Turkish barber. These are moments that set you off on a particular course you might never have chosen. You may choose the route inadvertently and some thing or some force will get hold of you and propel you like fluff to where it wants you to go. The bird feather falls to earth but could land just about anywhere. Of course, it may be just a small tilt on the rudder or something more powerful and deliberate that turns the boat around and sends the sailor on his way. Small or large, whatever your actions may be, events can steer you in a direction over which you have no control.

I was thirteen and three-quarters. It was May and we were outside in the Tullis schoolyard, breathing the crisp morning air. There was a suggestion of green shoots once again pushing out from the raggedy, hawthorn hedges; the sycamores were showing tight, little buds along their boughs and the pale yellow daffodils spawned peeping, half-hidden heads along the earth banks outside the school's iron gate. The sky was predominantly blue and there was no breeze to worry about. The warmth of the sun was on our faces.

Mr Shifner was having a migraine for which he took a spoon of syrup from a green, unlabeled bottle and sent us outside to consider the proper articulation of verbs and pronouns without his intervention. Most of the goons in my class were beyond educating in such esoteric matters but since the General Education Act every gormless Jim in the country was expected to surrender to a small amount of learning. I was bent against the sill of a ground floor window, in the company of these simian dodos, wishing the migraine break was over and we could get back into the classroom for a bit more of *The Self-Help Grammar of the English Language*.

Weary of English grammar, I amused myself with Latin verbs, two at a time, third person plural to first person singular. I sound like I was just being clever: I most definitely was. Momentarily, I was distracted from my conjugations by the stonework around the mullions, noting that it was poor and broken and in need of pointing. You could pull stones out from the crumbling mortar. If Mr Shifner had seen me doing that he would have given me a work detention. That did not bother me one bit. So, I pulled a large lump of hard stone from the mortar and weighed it in the palm of my hand.

There were three other boys close by and I sensed them as they insinuated their presence. In my life then and the life that was to follow, these boys came to assume some importance. There was Tom Burns, farming stock with just enough brain, potted like dry compost in a shaven head, to half fill his dad's clay pipe. The shortness of his hair accentuated the bulbous nose that squatted like an intruder on his round face. Beside him, sitting with his trousered bum on a wooden log, was Joe Sharpe, another farmer's boy. He had none of Tom's rounded, over-fed look. He was pale-skinned, yellowish, thin-lipped, already topped with a light growth of soft hair on the slim ledge beneath his nose. There was a smear of meanness that hung about him, like stubborn sweat. Then there was Rory Fraser, squatting on his worn heels, fair hair, blue eyes, skilled at spitting mainly, forever sniffing up fresh ammunition. He had large ears that lunged forward like clam shells and his blue eyes were shiny, as if he had just had a lot of bad news.

I was there, close to the window and its mullions, but I thought I was quite invisible to them. Usually I was just a thing that suggested its presence but was never really there. On this occasion, however, they had time on their hands to fix their focus on me and my unnecessary existence.

Joe rose off his log like an extending toad and moved a series of small, unambiguous steps in my direction. He leaned forward. "The old man still in jail, Seany?"

Tom raised his head and shelled a nostril with his thumb. "His da's in jail, Joe, that's fer sure."

"Time passes very slowly in jail, you ken," said Rory, sniffing, like he was consuming a hearty meal.

"What did he think he was doin'?" asked Joe. "I'm talking aboot yer dad."

"Think he knows that, Joe," said Rory.

"Do you, Sean?" He stared at me. "Did no one ever tell your da' no' to wave a knife aboot?" I looked at them but my eyes revealed nothing but empty rooms. "Knives are very dangerous, Seany," said Joe.

"Pretty dumb behaviour," said Tom, looking back at Joe. "Bit of an erse to think he could do that and get away with it."

"Who asked you, you dopey bugger?"

"Scuse me," said Tom. "Just sayin'."

They wanted me to react and I was happy for the price of two specks of farmyard cow dung to deny them that pleasure. I maintained a look of blank congeniality.

"My dad says, interesting fact, your old man did that murder unprovoked."

"Got twenty-five years in jail for his effort," added Tom.

"Got to say, fuckin' deserved it," said Joe.

"That's what I was saying, Joe."

"Not very civilized, I'll say that much."

"My dad said he skinned him with a knife," said Rory.

"Man's a fuckin' animal," said Joe. "Who'd skin another man? With a knife?"

Tom smiled, wrinkling his soft nose and exposing grey-brown teeth that looked like they'd been eating mud. "After aw, he's no a fuckin' potato," he said.

There was a long period of silence but maybe it was just five seconds. "Mind you," said Joe. "He was entitled to be cross. After all, Mr Mercer fucked Seany's mum first," said Joe. "So they say."

"Well, someone did," said Rory.

"You'd give her a poke, would you no' Joe?" said Tom.

"Just like your dad did," said Rory.

Joe looked back. "He did fuckin' no'." He moved a step closer to me, his pitted skin close up against mine. "No' him and no' me," he said. "Wouldnae touch her with fuckin' gloves on." He waited a moment and then turned and tossed a stone into the ploughed field beyond the fence. The dry earth threw up some dirt. "She wis a fuckin' gypsy." He threw another stone that clipped the fence. "Dogs an' fuckin' gypsies, I dinnae ken! Whit's happened to oor fuckin' standards?" Rory spat a gob of mucus. Joe crabbed back over to me by the window. Again, he held his face close to mine. I could see the open pores of his skin. "Peg on nose time, I'm thinkin'."

"Think she enjoyed it?" asked Tom, still smiling, his disembodied voice sweeping in from behind. "I ken I would."

"She wis a passionate woman, Tom. As a matter of fact," he said, glancing at his fingernails. "There's a good reason why gypsies are born with their legs apart." He looked over at Tom who accepted this as an undeniable proposition.

"What do you fuckin' expect?" said Rory. "Ma dad's horse would've taken advice before he fucked her."

"Stands to reason," said Joe.

"Aye, it does," said Tom.

"A horse is a valuable and discriminatin' creature," said Joe.

I will not bore you with more charms from these pygmies. Suffice to say that the bonhomie towards my dead mother did not last very much longer. That was just about as far as Joe got with his eulogy to her memory. A black cloud, full of Helman ghosts and forgotten grief, had imbued itself within me and for the next thirty-seven seconds, to my eternal shame, I became unhinged. For the first time in as many years, I had left the room inside my head and I entered the battle zone. I was on Flodden Field or Waterloo. I was my father at Kandahar meting out the slaughter. I was a urinating Pashtun woman. I was not wholly in charge of who I was or where I was or what I had become. The purple mist descended and the once reliable self-control system was debilitated to the point of total malfunction. In common parlance, the shit hit the rotating blade. By the end of thirty-seven seconds, Joe had two broken ribs and a tooth hanging out of his skinny mouth. Tom had a lip thick as a sea mussel, an index finger bent ninety degrees to the left, with a dislocated crack along the shaft and a high pitched ring in his right ear where my fist had exploded the pressure in his eardrum. Rory never left his wooden seat; he did nothing at all, other than land a gob on the left side of my head. Most of the damage was inflicted with the stone I had pulled from the pointing beneath the windowsill. It was flint or some variety of sedimentary chert, acting as a crude knuckle-duster and almost breaking my own fingers in the process.

I noticed later that I had blood on my hands and I was not at all sure it was mine. I dabbed at it with my pinkie finger and touched my tongue with the tip. The taste was metallic and salty. I wiped my hand on my sleeve and reflected on this uncharacteristic physical outburst. I had shown that I was capable of volcanic violence.

The worst of it was that they kept me out of school for my violent outburst, but it had provided a solid enough indication to those who dared to enter my airspace that I had a psychotic nature. On the whole I did not have too much trouble after that. It taught me what could be achieved with a well-thrown fist and a big stone wedged between your fingers. It taught me about playing fair too: on the whole, forget it. Marquess of Queensberry rules and all that fair play bollocks were an unnecessary luxury.

So, my fists had spoken for me and I didnae feel too sorry about it. Of course, I would like to think I was better than a blossoming psychopath mapping out a future life in gangland. After all, I had a neat little brain on my shoulders that told me I possessed the flower of intellectual promise.

Then again, neither do I want anybody to think I had nothing on my mind but crunching numbers and working algorithms. I had a real love for books and there were times you could not thread skin between the tip of my nose and the page I was reading. People could find that annoying. Aunt Marion expected me to pull my weight around the farm – after all I was the closest thing to a man right there. There was many a time when I could see she wanted to bawl me out for not chopping logs, not cleaning out the klinkers from the old fire grate or not doing a proper job of mending a broken wattle fence so a goat got out and ate the small saplings at the end of Hograt field.

She would yell at me to pull my weight when she had lost the will to cope or was just narked at what life had thrown at her. "You're the man here," she would say and I would look at her vacantly. My eyes sometimes dipped - because I *was* the man, even aged thirteen and three quarters.

I will grant you I was sometimes lazy, but I was not the first to be overawed by the prospect of a whole twenty-four hours in any one day. That was a lot of time to get through. Or maybe it was not laziness. Maybe it was the selfishness of youth, that unassailable belief that my squeaky little life was designed to stand foremost and eclipse every other. I knew there was more to me than splitting logs, sweeping shit and hoeing weeds. I had a good pair of hands and I knew they were for more than pulling teats on the cows. At the same time I was well aware that Aunt Marion took some pride in the fact that I could read quicker than her. She took pleasure from knowing that I could explain a binary numeral system by a simple note on a piece of paper, without a word from my silent lips. She knew that as well as skinned knuckles I had electricity between my ears.

People think that a man of few words has even fewer brains, but wagging your tongue in the breeze all day is a waste of energy. The man who speaks less has more time to think. He's no' wasting precious moments on his lips when he could be workin' on his brain. He has spare capacity to ponder targets, strategy, resolution. He sees the wider picture, unaffected by the drowning pull of words.

Nevertheless, whilst being dumb had its up side, it also had its down side. There were a lot of times I felt like I was trapped inside myself. I felt like someday I would have to talk, yell or roar out loud or else I was going to explode. At times it felt like I had my head in a bottle and the air was being sucked out. These times felt like I was experiencing death by a thousand suffocations. I was a bee in that bottle and I was using up all my air.

Maybe it all started with the batterin' I gave those boys. A flint from some distant, chalky ground ending up as a knuckle-duster in my clenched fist. Breaking those ribs and spilling that blood seemed the perfect way to get these snakes off my back. I found myself less anxious when I came to be around them. I looked them in the eye and, to my surprise, it was often enough they who looked away first.

If my fists were good enough, I was becoming a sharp shot with the rifle too. With practice, I could pick off a flea on a pig's arse when I got my range right. Lizzie and Aunt Marion knew that I was using the rifle now, but then we lived on a farm and it would have been unusual not to have a gun. Killing is what farming is all about. There were rats in the barn and you had to shoot them. Good practice too. Rabbits were good for Lizzie's stewing pot, particularly if taken with a good, clean blast from the Snider-Enfield. I could skin a rabbit in less than a minute, like I was peeling fruit.

Yet, at first, the shots I was firing off around the farm got Lizzie all shaken and excited. "What's all that bangin' going on?" she said.

"I dinnae ken," said Aunt Marion. "Probably the sound of you droppin' stuff."

14

THE BOMBO BURN

1½ years later

P eople often make the mistake of thinking that when something is done, it's done. Nice and tidy. Like fights in playgrounds. When I was fifteen and a third years old, I learned how things are not always entirely finished when you thought they were. We all move on, but not necessarily together. This enlightenment came at a time when my legs were knee high in mud water oozing through the Bombo Burn.

There was a field running west from Salmon Cottage. We didn't keep anything much on it. The ground nearest the house was fertile enough and, with work, could have been productive. Sometimes you have to decide if the drop of sweat you earn is worth as much as the bucket of sweat you expend getting there. Balance is the critical issue, albeit sometimes you lose it and all the decisions that follow are skewed by that lack of equilibrium. With this particular field, as the grass swept down to the burn, you got the feeling the brown soil would be richer, more sympathetic to the whims and vagaries of an aspiring crop; or would be easier to squeeze out just a bit of scruffy grazing for the sheep. In fact, the truth is the earth grew sandy and dry and nothing much would grow. It had been tried but it stubbornly refused to yield anything edible. Even the sheep stayed away.

I was down at the dirty end of that stubborn field, behind the prickly sow-thistle, where the Bombo Burn snaked past, winding onward to the next open ground where it meandered to a modest flow, carrying the rain off the distant hills, all the way to the firth and beyond to the open sea. I was in the cold, muddy water, and as I say, it was up to my knees and seeping in through the loose stitching of my boots. Where I was stood, there was as much mud as there was water. The banks on either side of me were made up of the same dry, sandy earth as the field itself and they were crumbling and breaking down into the burn. There were rocks too that had rolled off the top and into the water and, together with the sand and the earth, they were strangling the flow. I was the human dredger, armed with a pick and a scooping spade, in an effort to mend nature's havoc.

I'd been so lost in my own thoughts, so intent on completing the sedimentary excavation, I neither saw nor heard them coming. More fool me, but the first thing I knew was when I felt a large gob hit the back of my neck. I ran my fingers over it, thinking that maybe it was slopping out time for a seagull or a puffin. I looked up to see not the bird loosening its bowels, but Rory Fraser, smacking his lips with two straight fingers, blue eyes big as plates on the kitchen wall.

Joe, his skin dull as the overcast sky, was at his side. "Nice wan," he said.

"Thanks Joe," Rory answered.

"We've no' seen you in school for a while, Logan," said Joe. "You're neglectin' your education. Ye'll no' make the diplomatic corps at this rate."

My eyes rose up from the water but there didn't seem too much point in responding, even if I could.

"That's not good Sean," said Joe, smoothing the light growth above his lip with a skinny hand. A potential moustache but without ambition; a frustrated, pointless work in progress. As if, like a plant, it had been starved of water or decent soil.

"Try no' to wet yoursel'," said Tom, laughing so loud you would think the world's funniest man had just walked into Tullis. Slowly his laughter subsided. "That was funny," said Tom, in case we didn't know.

"Last time Sean, you got away with it, but I've got a long memory for these things."

"Aye. Unfinished business, as they say," said Tom, taking a step forward. "We're better prepared this time, are we no', Joe?"

"Aye, could say that." He pulled an object from his pocket, flicked his arm out to his side, and I watched a blade unfold with a sharp, ugly point. I'd read about these things. It was a flick-knife, something I hadn't seen before. But it wouldn't take a genius to know it could do some damage. I leaned on my spade and pushed the hat back on my head. Given the weakness of my position numerically, I had an urge to reason, but for that I required words. If I had had words, I would have asked them what it was about me, my mother and my father that had them chasing their tails to subdue me. Did they know the first thing about my mother? Did they know one thing about my father? Every word they uttered was twinned with ignorance.

It has to be said, I did have some concern that things might end up as last time in the Tullis schoolyard, except it would be *my* ribs pointing the wrong way and *my* teeth floating like duck feed in the water. The knife would be sticking out of *my* gut like a shark's fin. That would be a bad result. I wondered if that was the kind of balanced outcome we look for in life. Still, they were not the brightest boys. They wanted revenge? They wanted to avenge a thumping they already got. Was it an eye for an eye they were after? With the knife entering the equation, it seemed to be more than an eye they were looking for. Even if I could speak, could I have ever found the words to persuade them that revenge was pointless? After all, to my mind, revenge was everything.

"That Lizzie of yours," said Joe, looking up towards the house. "I was thinking of askin' her out."

"She's your type, Joe. On the big side, of course," said Tom. "But you'll get plenty cuddles!"

"I'm glad to hear that," said Joe. "I'm no averse to cuddles. But a nice nature, Tom. She's got a nice nature." He looked back at me. "We might be very good together."

"Oh aye," said Tom. "I'm thinkin' poetry here."

"I might be interested in giving her some poetry of ma ain. I have to say, I've been thinkin' aboot her a lot," Joe persisted. "She's got great potential." Rory smiled at that and Tom chuckled and wiped the spit off his lips.

To Tom, this was better than the clowns at the circus. He liked it when Joe was funny. As for me, I could sense my temperature rising. I could tell that for once he was right to focus on the arithmetic. In other circumstances that might have been good news, but the calculation here was relatively elementary: there were three of them and just the one of me. There were no witnesses. There was no escape. Joe was smug, his smile thin and wide for a small head and I could see his stained teeth between the lips. He still had the open blade in his right hand.

At that moment Tom took it upon himself to launch the attack by jumping off the sandy bank. All this intellectual jousting had evidently palled on him. He had appreciated Joe's sense of comedy, his genius at setting the tone, but Tom was impatient to get to the point. It was time for the punch line. It was time to bring on the clowns. He wanted to sort me out with his fist before the clock ticked off another wasted minute. Joe could stab me later with that great knife of his.

Had he landed on me with his full weight, I would have gone down like a boxer with jelly legs. Luckily for me, the sand crumbled under Tom's feet and he was a fraction slow or sluggish with his elevation off the bank. I had just enough time to pull the spade from the water and swing it against his chest.

Doubtless, I am to be congratulated on the zip of my response. That in itself would have been quite a satisfactory result – another couple of ribs would have got popped, a small amount of blood may have been spilt and it would have been over, at least so far as Tom was concerned. The other two might have taken fright at the sight of gore on my shovel. Nothing to write to the Marquess of Queensberry about. I might have got my legs out of the water and made a run for it. Up to the house, barred the door. Got you again, you bastards! Unfortunately, the spade was a heavy, sharp-edged old tool and when I dragged it up it was slow coming out of the water. Tom was also slow to elevate because of the soft, sandy terrain and the bulk his own physicality placed upon it. The spring was gone from his launch. When the jagged top edge of my spade connected with the unfortunate Tom, instead of breaking his ribs it caught his neck and ripped a hole in it. It was like pulling on a string as the tear unzipped his face as far as his mouth. He lay beached on his back to one side of the burn, the soupy water swirling over his cotton drills and tugging at his feet, the blood gushing from his neck and left shoulder and slicking red across the stones. The spade had left a hanging flap that would have folded neatly back against his Adam's apple. All sorts of anatomy was visible, hovering inside the open flesh.

Joe and Rory jumped down off the bank themselves, one after the other, their faces all of a sudden cast greyer than wet ash. They stood on either side of Tom, not knowing what to do. You could see what looked like Tom's windpipe through the hole in his neck, but there was a lot of blood and it was flowing freely down across his shirt, obscuring the view.

"You've fuckin' killed him!" yelled Joe, waving the knife at Tom then me. "What the hell have you done?"

Rory said: "He's no' dead."

"You've fuckin' killed him!" Joe shouted again.

My own thought was that it'd take a slash more than a spade in the neck to kill a slob like Tom. Then again, he didnae look bright as a button on a picnic and it wasn't long before my confidence in his recovery was in my boots. I worried in that moment that I had inflicted a potentially mortal injury. Still, I knew that a spot of elementary medical care might assist, so I walked a few steps back and demonstrated a movement against my neck and then I raised my thumb and pointed at Tom. I wanted to convey to the imbeciles that they should pull the flap back over and push two fingers against the wound since in my opinion that might be the best way to stop the flow of blood. On the surface, I stood there quite calm. I could have been demonstrating how a man would mend a fence for all my coolness and if I had raised a hand I swear it would have been as steady as the horizon behind it. But inside, I was doing somersaults.

"Rory!" shouted Joe. "Fer fuck's sake, he's meaning put your fingers in his neck! Fingers against the fuckin' hole on his neck, to stop the blood!"

"I'm no' puttin' ma finger in no fuckin' hole!" responded Rory. "Fer once, why don't you put *your* fuckin' finger in the hole?"

"*Ma* finger's no' big enough for the fuckin' hole!" Joe yelled.

"Whit you sayin'? I've got fat fingers noo?"

I raised my palms, as if it was obvious that this was the only way to stop the bleeding. I lifted two fingers and gripped them with my other hand, in an attempt to signify that this was a technique supported by even the most rudimentary study of *Gray's Anatomy*. With some difficulty, I climbed up onto the sandy bank. They seemed paralysed with fear or revulsion at the sight of an open throat.

"Anyway," shouted Rory. "You may no' have noticed, but I've got a ring on ma finger!"

"Well?" said Joe.

"Well, ma finger will no' go in the fuckin' hole, will it? No' wi' a bloody ring on it!"

Tom gurgled small, oxygenated bubbles and more blood flowed from his wound.

"I'll hold your ring!" pleaded Joe. "Give me yer fuckin' ring and I'll hold it for you!"

Rory stood seemingly astonished. "This was ma fuckin' grandad's ring!" he shouted. "It never leaves ma finger!"

"What?" Joe exclaimed.

"Third from the right! Never leaves ma fuckin' finger!"

"What you sayin'?"

"It's a bad omen to take it aff!"

"Aw Christ," said Joe. "Aw Christ! Fuck! It'll be a bad omen if Tom's dead an' all!"

"Hey!" said Rory. "You brought us down here! You fuckin' sort it out!"

15

THE VOICE

There was more gurgling, gasping and gentle fizzing from Tom's throat as the air escaped. I stood on the bank and I was looking down at the pair of them. I was pointing at each of them, jabbing fingers at the body below their feet. They went on shouting profanities across the mud and water between them. I could feel the sweat dampen my forehead. It crossed my mind again that Tom might die and so my life could very well die with him. I was not sure I was ready to give up on it yet. Not just as things were getting interesting. The whole idea made me very nervous indeed.

It's worth noting that I had done some chemistry and some elementary human biology. I had also recently obtained that copy of *Gray's Anatomy* from Mr Shifner's library (which he was no' getting back, by the way). Therefore, I recognized the importance of the thyroid cartilage. It crossed my mind that the spade may well have cut the thyrohyoid muscle and even split the cartilage itself. Or worse, that old fanny, the *brachial plexus*. I felt a sense of rising panic that began in the pit of my belly, scaling ma insides and sendin' a light tingle through my pectorals before launching a flush of warmth to my already over-heated head. Tom gasped and gurgled. Joe and Rory continued to shout bollocks at one another.

"You put your fuckin' finger in!"

"I tellt you, I'm no fuckin' doing it!"

And more of the same. More gesticulating, more yelling they would no' put their fuckin' fingers in the fuckin' hole. Joe jabbing the knife in the air to make the point with emphasis. Well, I should have seen it coming. Out of the extreme comes the moment. Something that was propelled, switched on and empowered. It rose from somewhere in the gut and, amidst the trickling of the burn and the splashing of the mud, it emerged between my teeth and across my tongue, threadin' through those half-open lips, burstin' from ma mouth like air from a cave or light through a window.

"It's fuckin' simple!" I yelled, not expecting these to be my very first words. I peered at Tom and I stepped a pace towards him. I looked again at Rory and Joe. "I'll tell you this: he is gonnie die unless you stop that bleedin' from his neck!"

It was a strange sound to hear these words come from my mouth, as the blood seeped from Tom's throat and coloured pools took hold of the Bombo Burn. It was distant in my ears and sounded not like me – or what I expected to sound like me. It was remote, as if it it came from someone else. The tone of the voice was neither high nor low. I sounded like a boxer after a long fight. There was more air to the voice than proper volume, but I recognized it as a more or less satisfactory and surprising first step. I was not yet ready for a public oration but I'd said my first words.

I looked at Tom and back again at Joe, who stared at me.

He dropped the knife and it clattered against the rock. Rory looked up from Tom, his blond hair blowing across his face, his eyebrows curled into a question. "That's just my opinion," I said and I coughed. Still they said nothing and I continued to cough. "I'm no' qualified," I gasped. "You know that! I'm no' a doctor or anything, but that's how it looks to me: you need to stop the blood." I took a towel out of the bag I had left on the grass mound close to the water, screwed it into a ball and tossed it towards them. Rory caught it with his right hand. I was still outwardly calm but, if truth be known, I was just beginning to take in what had happened. Still, I was concerned about Tom's prospects in the full drama of life. "Hold it to his neck Rory," I rasped. "Hold it hard against his neck." Rory kneeled down on the bank and pressed the towel against the wound, intermittently staring back at me. I scratched the hair on my head. "That's a lot of blood he's lost," I said as I walked away up the field, dragging the bloody spade through the sow-thistle weeds. "He'll need stitches," I called out over my shoulder.

"Where the fuck are you going?" shouted Joe.

"To get the cart. We'll need to get him a doctor."

"You need to help us!" shouted Joe.

"I'm getting' the horse." I said. "Hold the towel against his neck. Hard."

We took him down to Tullis, to the woman called Nancy Carter. She fussed and tutted. When the blood stopped flowing, she took her needle and thread and said: "You may no' want to watch this bit."

I said: "You done this before, Mrs Carter?"

She said: "No, but I've sewed all my life. Hats and socks and a pully for ma grandchild. Can't be that difficult!"

"I thought he was gonnie die."

"Bad scratch," she said. "But I'll need to get they stitches in."

I left them there together and made my way back to the house. I had a strange sensation in my throat. I coughed a few times and that seemed to help. There was nobody home, as I expected, so I took the kettle off the stove and poured myself a cup of tea using the leaves from a wooden box in the wall cupboard. The tea was soothing as I sat there thinking about what had occurred. Something had switched itself on, after all these years. What it was, I didnae have a clue. All I knew was that something had come out of my mouth and it had sounded pretty good. It was well articulated and it came out free of saliva or unwanted pauses. Words, for god's sake! They were genuine words with proper syllables, as found in the *Oxford English Dictionary*! They just fell oota ma head like loose teeth.

I was still concerned about Tom. I hated the fat fool but I hadn't planned on being responsible for his death. But he was sitting up when I left Mrs Carter's place. I have to admit I had thought to myself, here we go again: if he dies I may find myself in a new cell. Well, it happens. My father would be so proud, what with taking after him, a stella career in criminology, going straight from the classroom to the jail.

I drank the tea in the deepening gloom. I picked a *Darjeeling* or some such leaf from my tongue and wiped it against my leg. I poured a second cup and then stepped out into the yard. I cleared my throat and said the word 'beautiful' and out it came, a little husky, but it was there, resonating in my ears. Another word, another milestone. I had not imagined it. I looked down the field towards the Bombo Burn. "Beautiful," I repeated, and it was still there. I felt another flutter of anxiety that it would disappear, that the words would cease. "Beautiful," I said again, with a more syllabic intonation. Music never sounded better. The early evening was cool. I looked again towards the Bombo Burn.

An hour later, I did not notice Lizzie as she climbed over the gate and playfully threw a stick at me to get my attention. "Hey!" I shouted. "No need fer that!"

Her knees just went from under her.

16

RETRIBUTION

1 year later

Of course, nothing had changed physically. I had power in my lungs, vibration through my voice box and a resonator in my throat, nose and sinuses. I was doing nothing different: the air stream poured from my lungs through the vocal folds of my larynx, perched atop my windpipe, just as it always had done. Except now it produced sound. Now the parts all worked together to provide an effortless voice. Now that I had found that voice, I could speak and articulate the thoughts in my head to those on the outside and, after fifteen and a third years of silence, I had things of importance I very much needed to talk about.

Finding my voice was one thing, but other pressures were still driving the air out of the bottle and suffocating the life out of me.

"Christ, you're talkin'," said Lizzie. "Be thankful for that."

"You can pay a visit to the church if it makes you feel better," Aunt Marion announced.

"Thanks," I said. "But why should He get the credit?"

"Did *He* no' bring about this miracle?"

"I never blamed *Him* for it in the first place, so why should I give *Him* any thanks for its passin'?"

I was happy enough to have found my voice, but I was troubled by the other dark questions that kept pressing in on me, through the night and dampening my spirits by day. I could not stop these thoughts crowding in on me. Questions that racked me from my earliest days, when I knew I would in all likelihood never see either of my parents again. Questions that were basic and sometimes vengeful, like who had done this to my parents? Why had they done it? My dear mother was dead and my father was gone. But who were they? If I were a man, would I go looking for them? How could I find them? Was that it, forming from the miasma of loss, a desire to find and obliterate those responsible? Were the questions no more than small steps in the quest for my own personal justice? With increasing clarity, I could see it was the search for retribution, atonement, satisfaction, justice and my own personal equilibrium.

Retribution is polite speak for an eye for an eye: you killed my dog, so you better hide your horse. Retribution sounded better than revenge. Retribution flows from justice whereas revenge seemed to me like something base and selfish. Nevertheless, I had in mind some resolution of what had been done. It was by no means finished. It was not a laudable, sophisticated or intellectual response, but it was curried over many years – and just now, it was little more than an aspiration.

Then again, aspiration and ambition is all very well but I had no real idea who the perpetrators were. Were they alive? Could I find them? If I had the chance would I take it? Maybe there would be a time when they would think themselves happy, these criminals. Would they have wives? Would they have parents, brothers, sisters around them? Would all the smiles turn to grief? Would the taste of fruit osmose into ash? Perhaps the bigger man would offer forgiveness. To my mind, that was a seductive nonsense that I would have little part of, a humiliating placebo for an illness that demanded a more direct remedy.

As I sat, quiet is the truth but - by virtue of a recent miracle - by no means dumb, I pondered heavily on who had in fact done this and why. I had small grains of knowledge on the subject but they blew ahead of me like dust in the wind. However, when there are things out there that you do not know, and you want to know, it may be a good strategy to sit back and think about the things you *do* know. When you know what it is that you do know you can then perhaps work out what it is that you don't know.

I knew well enough the hand that was dealt my mother. We still ate together off the same kitchen table in the same room where it happened. Yet I would not get rid of that table, not for all the books in Mr Shifner's library. Each time you sat at the table you dined with the dead. You put your hands where it was done. Then again, you need that sometimes because the brain is quick to protect; it draws a greasy film across those experiences it does not want you to know or remember. To my mind, I had to hold onto these things.

Yet, given I had the raw facts, what else did I know? I pursued my investigation with the person who I considered knew the most.

"I'm havin' these thoughts," I said.

"Thoughts?" Aunt Marion replied, not even raising one

eye. "I still cannie believe I'm hearing your voice, let alone your thoughts."

"Well, you are."

"I'm no' sure I'll ever get used to it," she said. "I hear your voice now but I wonder who it belongs tae."

"Just me."

"Sometimes, I think it's your father back there."

"Is that right?"

"Then I see it's you."

There was a silence. "Funny you should mention that."

"What is, is what is."

"My father," I said. "I have to understand more about what happened there."

"What happened?" she said.

"Aye, what happened to him." I was hesitant.

"I've told you plenty already."

"Well, about my mother then."

"What about her?"

"What happened to her?"

"I thought you knew already."

"I have the bare facts. Ma mother's dead. My father's in jail. That's all blindingly obvious."

"So?"

"There's lots I don't know."

"You're intelligent, Sean."

"Maybe."

"So work it oot."

"I will work it oot."

"Faster."

"I'm trying," I said. "But I'm no' seein' who the people are here. I cannie see how one piece of information connects with another."

The greater intelligence is the gift of analysis. That was

something I believed I also had. "What I'm after doin' is piecin' the events together."

"The events?"

"Yes, the events. Everything that happened that night."

She looked me straight in the eye. "Why do you no' want to just let these things go?"

"How can I let them go?"

"People have to move on in their lives."

"I'm no' wantin' to do that," I said. "I'm no' sure I could - even if I wanted to." I rose to my feet and stood by the fire. I turned towards Aunt Marion and I noticed the grey in her hair. "I would be dishonourin' them."

"What do you want to do?" she asked.

"I don't know, but I want them to know I haven't just let things be."

"Maybe they would want it that way."

"They can't tell us now."

"And where will this take you?"

"I dinnae ken that either."

There was a long silence. "I always wanted you to know what happened. I never tried to hide it from you."

"I know that."

"Is it revenge? Is that what you're after?"

"That's an ugly word," I said. "Justice is what I'm after."

"Say it for what it is."

"Revenge then, if it makes you feel better."

"It may not end happily."

"It has that reputation."

"Revenge is an angry emotion."

"I'm angry, Aunt Marion. Make no mistake."

"That's what I'm worried about," she said.

"Which is why I call it justice." I turned away from the fire. "I've no equilibrium in my life. Everything is skewed around this one thing. Somehow, I have to find some balance."

"Diggin' graves is dangerous work," she said. "You can fall in."

I sat down again and sighed. "I'll tell you what I'm thinkin'."

"That would be a good start."

"I've no' got the whole picture here, not by a long chalk."

"Fine. Let's hear what you're thinkin'."

"But?" I said.

"But remember one thing: put a seed in the ground and you dinnae always ken what will grow."

"You're full of worthy homilies the day," I said.

"I've got one more. Have you heard of this one? It's what I said about graves being dangerous work."

"Which is?"

"Before you embark on vengeance, first dig two graves."

"Seekin' justice is dangerous? I knew that already."

"Perhaps."

"Be careful what you wish for? Is that it?"

"That too."

"It's good advice," I said emptily, although I knew it was.

"You could leave it alane," she said.

"There are wounds that willnae' heal." I was becoming impatient. "They stay green forever, like it or no'."

"Seekin' revenge is what keeps them green," she said.

"Anyway, after all these years, why on earth are you tryin' to discourage me?"

"I'm no'," she said. "I've told you everything. I've never kept any bit of it away from you."

"Yet you're no' convinced I should go after those responsible."

"Ye make your own choices," she said. "You say you've no choice, but you do."

"Well, I've chosen."

"A fool walks with his eyes closed."

"You're thinkin' I'm a fool then?"

"No."

"You think I don't know what I'm doin' here?"

"You cannie know where it'll lead. That's all I'm sayin'."

"My eyes are open," I said. Aunt Marion did not answer. "I cannie see through walls but my eyes are open."

"Maybe I should've said nothin'."

"I wouldnae've blamed you," I said. "You *could* have said nothing."

"That might have been dishonest. That's what I thought at the time."

"You've been true to yourself, Aunt Marion."

"Your father might no' thank me."

"Maybe no'. But father is in a jail and I'm no' my father."

We sat in silence for a while and then I leaned forward, elbows on my knees. "I have to work it oot," I said.

"You know all there is to know."

"I'm just thinkin' aloud."

"Go on then." I looked at Lizzie who was by the kitchen table. "Don't look at her," said Aunt Marion. "Lizzie knows as much as I do. She may be on the clumsy side but god her heart is in the right place. So, dinnae worry aboot her." Lizzie smiled and lowered her face to the table. "Most of the time," she added.

17

SALMON COTTAGE (2)

The night had begun with a lot of men coming up the track to Salmon Cottage, shouting, angry, making a whole lot of noise. It wasnae dark yet, but it was afternoon and the sun was down and the light, I dare say, was getting on the gloomy side. My father, of course, was not to be intimidated. Afghanistan and the life of a soldier had hardened him. He confronted them outside the house, maybe on the porch. Or maybe by the big old gate somewhere. Not to discuss potato varieties, but to know what the hell they were doing there. My mother was inside. Was she sick with fright? A little maybe, who wouldnae be, but she came from a place where fear and violence were daily visitors. She almost died the day my father met her. How many of them were there outside? I would come back to that. Best do the headcount later, but my father was on one side and on his own, in the thick of it, not intimidated, but confronting or perhaps seeking to contain.

Meanwhile, my mother was in the house as she always was. Let's say agitated, not terrified, maybe shaking a little by the window. As I say, she wouldnae frighten easily. Then what? A discussion with the men, pushing against the gate, a few insults traded. Fingers up, jabbing and some bad feeling. Drink had been taken of course and that never helps. Tempers getting heated. Blame handed out with spit and red ears. Then someone got hold of my father and he ended up face down, maybe getting kicked, lying in the dirt, wondering how did we get to this? One man, against how many? What did he think he was going to do? Blow them away with a sermon? Like Moses on the Mount? I suppose then there was a scuffle and it turned into a fight. A lot of heat over nothing you might think. He was trying to stop them, but they pushed on through the open gate and some at the front went into the house, like they had a right to be there. Windows were broken. Nothing serious. But suddenly, there was a shot. Everyone stopped, and out came Mad Bob with a hole in his stomach. Someone said he came from Dysart. Most bad stuff does but it's no' conclusive. Montrose, Aunt Marion pondered. She'd heard that old bag Wallace, whose husband was a butcher, worked at Skene's abattoir, she heard her mention it once.

"So," said Aunt Marion. "You've got Mad Bob from Montrose."

"Or Dysart," I said.

"But Mad Bob nonetheless. That's what we know."

"In any event, a man with a lot of daylight passin' through the hole in his belly."

"Cannae be too many of them aboot," said Aunt Marion.

"You ever been to Disarm? The place may be full of them."

"Montrose," she said.

"Whatever," I agreed. "Not a lot there to go on."

"What else d'you want?" she asked.

"A surname?"

"Weir," she said. "Weir's the surname. Did I no' mention that?"

"No, as a matter of fact you didnae."

"Well, it's Weir I think. Mad Bob Weir."

"How d'you know that?"

"That he was mad?"

"Naw. How d'you know it was Mad Bob Weir?"

"He wis at your father's trial," she said. "He was the peacemaker, you see. That's what he said. Your mother shot him. He was the man wavin' the white flag."

"That's no' true," I said.

"Well, that's neither here nor there. That's what he testified, I heard it with ma ain ears. And they chose to believe him."

"Father then went for his gun?"

"Aye, but what chance of that workin'?"

"The gun was in the house?"

"Inside the house, up on one of the rafters."

"What did he do then?"

"He used his fists, what d'you think?"

"What about the fish-knife?"

"Aye, that too."

"As Ben Mercer would testify."

"If he was no' dead."

"Then what?" I asked.

"By all accounts, he got clocked on the head with a table leg."

"Christ, who would do that?"

"Big gash on the head," said Aunt Marion. "The hair didnae grow back."

"Then they…" I said.

"Don't rush now, Sean."

"Then they killed her."

"They did. But first they broke her spirit and then they broke her bones. Then they killed her."

"I know that," I said. "You told me that already."

"Right enough, but it's part of the story."

"I was lookin' to be sensitive."

"I know."

"They beat her to death," I said. "It was only then, when they'd finished...." We were silent for a minute. Then I asked: "Okay now, how many are we looking for here?"

"I'm no' sure," said Aunt Marion, "how many *you're* lookin' for. But there were four. Maybe five? Naebody took a roll-call."

"Ben Mercer was dead, so take him out of it."

"Must have been three or four anyway," she said.

"Aye, definitely three or four."

"Could be there was more, I dinnae ken."

"But where were they from?"

"Hard to say," said Aunt Marion.

"There's Mad Bob Weir from Dysart," I said.

"Montrose."

A thought crossed my mind, cutting in and out like a page that keeps dropping from a loose book. It gave me an uncomfortable feeling. "Do we live amongst these people?" I asked. That was a question that had preyed on me for years. Were we the only ones who did not know?

"None of them came from round here," said Aunt Marion. "None from Tullis."

"Not that you know of."

"Not that *I* know of anyhow."

"You could be wrong?"

"I could be."

Then again, I was not so clear about all that. Some of them had faces that were known to my father - of that I was sure. He knew who was on his farm that night. So it was likely they were native to or at least loosely acquainted with Tullis. The one with the table leg skills on my father's head was portly, that's what my father had told Aunt Marion. Portly. Or fat to the rest of us. "Had thin, fair - or even red - hair on his head, but it was a while ago. Hair may have gone by now."

"Men and their hair are easily parted," said Aunt Marion.

"He took charge. Where he led, others followed." I paused. "But that's all we know about this man. There must be thousands close to that description."

"Well, there's somethin' else," said Lizzie moving towards them for the first time. She'd been sat listening but had said nothing. When we looked at her she seemed to lose courage. "Well, then again, it may be nothin'."

"Anythin' or nothin' might help," I said.

"Ok, I'll tell you anyway. I was at Fawcett's shop, you see and I overheard somethin'."

"When was this?"

"A while ago now. A few months."

"Okay."

"And it may be nothin'."

"Tell us, Lizzie."

"I was outside Fawcett's. I wasn't doing a lot, but I was just by the steps and I was lookin' around at things. I think I'd forgotten somethin' and I couldnae remember what I'd forgotten. Or maybe I'd dropped somethin'. No' too sure what though. So I was thinking about what...." She noticed Aunt Marion's look. "Anyway," she continued. "It was just that these two women come oota there and they didn't see me because it was cold and I had my hood up on ma cloak and a scarf on ma neck." Aunt Marion rolled her eyes. "Well, in any event, I heard them talkin' and I heard them say somethin'." Lizzie paused, aware that for this brief moment she had their full attention.

I nodded her some encouragement. "Are you gonnie tell us what?"

"They said somethin' like - I don't remember exactly, so dinnae quote me aboot this – somethin' like 'that one makes ma skin creep, I dinnae like it'. Then the other one said somethin' very strange. Well, it was right strange to me."

"Which was?" I said.

"She said 'dinnae be surprised' - or something - then, 'he was one of them did Salmon Cottage'."

"Anythin' else?"

"Well, that's all really," said Lizzie.

"He was in the shop," I said. "The person they were talking aboot?"

"Could be."

"He was in Fawcett's shop?"

"Mebbe. I dinnae ken. That's the impression I got though. Tea?"

"But if she said 'that one makes ma skin creep' she must have been referring to someone she'd just seen?"

"Aye."

"Most likely in the shop?"

"Yes, I suppose."

I turned to Aunt Marion. "Aunt, you said he was a redhead? Or reddish? And the hair was thin?"

"That's what your father told me. He didnae remember much, no' after the table leg bouncing aff his heid."

"But those were the words he used?"

"Yes, I think they were the words he used. At least, thinnin' hair and red hair."

"He would no' be young now, would he? He might have little hair and it could be red or fair or grey-fair."

"Mebbe."

"And maybe that was him. In Fawcett's shop." I turned back to Lizzie. "Before that, had you been in the shop yourself?"

"Aye. I had to buy a lathe stone for the knives."

"Did you see anyone in the shop?"

"No," said Lizzie.

"Could he have been?"

"Aye. Now I think on it, there was someone in there with Mr Fawcett."

"What did he look like?"

"I didnae see him. He was in the small room behind the counter."

"Who was?"

"Somebody was."

"How do you ken that?"

"Ken what?"

"Ken he was there?"

"Because Mr Fawcett carried on talking to him, even though he was serving' me. I thought that was rude."

"You couldnae see this man?"

"Naw," Lizzie answered. "That's what I already said."

"But you heard him?" I persisted.

"Aye."

"And what did he say?"

"Just small stuff. I dinnae remember if he said anything."

"Okay." I thought about this. "He may be from round here then," I concluded. "Or why would he be there?"

"Oh, he's definitely from roond here. He said it was a short ride from Buckhaven, even in this weather."

"You said you didnae remember what he said."

"I didnae. But I remember him saying that, aboot Buckhaven."

"Okay," I said.

"Oh, and he had a horse outside. A big chestnut mare with four white socks. I remember thinkin' it'd been sweatin' a bit. A *lot* in fact. There was foam all around the girth and I never like seein' too much foam under the girth."

"Anything else?" I said.

"It was cold. I felt sorry for the horse."

"Anything else about the *man*?" I said.

"Naw. I told you I didnae get a look at him. He was in the snug behind the coonter."

"There's one other thing," Aunt Marion said.

"Yes?"

"Your father said he heard music." She stared at the fire.

"Not music, mum," interjected Lizzie. "Hummin'."

"Hummin'?" I said.

"She's right, actually," said Aunt Marion. "It wasnae music. *He* thought it was music and that's what he said to begin with, but later he said it was no' music at all. He said it was just a kind of hummin'."

"Yes," I said. "But he'd been hit on the head."

"With a table leg," said Lizzie.

"Mahogany," said Aunt Marion.

"Victorian," said Lizzie.

"Who says it was *Victorian*?" I said.

"Intuition," she answered.

"He *would* hear music," I said. "Or hummin'. Who wouldnae?"

"Aye, but your father could himsel hold a note. He was quite musical. He could sing well and he knew aboot music. He said he recognised the tune. It was a piano tune. He could play the piano, at least when he was a boy. Never had a lesson, but just seemed to ken which keys he should hit. Never had a piano himself. I was quite different. I had two left hands."

"So, he said he heard a piano tune," I said.

"A piano tune, yes. But the man was hummin' it," said Aunt Marion.

"I need to think about that," I said.

Who could hum the music of a piano? Was this a standard skill for your everyday killer? The answers raised only more questions. Of course, it was clear my mother had taken Mad Bob to task with the Enfield rifle. Nice shooting. Good ventilation. Alas, it had to lead to a mild escalation of events. Where was Mad Bob now? Mad Bob Weir. Self-defence was for the fairies. What was he doing? Maybe, if he was still alive I would find him and give him the second barrel. And then there would be balance and a satisfactory symmetry. I have always loved symmetry. There was the other man too. A friend of Fawcett? He let him sit in the snug behind the counter. That had the feel of a friendship or proximity beyond the paying customer. Could be from Buckhaven? There was a Buckhaven in Fife. Not far on a horse, but distance enough to work up a sweat. Particularly if you were carrying a portly man. Even a fat man.

"Is there anythin' else?" I asked. "Anythin' else at all?"

"Just one small thing," said Aunt Marion. "In fact two small things."

"Yes?"

"One was very tall. One of the attackers. Your daddy said he towered above the rest."

"Okay," I said. "And the other?"

"One of them had the tip of his finger missing. His index or his pinkie, I'm no' sure."

"Was he the hummer?" I asked.

"Might have been. I cannae say."

"Can't be too many people without a pinkie," I ventured.

"You'd be surprised."

"Does anyone want tea?" asked Lizzie. "It's stewin' in the pot."

18

THE BITTER TEARS

S ome while later I was sitting by the fire. It had been raining outside and I'd been and done my tasks, checking the sheep and putting feed in the hencoop. I'd been thinking about foxes biting the heads off the hens. Sometimes they took the hearts from the lambs. Give them half a chance, that's where they were headed. And never ate the carcase, just the heart. With the hens, they never did anything but bite the head off. Was that revenge? Or was it justice? Did the snooty hen give the grumpy fox a rude finger gesture from inside the coop? Is that what revenge or justice was, just takin' off the head, stealing the heart and leaving the body to rot?

I'd come into the house, sat myself down on the farm chair in which I'd always been told my father used to sit, and I lodged my boots on the fender. The steam was comin' off in tight, twisting swirls. Aunt Marion was applying her sewing skills to an old shirt of mine with more holes than a pea colander. Another time she would have told me to get my wet boots *oot the hoose*, but this time she said nothing.

Lizzie was by the oven, stirring a pot of parsnip soup. It *could* have been parsnip soup but I wouldnae necessarily have bet my darned shirt on it. I picked up a beaten copy of some poems I had long time ago diverted into my possession from Mr Shifner's library and I browsed the middle section. The page was dirty and the light was dim there by the fire, but I knew the words well enough.

"What's that you're readin'?" Aunt Marion asked, but I think she knew.

"Poems," I said.

"Poems?"

"Yes, rhymin' things."

"Well, Lord Byron, why do you no' read me wan?"

"I always think, you should keep a poem in your head."

"Why's that?" she said.

"Somethin' they lose when you take 'em ootside."

"Is that what's troublin' you?" She asked. "Takin' things ootside?" I looked at her and said nothing. My voice had been in my head all these years. It was no' exactly surprising that I would keep my poetry there too. "Just read me a poem, like I asked you."

"You heard of Landon?" I asked.

"I have not," she said. "I never heard of him."

"Her," I said. "Landon was a *her*."

"Well?" said Aunt Marion. "Let *her* be *heard*."

"Just two verses," I said. "Break you in gently."

"Should suffice," she answered.

So, I read the first two verses to her:

Ay, now by all the bitter tears
That I have shed for thee
The racking doubts, the burning fears, -

Avenged they well may be –

By the nights pass'd in sleepless care,
The days of endless woe;
All that you taught my heart to bear,
All that yourself will know

"People get their just deserts," I said. "If they wait long enough."

"Why does she no' just say so?"

"Come on, it wouldnae be a poem."

We didn't speak for a while. In our ears, just the sound of sparks cracking and spitting off the fire, the tough scrape of Lizzie's spoon in the soup pot, and the clicking of Aunt Marion's tongue as she pulled on the darning thread at the back of my shirt.

I pulled my overheated boots in from the edge of the fire. Aunt Marion put her needle down by the green thread on the wobbly, wooden table at her side. "I heard you shootin' your father's rifle."

"Just rats," I said. "Needs oil. Have to work a gun to keep it in condition."

I could hear Lizzie once more stir the pot. Aunt Marion turned towards her daughter with an eyebrow elevated somewhere near the rafters. Lizzie stared back at her and dropped the spoon in the soup. She fished it out with her fingers but yelped like a burnt cat when she felt the heat. She licked the spoon and burnt her tongue. The cloth that held her hair in place was smeared with neeps. She licked her burnt index finger and exhaled.

"Are you sharin' that soup with us or are ye intent on

suicide by a thousand burns?" Aunt Marion, sighed deeply, rolling the whites of her eyes. For a moment she looked like a dead fish, her lids wide open and unblinking.

19

THE FISHING TRIP

1900

N o tale about Fife can ignore the fish that swim in silver shoals along her shores. Of those fish, the *clupea harengus* is a smooth, slender, aquatic craniate with a white, lustrous sheen of a skin, speckled on its upper body. It holds a hint of bottle green and cobalt blue. The snout is a smear of black slate. The lower jaw protrudes to give the fish the scowling look of an old man with big gums and no teeth. There are many names for this slippery fellow: some call it the 'torn belly' or the 'wine drinker' – glamorous names for a simple herring. In those days there were plenty spilling around the rocky promontories along the coast of Fife.

From time to time we fished the herring. It was popular and a good price could be had for any fish netted without a prohibitive primary cost. The herring could then be salted, vinegared and smoked all in the pursuit of a modest profit.

Somebody would surely have carnalised it if they could see a return on their investment. In any event, a spate of herring taken at the right time - just before they swam north to the Faroes - was a chance to lay down some fat for the winter months.

It was early, the sun invisible, when Lizzie put out a breakfast of sourdough bread and cooked ham on a stone plate. Next to it was a pie disgorging a boiled egg like a dead eye and a pot of strawberry jam with lumps that might have been fruit many years before the Duke of Wellington met his mother. I helped myself to the pie, the egg and the jam and I slurped at the black tea. I enjoyed it all so much and, like a fool, I used my voice to tell Lizzie that I loved and adored her for the quality of her breakfast. It was a stupid thing to say but she smiled kindly nonetheless and dropped the butter dish.

When it comes to herring, you need a boat and you need plenty of hands to work the boat and pull the fish from the sea. The water is often rough and cold and you have to respect that. The closest farm to us on the Logan stretch belonged to a man named Harcourt, a gruff geezer of few words, but to me he seemed decent enough, although he liked to spit. I don't generally like the type of person who spits all the time. It seems unnecessary. The mucus is a slippery secretion but it's got its uses; after all, it protects the body from infection and is the kind of thing you see in fungi, bacteria and viruses. Your average body produces about one and three-quarter pints of mucus per day and, to my mind, it's no' particularly desirable that we all go around spitting out one and three-quarter pints of mucus per day. The streets would soon become unwalkable.

As for Mr Harcourt, he was the type who might speak a few choice words to you if pressed or if there were more than twenty-five hours in a day. For the most part he preferred to use two and a half words even if there were twenty going free. The two and a half words would, of course, be punctuated by a massive spit – hence the fraction. You could see Mr Harcourt's farm if you walked to the high field some six or seven hundred yards up from our own. He had some Blackface sheep, some wheat and a plague of weeds in a stony field and a strip of broccoli that never amounted to much more than pretentious shoots. In my view, he had too much sand in his soil. He owned nothing much to speak of, but then there was just him and his son Duncan to provide for. Mr Harcourt's wife was long since dead, buried and topped with a coarse *poa annua* meadow grass in the cemetery. Hers was one of the tidier stones complete with inscription, standing straight in death as she stood in life. Father and son had no need for much else, but they always did the fishing since they had the boat and it had proved it could be the source of reasonable profit.

As I said earlier, you cannot run a fishing boat on just two pairs of hands and a gutting knife, and old Mr Harcourt, off his own bat or because his son Duncan had persuaded him, sent a message down to Aunt Marion that if I was willing, I should join the fishing party. I was guaranteed a share of the catch and if there was money made he would see me right. Aunt Marion accepted those terms on my behalf, had Lizzie fill me with pie, egg and the historic jam and sent me on my way, like a crusty seadog, to join the crew.

Before I could leave the yard, the sun was already up if you could see it. No more than a diffuse, pale grey light across the fields. I looked at the darkening sky and became aware of a sombre portentousness in the air. Any shadows would not be around for long and the black clouds were already blowing in from Yellowcraigs and further east.

My instructions from Aunt Marion were to drop by at a house some way across the village, a spot well removed and a distance up the other side, at the end of three rough sheep-grazing fields. It was a house that had the benefit of a decent view down to the sea. It was windy up there and was quick to pick the worst of any bad weather that was coming through. The house belonged to a fellow called Calum Wilson. I'd heard of him and I knew him to look at – I'd seen him come out the post office from time to time and I noticed first the swagger he had about him, as if he had everything in the world to be confident about. I had never exchanged a single look or word with him before. Aunt Marion said Mr Harcourt wanted me to drop by Wilson's place to see he joined the fishing trip. He was lazy, he said, but would be useful. He knew little about fish, but he'd undertaken to come on board. Mr Harcourt said we needed all the hands we could get but he'd been let down by Wilson before, so why he trusted him to come I didn't know. If he'd taken a drink (which was entirely possible) I was told it was my job to persuade him to sober up and join the fishing party. The air would do his sobriety a whole lot of good.

I was thinking, a little sulkily, this detour was out of my way and we could manage the boat and a net with just the three of us. Calum Wilson seemed to me something of an idle bastard even with a boot up his rear end; it was common knowledge that he did indeed like a drink and I felt we could do without his *bonhomie de la mer* on our fishing trip. In any case, it was a common myth that more hands made light work; it depended what the hands were doing. If the hand had a finger up its rear end, it was likely to be doing nothing much more than tickling its prostate. It was hard to see how that would benefit the general popu-lace and its appetite for fish. Still, I wasnae in the mood to have my ears clipped, so I said nothing, just nodded with resignation at Aunt Marion and straightaway moved down the track leading away from Salmon Cottage. Sometimes you had to bite your tongue and take what's coming.

I cut through the village that, at this time, was still quiet as a pauper's grave. The only person I saw was Mr Fawcett brushing the earth off the step to his shop. He shouted across a greeting at me and I looked up and nodded. I now had a voice but I chose to use it selectively. I wondered who had been in his shop recently. There was plenty of time to work that one out. I had it in mind, when the time was right, to pay Mr Fawcett a visit to discuss the visitor to his snug behind the counter.

Once through to the other side of Tullis, I walked along the church wall, then jumped down and cut between the trees. I threaded my way along an old goat path, dodging the squads of heavy, black droppings, and at the end I crossed over a broken wattle fence that hung down from a leaning post. I picked my way through the heavy brambles, scratching the backs of my hands. This, I thought with a thin smirk, was at least the quickest way to Wilson's place.

Indeed, it took twenty minutes to get there whereas it would have taken forty by the road. It lightened my spirits a fraction. The route I had taken meant that I approached the house from the back, rather than the front. By this time the sun that had faintly risen with a pale chill in the east was already heavy and thickset in a solid blanket of grey cloud. There was a damp wash to the cold air and I could feel a light drizzle against my cheeks. That was how it could be round here, in these fields and woods we loved so much: one minute there was the threat of a little sunshine, face gently warming, the next you were wringing out the rain from a wet shirt.

Calum Wilson's place might have looked sweet enough on a dry, sunny day, its view caressing the green, leafy fields below, lightly skimming the Firth of Forth beyond. Today it was a depressing sight in the grey gloom. There was a back wall to the house ahead; the skim coat of lime plaster had parted company in many places and lay at the foot of the gable in broken, damp pieces, leaving the wall with the appearance of a crumbly cheese. The rubble looked to have been there a while but nobody had thought to clear it away. It was like somebody puked and didn't take the trouble to shovel up the mess. The woodwork around the eaves was flaked and blistered and the wood itself was split, soaked and plainly rotting. It was easy to see you might push your finger all the way in like it was old Miss Havisham's wedding cake. The windowsills were like a soft sponge and there was a yellow fungus like hard custard pasted on the uprights. Grey slates hung from the roof like stale biscuits. Some were broken or had disappeared altogether. Some leaned against the gutter, their ends poking out the front and scooping up the rain. Round the side was another desolate building, its's roof gone and a pile of wet timber stacked by the door.

I walked close by the house. Green logs lay beneath a leaky canopy and a coal box with a rotten, wooden lid that had been left open. It smelled of mould and sweating hay and fungus. The coarse grass at the back of the house had become a mud bowl where the rainwater was fast collecting in broken pools. I stood by the window towards the front of the house. I wanted to look in through the glass. It was smeared with thick grime. I wet the window with the rough sleeve of my jacket and rubbed noiselessly. I have to say I did think to myself, what the hell was I doing? Of course, that did not stop me, not for one second. I was intent upon my task and pressed myself to do a better job of it. I took a rag from my pocket and cleared a small funneled circle in the glass. I was curious.

Unfortunately, Mr Fuckin' Curious was *exactly* who I was. If you'd given me a riddle I would have chewed on it all night until my brain convulsed, by which time I would have solved it. Other times, I did things without a thought, as if instinct just took over and pushed me on in there. I'm no' sure it was the danger, but then again it might have been. Danger can make you do the stupidest things and, as I stood by the window with its clear, inviting, circle drawing my eyes through the grime, that day was no exception.

20

THE LADY'S LEG

Through the glass eye I had formed with my rag, I saw the end of a daybed and a blanket, some clothing and two male calf-high boots on the wooden floor, toe to toe like they were ballroom dancers picking out Polka steps. My eye was drawn further into the circle. I formed the impression I was looking at a naked leg, side on. It looked to be a pale leg with the slightest hint of creamy pinkness. Not a hair on it. Quite smooth. Quite beautiful I'd have to admit. It was so soft you could picture the dimples. It was neither a fat leg nor a thin leg. It was a slim leg but with texture and contours. Not just a bone, as you sometimes might see, but a leg with character and fullness. It was robust and, with some growing excitement, strangely I could imagine the taste of it, the sweet muskiness against the tip of my tongue. I could imagine running my hand from the calf and into that crevice behind the knee.

I have to confess my heart skipped as I thought about that leg. To this day it still does. Ridiculous, I know: it is, after all, only the lower limb and not uncommon so far as *Gray's Anatomy* is concerned. Nevertheless, it very nearly took away my power of breathing. A woman's leg was in front of me and I knew I'd never seen anything so desirable and so worthy of my attention. How had it taken this long? If the truth be known, I wanted to lick and drag my tongue from behind the knee, up across the thigh, and maybe enjoy the midlands before heading north, until my mouth ran dry as paper. I swallowed hard. I looked with my left eye and I felt something in both my balls. It was that tingle in the scrotum moment, accompanied by a profound sense of growth inside my trousers. I made myself breathe because I was going blue. My lips were very dry and I could feel my tongue against the roof of my mouth, clicking just a little against the dryness. I could hear the catch in my throat as once again, I tried to swallow. I moved my head a little to the right and traced my eye down through the circular hole in the grey-brown dirt of the glass. I was looking once again upon the woman's leg, and how soft the skin appeared as it curved, pale as cow's milk, towards her naked bottom. Her arm lay across the man's chest, her face below his ribs and close against his side. Were they sleeping? I thought I could hear the man snore. It occurred to me that the last thing a man should do in that company was snore. The very last thing he should do was sleep. A fullness pushed hard against the front of my trousers. What would have happened had there not been a sudden, unexpected movement? I threw myself back against the side of the house.

I hugged the building and edged my way towards the rear door, then turned the iron handle. I could have knocked but even my own mother would have said I was acting strangely that morning. I entered.

I was in a hallway. It was a small house and there seemed to be no upstairs to it. I could see the bare rafters. The walls were dirty and unpainted and the floors were blackened timber. I saw no one and at first I couldnae hear a sound. I could see there were two rooms at the front of the house, one on the left and one on the right. The one on the left turned out to be nothing more than a boot room, with some game and tackle hanging from the cracked ceiling. The floor was blotted with clods of dry mud. Coats draped the steel hooks by the door. Three rabbits with staring eyes hung from a rope attached to a cupboard handle. A bundle of snares were wound around a flat-headed nail, jabbed in the wall. There was blood, stained on the mat that lay across the floor slabs. I looked towards the other door, the door leading to the room on the right. The room I had been looking into from outside the house. I steadied my breathing, tried to make it even and smooth like I was in control of myself. All I could hear was my own heart beating in my ears. I could smell damp woodsmoke hanging heavy in the air. I felt it was time I introduced myself.

"Calum Wilson, you there?" Immediately, I heard the scrape of a chairleg against the floor.

"A minute now!" a male voice barked. "Who the hell is it? I've got a gun here! I'll blow your fuckin' head aff, if I have to!"

"It's Sean Logan. Now, dinnae fire! I repeat, dinnae fire!"

"And?"

"I'm here about some fishin'."

"Is that so?"

"It is so," I said.

Calum appeared in the doorway. He was a relatively short man with wild hair on his head, sideboards that ran from his ears to his chin, growing outways and joining together at the bottom. He had a pale, green-tinged skin. He had creamy puss in the corner of his left eye and he stood in his bare feet without any trousers. He had no gun. "What do you want, then?"

"Fishin'," I said. "You're supposed to be fishin'." He looked vacant. "Harcourt?"

"How old are you?" he said.

"Mr Harcourt sent me."

"And you are?"

"The larynx I understand to be a sensitive and useful organ that I've only just recently come to enjoy. Consequently, I say things only once, but I'm no' without heart and I do make exceptions for the slow-witted. For the second time, Sean Logan's my name and I'm here because you said you were doin' the fishin' with us." I could see the woman a few feet behind him. She pulled her gown tight around her waist. She smiled at me and bit her lip. Her eyes momentarily stunned me, like they were shafts of brilliant green light. "I was told you were comin'," I said.

"By the by," he answered. He looked at the woman and then back at me. "By the by."

"Well, you can suit yersel," I said. "I've delivered the message and I've put myself to the inconvenience of repeatin' it."

"You're a cheeky fuckin' sod," he said.

I looked at him. "Really?" I said. "I never thought o masel that way. Anyway, I'm no' waiting roond here jabbering to you." I looked at the woman. "Morning, Mrs Wilson, please forgive my intrusion into your hoose. I chapped the door but..." And I took my leave.

The man annoyed me. He was that type with no care for anything. What did he stand for? He was as limp as he was loose. Stood there in his pimpled bare legs, he was the very epitome of *slack*. Or so I thought. No matter what personal view I took of him, I had indeed delivered the message and I was damned if I was going to prolong the chit-chat.

The woman turned away, stifling a yawn, as if she was bored by it all. I didn't see her smile. If Wilson chose not to turn up that was his call. I turned on my heel and made my way out through the back door of the house, the way I had come. I cut around the edge of the boggy field without a backward glance. If I'd looked I might have seen the figure at the small scullery window, watching my retreat.

I didnae think it likely that I would be followed and I had no regrets about that. I joined the old farm track that ran straight down to the shore between the twin spines of two moss-covered walls. I followed the path along the water's edge until eventually I came upon Mr Harcourt and his son Duncan at the small quayside. This quayside could take two small boats end to end but it was rarely used and almost never by two boats at the one time. The quay stones were breaking up with the persistent heavy swell and over time they were toppling piece by piece into the grey water. The waves and the rising, falling tide, continued to push into the fissures and split them wider apart. No matter how long you waited, one day the sea would have its way.

The wind had picked up. It had sent gusts to batter them as they worked to prepare the boat. Duncan was tarring a split in the side of the hull. It was amazing how these old cups stayed afloat. The rain came harder on the back of the wind. My jacket was already heavy with the wet and the spray I collected during the walk down from the Wilson farm. The boat itself was made of wood, perhaps twenty feet long, painted black with a white stripe along the top edge, two sails, one large with a box top and the other the size of a handkerchief, with a couple of good oars on board just in case someone messed up the navigation. On the port side was painted the boat's name, in black letters against a white background: *Firth Wind*.

The boat was done and ready to sail. They had stowed the oars and other equipment, fixed the net and stored it in the bow and finished off the tarring at the hull. By then the wind was creating a big squall and the tops of the waves were splashing hard and white against the boat's ribs.

"Take it he's no' comin'?" said Mr Harcourt to me as I had approached.

"No' too keen on fresh air today," I said.

"Thought not." He said. "Lazy sack of shit." He spat against the quaystone.

I had looked at the boat. "Are we okay with three?" I asked.

"Four," he said. "Thought this might happen. Should be right with four though." At which point fair-haired, blue-eyed, projectile-spitting Rory Fraser stepped out from behind the sail and grinned at me.

"It's goin' to be some trip, Logan," he said. "Hope you can fuckin' swim boy!" Not an idle question, as it turned out.

21

THE MCLEODS

1897

There is that moment in a human life when an event occurs that stands every other in its wake. It's the big syntactic pivot, the word around which every sentence is formed, on which each existence will turn, changing what came before and transforming all that follows. It's the moment that will cast a conspicuous, indelible shadow, a grey unbroken wash, for good or bad, across the length of a person's life. It's the jump of a train from one set of tracks to another as those aboard head in a direction they had never foreseen, invited or anticipated.

Keira McLeod had that experience when she was seventeen years old. She was a woodland farmer's daughter from Blairgowrie, birthplace of the Scottish raspberry, a small Perthshire town at the foot of the highlands, where the Cairngorms flatten out from blue-grey mountains to green foothills. It is a wet place that feels as if all the rain off the hills had to go somewhere and it chose to come here and ease itself through a funnel into the River Ericht. Keira lived in a black, slate-roofed farmhouse on the southernmost edge of the Meiklour Wood, not so far from General Wade's post-Jacobite military road that carves its way through the highlands, to the northwest by Loch Ericht.

Keira's brother Ian, lived across the landing in a room with a broken window latch, so that the case leaned to one side and the gap was filled with old paper and horsehair. The draught still found its way through and breezed across his head as he slept in the iron bed beneath. He was always getting colds. Their mother lived along the landing. Her father was dead. In his place was her father's cousin who had offered a home to them when it was plain they would never survive alone. When he was there, he would slam the bedroom door at night. Sometimes they heard him pee in the outside toilet. Sometimes he farted and belched before he had finished the final drops. At the centre of the Meiklour Wood was a natural spring loch known as the Hare Myre. In the days that followed, Keira could not go back there because of what happened. Her brother Ian coped better by spending as much time as possible in his simple, wooden boat. Somehow, by being on top of it he was able to keep any demons at bay. Sometimes he put a line out and took some trout and these he would bring back to the house. Their mother would cook them on the stove. Keira found them hard to swallow – the eyes always stared at her.

The house in which they lived was a wood frame, leaning sack of shit. It was a place designed by an idiot and built along a low ditch into which it threatened to slide. It was constructed by a moron in the wrong stupid place, is what her father's cousin always said. It should have been built higher up where the earth and the grass were relatively dry, removed from all this damp, seeping into your bones.

The man had a point. The house had two floors. The roof had a dip halfway along the ridge as if it struggled to support its own weight. It had uninvited pigeons in the loft, the occasional string of nesting bat and a woodlice infestation around the front porch which had once been painted green. The door had no colour to it now. Keira thought that the pigeons maybe got in because they tore themselves a hole beneath a missing slate that nobody had bothered to replace. The woodlice got in because the front porch was a holy Mecca crying out to them like they were god's special children, drawing them into its darkness and ballooning moisture. Sometimes you thought you could actually hear them crawling beneath the hearth at the front door, like they were tiny soldiers on military manoeuvres. Her brother Ian used to eat them as a small boy and said they tasted like "strong urine". Keira loved her brother, with his pants hitched up halfway to his chest, but she had no urge to sample bodily fluids.

The house had a name: *Merrylees*. "*Merry* means happy in ma book," was Keira's complaint.

"Did naebody tell you?" asked her brother. "The *lees* are deposits of dead yeast. They sink to the bottom in a beer vat."

"Whoever the idiot was to come up with that name already spent too long with his heid under the beer tap."

"I agree," said Ian. "The two words are antithetic of each other."

"In any event," she answered. "I can see plenty mulch but there's no' a lot of happiness."

Merrylees was near to - and over-shadowed by - the dense, red-brown wood of pine trees that surrounded it, pushing in with roots that squeezed out its life like tightening ligatures. Whilst enjoying the heavy scent all around, still it was always damp, even in the warmth of summer. Damp from the moisture that dripped off the sweeping, evergreen needles whenever it rained, theirs was a house that never offered much comfort. The fire in the iron grate never did any more than spit out a small, petulant flame, as if it were saying, I am alight but under duress. The house smelled faintly of fungus and was usually cold, giving rise to intermittent hacking coughs, sore knees, wooden stairs that creaked under your weight and small oil lamps that never worked like they would out there in the ordinary world.

Keira's mother was Alice and she had her own way of dealing with the cold that covered their bones like frost on a gate: she moved around a lot. She was always active, she never stopped working morning to dusk.

"She's a fuckin' woodpecker," her father's cousin took time to remind them all. But a useful woodpecker since she made a lot of jam out of plums, raspberries and other red berries that some people said were poison.

"I've never had a death yet," she proudly told anyone who would listen. She swept the floors so hard you could see sparks fly off the brush. She hammered a nail in the wall and hung a coat off it. She banged it in so hard she could have hung a bridge off it. She scraped mould off the bedroom wall like she was taking soot from a chimney or dredging scum from a canal. She chopped dry kindling for the fire that refused to burn (because it was still green, she never gave it time to grow old and die), and she did not stop for tea, argument, urinary convenience or two civil words for fear of being accused by God of momentary indolence.

Her father's cousin was called Graham. "Graham," he said. "Spelt with a silent aich." A word said to mean 'grey home' or 'warlike'. For Keira, both meanings had resonance when applied to that bastard. Aggressive and unloving, he was full of gruff whinges. His scope for genuine complaint was limited because, having taken them in, subject to 'conditions', he contributed almost nothing to the betterment of his cousin's family. Graham was a mean-spirited, uncharitable kind of man who felt that existence, in spite of all his blessed gifts, had dealt him an unfair hand.

"Never had a leg-up," he whined. "No' like you lot. Livin' like fuckin' princes."

"You know why that is?" her mum would answer in braver times. "If you were offered a ladder up, you'd thieve the ladder."

"Aye, but the house," he began.

"Oh aye, the one you got frae your parents. Lucky old you!"

He was a man who liked to spit in the fire and watch it sizzle. He swore at the two children. "Dinnae look at me," he told them. " And dinnae look to get anything aff me."

He was a discontent with tiny, greedy thoughts that he wore in a hungry space he called a brain, wedged beneath a filthy tweed cap he rarely removed.

Graham, like any man, had his dreams. He'd thought there would be more to his existence than was found at Merrylees, by Meiklour Wood, and he was disappointed. Every time he checked his cup, it was nearly bloody empty. "What's this then? Bloody nothin' as usual!" He always reacted with surprise.

"I dinnae ken why you're so surprised by your ain failure," said Keira's mum. "Can you no' see?" His increasingly feeble mind was unable to comprehend this miserable lack of success at any venture he embarked upon, far less doing anything to change its course. He surrendered himself to his failure and lashed out venomously against those who witnessed his fall. To his edited reckoning, it was not he who was at fault. They, that is those around him, were all responsible for what had happened - or what had not happened - in his life. His eyes were sharp drill holes, the type that might be filled by a judiciously hammered peg. He had a level of insight into his condition: he recognised the cup was broken and beyond repair, even if he did not recognise that he was responsible.

Her father's cousin worked hard to assuage the rising tide of negativity by consuming alcohol he expertly brewed in a lean-to, straw-covered shed at the back of the house. In here, he devised a giddying concoction, sweetened with a sugary sauce to make the alcoholic acid digestible. If anyone said he had few friends, that person would have to correct himself. He had no friends.

Keira was not particularly unhappy but the stone was in her shoe and she'd learnt to live with it. She did the equivalent of walking on the side of her foot to lessen the pain. She could remember much happier times. Merry moments when home-brew did not smear its blur across Graham's life, when he had given some small pleasure to others, when he had worked to provide something for his adopted family. Those were times Keira fondly remembered, even if the passage of years had exaggerated the warmth of her memory: brief occasions, when he might have talked to her, looked at her with gentle eyes. Once he even played a game of cards with her. Whist was the name of it. She enjoyed it at first but then he took the pleasure from it by pulling the head off one of her dolls for every game she lost.

"That'll teach you," he said. She didn't know what. She had a row of dismembered dolls that summer; then the corpses disappeared and she only had the heads.

Keira also remembered hide and seek with her brother, Ian. She could picture her mother smiling on the doorstep. Another speck of silver memory in the inky darkness. Those days slowly melted away and as Graham's skin grew tight and yellow, his temper grew meaner. Too much drink played all hell with his constitution. He would get to his feet and bowl over in pain as some part of his body protested against the assault on his liver. He lived in a deadly cycle, his brain shrinking from the abuse, his guts straining with the poison. If he resembled anything good, paternal and human by the time Keira was seventeen, it was only ever because he wanted something. He hung around most of the day, doing nothing very useful, staring at Keira to make her uncomfortable. He seemed to enjoy and delight in that, just looking to make her feel awkward beneath his gaze.

In the face of all this, there were times when her mother, Alice, would try to control Graham. But the bravery had long since deserted her. He had taken to beating her hard with the back of his hand and sometimes a wooden paddle he kept in the brew house. "Where's the fuckin' boat?" he was shouting. "Where is it?" There was no boat. There was just a paddle which he used to break her mother's nose more than once when she answered back at him. They could hear his hand when it connected with her face.

Keira's brother Ian, had sometimes tried to intervene with limited success. It was not his fault although he would say it was. When he was a young boy he was strong and determined and would push Graham away so that his mother and sister might escape the full extent of his brutality. For his efforts he often had a fist battered into his own face. Sometimes, it was a brick-like punch to the head and Ian would see the stars – sometimes the entire galaxy. Keira would bring him round with a cold towel on his head.

Graham once slashed Ian's lip with a jagged ring; the wound bled for a whole day. Each time it stopped and he moved his mouth the blood started up again, dripping down his chin. He still had the scar along the strip beneath his bottom lip. Sometimes Graham would have him on the floor and he would kick his ribs until the blood came out of Ian's mouth. He would bite his own tongue. He was a young, modest boy though, and he never would have claimed he was given to huge acts of bravery. There were times when he was shameful that he had turned away as the blows were coming down; sometimes he got on the floor and put his hands over his ears. You could not blame him for that but it caused him quiet guilt for the rest of his life. He never said as much but Keira knew it. They both remembered. Graham remembered nothing at all. All this led to the one moment I was talking of, the moment that changed their lives forever.

22

MEIKLOUR WOOD

K eira was digging carrots in a field to the north of Meiklour Wood. Through some rapturous quirk of Paleozoic geology, the field stood in a rift valley where the soil had turned light and sandy. Here the thick, wet earth around most parts of Meiklour Wood gave way to well-drained loam. That kind of rich, dry soil had a fertility that seemed to suit the carrots like no other place; they grew big as table legs and tall too, virtually leaping out of the ground.

Keira had been out for an hour – she'd lost any idea of what time it was – and she'd filled a large, wooden basket with enough carrots to take back to the house. She hummed as she went about her work. She was taller than most, slim as a young tree, and her arms ached from all the pulling. She had soil marks on her skirt, but she didn't care too much. She brushed the dirt with her hand and was then on to the next clump. She was seventeen years old, gone February, her skin was good and her dark hair hung lightly curled by the damp air, just loose to her shoulders. She had what you might think were the greenest eyes, but when you looked more closely at them you'd see that they were flecked with grey. That was what made them so striking. They were set against the clearest complexion. You found your own eyes were drawn to hers. You never knew if they were green or grey or even blue.

As she worked, from time to time she would look up and see the red deer. There were stags as well as hinds, the former distinguishable by their size and the huge antlers they bore that they would be rid of come the spring. Sometimes you'd hear the loud bark and clatter of their antlers echoing through the woods as they jousted with one another. Often they came down to take a look at her as if she were some curiosity worth peering at. Sometimes she couldn't see them, but she could tell they were out there, gazing with their glistening, unblinking eyes. They might have thought she would have something for them. Maybe some carrots, because clearly she could spare a few. Still, Keira was not breaking her back in order to feed the deer; they could come along later and scavenge after she was gone.

The carrots she gathered she placed in the large willow basket on the ground. Some she would take home and some she would leave in the wood store beneath the canopy of trees to one end of the field; they could be cleaned up and some would be put through to Perth market whilst others would be buried in the big, old, rusted tub of sand at the back of the house and kept for use, as and when.

The work was hard, doubled up as she was, and she could feel it either side of her spine. Yet, the sight of a basket growing heavier with the stacked carrots was satisfying. That was a good sight to her and she thought that she'd work on a little longer. She'd take another load to the store then fill up one more time and head off home, careful not to overload the basket. Sometimes she had to drag it on a rope. The light was fading and it had begun to drizzle ever so lightly, but not too much to trouble her.

She had a basket close enough to full when she had a sense that she was not entirely alone. She did not know if she saw something move or heard the ground carry the weight of another person, but she knew there was something or someone out there. It might have been a deer or some other animal. Who knows, there were wild cats out here, at least that's what Ian had told her, and foxes too.

She stood up straight and looked across to her left, down towards the Hare Myre water but saw nothing. As she turned back, she glanced over her right shoulder. She jolted when she saw Graham standing there, leaning to one side, his face blue-grey in the early evening light, his chin unshaven, his big hands by his sides. She saw him and he saw her, but neither said one word to the other. There was nothing unusual in that. Over many years, she had got used to his morose nature. Sometimes he said not a word for days, brooding over something that he chose not to share. However, today she felt that silence keenly as he looked her over. He had on a long, black coat and some cord hung from his waist that was doing a poor job of holding up his trousers. Even from where she stood, legs stretched across the ditch, and though not a huge distance away, she thought she could smell the staleness off his body and the drink coming away on his breath.

"Put the bloody shovel doon," he said. She shivered. She had a sense that something bad was about to unfold and she would have no power to stop it from happening. Still, she put the shovel down as her father's cousin had told her.

23

MERRYLEES

W hen, some time later, Keira found her way back to Merrylees, she placed one hand on the door and leaned towards it. The snib was unrestrained and she fell in, across the threshold. Her mother Alice was making jam. She stood with some small pots by the kitchen table, some sugar, a can filled with cold water and a hot, red, sticky tar bubbling in the pot. Alice looked up, stopped what she was doing, dropping a stone pot that smashed against the floor. Looking at her daughter, it was as if her mother understood that something had happened before Keira even spoke.

Her mother stood in a daze, as if a strong light had been shone into her eyes, before she moved towards her daughter. "I've made too much," she said. "It's gone past the settin' point." Keira said nothing. "Put your finger in it, you'll see it doesnae wrinkle."

Keira's brother, Ian, was seated in a chair by the fire. He had stood up, his face pale in the grey-orange light. He came over and stood by her side. His mother took Keira's other arm and together they brought her in and sat her down on the couch. She was trembling all over and they could feel it through her clothing like an electric charge. There was no hiding that her dress was torn all up one side. Ian had still not said anything, but he looked at his mother as if seeking reassurance from her. He went to the metal urn by the sink, and filled a glass with milk. He brought the glass back over and put it in Keira's open hand. He did not touch her. "What's happened?" he asked, when no one else had spoken.

Keira told them everything, from the moment she had looked up to see Graham looming over her in the carrot field. Her mother stared right back at her whilst Ian turned away, faced the window. When she had drunk half the milk, she put the glass on the table beside her, wiped her hands and continued with her account, recalling events as if she were recounting solid, historical facts. She was careful not to make judgments. She did not know why it had happened but she knew that she could not hope to repress telling what had occurred even if she had wanted to. It came out in a steady, unbroken stream. She thought they might say something but they stayed quiet. Her mother had sat close to her on the couch and had put one hand on her shoulder. The hand was light against her, hardly touching. Then she moved away, far enough for Keira to notice. Ian did not leave the window, just his broad back to her and his head dipped to look at his feet. As each word came she felt the better for it. She already knew that her life had changed. In the heavy silence after she was finished, it was in her mind that they might still blame her. She was confused but if she carried guilt for this, if she had encouraged this attack by her own actions, she believed they would tell her so. It was only right that they should.

It was dark now when Ian took the poker from the coal

scuttle next to the fire. The grate spilled a small glow but little flame. "I'm gonnie fix that chimney one day," he said.

"I heard that before," her mother said.

"I'll make that fire really blaze." He jabbed at the small, damp log and the embers splintered into red sparks. "I promise you that," he said.

"Forget the bloody chimney. The bloody chimney's the least of our worries."

Her mother had sworn twice in two sentences; that was unusual for her. She took her hand from Keira's shoulder, stood by the table and lit the kerosene lamp. She moved over and stood by Ian. Her face in the yellow light was anxious and strained. She looked at her son and he nodded back at her, as if he knew what she was about to say. Without the need for words they understood what they would do. She turned her face, her eyes passing from him to Keira. "You'd better come with us," she said. "We do this together or not at all."

Keira had no real understanding of where they intended to take her or what they planned to do. They had said nothing, passed no comment, articulated no judgments. Did they think she was responsible? Did they blame her for this? Had she brought this calamity upon her, upon them? It crossed her mind that they would take her out and punish her for an event that she should have prevented.

"I'm no' havin' this any more." Alice said, "Things have to be brought to a conclusion." She looked at Keira and again at Ian. "Now's the time," she said. She took the poker from the fireside.

24

RETURN TO MEIKLOUR WOOD

They marched like doomed victims to Hare Myre water, in the middle of Meiklour Wood, at least in part their minds full of grim intent and their hearts as heavy and suffocating as the gloomy darkness that surrounded them. Their eyes had adjusted to the poor light and, true to form, they found Graham at the same old fir tree where she had left him, slumped like a bloated corn bag, not so long before. He was on his back still, his neck and head against the brown, sappy bark. They could see his wasted silhouette stretch from the base of the tree, his knees a little bent, the toes of each boot parted and pointing to either side. In the murk, one could almost see the carrot basket, lying exactly where Keira had left it, a heap of green top shoots sprawling out one end, a small distance in from the edge of the field. Graham was half asleep in a whisky stupor, exorcising demons through a deep strangled snore, the green bottle empty against his chest. Keira stepped back from her mother's side. She would not approach any further. Ian stood over Graham and lay a hand on him, roughly shaking him by the coat.

"Wake up!" Ian yelled. "Wake up!"

Graham's eyes flickered open and he saw Ian and also Alice, who stood behind him, and at first he had the look of somebody who might have been pleased to see them, as if it was a nice surprise, them turning up just at this juncture.

"Aye, what you wantin' then?" He looked, of all things, to be smiling, but it was a nervous, devious smile.

"Bastard!" Ian said. "Filthy bastard!" Then they shouted in his face, Ian and their mother. "Ya filthy, rotten bastard!" They jabbed him with their fingers and Ian slapped him with his hand. As they did so, you could see the fear rising in his bloodshot eyes. "What did you think you were doin'?"

"Ah was... nothin'!"

"What were you doin'?"

"I tellt you, I was... what the fuck are ye on about?"

"You ken what I'm on aboot?" Ian said. "You ken you filthy git!" He shook him again, harder this time. His teeth must have rattled. "What did you do with her?"

"What? None of your business, you. None of hers either!"

There was no exculpation, no plea in mitigation. Ian shouted at the older man and against the light from his oil lamp you could see the spray of saliva shower off his lips. You might have thought it would end there, but then Ian swung the iron poker and beat it hard against Graham's head. He beat him maybe seven or eight times, until his face was broken and pulpy and the flesh was torn off his nose and his teeth hung in bits from his jaw. The poker was now bent some two thirds of the way up its iron shaft. The years of hate he must have sucked up.

Even then the old fool spat the blood from his mouth. "I'm no..." he began. "Cannae..." He tried to speak but no words were coming.

Keira had looked away when the violence began, but now she lifted her head just a little, hoping it might end. She had half-expected them to beat her - not him - on some notion that she shared some blame for the attack. Instead they were beating Graham to death. He lay still on the ground, raising a hand up towards her mother, the woman he'd taken in, with her children, when her husband died. He looked at Alice as she came close.

"You bett.. better be helpin' me!" He said. "Get him aff me!" He expected mercy from her at least, but he could tell quickly from the wide eyes that she was not in the mood for pleasantries or reprimands. His expression implored her to look at him and recognise this was only who he was, the man she had shared much of her life with. His eyes begged her to show some mercy; but forgiveness was beyond her. Alice took the poker from Ian's hand, raised it above her head and drew it down hard against him, catching the square edge on the top of his left eyebrow. The side of his face peeled away like she was pulling the sheet off a mattress. Like her son, she rained blow after blow upon the head and body, each met with a dull thud, and she went on until she was exhausted, until the man's eyes did not look back at her.

Graham lay flat now, a few feet from the tree, his head battered, unrecognisable, pouring out its memories with broken thoughts weaving a slick in and out of the bone and the blood.

"There's your retribution," she said, shaking and gasping for breath. "I should have taken it sooner! God forgive me!" She dropped the poker, wiping a spray of blood from her cheek.

25

HARE MYRE WATER

1 hour later

Later that night, Ian came down to retrieve the body. There were no flies yet, but he kept swatting at them as if they were there, invisible but swarming. Ian was a strong man, his muscle hard from chopping wood and the physicality of farming trees. Still, he had some difficulty raising Graham's body and placing it on the floor of his barrow. They tell the truth when they speak of a dead weight; Graham had become an inert lump that held the ground in its grip, reluctant to budge. Once in the barrow, he trundled the small vehicle along and the vibrations caused an arm to fall out and it clapped against the trunk of a tree. Ian wheeled him to the small wooden boat, with its paint broken and blistered and lifting, a boat that was berthed against the low jetty to one end of the Hare Myre water. It was a long way with a barrow on a steel wheel and the lifting grips carved heavy grooves into the palms of his hands. Of course, he knew it had to be done and it had to be done now. Leave it till morning and who knows what busy-body would find him. He tipped the corpse onto the wood-planked jetty like bricks falling from a hod. He dragged the weight from the jetty and, with much pushing and shoving, cajoled the heavy bundle into the boat. Like a bag full of hammers, it fell stiffly with a clatter, its limbs twisting awkwardly.

As the body lay there, face up, stiffly gazing at the stars, the face of the man in the increasing gloom was only recognizable in parts and it didn't hurt Ian too much to look at him. He recognized the shape of the small round jaw. Even the ear looked familiar, although partially detached from the skull. He looked at his father's cousin and felt no remorse. Nothing. He did not remember any good times and it is only the memory of good times or the prick of conscience that feeds remorse. He felt neither. He filled the black coat pockets with sand, pebbles and heavy rocks that he picked off the shoreline. He lifted a large lump of stone and dropped it as gently as he could against the body in the boat. He rowed out to the middle of the cold water and watched and heard the ripple of the surface as they went. One time he thought he caught a noise from the dead man, but he laughed at himself when he looked down to check. "You fool," he said to himself out loud. It must have been the oars grinding against the rollocks as he pulled the blades through the water.

The light rain had stopped by the time he took the rope from his pocket. He attached it to the large lump of rock as if he were tying a food parcel. He cursed himself for choosing a smooth rock; a jagged edge would have been better to make the rope stick and stop it from sliding left and right. Still he thought that it would do the job, once the tension was on the rope. He took the loose frayed end and pushed it round behind the dead man's stiff neck before tying a large granny knot just beneath the chin. He had thought he might do a cow hitch knot of some kind but concluded that a cow hitch might well slip, and out would pop the man with all that gas in him like some freak at the fair. Instead he chose a reef knot, better than a granny knot, though often enough tying one produced the other accidentally. It was right, he thought, they called it a granny knot. After all, a granny knot got its name from being tied around the neck of a grain sack. Tying this rope around the dead man's neck was just keeping up with agricultural tradition. This could be a granny knot, he thought, and chuckled grimly. He was almost family. It was hard not to make small jokes: it would keep him sane. He felt Graham's stubble brush against the back of his hand. He accidentally touched his Adam's apple too, resting like a fat egg. One for the urn, as they say in Japan. Ian was amused by something else he remembered: in Japan it was said you could measure a boy's puberty by the size of his Adam's apple.

He took hold of the corpse's coat and lifted him to the edge of the boat, where he balanced him like a plank to one side of the splintered bow.

"Goodbye," Ian said. "Sorry," was his last word, but he didn't know why.

He tipped the body over the side and it slipped gracefully into the water with a quiet slurp. For a short while, it floated close to the surface, the toes up like a pair of fins. He could see the dead man's face lit by the kerosene lamp, rippling beneath the water, one eye just a little open and the other an empty hole. He threw the large rock into the water next to the corpse and he thought he would see him sink straightaway. When the body did not go, he poked at it with his oar but it resolutely bobbed on the surface like a half-sunk canoe. He was thinking hard what he could do to send the man to the bottom when, a second or two later, the body disgorged a large bubble of gas and then harpooned from sight. Minutes later, he had to believe that his father's cousin was now at the very bottom of the loch. Ian stared into the water for the best part of an hour, drifting only a little way to the east where the water fern spread its easy growth. Then he picked up the oars, eased them noiselessly into the rollocks, and rowed back to the shore.

They said to anyone who asked - and in all honesty, there were not many - that Graham had finally taken himself off. It was not so unlikely. They confessed that they were not that sorry. They said they thought he'd gone to Glasgow but they couldn't be sure. He'd talked of London often enough. He had no close family to speak of - *they* were his only family. After a while if anyone really cared, they at least stopped asking.

26

ESCAPE

I an took over the running of the farm and, to his credit, made a good job of it. Graham's death liberated him, took a weight off his back and injected a new energy. It was in truth a strange kind of farm; the crop was the trees he harvested and he was known as a logger or, as they sometimes called him, a lumberjack. From year start to year end, he felled the trees, from birch to oak, in every type of weather. He immersed himself in the work; planting ever more saplings and making more efficient use of what he already had. He built a small one storey woodshed to the north side of Meiklour Wood, on a spot cleared of shrubs and trees, with a pleasant raised view out over Hare Myre water.

Sometimes Ian fetched his Tonkin bamboo rod from the rafters above the woodshed, dug up some fresh worms and oared the same old boat from its mooring out to the middle of the Myre. There was freshwater trout here, spearing the water with their pale cream bellies and speckled backs, and they could be caught if you considered carefully your fishing strategy. Before putting two feet in the boat, Ian pinched a wedge of gritty dirt from the ground and rubbed it into his hands. He knew well enough that no fish came near a worm that harboured a whiff of humanity. For good reason, they were scared. A fish could recognise his assassin by the smell of his fingers, that's what he believed. He sat on the middle seat of the boat, stretched a fat worm between two pre-tied gang hooks and presented his line to the water. He thought of the man he had killed, as the line sunk from view. On the whole, he liked to keep the line a little short.

Ian built up the timber business, drew a modest profit and did not pour the profits directly into his liver. He had his own supplies of hardwood timber, including plentiful oak and elm, but he found ways of importing the same resources from elsewhere, the Scandinavian coastal conifer forest mostly (along the Norwegian coast from places like Lindesnes and Senja), and he developed good business contacts supplying, in particular, the growing demand there was for the wheels of horse-drawn vehicles. Still, the home-grown Scots elm was as native to Scotland as a bunnet to a Dundonian. Ian knew well enough that 'Loch Lomond' was no more than *Lac Leaman* in the Gaelic vernacular: 'Lake of the Elms'. The place here was full of elms. Their slippery barked trunks could be cut into long, straight planks and it was not long before Ian had an additional shed with a small yard next door where he installed a power-driven saw to get through the work – a saw that bit quicker and to a better finish.

After a year or two, he had orders from all over - builders as well as farmers in the area - as far away as Cupar, Stirling and the cities of Glasgow and Edinburgh. He was making a success of the business - one that Graham had only ever flirted with and taken nowhere. Furthermore, Graham was lucky enough to have a prime view of that success through one hundred and twenty feet of Hare Myre water.

Yet of course, it had to be said, with success came other issues, not all of them welcome or expected. His own sister came to be of growing interest to families from Tillicoultry to Cardenden who had sons looking for wives who might provide. Sure enough, Keira was an attractive girl, yet any fool knows that looks fade but gold keeps its colour. One of those sons who took an interest was from a Fife family, living some distance over the other side of Perth. Like himself, the family had a farm, albeit on a smaller scale. How well they farmed he did not know, but if he was honest, he could see pretty early that this man's people were a hard lot.

"Bunch of thieves," said Ian. "Greedy and conceited."

"I agree with you there," said Alice. "That mother would steel the skin off your back if there was profit in it."

"Why then are we encouragin' her?" said Ian.

"She's best off away from here."

Ian met the son a few times and there were moments of jocularity when he would perhaps grow upon him a little but, in his heart, he always sensed that the whiskered man pursuing his sister, whilst bright-eyed with a sharp, caustic tongue on him, was not being true to himself or anyone else. He was a man who might laugh the loudest but his eyes were glassy beads that moved furtively from one scheme to the next.

"He reminds me of Graham," he said. How often did a daughter choose the wrong mate? Graham had not been her father, but he was in that role. "He's no worker, that's for sure."

"He's young," said Alice. "Give him a chance."

"He's idle," said Ian. "He'll always be idle."

Ian thought the man could turn to fat or drink or women or all three, but the effort would be too much. There was laziness in this man, but there was a wily deviousness too.

Ian stood with his view across Hare Myre water. He recalled too well that he had once said to this bearded suitor that he was welcome to take away a load of planks he had cut to build a new roof on his own byre. He did not expect to be paid but he might have expected the fellow to make some small offer that Ian could magnanimously decline. He just took the wood all the same. Looking back on it, as he sometimes did, the man had never given any hint that he wouldn't be paying, and as it turned out he didn't pay. Ian's view was that effectively he'd stolen it - which may have been harsh, since perhaps it was a genuine misunderstanding - yet, in his more forgiving moments, he recognized that maybe he'd not explained the situation with sufficient clarity. People said he had other attributes. He had some money, he had something that looked like a farm. He had the backing of his family. For some that was enough and some to spare. He laid siege on Keira and she seemed to see none of the faults that Ian was sure were there.

If she was honest about it, Keira was more than ready to be taken away from the black grave she now inhabited. She couldn't bear to look at Hare Myre water, its mirrored reflection above the frozen, hidden depths. She avoided passing by that way if at all possible. Her brother Ian, on the other hand, appeared not to share her sensitivity. He was happy to fish the loch from morning to dusk if work would allow. She had seen him feed the worms onto his hooks, all the while knowing what was down there.

It was two years since the night of Graham's 'disappearance'. They had not spoken about it, neither what he had done to her nor what they had done to him. Whatever happened to that old steel poker? Was it at the bottom of the loch with the other secret? They never saw it again but she noticed a new one behind the fender. It was as if the man had indeed taken himself off to London. Sometimes, when you tell a story often enough and you tag on some mild embellishment, some little lie, you reach a point when you start to believe it yourself. The story becomes credible. For some people the truth disappears and the lies are all that remain and the lies become the imposters of the truth. So the story had become the truth and what had occurred could not be spoken of because it appeared that all parties preferred to accept that these things had not happened at all. And yet, this was nonsense and Keira knew it, her brother knew it and her mother too. Yet, not one of them could acknowledge it. When she thought about those events, it made her angry and frustrated that she would never escape all the lies and pretence. These were ghosts she could not hide from and guilt that she could never outrun.

Keira knew that the only possibility of a true escape from the hell that was in her head was to leave all this behind and go some place else. It occurred to her often that maybe marriage held that prospect, however daunting it appeared. Besides, despite the fact that the timber business was working, even with all this activity in the woodshed, growing another besides, it still only provided a decent income for Ian and his mother. She felt like she was surplus. She knew little enough about timber and did not have a man's strength to climb a tree or swing an axe. What could she give to a business like that? She could sweep the wood-shavings off the floor twice a day, but where was the reward in that? Besides, it brought on the bronchitis all that dust and mess. She knew that in time it was possible that the business would do a lot more, but just now there was not enough here for her and what there was, was no good.

Ian, at twenty-two years old, was himself ready to settle down. "I'm no' entirely repelled by the sight of women," he said one evening. "And they dinnae find me entirely obnoxious."

"Well, you'll be next then," said Keira. "You've grown up with two of the species, you must have learnt somethin'."

"Aye," he said. "I've learnt that the smell of money is the biggest aphrodisiac."

"You'll be married one day," said Keira. "When you're fat off the farm and need company."

"That'll be right," he said.

"Happens to us all in the end." Keira knew that there was more to it than just the money. For herself, it was becoming more obvious that every day she existed was another day to remind them of the fir tree at the edge of Meiklour Wood and the events that took place there. It seemed to Keira that Ian had largely come to terms. He could float on that loch for hours, a worm on his line, trailing out the stern. It did not appear to trouble him that there was a body pegged to the bottom with a big rock on his chest. And he had put it there. Their mother was a different story. She took to speaking less and less and most of all, she didn't speak a word to Keira unless it was torn from her. She turned in on herself and she spoke to God. She ate less. The skin sagged on her white-freckled arms. Always fidgety, she became fractious and prone to migraines and unable to sleep when she lay down at night. It was clear to Keira that the ghosts were tormenting her and every time she took a look at her daughter those ghosts glowed a little brighter.

27

THE WEDDING

1900

I n hindsight, when Calum Wilson asked her to marry him she didn't take sufficient time to consider the sanctity of the vows, the financial wherewithal of the bridegroom or the magnetism of his wit and general disposition. She had thought, putting it kindly, that his caustic, bruising sense of humour was refreshing in its freedom from pretence. Sometimes she thought it bordered upon bullying when he spoke so harshly to a farmhand or a coach driver, but she liked a confident man, a man who did not need direction. She enjoyed some occasions when he sparred with Ian and left her brother looking just a little pompous or sanctimonious. She did not dislike him for it and she felt it was no more than male bravura that would soften over time.

Beyond the idiosyncracies of personality, she had not

given a thought to his habits relating to hygiene, sexual experience or whether he wore his socks to bed.

"Does all that facial hair no' repel you?" asked Ian once, when she was cleaning out the woodshed.

"No," she answered. "You're forgettin' I grew up in the country with pigs and ferrets."

"You want a man like that to be the father to your children?"

"I cannae see any reason why not," Keira answered. "Funnily enough I've no' given a lot of thought to the mental health of his bloodline." She'd not reflected upon the physical or the psychological background, least of all considered the dangers that might be presented by forbears to which she might tether her own progeny.

"Is he good to his livestock?" Ian asked.

"Again, I've no' thought about that. I dinnae ken whether he kens his grazing from his silage. I dinnae ken whether or not he can fix a fence, or chase women or drink himsel to death. I dare say I'll find oot in the fullness of time."

It was true, she had thought of none of these things and, in hindsight, that was pretty much a mistake. The truth of the matter is she wanted to get on her way and he was the fastest route out of Meiklour Wood.

"Quickest is no' always best," Ian said.

"Should have stuck that on ma forehead, shouldn't I?"

Yet Keira knew that when she should have been looking beneath the hair on the man's face at temperament and other features, her desperation was such that she thought of little more than how soon they could read the wedding banns.

They were married in Kilconquhar Church at seven minutes past eleven on a Saturday morning in October, beneath an unusually crisp, blue sky, surrounded on all sides by wonky gravestones. They were there enclosed by a broken wall that stretched as far as the loch. In the distance, swans and ducks broke the water without a sound. Despite the clear sky, the days were cooler now and the sun would be gone by noon.

Ian chided her for the time she had taken to get to the church. To be late by seven minutes to her own wedding she had considered a useful ploy to signify that whilst she intended to offer love, honour and obedience, she did not intend the traffic to be entirely one way. She was taking no vows of punctuality. Seven minutes was the opening trade. Ian walked her up the aisle to stand beside Calum, who awaited her just below the altar. His hair hung down from his head untidily and his chin was rough with beard and whiskers.

Having delivered Keira to his side, Ian withdrew to sit beside his mother. "I don't suppose I'll see any payment noo," he said.

"For what?" his mother asked.

"The timber he took for his byre." He looked at the couple. "We'll call it the dowry," he said.

Alice sat close to him in the front pew, her thin body pressed against the hard seat, her eyes full of fear and regrets, cursing the cold draught that brushed the tops of her shoulders.

"Will there be prayers?" she whispered to Ian.

"Yes," he answered.

"Good," she said. "I like prayers and hymns. Something from the psalms would be a treat." She bit her lower lip and looked away. These days she was given to this kind of strange religious enquiry.

The remainder of the guests were broken parts of the Wilson family and those they called their friends. Mrs

Wilson did not speak to Keira until later in the day, when the celebrations were under way. She was unsteady on her feet and her breath betrayed the amount she'd drunk. She put her hand on Keira's arm, gripping it hard.

"Now, just a word of advice from someone who knows."

"What's that, Mrs Wilson?"

"You'd best mind some your ps and qs."

"Best behaviour," Keira answered.

"Serious. Better watch out," she said. "Better be watching him." She looked back over her own shoulder. "He can be... I mean, he's good, but just sometimes, no' so good. He's got a mean streak, if the truth be known to you."

"A mean streak?"

"Yes, yes." She drew her face closer to Keira's. "A mean streak."

"I've seen no sign of that," said Keira.

"Oh, you will," she said.

"I dare say, he can be rough sometimes. Isn't that the way with all men?"

"Maybe it is," she said, looking for a fresh glass. "But he's no' like all men. So take care now." She looked about her. "Ignorance is bliss!" she cried and then laughed. "Ignorance is fuckin' bliss!" She put her hand to her mouth, as if concerned that she may have spoken too loudly. She saw her son approaching and she dropped away out of sight.

The wedding turned out to be a two-day marathon. On the second night, Calum took Keira home to the house in Fife where they planned to begin their married life. It had been a rough, jolting journey up from Kilconquhar in a horse and cart and she was cold and hungry when they arrived in the small yard outside the house. As their vehicle drew up, she was alone in the quietness with her new husband. He'd said nothing on the journey but she was not concerned. She'd never wanted a man who blabbered all his life.

"This is it," he said. "Fer better or fer worse."

She climbed down from the cart after him. In doing so, she caught her shoe on her dress and stumbled forward. She would have fallen but caught the wheel of the cart and remained upright. At that point he laughed. She wondered if he would have laughed more or less if she had landed on her knees. The strange, removed look in his eyes as he laughed and the dryness of the laughter made her sense for the first time that their marriage might not be easy. She thought again back to what Calum's mother had said to her at the wedding.

The house was cold and empty and there was filth on the floor. There was a smell of wet clothes. There was a pair of muddy boots in the hallway and the mud had dried and was breaking off. She looked around and then began to clear the mess. She looked for a cloth and wiped down the surfaces. She put her hair up in a small, neat bun. She found an old brush with broken bristles and swept down the floor into a small pile that her new husband walked through once and then disappeared. She found cups in a cupboard, some plates and cutlery and a teapot. There was no food anywhere. They'd rely on the bread and cheese left over from the journey. The water came from a pump at the back of the house. There were no curtains but the windows were so dirty that curtains would have been unnecessary.

Her husband came back into the kitchen. He waved his arm at her, as if she should follow him from the house into the old byre next door, across the small yard. The roof of the byre had fallen in some while back but on one side, collecting damp and the feathered droppings off the many pigeons, lay the pile of timber.

"Is that the wood," she said. "From Ian?"

"It was good of him, I'm sure," said Calum.

"It wouldn't harm you to thank him," she teased.

"If it's thanks he's after he may as well whistle."

"Still," she said, her voice remaining light and playful. "The timber will rebuild this, will it no'?" She waved a hand randomly about her. "It may give us a new roof in here?" she said.

"Oh look at her," he said. "My wife wants a new roof already."

"What if we need an extra room?"

"What if we do?" he said.

"Well, I'm no' sure but..."

"Become the builder now, have you?"

"No..." she started. "I didnae mean..."

"Remember who y'are," he said. "Let's no' have airs and graces..."

"That's no' what I meant..."

"Building the new roof," he interrupted. "Whatever next will you be doing?"

"I just..."

He didn't cut her off again. Instead he looked straight through her and he said nothing. And that had the same effect. After a while, he said: "You boil an egg in four and a half minutes." She nodded. "Not one. Not two." He stepped towards her. "Four and a half minutes."

'Yes, okay," she said, avoiding his eyes. "I've boiled an egg before."

"Because everything has its time." His next movement was sudden, but at the same time she had the unlikely thought that in the right light, and with less hair, he was handsome. The whiskers were too much but they softened the hardness that came from his eyes. It crossed her mind that he was going to kiss her and, in all truth, she was not totally indifferent to the prospect, despite the tension that was in the air. After all, she was now a married woman and she understood what might be expected of her. So when Calum approached her in the old roofless byre, she saw a strange look in his eye and misconstrued it as the start of that marital process, the natural evolution that she imagined married life to be.

Once he was there, standing before her, without warning, the smile not moving from his lips, he beat her hard against the face with the back of his hand, first the left and then the right. It came so fast she was unsure it had even happened. He struck her a deep blow with a clenched fist in the soft hollow of her stomach beneath the ribcage. The pain was the worst she had ever experienced. She had not known he was left-handed. The breath escaped her and she fell to the floor with a startling crash. She gasped for breath. He stood over her, but she was hardly there a moment before he bent down and gripped her by the front and pulled her back onto her feet.

"I want us," he said, breathing heavily in her face. "To start off as we mean to continue." He put his short fingers around her throat and held her hard against the wall and its rough, wooden slats. She could feel the broken mortar crumbling against the back of her head. She was winded and struggled to breathe. Her feet were barely touching the floor, just the tips of her toes. "Let's no' start off badly," he said at the same time as she sensed that she was fainting. She pulled at his hand around her neck. She tugged at his fingers and tried to stop him choking her, but she could not get the words out, so tight was his grip. He drew his face closer to hers and she could see every pore of his nose, every line across his forehead and all the coldness in his brown eyes. "You're under my roof now," he said, blind to the irony of the roofless byre. "Any decisions to be made, I'll make them. Do you understand?" She felt a deep terror, a blush of fear that rose and engulfed her. He smiled. "You just have to nod your head." She looked away from him but moved her head. "Teamwork is what I'm after, see? We pull together and you do what I say. That way we'll get along fine. Are we clear? Mrs Wilson?" He dropped her and her legs folded beneath her as she slid back to the ground.

When he reached the open door to the byre, he stopped and turned to look at her. He could see that she was coughing and weeping. He smiled at her, showing the tips of his teeth. "Don't let's get upset about this. I want things to be right between us," he said. "Come on. Let's away in now." He spat a lump of yellow phlegm against the doorpost and watched it slide. His eye was caught by the wooden planks.

"What the hell are we going to do with this lot?" he said. She tried to speak but could not give voice to the words. "Wood's no use to us, but somebody might pay somethin' for it." He moved through the door, tossing over his shoulder as he went: "Come inside. I just got married. It's time we celebrated."

And so Keira's married life began.

28

POOLY POINT

We were set for the high seas: a vast stretch of water that separated Fife from Scandi-bloody-navia. Our trip was coastal but Mr Harcourt was muttering like a rusty hinge, about the wild weather, about the flapping net, and about Calum Wilson being a wee shite. The wind was picking up and there was blustery, showery, filthy weather coming. It was no' in the stars, it was in your face. There was just the three of us. And now there was Rory. My thought was that Calum Wilson would've been a liability and I was happy he was nursing his hang-over back on the daybed. Rory was also a liability and I'd have to mind my footin'. I'll admit I had a picture of Calum's wife in my head and she was on the daybed too, wearin' very little. As that thought slipped through my brain's connecting tissues, I pulled hard on a rope and the boat continued to be dragged by the wind through the dull water. I looped it and flung the bundle to one side. I had more to think about than Calum Wilson's daybed. I knew I had to take heed that Rory was still with us and I had to keep one eye on him for fear of what stunt, mucal projectiles or otherwise, he might wish to shower in my direction. He would not have forgotten the mess I made of Tom's voice box when getting' casual with a loose spade in the Bombo Burn. But Tom lived, what more can I say? A lot had changed that day.

The wind had taken hold of the sails, and they bulged to the front, like a couple of fat boys with their bellies out. The boat was now far from the quayside, drawn by the hard blow and already whipped by the lash of heavy rain.

Mr Harcourt, with characteristic brevity, called his boat a lugger. The pedantically disposed mariner - of which there are a few - would argue that the lugger was a small vessel with two sails on two masts or more commonly, three sails on three masts. That crusty purist would say that old Harcourt's boat didn't fit the bill. Whether the old farmer's boat bore any kinship with a *bona fide* lugger was a moot point: it had two masts and two sails, one large with a square top and the other a little bigger than a pair of Tom Burns' underpants. The rust-red canvas sails were hauled up each of the masts by heaving hard on a halyard rope. *Firth Wind* had a halyard made from baling twine, plaited into some- thing no thicker than my pinkie. When I had pulled on the rope at the quayside I had already felt the twine cutting into my hands. It was like handling a string of sharp knives. With a growing wind, alternating between south-westerly and south-easterly, the lugger was slicing a deep groove through the water, rising and falling with the waves. The cold, wet air became increasingly blustery, tugging at our hair and beating hard, gusting blows against our backs, and more than once I caught a look on Rory's face that showed concern at the fast disappearing land behind us. For the time being, I was safe.

Within a short time we reached Pooly Point – a crop of rocks a little more than a mile down the coast – and then we moved back in a little towards the shoreline again where we fed the net from the bow of the boat. The net was black cotton, coated with creosote to keep it from rotting and weighted to make it sink and sit low in the water. Cork floats hung along the surface, holding the net from running too deep. The herring were happy to flip-flop along the bottom during the day and then rise intermittently to feed on the plankton. The task was to feed the nets into the water and allow them to drift on the tide and so catch the herring. A man could show his skill here. He had to know where the fish might be at any one time, and at what depth and if he got it right he might fill his net. On the other hand he might get it all wrong about the movement of the herring but stumble blindly into them and fill his net by luck rather than skill.

The wind was still hard upon us and the net was all out, drifting, as Mr Harcourt intended, towards the shore. From the moment we had rounded the rocky outcrop that formed the point we felt the full force of the gale and the driving rain, baring its teeth at us, lifting the ripped, whisked waves ever higher, pounding hard breaks against the boat and rolling it like a child's toy in a tub. At this stage, the child in me would have opted for dry land. Old Harcourt squatted at the back of the boat, head down against the rain and the spray off the waves catching in his beard. He was not alone in thinking they could only keep this up for so long. A beluga whale would have turned back by now. It was my feeling that we were not far from having to do the same, but there was no telling Mr Harcourt because he was in charge.

"No' headin' back, Mr Harcourt?"

"The fuck we are," he shouted back. I wrestled with ropes that slipped through my fingers and flapping sails that cracked against my ears. Rory was over the other side, slipping and falling around the deck, tugging on ropes like mine and hopelessly holding a hat tight against his head, strands of blonde hair whipping in long streaks beneath the rim.

At that point, it could not get any worse. Suddenly it did. Just as old Harcourt made the decision that I mebbe had a point and they had to give it up and return to shore, the net became snagged. The saltwater continued to crash against the side of the boat, cascading wave after wave across the deck. I never knew the sea held this much water. Duncan slipped and cursed as he grasped at a halyard that had broken free from its stay. He slid across the deck, on his back, his legs above his middle, like a rolled turtle, crashing like a curling stone against the other side of the boat. Harcourt remained at the helm keeping the bow pointed to the east, but cast a worried look at Duncan who waved a reassuring hand back at him. I staggered to the bow, rolling with the undulations, gripped the net with frozen fingers and pulled for all I was worth.

The net was clearly snagged on a rock, well down beneath the waterline. The rain whipped hard against our skin and then the waves slapped over us, and another swell swept and swamped the boat. We rolled again. And again. Still I tugged at the net, the rain coursing across my eyelids, down my cheeks in tight rivers. I shook the wet from my face and pulled again on the net, leaning further over the bow of the boat, struggling to keep purchase with my soft, water-logged boots. There was a risk that the net would be ripped and lost, but I knew I had to shift it from where it was caught, and if I didn't achieve that we'd have to give it up and we'd lose the net altogether. Disaster! Rory, broken by many falls, had been sheltering to the north side of old Harcourt but, in truth, there was no cover to be had anywhere. Suddenly, he rose again to his feet and surged forward to where I was at the bow, gripping the side with both hands. He leaned over to the left of me, slipped his fingers into the holes of the black net and pulled. Even in that thundering storm you could smell the salt, the kelp weed and the creosote. We pulled together, our hands icy pink in the ripping, grey water, our arms pushing and jostling, our faces wet and determined. In the midst of our endeavour, I glanced at Rory. Whether through guts or fear, he was working as hard as I was. His efforts pushed me harder. I pulled again from a different direction, felt the net cut through my hands, and took the strain across my shoulders and back. And then, there came further disaster. Neither of us saw it arrive, focused as we were on releasing the net. The boat twisted to the starboard side and was caught by a wall of seawater. The vessel lifted and appeared almost clear and then crashed to the hollow formed by the waves. When I picked myself up, Rory's hands were no longer next to mine, they had slipped and gone from the net. He was over the side and already in the water ten or twelve feet away, waves crashing over the top of him, weighed down by his clothing, gulping for every breath like it was his last. Another wave like the first and I knew he would be gone.

29

THE HAYSTACK

I had the sense - but little more - to throw off my sodden jacket before I plunged over the side. It was a challenge to get into the water, given the rise and fall of the boat, and I thought for a minute I'd get nae further than a little gentle crushing by the vessel itself. Old Harcourt shook an arm at me and shouted words that I could not hear but I was away by then. I hit the water and immediately came the extreme chill driven like nails into my bones. Every now and then I caught a sight of Rory across the tops of the waves and I swam as hard as I could in his direction. He was moving with the tide, as was I, but his head was bobbing very close to the waterline, disappearing below and then up again. Soon he would swallow a bellyful of water and the head would disappear for good. I kicked my legs and pushed to reach him. I saw the boat move further away as I flailed hopelessly in Rory's direction. I was struck on the forehead by something hard, floating in the water just above the surface, probably enough to cause a gash but I was still conscious. A piece of driftwood shaped like a pole revealed itself and, with my two hands, I pushed it hard towards Rory. It speared some way through the water.

I shouted at him but he seemed to be losing the fight. I went on, swimming towards him, slowly closing the gap. He was closer now and I could see his eyes were open and they were filled with a stunned terror. He clawed with his fingers and paddled with his arms like a human windmill. He kicked with his booted feet, the clothes he was wearing pulling at him, sapping his strength and sinking him. As I drew close, I put out my hands in an attempt to lift his head above the water. He raised his own hands, grabbed hold of the hair on ma head and pulled me right under the water. All life blurred before my eyes and what was left began its slow, inexorable ebb from this place to the next. I struggled to shake off Rory's grasp but he was a man possessed. I had a sense of how easy it would have been to let go. Aye, let go, slip away. I was shivering as my metabolism slowed and my muscles were beginning to seize, making it harder to move my arms to save myself. I was entering the worst four minutes of my life.

He told me later he was thinking of his father, his dear dead father, who loved fruit chutney on his biscuits. He let go of me and kicked out to draw himself nearer to the driftwood. I was almost done, exhausted, gasping, vision blurred to within a few feet, mental processes becoming weary and slow. When his hands struck another time, hard against my head, I held on but I thought then that he'd killed me.

When the tide is coming in under those conditions, it is like a sliding, unstoppable blob, dragged across the seafloor, the moon pulling with a force we can only imagine. An incoming tide carries a person or anything in its grasp towards the shoreline with the same impossible grip. The struggle to close the small distance in the water between

myself and Rory was far greater than the small effort
exerted by the sea to drag us close to the rocks, but then
disgorging us without ceremony onto a seaweed mulch,
delivering us close to the shore. I could feel the reassuring
rock and sand of the gently sloping beach underfoot. I
gripped Rory's collar and dragged him towards the shore.
We lay above the shallow water, too exhausted to move. My
head was spinning. I felt light, dizzy and moderately
euphoric. My thoughts came back to me like I was reaching
for the pages of a book. I was alive.

Mr Harcout, with steely, sunken eyes and fish-hunter's
head, even through the thick buffeting of that storm had
seen us, Rory and myself, hang by nothing but our fingernails to the railway sleeper that had clouted me on the
head. He then lost sight of us as he wrestled to keep the
boat upright, battered by the gusting wind and spray. The
net was lost on the rocks, still snagged below the
waterline.

Mr Harcourt had guided the boat closer to the shoreline,
but by that time the main sail was ripped and there was
little control coming off the rudder and there was a real
danger of splintering themselves against rocks that scraped
the belly of the boat. Still battered by the fierce wind, he was
able to find some shelter on the lea side of the point and the
gale there had eased enough to allow them to bale out some
of the water sloshing around the deck. They tightened up
the main sail and, after a while, they limped home to the
quayside.

Only then did Harcourt and his son allow themselves to
think what may have happened to us. Once they had
dragged the boat up the beach and secured it to a mooring
spot, they headed off on foot up the coast to the small
stretch where Mr Harcourt was thinking we might have

come ashore. He and his son knew it was not a given that we had come ashore at all.

They searched the coastline, threading like drunken weavers, up and down over the dunes, through the long rolled leaves of the wet Marram grass, a seaside mile this way and that way. As they did so, the rain was still chucking down on them but the wind was blowing itself out. Shouting our names, scanning their eyes along the shore, Harcourt was tired by his efforts and was about to turn back again, but instead he walked towards the fields that cushioned the water's edge.

When Mr Harcourt approached the old barn, he had a sense that he would find us. Maybe the grey hair on the back of his weathered neck prickled up. He shouted out my name, like he had a hundred times already. He was surprised to see me emerging from the top of a haystack, Rory right behind.

"You're alive then?" he said and spat a gob by the door.

"Just about," I said.

"What you doin' up there?"

"Trying to get warm."

"You cold then, are ye?"

"Yes." My teeth were still chattering.

Mr Harcourt stared back at me and then looked at the ground. He appeared embarrassed. "I suppose you would be. That's no' surprisin'. You both okay?"

"Aye," I said. "Still breathin'."

"Strange decision, jumpin' over?"

"I had nae choice," I said, making my way down to ground level.

When I reached him, he put his hand on my forearm and moved his mouth closer to my ear. "Where's Rory?"

I pointed. "He's up there."

"Is he alright?" I nodded. "I was told you hated that boy."

"I never hated anyone," I said.

"Best get goin' now," Duncan said, intent on steering his father out from the gloom of the shed.

"He's okay then?" said Mr Harcourt, pointing at Rory who had emerged and was sitting on the hay with his arms around his knees, pale and shivering and not speaking.

"I think so."

"You alright to look after him?"

"Yes," I said.

"Fine." He turned at the entrance. "Net's fucked," he said.

"No' the best result."

"Small price," he said. He spat one last time before he headed out into the rain.

What I failed to explain in any detail to Mr Harcourt about the haystack was its most useful property: heat. The haystack came to me from another book extracted from the farming section of Mr Shifner's library. It may have been catalogued incorrectly because it was not a book purely about farming. It was about five boys from Massachusetts in America who, after a violent thunderstorm, took shelter on the lee side of a haystack. They were soaked through and shivering, so they got *inside* the haystack. The reason for getting inside the haystack was that they knew there was always heat in these places. The heart of a stack can get hot enough to start a fire and sometimes it does. Once they were warm they thanked God and became missionaries in Asia. Those missionaries gave birth to the *Haystack Movement*. There you go. Not to mention a twelve foot granite monument in Massachusetts to celebrate the fact.

It was with this little anecdote, culled from Mr Shifner's rosewood library (farming section), that I came to the view that I did. We had been on the beach a while, Rory and me. My head had taken a blow from the railway sleeper and was still spinning and pounding. I had likely been hypothermic, finding it hard to think, the cold eroding my brainpower. Rory was no better than me and was shaking and shivering and all folded up like he was going to die there and then, face as pale as the hair on his head. I knew we had to get warm but we had nothing for a fire. All we had was our wet clothes and it was hellish cold out there. I dragged Rory along and up the beach with me, bent over, hunched up, trotting. We moved along the field to the old shed I had passed often enough, but a distance in from the shoreline. We got in under cover and I pulled a ladder away from the wall and leaned it against the stack of hay that sat inside. Rory climbed the ladder, struggling all the way, almost falling off the top rung, throwing himself down on the haystack. He pulled the broken bales of hay to one side and dropped himself into the hole. I followed him in. I was no' too sure I'd get my legs moving enough to climb the ladder after him. I did get up there and stood at the top and then placed myself in almost the same gap, splitting more hay and spreading it across us. For a second or two there was no noticeable difference and I began to have misgivings about those bastards in Massachusetts. I was thinking mebbe they were bogus and that granite monument may have been a waste of time and money. Then suddenly, I felt the warmth seeping in and the chill eased out from my frozen bones.

We lay in the hay in the half-light until Mr Harcourt found us. Before that, Rory said: "Thanks."

"That's okay," I said. "Joint effort anyway."

There was a moment's quiet, then he said: "You didnae have to come after me. In the water, I mean."

"I know."

"I'd probably have made it okay on my own."

"Probably."

"I thought I was bloody drowning," he said.

"You were."

"Then I thought I was dreaming that I was drowning."

"You were drowning."

He paused. "I saw my dad," he said. "Strange memories come to you." He chortled at the thought.

"It was a serious situation," I said.

"It was bad enough."

"You didn't die anyway," I said.

"Came close though."

He said nothing for a while. Then, he raised his eyes at me and nodded.

30

CONFRONTATION

Mr Harcourt had experienced pleasant relief when he found us, alive and well. He knew that in a different life he might have had two dead boys there. How would he have coped with that? He'd buried Mrs Harcourt and that had been bad enough. She was a grown woman with a life behind her: she'd had her time. But two boys, that was something different.

Mr Harcourt and his son, Duncan, left us and went straight back to the boat. They were worried that in their haste they'd not secured it properly, but it was there, beaten but none the worse for its ordeal, apart from the ripped sail. The tar used to fill the split bow was still holding good. They checked the boat ties and gathered up the belongings they intended to take back with them to the farm. Their clothes were still damp from the sea but they were warm enough from the work they were doing.

The horse called Ballymena was still tethered beneath the shed roof by the track, not too distant from the quayside. Ballymena cut a forlorn figure, his gut hanging low to the ground, one hindleg slightly raised and the tip of a hoof resting against the mud, like a petulant ballet dancer. His hindquarters poked out from the iron roof, wet through from the rain and he heralded their appearance with a shake of the head, as if to rebuke them. Duncan hitched Ballymena to the old carriage and then loaded their gear into the large chest that sat between the rear wheels. They wasted no time and shortly they were on the broken track, putting distance between them and the water, wheels sliding in the mud and heading home. All the while Mr Harcourt muttered and cursed, his thoughts on the net that was lost and the lives that weren't.

"Bloody man!" Harcourt suddenly shouted aloud, as the carriage slithered in the mud. "Bloody old dog!"

"Wilson?" shouted Duncan.

"Aye, Wilson!" he shouted back. "Might not have happened but for that fuck wit!" He whipped the horse.

"Can't change that now, dad."

"We were a man down," he yelled.

"There's no harm done, dad," said Duncan.

"There could have been," shouted his father.

"He'd have been a liability."

"There could have been two dead boys! No' to mention you – or even the both of us!"

Harcourt cursed Wilson again as they cleared the crossing and followed the track up to the left. Who knows, with an extra man they might have manoeuvred the boat a little less close to the rocks, thought Mr Harcourt. They might not have snagged the net. They might have weathered the storm a damn sight better than they did. They would've had an extra pair of hands to pull up the net when it did snag. They would've at least had a chance to get out of that situation. They might even have caught some bloody herring too! Instead, they had nothing for their trouble but a boat washed out, a ripped sail, the net lost, not so much as a tiddler caught and two boys half-dead in a haystack.

Wilson's farm was on the far side of Tullis. To pay him a visit would have meant a round trip of less than thirty minutes. To Mr Harcourt's mind, that thirty minutes was time well spent. It was a minor deviation. He could get this thing off his chest. It would do no harm to drop by and let the man know he was a prize arse. Duncan said it might be better to let it lie, so far as he could against the clatter of Ballymena's hooves and the rumble of the wheels on the stone and through the mud. He said he had to let things settle down, but his father was beyond the point of listening. Old Mr Harcourt muttered something inaudible and pushed the horse a little faster, smacking both sides with his whip.

The sky was still grey and leaden, hanging like a slate cloud over the Wilson house. The coach, with Balymena behind, took the last bend at some speed, up a track heavy with mud between two chest-high walls, the coping wet through and covered with dull green moss. They pulled in at the front of the house and could see traces of black smoke leaking from the broken chimney cowl.

It so happened that Calum was standing at the window as Mr Harcourt drew his carriage up outside. He put down the watch chain he'd been swinging through the air in front of him. "What's that old bastard want?"

His wife joined him by the window. "Maybe he wants to sell you a fish," she said.

"Looks like a drowned rat."

"Please be nice to him."

"Or a turkey," he grunted, pulling up his braces and looping them over his shoulders. "Turkey brains." He scratched each of his testicles in turn and then left the room.

Mr Harcourt was about to rap on the door when it swung open and Calum's face appeared. "Whoa!" he said. "Good morning, Mr Harcourt. How can I be of service?"

"Good mornin' ma erse!" Harcourt shouted back. "I needed you on ma boat this mornin', no' now!"

"Other priorities I'm afraid," said Wilson.

"Almost lost that boat of mine," said Harcourt.

"Maybe you chose the wrong weather, old fella!"

"We were short of hands!"

"Need to calm down," he said. "Bad for the heart an' all that."

"You said you were comin'?"

"I tellt you. Something came up."

"You should've been there."

"Yeah well," said Calum. "I'd better things to do." He stepped back a pace as if to close the door. "Is there anything else I can do for you?" As he began to close the door, Harcourt wedged his foot in the gap.

"Can't rely on pig-shit like you for anything."

"Is that so?"

"Those boys nearly drowned!" he yelled.

"Well, if they're still alive they've nothing much to complain about, have they?" said Wilson, through the gap.

"Rory Fraser," said Harcourt.

"What of him?"

"He'd no' be alive if Logan hadnae fished him oot."

Wilson opened up the door a little more. "Sean Logan?" he asked. "The dumb one?"

"The one," said Harcourt, "who was here to get you this morning."

"Oh aye. That cheeky fucker."

"He's no' dumb either."

"I noticed that mysel. Right enough, he's a cocky gob-shite."

"Speaks more sense than you ever did."

Calum opened the door fully and stepped forward onto the step. He pushed his face very close to Mr Harcourt's and breathed over him. Duncan, who had been seated on the carriage throughout, jumped down and moved towards them. He was thinking he might kick Wilson and he and his dad would run, before things got out of hand. Calum held up his hand at Duncan but continued to press his face into Mr Harcourt's. "Listen to me you old pisser! As it happens I stayed at home today. I stayed at home because I dinnae like your boring old shit fillin' up ma heid. I dinnae like your manner either. Now get your rutty old face out of my yard and don't take any more of your fuckin' liberties!"

"You're an erse," Harcourt said.

"And you've the fuckin' nose for it."

Harcourt's face was puffed with fury and there were little red blisters raging on his cheeks. He did not say another word but his eyes were fired up. Duncan pulled him back towards the carriage and the two climbed on board, shook and slapped the reins and thundered out across the small stones, sliding along the dirt track towards Tullis, Mr Harcourt's face as dark as the track beneath them and thunderous as the clouds above.

Calum stood outside his door and laughed aloud. A dull day had turned out quite enjoyable. He laughed some more and showed his yellowing teeth. "That old erse wouldn't like that, would he?"

"Why d'you say that?" his wife said, appearing behind him. "He's just an old man."

"Thinks he's the only bastard who can fish that bit of

coast." He turned towards her and stepped up close by the door.

"He's an old guy," she repeated. "He means no harm. Why do you bully him?"

He stood before her and pulled the shoulder band off her blue smock, threading his thick hand inside her shirt and holding her nipple between his thumb and forefinger, like he was working a ball of clay into a narrow pipe. She had an idea he was going to squeeze it hard and crush the nipple. She sensed it coming and she knew that it would be painful, but he did not squeeze. He ran the sole of his finger across the top of the nipple and then took away his hand, as if he were bored. He looked at her. "On your own tonight," he said, "I'm no' here." He turned for the boot room.

"You're goin' out in *this* weather?" She lowered her eyes when he turned back.

"I've some business in Cupar."

"What kind of business?" she said.

"The kind that cannae wait."

"Are you coming back tonight?" she asked.

"I may go to Perth."

"That doesnae exactly answer my question."

"Then again, I may not."

"Are you back here or no'?"

"What d'you think?" he said, moving back towards her. "What d' you bloody well think?"

"It was just a question," she said.

"I told you I'm no' here tonight."

"That's what you said."

"I think that's enough, don't you?"

"I suppose it'll have to be."

"That's right."

Later, after her husband had gone, after she'd eaten

some stale biscuits and the broken half of an old fruit cake; when she'd drunk some warm, weak tea from a cup with a broken handle; when she'd washed it down with a half glass of whisky; when she'd applied some ointment to the heavy bruising around her eye where the bastard had hit her on his way out; then she looked out of the window towards the Firth. It was enveloped now in a heavy, velvety darkness. She knew it was there but she could not see it. The rain was still on. She could hear the pattering drum of broken drops as they struck the slated roof. She knew Tullis was there in the inky blackness, its people just down below, but there were no lights to betray its presence. She knew that that boy Logan was down there somewhere too. A strange boy, the way he'd looked at her. Foolish to call him a boy. There was nothing of the boy about him. Saved the other one from drowning, old Harcourt had said. But who will save me from drowning, she asked. Who will pull me from the spinning, dark water that sucks me down and steals the breath from me?

31

HORATIO'S DEATH

About the same time as I was doing haystacks, my father was dying in his cell at Peterhead Prison. It was November, a month I hate anyway. When she heard, first thing Aunt Marion said was he must have given up. He'd chosen not to live. As if it was a free choice. I was not so sure it was as simple as that.

"But why do seventeen years of a twenty-five year sentence and then give up on it?"

"Who knows."

I couldnae make head or tale of it. Why decide at that time, with the blue sky on the horizon, one foot tiptoeing out the cell door, the milk and the honey sliding into your peripheral vision, why would you decide then that you were ready for a more permanent incarceration, in another box? A little tighter albeit more attractively furnished in scots pine with ornate handles. It made no sense. Aunt Marion said she thought he simply turned his back on it, disappointed, like he had been given bad news about the weather and had decided not to venture out. I could not fathom why he had not held on a while longer, why he just gave up the ghost. I said as much to Aunt Marion, as we recovered from our grief.

"His past haunted him," she said.

"But why just give up like that?"

"People do."

"It seems cowardly," I said.

"He was never a coward," she said.

"But he gave up."

"Don't think of him as a coward."

"Why did he no' keep going?" I persisted. She was annoyed at me, but I was annoyed more at him.

"He was never a coward," she repeated.

I was being harsh, I know that now. Sometimes you have to kick someone to save yourself. I think it was true that the assault on my mother hung like something rotten in my father's gut. It never quite escaped. It gassed up inside and leaked out in little poisonous bubbles all around him. His every step was shadowed by her death and the manner of her death. Every breath he took was yoked to that unspoken bitterness, that leaden bile in the pit of his stomach.

What I heard is that sometimes in the prison they would be sent out into the highlands in small teams to burn the heather. The purpose of doing so was to bring on the green buds, to encourage the new grass. They still burn the heather. New grass means bigger and fatter sheep. In the midst of all this, the men were herded around the fires. Surely, some would think of escape, a mad dash through the smoke? Then again, escape to where? Freedom? Fresh linen? The smell of the farm? The babble of the Bombo Burn at the end of the field that produced little more than prickly weeds? There was no place to go even if those prisoners had the strength to run, whether directly into the fire or away from the heat. They were hobbled. Even then, I could imagine my father staring at the yellow flames, nestled amongst the red embers, and he would never stop seeing her face. My mind tells me that that was what kept him going and paradoxically, in my view, that was the very thing that killed him. A small touch of pneumonia, if that is what it was, did not need to be the death of anyone.

Then again, there were times too when I could imagine my father would have sat back in his grey Peterhead cell and he may have thought about the old wall at the front road to Salmon Cottage, running his hand across the damp moss on the coping, and he would have seen himself looking down at the spray of sheep fanned out across the green field. Immediately he would have thought of her and the times they had had together, when they had sat upon the same wall, enjoyed the same view and shared the same pleasure at being together, there, then. Or else he might well have eaten something his sister Marion had left with him on one of her occasional visits and just a flavour of wild sage, just a taste would have done enough to bring back the sharp memory of his dear, lost wife, Tatiana. Her name itself was like the last breath escaping from a corpse.

Aunt Marion said he had never forgotten my mother. Her memory, she said, was sharp as bright sunlight, all the way to the end. Then again, I must confess my own view on that is a little different.

I still cannot make sense of why my father died. When I think hard about it the truth pains me as much as I am sure it pained him. I have to ask myself, what if he was becoming aware that his memory of her was fading? What if he thought that he was actually forgetting her? What if he thought that was one ounce too heavy to bear? You can lose the thing you love the most, but how can you forget her altogether? How can you lose the memory? How can you drop the rope that tethers her to the shore and see her drift away like that? It's like she died twice. But then how can you keep any memory fresh? He should have asked himself that question. Memory is no different from apples: over time, they lose the green skin and the water and the little seeds. A skinny old husk is all that remains; that is memory. He should have asked himself how anybody could hope to keep the picture from fading. You can beat this old boat with the weather for one season, maybe two, but eventually the mooring works loose and the memory drifts away or is swallowed up by the water. Memory, in the end, is no more than the shitty sludge that is left over once everything else is gone. And so, with regard to my father, I am more inclined to the belief that it was because the years were rubbing away the memory, like the gilt coming off a gold picture frame, that he decided that it was his time to go. Before the whole fucking thing disintegrated to dust in the bone of his hands. The spirit left him and he had no desire to keep it back. The detail of his memory was becoming so blurred I do not think he could reconcile losing the clarity in his mind. It was fading from memory, the clear shape of her ears and the deep green of her eyes. He didn't like to see the dimple in her sallow cheeks fade away; or lose from his mind's eye the neat precision of her features.

In a sense, my father was going blind. He was no longer certain of the accuracy of what he could see. He had worn her shawl against his skin every day of his life since that hated night, all through his prison years, but my belief is that he'd begun to realise that there was nothing left of her in it now: no smell, no fragrance, nothing. It was no more than a rag you might wipe your stupid hands on. It was no longer her; if anything, it was him. I could imagine him wondering if his memory of her had in fact become a memory of somebody altogether different; did he worry that the person he remembered during the long, cold nights in his draughty Peterhead cell or out in the field damping down the fires, or even in his head, might never actually have existed?

I believe now that he worried that the woman he remembered was not the woman he had known. He could not live with that. It was like being unfaithful, promiscuous with another woman. He was coming to terms with the idea that memory, as it turned out, was little more than an invention; nothing more than what is left when a man's disintegrating head has forgotten all the other shit that ever lived there.

These were the voices that crowded my own disintegrating head on the day they brought my father's body down from Peterhead. I knew a lot of this was conjecture, speculation and the rest but it made some sense to me and it made it easier for me as I opened the farm gate to let my father's body pass through. He was a long way dead and even with the lid hard down on a cold day there was still a chemical smell of formaldehyde in the air. After eighteen years his pale, grey, plugged body was once more come home to Salmon Cottage. It had been a long time for my father and jail years must be the longest. This was his farm and yet you could not help but feel that his ownership had been painfully brief.

Earlier, I tore off the lid and checked that he was there. We laid him out in the back room. He lay on a white sheet, so still, so ready to face all the shit that was coming. I had no memory of his face, barely having seen him. He was like a stranger in my house. Yet, I could see parts of me imbued within his features. We had some of the men and women from the village come by to pay their last respects. I looked at them but we shared few words. They took their own good advice and did not speak beyond formalities. Mr Fawcett came on in after he'd locked up the shop for the day. He'd taken off his apron and wore a black tie. His shoes were shiny brogue. I didnae mind him comin' too much but I took the opportunity to remind him that he'd obligations not just to the dead, but to the living. He looked at me a little puzzled.

"What d'you mean by that Sean?"

"No, another time," I said. "I can explain to you later what I mean."

"Very well."

"But I want you to think on this between now and then: where does your own responsibility lie?" He looked uncomfortable and drank a large glass of gin.

Others chose not to come at all, and they were wise. Forgiveness is not a bottomless pool. Once the formalities were over, the coffin was closed up once more and the body was put on the cart, ready to be wheeled to the cemetery in Tullis. Stupidly, before we left on that last journey, I once more pulled out the nails and took a long, final look. I was not surprised to find him still dead and again, for the last time, I hammered down the lid. Aunt Marion put a hand on my shoulder and Lizzie took hold of my hand.

Initially I'd some small issues with the minister. He was a man of forty or so years. He was known to smoke a clay pipe at the altar when he thought it was just him and God present, and he usually carried a liberal dash of breakfast egg on his robe.

It was immediately apparent on our initial meeting that the minister was reluctant to undertake my father's burial. He gave me some suspect shit about there being limited space in the cemetery, when I knew fine well his reservations were more to do with my father lowering the tone than causing subterranean congestion.

I'd thought things over. I went back down to the church, the one with the fish on the roof. The old boy was on his knees, silently declaring his transgressions to an empty altar. I sat at the back of the church and let him finish. He was there a long time so he must have had a lot to get through. Still, eventually he lowered his head and then turned back down the aisle. The lights were low in the church, a few small candles up there on the pillars at head height, and so my voice to him must have seemed at first disembodied, rising like smoke out of the darkness. Did he think that God was speaking to him?

"Good evening, minister," I said.

"Who's that there?" he answered, craning a flat hand suspiciously to his brow to see me better, as if he had sun in his eyes. He held his other hand across his heart, as if to protect himself from celestial attack.

"It's me, Minister. Sean Logan."

"Oh," he said. "Sean Logan. What are you doing here?"

"Meditating," I said.

"God will guide you."

"Aye, that's possible."

"As I said before," the minister said. "I'm truly sorry for your loss, Sean."

"Funny you should say that, Minister."

"Oh?"

"I want to consider the arrangements, if you wouldnae mind."

"Well, as I was telling you before..."

"Did you know my father?" I asked.

"I didn't," he said. "He took his vacation, as it were, before my arrival here. I knew of him though."

"He's up at the farm now," I said.

"Good."

"To be frank, looking alright. Looking very relaxed in death."

"Oh yes, I'm sure he does."

"Looking forward to going into the ground."

"I see," said the minister.

"I didn't know him well. I hardly saw him. He always liked the quiet, I'm told. He wasnae a difficult man, he usually got on well with people. I'm sure you know the type." The minister smiled. "With that in mind, I'm thinkin' that the cemetery here is the ideal spot for him," I said.

"Well," said the minister. "I thought I'd said, but there may be a difficulty there, Sean."

"I know what you said. But why would that be? My mother's here already. He'd want to join her."

"Well," he said, moving up the aisle towards me. "To put it plainly, he's a convicted murderer, Sean. This makes it difficult for people round here, you understand, to just put him in the cemetery, like any old Joe." He laughed lightly.

I sighed and folded my arms across my chest. "Maybe I'm not being clear, Minister."

"You're doin' well enough," he answered.

"In case I'm no' getting' ma point across. For all my education and my having read the Bible from cover to cover, sometimes it's difficult to express clearly what I think."

"Yes..." he said.

"Would you like to sit down, minister?" I pulled him by the hem of his black gown. His knees caught against the front of the pew and he slumped like damp mud off a shovel down beside me. "I should really explain so that we all know what is going on. Please try and understand this, if you would: there's a man, my father, in my kitchen and he's lying comfortably enough, but he can't stay there forever." I paused and looked in the direction of the altar. "Two days from now, it's my earnest desire that we put him in the ground to rest. He's been in the house too long already. As you can imagine, it's a more permanent arrangement I'm lookin' for. The ground I want him in is here, right outside." I helpfully pointed at the door to the church that I had entered by. "Somewhere close to my mother's own grave. I'm sure there's space. I think he deserves that after all he went through." I could hear the wind under the door. "What I'm expecting are some words of condolence spoken over his body, if you could please manage that for me. I want him to be remembered by those who wish to remember. I want him remembered as the good man he was, if possible. Sorry to ramble on Minister, but do you understand?"

"Well, as I have said..." I didn't hear what he said, but dug deep into my waist pocket, extracting various items, and I placed three gold coins on the back of the pew in front of us. He stopped talking and looked at them. "There's three, which should be ample to cover expenses. There will be a couple more when it's done. Now," I said. "Is that all settled, Minister? Can we go home and get on with the preparations?"

The minister had a nervous look about his face. He was leaning away from me and his eyebrows were raised in a frown atop his forehead. He still had his Bible gripped hard under the white knuckles of his right hand. He got to his feet, and pulled away. "There won't be a problem," he said, quickly placing the Bible under his arm and scooping the coins into his hand. "But you know, Sean, I'm not sure there's any need to make threats." He walked away towards the small door to the side of the altar. "Goodnight Sean," he said, before he disappeared.

I looked down at my right hand. I had my father's fish knife in my grip. I had taken it out when looking for the coins. It must have been momentary inadvertence. I stood up and walked out of the large door at the rear of the church and meandered slowly through the cemetery. I looked around and found the plot where soon my father would find his final place of rest.

32

THE FUNERAL

T he minister was as good as his word. He put on a decent burial and the occasion did not lack dignity. Towards the end, he either spoke some Gaelic or said something inaudible. He wore spectacles to read the blessing. When we filed out I was aware of the troubled look on his brow and it seemed to me every time I stepped near him he turned a shade pale. As he stood on the church step, the sweat on his forehead made him glisten like a honeyed nut. When I was up close I could smell the pipe tobacco on his breath. Yet, he had said good words. He'd had the sense to tread lightly on the repentant sinner theme and I thanked him for that. I pulled my face close to his and squeezed his limp hand. I noticed the shine of the open pores on his nose. He looked at me as if I was something sharp that could cut him badly. I delivered the promised coins into his open palm. These he shuffled slyly into one of his many pockets.

There were people at the funeral service I had not expected. There were even faces I did not recognise. Why do people go to funerals? They're not going to be missed if they don't. If it's jokes they're looking for, look elsewhere. Maybe some seeking respite from the cold, late November wind. Some to check the nails, make sure the lid was banged down nice and hard. Others, like a lot of those gassing women, would think it safe to turn up now, that the secrets would die with him. The soldier-farmer and his foreign wife were both dead after all. Nae bark left in them. I even saw Joe and Tom, my old adversaries, lined up outside the church gate like they had doubt about the wisdom of entering. Mr Shifner sat at the back of the church, looking much older now, his sideburns streaked with grey. He shook my hand at the door of the church as he left. "I've not had to buy another book since you left the school," he said.

"I'm sorry to hear that, Mr Shifner," I said. "I can't believe I'm your only success."

My father was in the earth, already breaking down into his constituent parts. He was close enough to my mother's grave. Somebody could have made the kingdom of heaven easier to enter by making the ground a little softer. It had taken two men one and a half days to make a hole deep enough. The ground was so cold that the walls were like flint. Nevertheless, I did not begrudge the little extra I had to pay to have them dig a decent cavity. I was not of a mind to bury my father sideways just to save on the gravedigger.

When it was over, Aunt Marion stood by the church door and she too had her share of words with the minister. She said that at his next funeral he might wish to remove the egg from the front of his robe. Lizzie meanwhile hung behind her and kicked small stones off the step. She was an awkward woman, I thought, but then again, with the right tilt of her head, she was pretty. Some people were like that; it depended on the light and nobody had seen it yet.

I was still at the graveside when I noticed Rory Fraser

hovering somewhere to my right. His fair hair was still long but he tucked each side back behind his wagging ears. He was wearing dark clothes, his sleeves were too long and the top button of his collarless shirt was tight against his neck. He wore no socks. He looked like he had been dressed by a psychotic blind man but seemed unaware of this fashion calamity. He coughed productively but today there were no graveside projectiles. I looked at him and he looked at me. We looked down at the coffin in the hole. They had not yet filled him over with earth. The men would be along shortly with their shovels.

Rory stood tall and put the black hat back on his head. "I'm sorry for your loss," he said. In the same breath he walked from the graveside, along the pathway between the slabs of stone. He then gobbed hard against the slim trunk of a rowan tree, his spittle flecking against the last remaining red-yellow, age-puckered berries.

33

MR HAMILTON

With my father gone, stiff and buried, to my surprise and with a little shame, my own anguine response was to shed my skin and regenerate myself with new purpose and direction. I say *shame* because the last thing I wanted was my father dead in a freezing coffin, little good to anybody but multiples of legless larva. Undoubtedly, the effect of his dying was to galvanise me. I found a confidence I did not have before. I was like a man who began to understand what he wanted, who all of a sudden recognized his direction of travel. I've heard since that this is not so unusual when a parent dies; death removes the shackles of the past, as if the nagging voices lie still at last.

I set about reroofing the house. This involved stripping off the old Welsh slates, lining the timbers with sarking boards and relaying the restored slates across the top so that they fitted snugly together. The old wooden 'snake' fences around the pasture field were pulled out and rebuilt. I cleared away the sandy scrub that wasted the earth of the field leading down to the Bombo Burn. I put in some

Blackface sheep, partly to keep the weeds down, albeit typically they might have preferred a more hostile home than the hills of Fife. I supplemented their numbers with half a dozen gorse-eating feral goats who specked the field in their white socks and black charred necks. I then set about rebuilding the wall on the east side of the house with whinstone reclaimed from higher up the burn, in a spot some way before the soil turned to sand. I took a large sledgehammer to the soft stone that lined the west side of the byre, bagged up the chippings and shoveled them onto the track along by the burn. I took down the old gate that stood at the mouth of the farm; we all knew it had never served to keep anyone out, so I replaced it with one fashioned from old roof joists that I cut, sized and treated. The gate now released swung freely open, without a sound or a squeak of protest. I put a steel bolt lock on it. The invaders would have to come over the top and take their chances. That's what the Enfield was for. I planted more seed potatoes or tubers in the field to the east of the house, where I knew the soil was good, and stoned the track from the road to the house, sprinkling the surface with barrowloads of small chips and sand from the shore. Carriage wheels would no longer stick in the ruts. I pulled out the old fire that Aunt Marion had always cursed because it smoked so badly, rebuilt it and mended the cracks in the original chimney with shovels of wet lime. I glowed with pride when there was no trace of black wood smoke leeching from the lining. Aunt Marion was appreciative and, for once, eyed me as if I were the latest in a short line of deities.

"No' completely useless then," she said.

I took down the rotten ash trees over the other side of the river, sawed them into lengths and split the logs. I stacked them in neat rows off the ground to lose their sap and moisture, where they would lie for another year.

I laid hands on a Scots Grey cockerel and a posse of Scots Dumpy stumpy-legged hens and constructed a house out of rough wood and a run from torn fishing nets. We took more eggs off them than ever before. We had three horses now, two being of good Clydesdale stock, heavy and massive with the plough, they could turn the earth all day. I found work for these horses, miles around, running the plough through neighbouring fields and I earned a decent amount for it. I discovered in the process that money begets money. Finally, I had the blacksmith cut an iron fish from a steel sheet that he soldered to a stout bar to serve as a weather-vane. He attached it hard against the top of the front gable of the house. Often I would stand beneath it and enjoy the rusted fish as it turned in the freshening breeze, most times blowing south-westerly across the rooftop. The farm took on a prosperous appearance, giving it the kind of rude health that it had not seen for many years.

I was pleased with these achievements. It was good to wander around the farm and see it the way my father would have wanted it to be, its walls dark and solid, copings sharp along the top, its roof neatly tucked against the rafters, slates secure, free of draughts and leaks. The work had done me good physically: I already had my mother's dark, broody looks and these had not faded and I was leaner now than I had ever been. I had a back that was broad and straight.

With all these changes taking place you might assume that I would have moved on in my own mind, but there was much at the back of my thoughts that I suppose I was reluc-tant to confront. The choir voices were never still for long. All the roofing and the fencing, the roadwork and the logging, pulling weeds out from gutters, none of it got rid of that need to know more. And when I knew more, I was beginning to recognise that I'd have to do more. To make this go away, I'd have to settle old scores. If I knew how and by whose hand my mother died, I could not put that to one side and carry on with a stubborn grip on the plough. I had come to recognise that fact. I may even have always known it. With knowledge comes responsibility. I had to take it on, aware of what I was doing and what it would cost, not like a dumb fool stumbling into an open hole.

I have made reference already to that useful book misappropriated from Mr Shifner's rosewood library titled the *Nuttall Encyclopoedia*. This linen bound heavyweight provided a grand source of incendiary information for a young man entering his late teens with a passing interest in guns and small explosions. I had enjoyed firing off the Snider-Enfield. The pleasure was such that I had worked my way through most of the "Boxer" cartridges. That is not to say I wasted any; I did not miss many targets because I was already intent on making sure that every bullet counted. I shot a seal in the water off Pooly Point and Jacob Snider would have been proud of me, buried down there at Kensal Green Cemetery. It was a moving target after all, dipping in and out of the water, but I popped a steel ball straight between its ears as it craned its neck in search of a mackerel or a tempting sea trout it would never enjoy.

In ordinary company, killing a seal for idle sport may well be considered as an action of sub-average morality, but I have to say that it was important to me to have some proper sense of what taking a life really meant beyond the abstract notion. Common killers rarely have any sense of what they're doing before they do it. When such a person takes a man's life or attacks a woman or commits some other vile felony he might very properly find that he has no capacity to withstand the psychological effect of all that blood or all that pain inflicted so recklessly. Worse than the mere physical discomfort there is always the unquantifiable complexity of guilt, that cloying excess of conscience. Of course, plenty others who undertake murder or other violence might just as well be snapping twigs off a log for all the feeling they have after their crimes. I'd read about brutal killers who murdered and raped and then helped themselves to a sandwich from the larder as they were leaving. I felt it was only right that if I was going to kill somebody I had to do my research and discover what emotion I might some day have to deal with. Once aboard the assassin's boat, there are no liferafts: it's sink or swim.

As it was, I did not feel much at all when I shot that seal. It sank and it was gone. So there was blood in the water. So what? God's peace go with you, dear departing semi-aquatic marine mammal. I concluded that my lack of empathy was not going to be an especial burden upon my conscience. This was in some ways a surprising and disappointing discovery; what marks us out as civilized human beings is our capacity to suffer guilt, sadness and remorse for unconscionable acts. Shooting the seal told me that I had very little to fear in that department. To my mind, I'd all the makings of an extremely cold killer with an undeveloped sense of conscience. More importantly for now, on a more practical level, I knew well enough that if I was to develop my aptitude for guns and minor explosions, I needed to get my hands on some new Boxer cartridges.

There was an old fellow with a purple nose living in Tullis, somewhere near the cemetery. He was not yet in it, but his home was conveniently close. He had round shoulders and short, bandy legs, carried too much weight and often wore a blue felt hat with a green bandana. At the time,

I didnae know where exactly he lived but I knew that it was one of three or four houses near the church. This man did not do much around the place and was often not seen for weeks at a time, but it was known that he drank a lot of wine, invariably red, which was delivered by horse-drawn coach from Alsace, a busy spot to the east of France. Sometimes he'd a small delivery of cheeses with his wine. Musty cream cheese behind a thick skin and smoked goat cheese from Germany. As I came to discover, he didn't mind telling you that he knew all there was to know about every little thing you didn't even know existed. I realised very early on that if you told him you'd three fat hairs growin' out of a mole on your chin he was so sure of himself that he might very well correct you on that. He might say there were four, and you'd be wise to check your chin to see that you'd not miscounted. He was a walking encyclopedia. He'd a breadth of knowledge that would fill the shelves of old Mr Shifner's rosewood library. I figured that if he was just partly right about some of those things he'd know where I might be able to get my hands on some new cartridges for the Enfield.

His name was Mr Hamilton. I found him one night in Tullis village, sat atop the cemetery wall, reflecting on the dead within, one of whom was by then my dear father. I'd circled round the village every afternoon and evening for a week before I stumbled upon him.

"Mr Hamilton? It is Mr Hamilton, is it not?" I asked, to which he said nothing. "Sean Logan," I said and put out my hand, but he only looked at it as if I had shown him something peculiar. He turned his head to study the graves. Not to be discouraged, I sat down beside him. He looked back at me and then away again and I thought of something to say, to break the ice. "Can I ask you why you're looking at the cemetery stones with such great interest?"

He said nothing immediately, then wiped the top of his nose. "I was no' aware I had to ask permission to look at some old graves."

"Carry on, Mr Hamilton. Dinnae let me interrupt your meditation."

"Thankyou. I will."

We'd been silent for thirty seconds when I said: "Do you know *funus* is the Latin word for funeral?"

"Yes," he said.

I fell silent again. "Do you know in Japan they pick out the Adam's Apple from the cremated bones?"

"Do they indeed?" he said.

"Yes, they put it inside the urn."

"I see."

"One for the urn is what they say."

"I see."

"In Japanese of course."

He looked away again. Then his eyes drifted back to me. "Are you like me?" he said. "Do you find the dead a terribly interesting subject?"

"No' really," I said.

"Are you frightened of it?"

"No."

"But you've had death in your life. I know that much."

"I have," I said. "But I'm no fearin' it."

"Your father's dead," he said.

"He is, as a matter of fact."

"And your mother too."

"A long time ago."

"But to you, it's like yesterday." I did not answer. "Well," he said. "If you must know, I was calculating exactly how many bodies there are in this yard. Including your father and mother." I liked the way he called it a *yard*. I could tell he had some wine in him. "You see, in this yard, it's easy to count each stone left to right, then count each row left to right, do the appropriate multiplication, then add in the nobodies at the end who havenae a stone at all. That would give you...? Any idea?"

"Well," I said. "That would give you seventy-nine bodies."

He looked at me with an eyebrow raised in a squiggle and then he smiled. "You might cut yourself with all that speed." He tapped his unlit pipe against the wall and it made a clunking sound in the silence. It was wood, a briar pipe cut from the root burl, chosen for its ability to absorb moisture and its resistance to fire. "Seventy-nine you say? The number seems on the heavy side," he said. "But in any event, are you no' ignoring something?"

"I'm no' sure about that," I said. "It's not my habit to ignore things. Mr Shifner used to say I'd be a sight better off if I did because then I'd have more time for what was really important. But I find detail every bit as important. "

"Aye, you've a point. But some of these bodies are layered," he continued. "You've got them double-stacked, you see. Could be treble-packed, I don't know. You cannae say how many you've got underneath the ones on top. See what I mean? So how do you know how many bodies there are in here? Had you thought about that?" Mr Hamilton appeared satisfied with his logic.

"I allowed for double-layering," I said. I moved my face towards him. I did so because I did not like the way he kept on looking away from me and I had learned that the quickest way to get someone's attention was to move yourself into their physical space. This made them uncomfortable and, often enough, submissive and receptive. However, Mr Hamilton did not appear uncomfortable or submissive and showed no signs of being at all receptive. "But they're no' all double-layered. When I laid my father here to rest no' too long ago, I was not wantin' anybody shovin' up from below."

Mr Hamilton gave me a look. "Go on," he said.

"So I checked it all out, you see, Mr Hamilton. Turns out there is some regulation about all this. Double-layers is fine. Trebling is no' permitted under borough byelaws. Therefore, the answer to your question is still seventy-nine."

He raised his eyebrows. "Well," he said. "If you're no' pulling an old man's leg, I owe you an apology."

"I'm no' looking for apologies," I said.

"Good. In that case you'll no' get one." He paused. "You may as well tell me, then."

"Tell you what, Mr Hamilton?"

"Tell me what you're looking for?" He screwed up his eyes.

"It's good that you ask me that," I said. "I'm lookin' for some advice."

"I doubt you need much advice from me."

"I'm looking for Boxer cartridges and I'm looking for advice about where I can get ma hands on some."

"What do you want them for?"

"My Enfield. No point havin' a gun if you're no' going to work it."

"Do you like guns?" he asked.

"Yes, I do like guns," I answered. "Well, at least, I like the one I've got."

"It's true that you'll do a gun no favours by locking it in a drawer," he said. "Enfield you say?"

"Yes."

"The old Snider-Enfield, hey?"

"The very same." There followed a long silence.

"The one that did Bobby in?" he asked, carefully weighing his words like they were plums.

I looked at him. "Go on."

"What's it you want me to say?"

"You said 'the one that did Bobby'."

"I may have done."

"You did."

"And if I did?"

"What d'you mean by that? I should like to know," I said. The old man hesitated, looking at the briar pipe in his hands.

"Like to know what exactly?" he asked. "Sean isn't it?" I nodded. "What would you like to know, Sean?"

"I've heard of this fella Bob from my Aunt Marion."

"Is that so?"

"She said my father talked about a man called Mad Bob."

"It's a common name," he said.

"I'm assuming Mad Bob and Bobby are one and the same?"

He sighed. "It's Bobby Weir she might be talkin' about," he said. "His friends call him Mad Bob."

"Well?" I said. "That all fits." I hesitated. "Is he still alive?"

"As far as I know."

"Do you happen to know where I might find him?"

"It happens I do," he said.

"I would be most interested."

"Is that so? What about the Boxers then? The cartridges? Are you no' interested in them any more?"

"Of course," I said. "More than ever. I may need quite a lot. I've still to get my eye properly in."

"I might be able to help you with that an' all," he said. "It may turn out there are other things I can do for you." He was looking at the pipe in his hands again. "You interested in guns then, are you?"

"As I said, I've only got the one. When I pull the trigger on an Enfield it's an enjoyable sensation to me. The feel of the trigger when I squeeze it. The smell off the barrel when it's fired. That's what I like."

"There's nothing wrong with the Enfield," he said. "But are you no' looking for a bit more than that?"

"Like?"

"There are newer, better guns out there."

I waited for him to continue but he fell silent. "You said there were other things you could help me with? What did you mean by that?"

"Oh yes," Mr Hamilton said, half tilting his head towards me. "I think I maybe can. It's probably time that someone did help you." He got to his feet. "It may be best if you come round to my house tomorrow." He walked away and then turned back. "You know my house?"

"Yes, I think I do."

"I've got a lot to show you and some things I ought to tell you," he said, as he looked back at the cemetery and pondered the bodies beneath. He turned and walked away, quickly disappearing from sight.

All the voices in my mind, until now so quiet since the death of my father, were suddenly singing in my ears.

34

THE ENFIELD REVOLVER

Next day, I was around at Mr Hamilton's house at twelve minutes to ten in the morning. It would've been earlier but I did not in fact know where it was. I had a good idea where it might be but that is not quite the same thing. I got the wrong house and was chased from a fat lady's backyard because she thought I was stealing her hens' eggs. She swung a long broom handle at me with some athleticism, as if whatever threat I posed, it was one that would respond well to a pole across its legs.

I was down there early because I wanted to see Mr Hamilton before he'd had his first glass of Vosges, but when I knocked hard on the right door, he opened up, already armed with a red-brown liquid in his fist.

"You came then?" he said.

"Didn't I say I'd be coming?"

"You better come in." He closed the door behind me.

It was a wide door followed by a smaller door, very low it was and I stooped my head to enter. It creaked on its hinges as it snuffed out more of the light behind me. He ushered me through the dark hallway, along a hard wood floor, into what seemed to be the main room of the house: it stretched from the front of the building to the back and was gloomy, the morning sun struggling to filter through the gaps between the shutters.

"This is my office," he said. "D'you have an office, Sean?"

"No, I don't have an office," I said. "It's certainly a grand size."

"I live in here. It has to be big. It's where I have all I need." He waved his arm at the desk by the window. "Organised chaos. I ken where everything is – if you just give me time to find it."

It was indeed a large room, dark walls and a wooden floor that echoed under your feet as you crossed. On the walls, there were oil painted pictures in large gold frames, depicting wild animals – leopards, elephants, stags, dogs and other four-legged flesh-eaters. Behind the picture frames there was an old patterned paper. I had not seen that before except in books depicting the palace at Versailles, before the revolution. Also some on the walls of the large royal palace in London. Thick, velvet, burgundy drapes hung at each side of the window, uniting with the shutters to hold out the light and keep any heat in. They were faded along the edges by occasional glimpses of the sun. There was no' much heat on this occasion since the stove was out and sat like a dead tooth at one end of the room.

"Sit down, sit down," he said, as he flicked a cat from a wide cushioned stool in front of his desk.

"I see you keep cats," I said.

"Hate them myself. They're utterly selfish. You like cats?"

"We have some."

"Farmers always hate cats, don't they?"

"Not always. They keep the rats down. They can be

useful." I said. "Like most things, an upside and a downside."

"I'm sure that's true. I once had an albino rat. Blind, as you'd expect, and kept walking into things."

"Rats don't live long," I said.

He clicked his fingers. "Just a year at most and they're dead."

"Makes you wonder why there are so many."

"Do you know, they often die because they've passed from being hunter to being hunted. There's a justice in that, do you no' think?"

"Someone else's supper."

"Have you ever thought what it must be like to be the hunter and later, to have the tables turned on you? For the hunter to become the hunted?"

"Not very pleasant, I imagine," I said.

"It's all about changing perspective, seeing things from the other end. Like looking down the wrong end of a telescope."

"Or the wrong end of a gun?" I said.

"Yes."

"Very dangerous." I shifted in my chair. "Are you telling me I'm the hunted one here, Mr Hamilton?"

"Things are never that clear," he answered.

"I prefer to be the hunter."

"Rats have proved, you can't always choose." He clapped his hands together as if he wished to change the subject. "But, I promised that I could show you something more interesting than cartridges, did I not?"

"Yes," I said. I sat with one hand on each knee. "It's given me a restless night to think what you were meaning."

"Let me show you something then that I've found very interesting and which may give you more restless nights before you're done." He took a large gulp from the glass he held in his right hand and placed it on the blue, leather inlay of the desktop. He lifted an intricately crafted key from his waistcoat pocket and unlocked the bottom drawer of the three-drawer, Georgian desk. He pulled it open, and it squeaked as it came, as if the drawer was reluctant to release its contents. He took out what looked to be an old, oily cloth, but there was clearly something inside it. He moved his glass to one side and laid the cloth on the leather top of his desk. Carefully he peeled back each corner. Mr Hamilton looked at it affectionately. "You said you liked the Snider-Enfield," he said. "Know what this is?" I shook my head. "It's a close relation. One of the family. An Enfield Revolver." He picked up the gun and looked at it side on. "She's perfectly lovely, isn't she?"

35

OFFICE PYROTECHNIA

1903

As it transpired, the Enfield Revolver was just the first in line. Each time he disappeared off somewhere, I knew Mr Hamilton would be back with an addition to the family. The strangest thing was, he didn't wish to keep any of them. He wanted me to have them and use them. He said there was no point him hiding these beauties in a drawer. He wanted me to take them to the farm and make good use of them. Shooting rats or cats or anything else with a heartbeat.

Another thing was the way Mr Hamilton had what he called *the office* for his private interests. After my visits became a little more regular, it got me thinking that it was high time I had an office of my own to house those discoveries in my life that I was not inclined to share with others. To some degree I was already in a position to offer that level of desirable bureaucracy: I had a big shed – it had once been a byre, the hay pens were still there, stinking at one end – a shed that I was gradually filling with those little pieces that were assuming importance in my life. This collection of guns was growing and I had to find a home for them. Somewhere I could take them apart and clean them properly and then store them the appropriate way. I was concerned that they should be kept secure and I was worried about the risk of fire.

I'd purchased some timber from a merchant in Blairgowrie. I also bought off him an ample supply of screws, nails and other tools and bits of ironware. He delivered them to my door, having said he would be in the area anyway. I avoided Fawcett's shop for these supplies because he was a complication; I would visit him soon on other matters. For the present, armed with this equipment, I set about making an imposing wall cupboard. It was not difficult, not for a young farmer like myself used to putting iron and wood together and making them into something productive.

In that shed with the big double doors, I had a large table that was heavily topped in granite. The granite had been expensive but necessary to further my growing ballistic endeavours. It was not long before I had reached the evolutionary phase of my apprenticeship in weapons technology where it was not beyond me to cast my own personal bullets. This was not for reasons of pretension or a particular delusion of grandeur; it was simply to allow me to obtain the quantity I required and of the quality necessary for my overall purpose. To tell you the truth, I'd no idea how many I'd need, so I just kept on making them until I knew I had enough. It was also economical – that is once I had got the hang of it and had reduced the initial wastage. I needed nothing more than a fire, an iron pot and a heavy ladle. I melted down the lead, skimmed off any crud and bubbled it all into a silvery texture. Mr Hamilton had become an ardent supporter of my enterprise and was very useful in obtaining moulds for me - special shapes for individual firearms - and, in truth, it seemed that no challenge was beyond him. I poured the liquid into the moulds and when it cooled the bullets dropped out. With a degree of learning, it was not too hard. Of course, you needed to size and lubricate the bullets, but the whole process of manufacture I found immensely satisfying. As a result I'd more bullets and cartridges in my office than I would ever have use for. At least, that's what I thought.

The cupboard I was building to house my weaponry was supposed to be five feet wide and eight feet high. I paid a second visit to the woodshop in Blairgowrie to obtain more timber, screws and nails. He struck me as a strange sort of person: he talked night and day about fishing and how he loved iroko wood, that all you could buy around here was spruce and elm.

When the weaponry cupboard was finished it was easily ten feet wide by twelve feet high with a pine shelf along the top and bottom. I had a modest, wooden stepladder for reaching the top stuff. In the middle of the cupboard, sitting on two strong brackets and appearing like the sun around which the other planets rotated, was my father's Snider-Enfield. Circling it, as if following the numbers of a clock, at one I had the Enfield Revolver, with its rugged, all-metal, large trigger look. It was a gun with a warm, cherry wood handle grip that sat comfortably in the hand. You could hit your target at twenty-five yards, but it had a range of up to two hundred. I never hit a damn thing at that distance. At the two o' clock position I had to have the Lee-Enfield, a bolt-action rifle, a standard in the Great War that was coming sooner than we all knew. A range of two thousand yards and a ten round magazine, using the Lee-Enfield I could take the spot off a man's nose whilst resting a cup of Darjeeling tea on the barrel. Or nearly. Next on the clock was a Mauser: a semi-automatic pistol, a classic with a pencil thin barrel and a broomhandle grip. At the four o'clock position, I hung the Webley Bull Dog, a small but powerful revolver you could put in your pocket or, if you were a respectable lady with interests to protect, you might keep it in your handbag. The Webley had a revolving 6-round cylinder into which you just slotted the bullets and you could hold it very easily with just one hand. A pretty gun, primarily nickel with wooden grips, the type used once to assassinate a President of the United States. President Garland was his name or so I read in a periodical newspaper in Mr Shiffner's library. Next I had the German, four-barreled weapon known as the Reicher. The Reicher had to be for fun-loving aesthetes only; I did not see how you could kill anyone sensibly with it. It was the invention of a madman. Down at the bottom I had the classic Colt pocket revolver, although you would need long pockets to keep the barrel warm; it was the 1849 model with six chambers, and it used cap and ball ammunition, loaded from the front with loose black powder - a mixture of sulfur, charcoal and potassium nitrate - and a bare bullet. The underside of the gun body was angled down towards the dark wood grip, as sweet and comfortable in your hand as you could ever hope. You had to cock the Colt each time you fired it and that could make your thumbs throb. You needed tough old paws like I do. It was heavy too. This was not one for the handbag. Up the left side, I'd a Cook & Brother Carbine, a dinosaur in this company with its muzzle-loading musket. Then, the curvy Devisme revolver, a nod to the Frenchman who was better known for all the military swords he used to make; a gun forged with elegance and charm and an unusual octagonal barrel. Very French. It had the words *Devisme à Paris* engraved along the top flat of the barrel. Finally, a pair of the most brutal guns you ever saw, they never had a name that I could discover but they would strike fear into the toughest opponent: like a rifle, big trigger with a decent wood stock that tucked into the crease of your elbow; then a long breech and two very short barrels, one on top of the other. Big recoil but if you hit the target you would never see it again.

Those were my guns, part of a growing inventory, and I kept them in my brand new gun cupboard courtesy of the Blairgowrie timber mill. I made more bullets and cartridges as the days went by until I had a stock big enough to start an Afghan war. Of course, I was no' the only guy to have had an interest in things that go bang. Alfred Nobel was still warm in his grave but luckily for me he'd spent the best part of his life perfecting the invention that was to change the world forever: dynamite.

I borrowed from Mr Nobel's knowledge. I went to the library in Stirling and viewed a copy of *Pyrotechnia* by Vannoccio Biringuccio, a book that had been around for three hundred years but which contained the basic chemistry essential to a fledgling powder monkey. By the look on the librarian's face, I don't think anyone had looked at it in three hundred years either. I could tell he didn't want to let me get my hands on it but the letter in my pocket from Mr Hamilton was enough to persuade him. I discovered that basic chemistry was still basic chemistry and there was easily enough information there to provide the guidance I needed.

As I mentioned, Mr Hamilton was the source of my

growing armament collection. He said it gave him real pleasure to satisfy my curiosity on this subject and to provide
me with ever more interesting and varied weaponry. Even
books on the subject were not beyond him. So far as the
bomb-making was concerned, he obtained some of the
ingredients for me and, by trial and error, I put them
together: three parts nitroglycerin, one part sawdust
(although sometimes I used clay) and a small admixture of
sodium carbonate. It goes without saying, it was important
to obtain the correct mix: nitroglycerin is shock-sensitive,
particularly when it's pure, and it blows up with very little
encouragement. You get messy results when you have an
unplanned detonation. Once I had the correct mix I could
shape it into short sticks and then wrap them in paper. The
other thing you had to remember when you stored these
sticks was that dynamite boxes have to be turned regularly,
otherwise you get pooling when the nitroglycerin sweats.
That, I very quickly learned, created a dangerous situation
so far as involuntary and undesirable explosions was
concerned.

"What are you doing in that shed?" Aunt Marion wanted
to know when I emerged one day blinking into the light.
"You're spending your life in an old shed," she said. "What's
that about?"

"Hobbies," I said.

"What are you needin' a hobby for?"

"Relaxation," I said.

"You need time out on the farm, getting the jobs done,
fences mended, all that. No' a hobby."

"I do that and plenty more," I said. "The farm's looking
good just now."

"It could always look better," she said.

"It's lookin' a lot better now than it ever did."

She paused. "That's a big lock and chain you put on the old shed door."

"There are bad people about."

"Nobody comes here. What're you needin' a lock on it for?"

"In the first place, to stop people from go-in' in there."

"And why's that? What needs kept under lock and key?"

"Dangerous material," I said.

"Like what?" I didn't answer. "What kind of hobby needs dangerous material?" she said.

"Just the stuff you need on a farm."

"We never used to."

"Times have changed."

"What's it for?"

"To keep us safe."

"To keep us safe?" she repeated. "That all?"

I sighed. "I've got guns and I've got bullets in there, Aunt Marion."

"Oh?"

"Now, please don't pretend you didnae know."

"Your business is your business," she said.

"And I intend to use them."

"That's what I was fearin'."

"I know what I'm doin'."

She hesitated. "I'm scared for you, Sean."

"I won't do anything daft," I said.

The truth is that the work on the bullets and the dynamite and the growing collection of guns, these were the things that were keeping me going. I touched her hand. "I'm doing what my father would have done."

"Are you sure about that?" She turned away. "Let's get in for supper, it's cold out here."

I stood there for a minute. Joe and his friends had always

tormented me over my father. They didn't have to any more. My father had served more years in jail than anyone deserves. Of course, he never reached the end of that sentence. He was now dead as the dark hole he slept in, a slit in the ground behind the broken wall at the Tullis cemetery where Mr Hamilton combed the bones with his estimates and calculations. Neither two farthings for his dreams nor a care in the world. The threads of what had been his bumpy life were disappearing into the dust as fast as light fading at the end of a long day. His time was served. On the other hand, I was twenty years old with some stubble on my cheeks and a shed housing an eclectic range of international weaponry and homegrown explosives. Add to all that, for the first time I'd discovered I had an interest in a woman. True, she was married to a donkey brain but that didn't make me desire her any the less. Marriage wasn't the same thing as ownership, or so I believed. In any event, as I stood there in the yard, I was ready to shake off the brown paper and explode into life. I didn't know then that I was not the only dog in the pack wanting revenge.

36

CHITTED TUBERS

Sowing spuds in mid-March is not easy work. Backs are bowed, hands are cut, fingernails break, sweat drips and tempers fray. The fields are ploughed by horse, then ripped open with long trenches, each up to eight inches deep. The base is padded with manure scooped from cows, horses, hens and any other livestock, mixed and turned. The chitted tubers are set into the trenches by hand, one at a time, a foot to eighteen inches apart, being careful to keep their shoots intact and pointing upwards towards the prospective sunlight. The fields are packed with busy farmers, their arses in the air, cursing, laughing, sweating and sometimes fighting. The children are out there too, in open shirts and muddy pants, there's gaiety and noise, despite being roped in and forced to work. There is the occasional flash of colour – yellow or even red – off some-body's clothing, and sporadic shouts or laughter carry down to the next field where others lift their heads to ask what the hell are they doin' up there. To which you can add the inter-mittent whinny of an awkward nag and the sound of a hoof scraping at the ground as if that was the way out.

Salmon Cottage had three fields ploughed, turned and ready for sowing, each shielded by an old hawthorn hedge along the boundary. The neighbours had fields of their own, all in varying states of readiness. Some, more work-shy or behind with their preparations, had stretches little more than half-ploughed or half-manured. Others looked fondly over their land, but they were so far behind in their preparations they could do nothing but daydream of when the ground might be good enough to take a flowering tuber. The truth was you could bury six pieces of silver in some of that grassland and you would harvest nothing more than a ten percent return and a hundred percent sore back. In their hearts these people knew that the earth of their barren fields would see another season without a decent harvest. Nevertheless, come the first day of the third week in March, the families from all the farms would come together and, as a makeshift unit or cooperative, would work their way round between the hawthorn hedges and the fencing, sowing the potatoes as they went. Any field not ready by the time they got to it would be passed by for another year. So it came about, that those from many miles around gathered at the Tullis village hall where they set about discussing which of the many fields were ready for sowing; and planning which to sow first, which to sow last and which ones they had not the slightest intention of sowing at all.

I attended the meeting. The village hall was an austere, wooden rectangular box with a leaky roof and rough timber cladding along one side. I sat there with Aunt Marion, rolling her eyes like a dizzy trout, something she did a lot these days, and Lizzie too on the other side of the table, clicking her tongue impatiently.

"Bloody waste of time," muttered somebody without elaboration. There was the usual round of cursing over which fields were ready and which were not. In the end it was agreed to take on the worst field first and that was to be found in a shady, sunken spot, penned by an old rope fence that the sheep took to eating. The field was flooded at one sloping corner by the heavy rain of weeks before that petulantly refused to drain. With part of the field still underwater, there was debate as to whether it could or should be sowed at all.

These protracted discussions meandered to their conclusion and, once resolved, the community separated into its constituent groups, thereafter launched like swirls of hail upon the many fields. The sowing might take a week, depending on the weather, their state of readiness and their willingness to work. Their owners fought their cussed battles with one another along the way; one would be dissatisfied at the way in which the sowing was conducted and the amount of effort that was expended. Others would share those grumbles and make up a few more.

Keira was also at the village hall, but she wore a dark, hooded cloak and held herself at the far side where the light was poor and where people would have to come up close to recognise her. Her day had not started well. That morning, expecting her husband to join up for the sowing, she had been surprised to find him in the yard, mounted early on his grey horse just as the sun was rising. She stood by the front door, not yet dressed.

"Where are you goin'?"

"Business elsewhere," he said, tightening the horse's girth.

"What about the sowin'?" she said.

"What about the sowin'?"

"We have fields here."

"I ken we have fields here."

"They need to be sown."

"Oh," was all he said, picking at his teeth with a fingernail.

"With potatoes."

"I am familiar with the potato."

"Well?" she said.

"Well I've pressin' business elsewhere. What can I say? You'll have to manage."

"Who'll do our fields?"

"I can see your difficulty," he said, cupping his whiskered chin. "I can see the problem." He steered his horse down towards the gate. "But there is fuck-all I can do aboot it."

She had learnt during their short married life that she had to tread carefully around her husband. That is what you did in a marriage. She was told you had to let him think he had his way and then just get to where you were going but by a different route. None of that had worked out. She reckoned there was injustice; the wrong she felt made her angry. She knew she should hold herself back and she knew he'd probably strike her if she didn't. "You've no right!"

He stopped and turned his horse around, moving slowly back towards her until his shadow lay like a grey slab across her face. With the low sun behind him she strained to see his features or even to gauge his reaction. She was not so deluded that she thought his face would be warm and generous. The sun behind gave him a breath of hazy halo as he sat up there on that horse, bearing down upon her. She tried to keep her eyes on him. His horse moved side on to her. It was fat and over-grassed and there was mud caked down one side of his shaggy, unclipped hind leg. The horse was called Marty. Marty released wind as he stood there in front of her and skitted nervously on the spot, as if he sensed the atmosphere. Calum then swung his crop down across Keira's face. She had been around Calum long enough to learn that speed of reaction was often critical. She pulled her head back from the arc of his strike. It was just the very thin end of the black leather tip that struck the lower part of her cheek.

"There's something you ought to understand," he said, still on his horse, but leaning well forward in the saddle. He pointed his crop towards her. "Because we seem to be on the verge of a bad thing here." She heard the saddle leather creak under him. "I'll be there," he said. "When it suits me to be there. I dinnae need you tellin' me when. I dinnae need you tellin' me what I am and what I'm no'. I hope you're understandin' me?" He turned the horse and rode a short distance. "I'll be away a week," he said.

"A week?"

"Just dependin' on how things turn out." He cracked the riding crop against Marty's neck and the shaggy beast lurched heavily forward. "You'll have your hands full," he shouted over his shoulder as he cantered away.

When Calum rode off, Keira had to confess that her first thought was that those soddin' potatoes could go mash themselves in a piss pot. It was his choice to do nothin'. His choice if the field didnae get sown. They would see how he felt about it when mid-winter came and the home potato was off the menu. She enjoyed the thought of him regretting his decision. However, on reflection, the adage that revenge was a dish best served cold soon lost its appeal: revenge was best served now, and very hot. Once she had cleared up the cups and plates she had hurled across the floor to assuage her anger, she began to think more clearly. If she did not get the potatoes sown then nobody else would and there was only one person who'd suffer when the time came. She thought to herself that she might as well go and lend a hand; the fields would get done. She might just avoid the cruelty he would show her if they didn't. She was saddened by her own weakness, her inability to stand her ground against the brute. She was cowed by the guilt of times past and for what lay deep in Hare Myre water.

Having rationalised her situation to such good effect, she pressed some ointment against her cheek to bring down the colour. There was little swelling but she smeared some paste upon it to make it less obvious. She then set off on foot for the village hall. When she arrived, the place was busy and the meeting had already started. Seated in the gloom of the far wall, she listened to an old soldier, who most people laughed at, pressing his case to have them sow his field. When he finally sat down she hoped he would get his way.

From her shadowed seat, she saw me there, close to the front, listening to what people had to say. A strong-looking boy with dark hair, she might have thought. At least I like to think so. Maybe she saw something good about this boy, come on, this man. The more she looked the more it might have become apparent - at least I hope it did - that I had some kindness about me that she might wish for; I suppose my eyes were always quick, looking round, like dry sponges absorbing everything. Maybe she glimpsed something of that. She may have noticed the slightest hook to my nose - not so unattractive - and the long, dark hair against my collar. It would be almost black in that grey place.

Did she think back to the day I arrived at the house, when the fishing was foremost on my mind until I saw her naked leg through the window? Did she remember me then? Did she have any recollection at all? It seemed unlikely. She had known my story, surely, as everyone else did in these parts. She, of all people, could empathise with someone whose parents had been through that kind of hell.

We spewed out into the waiting fields and began the annual sowing. The sun rose in the sky and settled a little early Easter heat on our backs. In went the chitted potatoes and a layer of soil to top them over. The process was repeated for many hours before we stopped for a bread and ham lunch and some flat, watery beer from one of the wooden flasks.

I will confess that I had seen Keira more than once across the field. The hood had dropped to her shoulders and the sight of the red bandana on her head had sent a flicker of heat through me. I had not seen her since that morning, some time ago, before the fishing that ended so disastrously. It occurred to me that whilst I had enjoyed the stolen intimacy of sight over her flesh (even just a leg), I had never yet spoken more than a formal greeting to her. It was a situation I would have to rectify. I wondered if she was alone or if her husband was out there too. I had not seen him since the day of the fishing trip, some time ago, but I knew too well that he was not the type to enjoy honest toil and would labour hard to avoid exertion.

Towards the end of the day, with the light fading just a little, I wandered over to one of the sheep sheds at the bottom of the field nearest the track that wound up from the village. There was water there in a huge rusty basin. I took off my shirt and threw it over a wooden hayrack. I washed down my arms and hands with the cold water. My skin was refreshed and tingling. I drank from the flask and lifted my shirt from the hayrack. I put on the shirt and I used my fingers like a comb, running through my wet hair. I made my way out of the shed and back up the field, avoiding the wet pools to one side.

Aunt Marion was waiting, Lizzie close by. "Where did you take off to?"

"Just havin' a wash," I said.

"He likes to keep clean," said Lizzie.

"I didn't know it was a crime," I said.

"The ladies like a clean boy," said Lizzie.

"What ladies? What you talkin' about?"

Lizzie pointed at a girl with a red bandana down the field. My eyes followed hers. "You've no' looked at much else all day. Half your tubers went in upside down."

"Don't be daft," I said, but I didn't look away from the red bandana.

"If you've finished discussing your ablutions, we might as well go," said Aunt Marion. "I'm no' spendin' the night out here just so you can smell nice." We walked from the field, through the creosoted gate, just me, Lizzie and my Aunt Marion. I looked up to the top field, searching for the red bandana, but saw none. "I'd think twice before chasin' that one," said Aunt Marion.

"What d'you mean?"

"Dinnae play the daft laddie." I displayed my petulance by kicking a stone off the track that ricocheted into the green hawthorn. A bemused thrush leapt out startled with wild, flapping wings. Aunt Marion and Lizzie turned to look at me.

"I'm just sayin' that ring on her finger is no' an ornament." Lizzie laughed and Aunt Marion cut me with a glacial look. Sometimes they seemed to forget that I was now a man, not the awkward schoolboy I used to be. I looked up at the darkening sky and began to jog down the broken track ahead of them.

37

BUTTERFLIES

The next day came quickly enough. The same morning melee of jostling people, colour, children dashing between fields like leaves blown in the wind, dropping baskets, spilling tubers. I knew at some point, amongst all the coming and going, my path would likely cross with hers and I spent the day in anticipation of that moment. You'd think I might have been better prepared. It was no' until I was on my way to lunch that I more or less walked into her by the old stone wall that bordered the copse behind the increasingly muddy Tullis track. She seemed to be heading back to the fields, maybe having eaten already. She did not say anything, just lowered her head a little and I think she was intent on walking right past me.

"Hello?" I said.

"Yes?" I looked at her and immediately loved the brightness in her eyes. "Hello?"

"You don't remember me?"

"Your name is Logan."

"So you do?"

"Everybody knows everybody. As I'm sure you know, there are few secrets in Tullis."

"Well, I'm Sean to you. We've met before, you must remember? Quite briefly."

"It's comin' back to me," she said, looking up. "I remember a very pushy fisherman."

"Better to be remembered as a pushy fisherman, I suppose, than not at all," I said. "We weren't introduced."

"Were we not?"

"No." I thought I detected a smile at the corner of her mouth. Was she teasing me? I have a good thick skin so I was not for giving up. "I remember *you* very well. I have a clear picture of you in my mind from that occasion when we met."

"You have a picture in your mind?"

"Yes."

"Well, that's a good place for a picture. You've a good memory then?" she said.

"For the important things, I think I do."

"Important things?"

"Test me if you like."

"What do you remember about frogs?" she said. "Or butterflies?"

"Butterflies?"

"What do you remember about butterflies?" she asked again.

"Facts, I suppose. But here's my question: do you know the three most beautiful butterflies ever to have existed?"

"No, I don't."

"That's a terrible thing. You may need to know sometime."

"I'm very grateful," she said.

"Begin with the Blue Morpho, glossy and mesmerizing, with a wingspan of aboot eight inches. Imagine that!"

"Yes?"

"Can you imagine one that size?" I wondered if I was boring her but it was she who started this. "And the Leopard Lacewing," I said. "Orange and yellow across the wings and even the edges – they're like black boomerangs, all tipped in white."

"Boomerangs? I've nae heard of such a thing," she said.

"A boomerang is a flat stick."

"A flat stick?"

"It spins about an axis that is perpendicular to the direction of its flight. You throw it and it's supposed to reach the end and spin back at you. And sometimes it does."

"I see."

"It's no' foolproof."

"You have your own?" she asked.

"Yes, I've made the odd boomerang."

"Is that easy?"

"Aye, they get better with practice. The Egyptians made them first, out of bones. They're no' that new to the world." I paused. "I didnae invent the boomerang." How did I get on to boomerangs? It was all going wrong.

"Is it easy to remember these things? Butterflies and boomerangs?" she asked.

"Most things are easy enough when you turn your mind to them."

She was about to move on but she hesitated. I could see she was slim with a narrow, lovely waist. "Three?" she said.

"Three what?"

"The three most beautiful butterflies that ever existed. What's the third?"

I looked into her eyes. "Well, you, of course!" I said. "I'm sorry. That's a bit forward of me."

"You think so?"

"You're the third of the most beautiful butterflies." She flushed a little. "You may even be the *first* of the most beautiful butterflies." I was not trying to cause any embarrassment and the words came out that way without me stopping them, as if I had holes in my tongue. I felt my ears pinken and was aware of my own embarrassment.

"Thankyou Mr Logan. I'd hate to be third."

"Sean."

"Well, *Sean* Logan," she said, moving away. "Enjoy your boomerangs and your butterflies."

"Have you hurt your cheek?" I asked.

"It's a scratch," she said, holding her hand to it. "An argument with a potato." She turned and walked away.

"You havenae told me your name," I called after her.

"It's Keira," she said, as she turned. "I'm sure you knew that already."

"I'll be here tomorrow," I said. "There are other frogs and butterflies you might wish to discuss."

"More beautiful than me?" she said.

"Oh come on," I said. "No' even close!" I watched the back of her as it became smaller and disappeared from view. Something had happened to me and I was not very sure what it was.

38

GASTROPODS

Next day I saw her right enough, but by design or chance, I was unable to find an excuse to speak to her. It was a pleasant, dry spring morning with some soft, uninteresting cloud overhead and a gentle, south-easterly breeze coming off the firth. Standing still, the air would have chilled you, but we were bent over the trenches, sowing and more sowing, and far from being cold, I would happily have removed my shirt. I worked through the morning on my own. Aunt Marion had stayed at home, complaining of influenza that made her bones ache and her head spin. Lizzie remained to look after her but I knew Aunt Marion would not make an easy patient.

Late mid-morning, I bumped into Keira on her way back from one of the sowing fields. She had on a long, green woollen dress, partially covered by a white apron, with a white collar at the neck and a dark, red cloak draped across her shoulders.

"Good mornin', Sean Logan," she said.

"I was thinkin' you were avoidin' me today."

"Why would I avoid you?" she asked. "I don't know you well enough to avoid you."

"You've no reason," I said. "I promise not to mention boomerangs." She smiled. She was wearing nothing in her hair today. She had it in a simple bun but several dark lengths had fallen free and they dangled in front of her ears. I could just see her teeth when she smiled, and they were white and even. Her lips were light pink and as they met she occasionally pressed them together.

"Are you thirsty?" I said.

"I have my own water," she answered.

"Would you like some of my water?"

"What is so special about your water?"

"Mine is from the Bombo Burn, water off the hills. There's no cleaner water for miles." She took the flask from me in her right hand. Her fingers were long and slim, but grey with earthlines from working the field, and the tips of our fingers touched as I passed it to her. She lifted the flask to her lips and tipped. I watched her throat move as she swallowed. The skin was white and smooth. I looked down her neck and I thought of everything that lay there. I will admit I had these thoughts but I tried hard to push them away. She lowered the flask and as she did so, the wind blew more strands of her hair forward. With one hand she pushed them back. The space between us was no wider than the width of her body. I imagined the gap like it was a ravine and I was looking for a bridge.

"What other butterflies are there?" she asked.

"There are many," I said. "Some don't even have names yet."

"Can you be a butterfly if you don't have a name?"

"If I can't see you, I'm no' sure you exist. Is that it?"

"Do you always answer a question with a question?" she asked. "If I was a butterfly, what would I be?"

"That's difficult," I said. I was so close to her now and I could smell her scent. It was light and sweet and I filled my chest with it. "There's one with wings of orange, red, black, white and brown and it's called the *Painted Lady*."

"Is that what I am, Sean? The painted lady?"

"Well, there's no doubting its beauty." I liked so much that she had spoken my name, I felt a warmth radiate from the words. "You can see them in Australia all flyin' together. They migrate south in huge numbers, all flyin' wing-to-wing, lightin' up the sky. It must be a great sight."

"You're a dreamer, Sean Logan. Australia is a million miles away."

"Ah, but imagine it. The sky filled with painted ladies, one end to the other."

"What else do you know about butterflies?" She asked.

"I know they're like women. They're no' always what they seem."

"And I wonder what you mean when you say that."

"You cannae judge a butterfly by its colour."

"Why can't you? You have to judge it by something," she said.

"Because, for all their fantastic colour, their wings deceive you."

"In what way do they deceive? A wing is a wing, surely?"

"They've no colour at all. They're transparent."

"But I've seen butterflies with coloured wings. Blue and gold and a load of other colours. Now, you're pulling my leg."

"Aye, but they're transparent."

"No' the ones I've seen."

"Don't you see what I mean? The pigment of the wing absorbs the light, but the reflective structure of the wing splits the light into different colours. The wing itself has no colour."

"I see," she said. "What a strange thing. Is butterflies all you know about?"

"No," I said, taking pleasure at her laughter but taking no offence. "I know about snails too."

"What do you know about snails that would interest me?"

"The thing about the gastropod, as it is commonly known, is that it moves very slowly," I began.

"That is no' very interesting. You've disappointed me now."

"Well, that's no' the *most* interesting thing."

"What *is* the most interesting thing?" she asked.

"The most interesting thing is the love dart," I said.

"The love dart?"

"Yes." I held up two imaginary snails, then hesitated. "I hesitate to speak of this in the company of one so young."

"You're pulling my leg. I've got a few years on you."

"That cannot be true, but I'll brave it anyway." I raised my hands again. "Now, think of two perfectly sensible snails. They fall in love. The church has blessed their marriage and they're out there on their wedding night, with some eagerness they take to the bridal suite."

"I hope you're no' going to make me blush," she said.

"I warned you!" I said. "Anyway, there they are," I continued. "Two snails circling the bridal bed in all their slime. A playful act, one side then the other, along and back. Suddenly, just as it gets very boring, each of them shoots a dart into the other."

"What?"

"They shoot an arrow into each other. Across the bridal bed."

"Why would they do that? You're makin' this up."

"No. You've heard of *Cupid's arrow*?" I said.

"I thought that was to do with love not snails."

"This is love," I said. "They are *in* love. When they go on to make love to each other the dart - or *Cupid's arrow*, whatever you want to call it – the dart," I said, "serves to enhance the reproductive capabilities."

"To make baby snails?" she said. I nodded. She stood there in silence for a short while. "How do you know these things?"

"I read a lot. There's a very good gastropod journal."

"You're teasin' me now."

"Am I?"

"Do you study?"

"I study and I talk to people who know about snails."

"And you study snails too?"

"I study snails minutely in their homes at night with a magnifying glass."

I looked right at her. I could see every hair on her head as it sat against her small, neat ears, above those eyes that were so big, so grey-green and round, shining out at me, still clear and sharp but with a flinty hardness to them that I had only just observed. Yet, it seemed to me what was hard could be fragile too. Was she like fine china? When banged down too harshly, maybe she would shatter into a hundred pieces.

"You're strange," she said.

"Fungus is strange. I'm no' strange."

"Strange in a good way," she said.

"I'll settle for that," I said. I looked into her eyes. "Maybe you know something about me now, but what do I know about you?"

"No' very much, I should think," she said, looking down at her feet. "There's no' much to know."

"I think I know a little about who you are," I said, scrutinizing her.

"I doubt that," she said, looking away from me. "It's no' in your books."

"Sometimes a person's eyes speak as much as a book."

"You study eyes as well?" she said, now looking straight back at me.

"It's just an observation."

"You won't see much in my eyes."

"But I do," I said.

She was quiet for a moment. "You will see nothing but tears."

"That's sad," I said. "But I've seen through the tears."

She looked away from me. She *was* sad and appeared anxious. She stepped back. "I think it's time I was going."

"Do you know snails aren't so different from us?"

"That's another strange idea."

"It's well known that before they fire the dart they also do that small dance to get to know each other better. They circle around each other, sometimes for up to six hours, as long as it takes really."

"Why is that?" she asked.

"Because they want to touch, bite, stroke and so on. You know the sort of thing. It's quite sensual but they're just gettin' to know each other."

"I see."

"I hope I'm not embarrassin' you?"

"Not at all."

"All this happens," I said, "long before they fire the darts at each other."

"Do you think I'm a snail, Sean?"

"I only mention it because you asked to know the most interesting thing about snails," I said.

"You're right, I did. I think you kept your promise," she said and smiled.

She began to walk away from me, but I held her in my gaze, and she answered my prayer by turning her face back towards me. "Do you like fish?" I asked.

"Still the fisherman?" she said.

"Not in the sea, I've had enough of that. No, I mean fishing with a rod and a line?"

"My brother used to fish a lot. I never did."

"You never liked it?"

"Not so much. I never learnt. It brought me bad memories."

"Well come with me tomorrow," I said. "I'll teach you properly."

"Do you no' care what people think?"

"It has to be very early. They won't miss us for a morning."

"They might," she said. "And people talk. How will you cope with that?"

"I'm askin' you fishing, that's all."

"Are you sure?"

"I'll knock on your door at six," I said. "I guarantee you will catch a trout."

"A trout?" she repeated. "This man makes big promises."

"I know just the place."

"And the talk doesn't worry you?"

"As I said, it's only fishing."

"And my husband?" she said, expecting the words to freeze as they fell.

"I'm not bothered by him," I answered.

"He may answer the door. What then?"

"It seems unlikely," I said, stepping closer towards her. "He's gone up to Perth, is what I heard."

"You've done some research then?"

"I was always a good student."

She nodded her head and smiled again. She pushed her hair behind her ear and then moved away without a further glance.

39

NO FISHING

Sometimes I had a sense - I had done for a while - that I was being watched. It was like being caught on the edge of a shadow that keeps changing the light, sparkling bright and dark, but every time you look up you can see nothing. It seemed as if it was always there, but search as I might, there was never any trace that it had been. I didn't know who would wish to waste their time watching me or why. Not Calum Wilson, he knew nothing of me. Not those school goons surely? I had long since seen them off. My life was no more interesting than the perambulations of my dopey Blackface sheep. Often less interesting I would say. On occasions, I might hear a noise, nothing much more than a twig breaking or a branch flicking or a flash of unusual light against a wall. Sometimes, I thought I heard stone crunching underfoot or the click of a shoe or a horse's startled whinney. On one occasion I thought that someone had been looking in to my shed through one of the broken slats. It seemed to me I could see some trace of a boot print in the mud where someone might have stood to peer through the broken timber. I filled the offending gap with a mix of black tar, but I was not convinced that it meant anything.

Of course, that's the point: there was no evidence to support this idle speculation. I had not seen a single person close by or hovering at my periphery. Nobody seemed the least bit interested in either following me or looking at me. I'd seen no suspicious behaviour whatever. There'd been no gates left open, no locks tampered with, no hens flapping their flightless wings at the late night intruder, no signs at all to bring this man - me - to the conclusion that anyone was taking the least bit of interest in my existence. Yet, that did not stop the niggling suspicion that someone was *on my tail*. Once bitten by paranoia, every shadow contains a shaft of menace. I looked over my shoulder many times through the day, like there was a bogey impersonating and mocking my every move. I took to peeking out of the keyhole on the shed door before I emerged, just in case there was somebody out there who bore me a modicum of ill will. I double-checked my guns and triple-counted my bullets before I turned in at night and same again the next morning. Yet there was nothing to indicate that anything was amiss and slowly, I lowered my guard.

This day in the second half of March, the sun was not yet fully risen but traces of yellow light already spilled like gauze across the endless sky. As I skirted around Tullis on my young horse, the shoeless, chestnut gelding called Master Henry, he skittered on the new macadam road that now stretched along the top path, his hooves unused to the altered sensation of the surface. I had chosen to take the longer route by the wider track in order to enjoy the freshness of the morning. Perhaps it was to ensure that I was not being followed; or perhaps at the back of my mind was the wish to put off my encounter, not through any lack of conviction on my part, but because I knew even then where it was likely to lead.

I had a decent rod with me, a single length maybe a little over six foot, made of a lightweight bamboo with a line made of horsehair. A lot of fishermen will tell you that when you fish for trout you need a rod with this kind of style or that sort of length and that these things are very important to a successful outcome. I don't believe any of it. Just give me a slice of whippy bamboo and a few lengths of horsehair. As for bait, worms would get you nowhere. For a fly, I fastened a piece of red wool with a couple of cock feathers taken from the coop. The trout would find it irresistible and I'm no' carin' what you say against that. I was largely self-taught in the fisheries department. I learnt all I needed to know about the subjects of rod, line and hook-making and the complexities of different flies employed for different times of year, from an afternoon poring over an abbreviated copy of *The Treatyse on Fysshynge with an Angle* published at the time of the Tudors in 1496. More magic from Mr Shifner's library. The subject of fish was exciting the same kind of nonsense in Tudor times. Fish were timeless but I had depth to my learning for I had also read *The Practical Angler* by W.C. Stewart just before Christmas the previous year. Clearly I was the first armchair fisherman ever. However, as matters turned out, all this fine knowledge gleaned from Mr Shifner's library and other repositories was to be so much wasted effort.

By the time I reached the house it was half a breath more than ten minutes past six in the morning and the steadily increasing light now hung across the grey-slated rooftop. I sat there on Master Henry, close by a privet hedge swamped by a choking growth of holly, admiring the scene with a small shudder of anxiety never far from the surface. I had a premonition that something – everything – would happen, followed by a very real sense that absolutely nothing would occur. There was little change that I could see since the last time I had been here. The windows, the eaves, the walls all carried with them the same sense of broken decay and dissolution. There were no longer great pools of muddy water around the house but the windows were still smeared with grime and, as before, the insides were hidden from view. My route had brought me to the front of the house and I pressed my heels against Master Henry's heavily coated sides and he skittered forward.

There was no sign of life. There was no smoke coming from the chimney. There was no pink bunting on the porch. There was no criss-cross guard of honour. I dismounted and tied the reins to a metal hook sunk into the stone wall. I put the rod against the wall together with an old bag filled with hooks, flies, feathers, a fish-knife, cotton thread, scissors, lump of stale bread and other toolery of mass piscine destruction. What if Calum had returned? He was an unpredictable fellow. I patted my horse's neck with one hand; he was warm from the ride but not sweated. I let him nuzzle the palm of my left hand then rubbed the flash of white between his huge eyes. I walked towards the door and with each step I took, the golden sky above me seemed a little lighter. I stood facing the door and then knocked hard. Three times.

40

THE THRESHOLD

I stood there, immovable as a deep-rooted tree. I had knocked three times, then another three, and then another three. Not a sound stirred except the heavy beat of my heart booming in my ears. I stepped back from the door and sidestepped over to the wall where Master Henry stood and shook his mane. I looked to the left and to the right and then untied the reins that tethered him. Perhaps I had misunderstood.

I did not see her that day or the next. I tried not to look out for her but every time I looked up from working the field her image was in my mind and her voice was in my ears. Those conversations simply replayed themselves over and over. Had I indeed misread the situation? I knew I was capable of pursuing my own objectives with a single-mindedness that sometimes eclipsed the sensitivities of others. I could misperceive a situation, read in things that didn't exist, leave out things that did. I could see steps along the path and I took them one at a time, no hesitation, because they would take me where I wanted to go. Once there was wind in my sails there was no stopping me. Others would let me pass, they'd stand aside, because I knew where I was going and I'd mow straight through them if they didn't shift.

On the third day I did see her. There was less work to do in the fields, the sowing was nearing the end. I put the saddle on Master Henry and rode over to the Wilson house. Maybe it was a stupid thing to do; I had not challenged too many brain cells over that decision. How was I going to explain myself to Calum Wilson, should he have been there? Invite him fishing? That cut very little ice the last time, I remembered. Still, I was not for stopping, hesitating, reviewing or rethinking or any other sensible activity that might have stopped all this before it began. I rode into the Wilson yard, tying Master Henry to the same iron ring as I had before. This time I stood at the door and was ready to beat it down, but as it happened, I did not have to wait very long before it opened.

She had on a white cotton gown, very simple in its presentation, embroidered at the shoulders and belted tight around her waist. Her skin was smooth and her eyes sparkled beneath the dark hair that hung against her shoulders. She wore no shoes and just a light shawl that covered the bottom half of her face, draping its way across her shoulders.

"I came before," I said.

"I know."

I looked at her. "Are you hiding from me?" As if by way of answer, she lowered the scarf from her face and I could see a blue cloud across her cheek, spreading from her eyes. In the gloom I had not seen that both eyes were dark and heavily bruised. "Good God," I said. "Who did this to you?"

"A wooden paddle," she said.

"Whose wooden paddle?"

"My own,"

"You did this to yourself?"

"With my husband's help. Don't worry, the worst is past."

"Is he here?" I said.

"No," she said. "He's not here."

"Where is he?"

"He came, and then he went."

"Why?"

"He didn't like what he saw."

"He's a fool."

"I won't argue."

"He's lucky he's not here."

"Would you beat him with a wooden paddle?" she said.

"Was it because of me?"

"Oh no," she said. "He knows nothing of you. What is there to know?"

"Has he hit you before?"

"It's not unheard of."

"Why? Why does he beat you?"

"He's got a thing about paddles."

"Does he not love you?"

"In his way," she said. "But I have imperfections, or so he says."

I barely heard her. "A man who beats his wife can have no love in his life."

"You say that, but you know what they say about fruit?" she said.

"No?"

"Fruit is seldom rotten all the way through."

"Some fruit," I said, "is full of maggots and shit. That sort of fruit shouldn't be eaten."

"He's gone now," she said. "He does this and then I don't see him for a week." She paused. "There's a pattern to it. I think he thinks I'm slow in the head, that I need to be reminded."

By this time, I had crossed more than the threshold. I had entered the house and was close upon her. I felt such pain for her that I wished to take her in my arms and hold her tight. The moment came as if by design but it was spontaneous and unintended. I had stepped forward and I held her against my chest. I pulled her close, such that I could feel the warmth of her flesh against mine. Gently, I stroked and caressed the side of her face. Her eyes looked up at mine. I wanted to squeeze her but I sensed what she needed most was touch not force. Still, our heads drew together and I brought my lips against hers and pressed them one upon the other, tasting the sweetness of her mouth. I sensed her lips part and give way to mine. There seemed no need for words now, but there were words aplenty spinning round inside my head, a torrent of questions and empty answers. I pulled my head back from hers and looked close into her eyes. Without a word, she brought her lips back to mine once more and we never spoke another word about trout or line or fly or rod or Calum or whiskers or Master Henry in the yard or guns that kill or Mad Bob or sharks full of maggots. I kicked the door closed with the back of my leather boot. The light dissipated against my shoulder as she led me through the house.

If I had not been so consumed by what tender pleasures lay before me, I might have chanced another look behind. I might have seen a figure peering down at us from the track along which I had just travelled. I might have noticed some chance movement that would have signified an intruder or identified the silent recorder of these current events. I may have even seen the face of that person as he masticated a strip of loose leaf chewing tobacco, intermittently spitting juice against the broken tufts of grass by his feet, his face insinuating itself between the boughs of a largely leafless, Rowan tree. The tree that protects us all from evil – but not this time. I did not look back and I did not see the fat boy rise.

41

CHINA POWDER

Interview day arrived for Mr Fawcett. I'd put off the moment long enough. It was early but the front steps to the shop had already been swept. I opened the door and that triggered a bell, somewhere in the gloom at the back of the store. As I closed the door behind me, Mr Fawcett's face leaned out from the small room behind the counter. Seeing me, he called a cheery "With you in a minute," and disappeared back into the recess. When he emerged he was wearing his apron; black with a white stripe. "Morning to you, Sean. What can I do for you?" he asked.

I approached the long counter, a series of planks spliced and glued together. I stood before Mr Fawcett, square on. "Customers in Buckhaven," I said.

He looked at me from the other side of the counter, with a look of strange puzzlement. "You'll have to explain," he said. "I don't know what you mean."

"You have customers in Buckhaven, do you no'?"

"Well, yes," he said. "Not uniquely Buckhaven."

"Customers and, who knows, friends and acquaintances?"

Mr Fawcett wiped his hands against his clean apron as if he were brushing down the pile. "Are you needin' more nails?" he asked.

"Nails?" I said.

"Yes. Or wire. I have a new three-strand alloy wire. Very ductile."

"Your wire doesn't interest me today, Mr Fawcett."

"This is a hardware shop," he said. "If you don't want nails or wire, or anything else, then I don't know what you're doing here."

"I think you know well enough."

"I must get on, Sean, if you don't mind."

"What do *you* think I'm here for?" I said.

"That's just the point; I don't know."

"Well, let me help you."

"Yes?"

"At my father's wake I had to remind you that we all have responsibilities. Do you remember that?"

"Yes, I didn't know for sure what it is you meant when you told me that."

"No matter."

"I assumed it was the stress of the occasion."

"Today I want you to think about your responsibilities."

"I don't understand," he said. "I wonder if you might get to the point." I walked to the end of the counter, casting an eye through the gap and into the recess. I could see a tall, green chair with a buttoned cushion and a high back. Mr Fawcett followed my eyes from his own position. "Is there something the matter?" he said.

I looked towards Mr Fawcett, leaving one hand on the counter. "We could talk for hours about this, but I don't have hours. Instead, I've a small experiment that I want to show you." I extracted a package from the large, outside pocket of my jacket. I placed it on the counter.

"I've to get the shop ready, Sean..."

"Just a few minutes of your time," I said.

"In half an hour we'll be fillin' up. We get a lot of early trade, you know."

"This won't take too long, Mr Fawcett," I said as I opened the package. "But we do have things to talk about whilst I set this up for you." I pushed down the edges of the paper to reveal a large pile of what looked like tea.

"What is that?" he asked.

"We'll get through this a lot quicker, Mr Fawcett, if I ask you the questions and then you just try to answer them."

"If I can, Sean. Of course."

"A little while back, you had a visitor in your shop, Mr Fawcett."

"Did I?"

"You did. He must've been fifty years old or so. Something like that. Red hair but perhaps not so much of that now. Thinning out, you see. That's what happens. He came into your shop, Mr Fawcett. A man. He sat down in that tall, green chair through there," I indicated the recess. "He made himself comfortable."

"I don't know who you're talkin' about," he said.

"He was a large man."

"That is not so unusual."

"I'm told he came from Buckhaven?"

"I know many people from Buckhaven."

"How many do you invite to take a seat in the recess?"

"What's this about?"

"I don't think you'd have a man sit in your nice clean, green chair if you didnae know who he was." His eyes moved to the left and then to the right, down at the counter, then back at me. I knew there was something he could say, something he could tell me, if I could only push him that far. I ran a trail of the tea from one end of the counter to the other.

Mr Fawcett looked unhappy with me. "What are you doing?"

"He may have had red hair. Is that jogging your memory, Mr Fawcett? He may of course be bald by now." I said. "You tell me." I looked at him. "Sitting in your recess. In the big, green chair. Who was he?"

"I don't know," he said.

"I think you do, Mr Fawcett," I said. "He had a chestnut mare outside, four white socks."

"Even if I did know, do you no' think that's my business?"

"It's my business now," I said.

"Can you clear this up?" said Mr Fawcett, indicating the grey spillage on the counter. "I don't know what you're up to, but I don't like it one bit."

I took a box from my pocket and extracted a long wooden match. These were luxury matches intended for a sophisticated gentry market. Designed for lighting endless candles in a big house. "Next thing I do is light one end," I said.

"What's the point of that," said Mr Fawcett. "It's only tea, is it no'?"

"Yes, it looks like tea," I said. "But it's actually China powder." I looked up at Mr Fawcett and he was sweating in spite of the early morning chill and the shop was still cold. "I make it myself out of saltpeter, which is essentially urine and a lot of old manure. I add some charcoal. And of course, there's a bit of sulfur. You have to have sulfur." I struck the match against my boot and I looked at the flame progressing slowly from the top and down the shaft. "I add water too," I said. "But no' too much." I paused. "And if you have all that," I said. "You've all you need for a good explosion."

"Explosion?" he said. "For God's sake Sean! Mr Logan!" He ducked and I lowered the match to the counter. "What are you doin' with the match now?" he said, stealing a look above the counter.

"I hope not to do anything with the match, Mr Fawcett," I said. "But that depends on you." I met his eyes down at the end. "I want to know who the large man was with the horse and the white socks. And the red hair. Not too much mind. Thinning perhaps. Sitting on your chair. I want to know now, because when I drop this match there," – I indicated the powder trail – "it will go all the way to there" - I pointed to the pile of powder at one end. "Then we will have the most wonderful explosion."

Mr Fawcett's eyes were riveted to the match. The flame was close to two-thirds down the shaft and the light shone yellow against my thumb. "I can't help you," he said.

"You've been here a long time," I said. "And this is a nice shop. And I've known you a long time. Let's not be picky with the truth. Please, Mr Fawcett, I'm serious about this. Tell me what I need to know."

"Well," he said, twitching. "Take the match away." He cleared his throat as if what he was about to say did not come easily. "I suppose someone should tell you anyway. I know why you're asking about this man. I can imagine why you wish to speak to him. That's no' my business. But he's dangerous, Sean. You wouldnae want to upset him." He moved a step towards me. "And nor would I." I said nothing, just waited as the match burnt down. "What happened to your father," he said. "And what happened to your mother too, of course. These were strange events and it was a strange time. I know all about that. Believe me I'm sorry."

"So you know why I'm asking you about the man from Buckhaven?" I said.

"It's Buckstone, Sean. I'm sure it's Buckstone, you mean."

"Buckstone?"

"Buckstone not Buckhaven. I can't say any more than that," he said. "You'd be better leaving it alone. These things happened a long time ago."

"Not for me."

"He's not a friendly man," said Mr Fawcett.

"I'll take my chances," I said. "Shall I put the match away?"

"I would appreciate that."

"Then tell me his name."

"Please Sean, I don't want to tell you."

"Sometimes, in life, Mr Fawcett, you simply have no choice."

"I've known you since you were a boy," he said.

The flame was now burning half way along the shaft of the match. I brought the heat closer to the powder. It continued to burn down, well into the last couple of inches. "There's no' much time," I said and I lowered the match still closer to the counter but kept my eyes fixed on him.

He hesitated for a moment, licked his lips nervously and blinked. "He'll kill me."

"He may not be the only one." Fawcett seemed unable to speak. "What's his name?"

"Traynor!" he said, desperately spitting out the word like it was hot in his mouth. "His name's Traynor. He lent me money when I needed it."

"You're in debt to him?"

"He took half of this place when things were hard."

"Was he at the farm that night?" I asked.

Mr Fawcett hesitated. "He would kill me."

"Was he at the farm that night?"

"Yes, I believe so."

"Where is he?"

"Buckstone."

"Where in Buckstone?"

"Don't go there, Sean."

"Where in Buckstone?" I repeated.

"Beyond the town. It's a farm. Decent house. Somewhere on the east side of the town, you follow the road out. I don't know exactly."

"On the east side of the town?"

"Yes, you can see the house from the road. You can't miss it. He lives with his mother, a mad old cow."

"Thankyou." The match was now burnt down close to my fingers. "The thing about this stuff is that it's very volatile when exposed to heat," I said. "Stand back." I dropped the match on the powder trail. It zipped along the length of the counter, sparking all the way.

"I told you what you wanted to know, Sean!" Mr Fawcett said, crouching down behind the counter, raising his arms to protect his head from the imminent explosion. The small flame ate up the trail of powder and reached the large mound at one end of the counter. "Watch!" I shouted.

There was a full but gentle noise, like an explosion wrapped in soft wool, and the powder ignited, creating a large cup of black smoke and a bright yellow flame ripping up the middle. There was a small pop and the smoke dissipated to the ceiling. All the while I was leaning on the counter, enjoying the extraordinary pyrotechnic spectacle.

I moved towards the door. "The thing to know about China powder is that it's a low explosive. You light this stuff and if you don't compress it somehow, then it just gives off that beautiful, soft deflagration, a bit of smoke and a bright shaft of yellow flame in the cup. Quite a sight, do you no' think?" I laid my hand on the doorhandle. "Purely decorative of course, quite harmless. Like a firework, but safer." I opened the door. "Thankyou for your time Mr Fawcett," I said. "Good mornin'."

42

CALUM'S RETURN

After I had gone from the house, Keira told me she floated on a small cloud somewhere above the Isle of May, by which I understood her to have enjoyed a sense of deep happiness, one which she told me she had never experienced before. It filled her and warmed every part of her. It thrilled me to hear it. She had colour in her cheeks and a shine, approaching a dazzle, in her green eyes. It brought life back into her. She hummed as she went about her business. She found it hard to sit down. It was as if the sensations she had wanted from life or imagined could be hers were rushing through her veins all at once, keeping her in constant motion. She tried to stop her mind from thinking, from poring over that overwhelming encounter. I say this not from arrogance but because she told me so herself. She said to me later that I had arrived at the right time in her life, that I was tender, smiling, warm when everything else she had known was cruel, mean, cold and brutal. She saw a twinkling in my eyes, so touched by her pain was I, before I wrapped her in my arms. I kissed her with lips that she said took her to a happy place. She floated, like air and bubbles and lightness, away from the torment and pain that had become her life. It had been so inevitable and so unstoppable, there was nothing with which she or anyone else could impede its progress. She knew it was coming from the first time she set eyes on me, over her husband's shoulder, the day I stopped by for the fishing. Or so she said and who was I to argue?

She recalled the embarrassment of that day when I appeared out of nowhere to collect Calum for the fishing on Harcourt's boat. How Calum had spoken to me like I was nothing, uncouth and rough. She was right, I did not rise to his rudeness: I had said my piece and then I had left. She said she liked that about me. At that moment, to her mind, I had won the battle – and it *was* a battle or at least a test of my resolve. She liked the look of a man who had no fear. Most men she knew would not have stood up to Calum. Most men took her husband for the brute he was and they were not prepared to step in his way for fear he'd turn on them with his fists or his gun. She knew I had no care for whatever he might do. Call it the foolhardiness of youth. I had the air of someone who did not care too much how you threatened him, I was not going to do anything that I didn't want to do. She thought that I was a fatalist. I had youth on my side and the young fear nothing because they know nothing. I'm not sure how true all of that was. I did have the fearlessness of youth but I also had a large dose of its igno-rance. It can be easy to say you've never feared fire when you've never actually seen fire.

The very first time we had made love, it had been with a deep want, a visceral conviction of total need that came from somewhere neither of us had known before. When I entered her, I entered a world I'd never experienced. I was no longer in my head, I was physically distanced from my head, and the electricity coiled round me and melted into her. It had arrived and happened so quickly. Later that morning, we shared our bodies with each other again, more slowly and with less intensity. The two of us experienced it all so deeply, I entered her again and again, it came easily and with a strength of commitment and purpose.

Nevertheless, I knew she sensed within my lovemaking a measure of calculation that never quite escaped me. She noticed that I looked at her intently during the moments she was at her most vulnerable, when I was in her and she was fast approaching the release that her body told her would come. Later, she said I looked as if I were studying her biological reaction to my careful ministrations like she was one of cupid's snails that I had talked so fondly about. I was studying her, that much was true, but not like some dubious laboratory experiment. That's not to say she thought I was *without* passion, just that there were times when we made love that I appeared to contain my emotion too well. It was as if I attempted to capture the moment like it was a scientific procedure that I had to note down very carefully for fear of losing it altogether. Then again, to some extent, I confess: that was the man I was, for my mind was everywhere in its complexity and hunger for new answers to old questions. It was little wonder that I'd subject the manner in which we made love to the same analysis as every other thing I did. The experience was so insane for me, I could only take it one image at a time. I would have exploded if I had not. In any event, she was astute enough to recognize that to rebuke me for intellectual analysis of what I was doing and experiencing was to call me to account for being Sean Logan.

She wondered if some might think, had they known, that she had an overly relaxed perspective on her predicament, but the danger inherent in our situation was neither lost on her nor was it something she ignored. She was aware of her husband's brutishness and the vengeance he'd no doubt seek if he were to find out what she was embarked upon. She was not stupid either: she dodged the issue, but in her heart of hearts she was convinced he would in fact find out. There were ears and eyes all over the place, lurking behind each and every corner, and sooner or later the news would leak like blue smoke from a cracked chimney and her husband would hear of it. When that time came, she had little doubt that he would respond with his own freakish cruelty. Maybe, it was she who was the fatalist, not I.

Keira appreciated too that the two of them might have been more careful. They might have hidden away in the house on those days that Calum was not home, but love is a release from such restraints and concealments: she wanted to be in the open with me, run across the fields with linked arms, hold my big hand and let all those around know that she could not contain her love in a dark corner of that miserable marital home. Love cannot live in the shadows; it can only survive if it takes to the open ground and is allowed to grow. Love needs light to flourish; it has to be allowed to breathe out in the wide fields and beneath the limitless sky. Take that away and the leaves would curl and wither and there would be no fruit off the tree before the love was dead.

Yet that was not to ignore the fact that she feared her husband. Sean Logan might not, but she most definitely did. And that was not terribly surprising. If he found out, his retribution would be truly awful. This coloured her days and made the highs so high and the lows – of which there were fewer - so crushing and breathtaking. She knew they'd taken risks and were continuing to take risks – gambles that were sometimes foolish and occasionally reckless. I led her, she said. I encouraged her.

We had lain on the damp grass up by the hills at Denton, where the view combed the pasture and stroked its way to the sea; where the Blackface sheep bleated; where we could watch these beasts dragging their coarse wool backs across the fields; where we'd hope that the two of us would be witnessed by nothing more than the silent wind and the open sky. Once, we had heard the voice of the passing shepherd just in time, talking to himself as you might expect, and we had lowered our heads to the ground to stay out of sight. He had walked on without seeing us, just a dozen feet away. It heightened the excitement. It made the two of us giggle like mischievous children.

The worst part for Keira was that she never knew when Calum might return. He took himself off and she would never be sure if it was just a day or days that he would be gone from her. Sometimes it could be weeks, but there was no predicting. He might come home at any time to find this situation going on in his own house, under his roof, and they had to wonder: what would happen then? Sometimes she would ask but there were risks inherent in doing so. Sometimes he told her. Mostly, he was plain unpredictable.

When the truth broke, she knew before he told her he knew. He arrived home on his horse, Marty, and he had led the muddied, sweated beast straight over to the trough where there was water and a small bag of hay. He pulled off the bridle and threw it on the wall and he slung the strap of a halter around Marty's neck and buckled it just a little too tight, with that sudden movement that speaks hostility. He undid the girth on one side, then removed the saddle and slung it astride the wall. He unbuckled the girth from the far side too and held it in his hand. There was something about his movement, a kind of quick impatience that betrayed the anger that was in him. He let the horse drink while the steam rose off his hindquarters, gathering around his flank and swirling in wispy tranches above and around his neck. He then took Marty to his stall and bolted the door with a sliding stab from left to right.

She saw the back of her husband from inside the house when he was removing the tack and stabling the horse. She ran a hand through her hair and straightened her clothing. She noticed the jerkiness of his movements as he approached but she did not know what he knew until she was close enough to see into his tight, little eyes. Only then could she see some trace of the rage that was consuming him, like red coals burning in the gorse. If there was fury, he still maintained the appearance of glacial calm and it made her think for little more than a moment that maybe she was mistaken. Could it be that there was nothing there to concern her, just the usual distance, the controlled angry hatred? He was not effusive but then he never had been. He approached her by the door, not three paces from the spot where I had first kissed her with my hungry lips, my breath in her mouth, melting the will to resist, before I took her inside and we took off our clothes and for the first time enjoyed our nakedness together. Her husband stepped in from the door and reached behind her head and stroked the brown hair with his hand.

"Any news?"

"No," she said. "Just the usual things."

"You sure about that?" he said. "Just the usual things?"

She looked at him, wondered at the hard edge, tried to keep his eye. "I said, just the usual things."

His hand gripped the hair at the back of her head and in one move he was dragging her down the corridor.

43

THE PRICE

She screamed, tripped, stumbled and fell against the small chest in the hall. He pulled her by the hair into the boot room. He banged her head off the upright jamb and blood quickly flowed from the wound. A picture fell off the wall. Once she was in, he slammed the door shut. He was still holding the leather girth. He folded its length in two and then beat her with it, repeated strikes against her body. He went on until he had no strength left in him. The buckle raked her sides like she was the horse for whom it was intended. She lay on the floor at his feet where she had fallen, blood running from her forehead and a deep cut on her legs and her hips.

Later, she felt sharp pain when she shifted her weight. She hurt all over. She could see herself turning purple, yellow and blue, but she was still conscious and she was still alive. He had slipped down the wall and sat next to her on the dirty, half-matted floor, amongst the sticks and the boots and the brushes and pans, the old blood and the spilled rabbit snares. There were tears in her reddened eyes. He was looking at the floor. He wouldn't bring his eyes to meet hers. They were red too, as if he too had cried.

As the days unfolded, as he slumped in the kitchen chair with the broken wood frets or looked surly coming in from the outhouse, he stared at her in his apparent hatred. He pushed the plate of food she served back at her. He took consolation in whisky for long parts of the day and night. He went out to drink and he became so drunk he had to lay across the horse's withers to get himself home, by which time he'd vomited down Marty's neck. Marty's sense of direction could not be faulted, since he always got him home.

All the while, when the drink had left his veins, Calum's mind turned and picked through the events. He dissected each and every moment of her betrayal, savouring each, like juicy flesh on a chicken. He sucked the bones and whilst the taste was good at first, as time went on it lost something. Maybe he loved her as much as he had ever loved anybody. No matter how hard he hit her with his boot, she had her own way of hitting back, and her way was quicker and seemingly more effective than anything he could inflict. He thought to himself that he knew he loved her and would always love her and to his mind it was a low, mean piece of feminine trickery that she should make him feel that way. She undermined the satisfaction he thought he had a right to derive from the punishment he had inflicted.

So it was, as the days passed he reached a point where he had to capitulate. He sat down to eat his breakfast and told her that she should join him. He made her eat an egg and some fresh bread. He poured her a glass of milk and encouraged her to drink it. He put jam on the bread and a thick dollop of cream and fed her the slice by his own hand. She ate it from him, albeit her eyes were twitching. He wiped the cream from the corners of her mouth and put the smear straight onto his own tongue. He struggled to understand the feelings that he still had for her. He was not such a stupid man, or so he told himself.

"I'm sorry. I may have lost control," he said. "You may think I hate you."

"You do hate me," she said.

"You're entitled to think that," he said. "But I don't know. I don't know what it is I feel for you right now." He looked at her. "I think I hate you sometimes," he said. "But then again, I'm no' sure." There was a silence.

"You almost killed me," she said finally.

"You're alive. Dinnae exaggerate."

"You almost killed me," she repeated. He looked at her. "How can you think what you've done is okay?"

"Why is that so surprising?" he answered. "Love makes a person weak".

"I can't pretend to understand."

"A man will always hate those things that make him weak."

"What do you mean by that?" she said. "It makes no sense."

He leaned towards her and for one brief moment she thought he was going to try to kiss her. Instead, he sat there looking at her with stupid, empty eyes above his dumb, whiskered face.

For ten days she had been a prisoner in her own house. He watched her closely. Her presence was both a reminder and an accusation. Her body still ached. The cut across her forehead crusted over. The bruising was largely confined to her trunk and her upper arms.

Keira had no contact with anyone and Calum did not seek company around the house. She was confined to desperate isolation. She could not speak to anyone. She could receive comfort from nobody. He watched her from the moment she rose to the moment she lay down. As the days passed, a change had come over him. The initial fury had petered out to nothing. Or nothing that made sense.

On the twelfth day, following many others during which he did little and said even less, he mounted his horse, Marty, and rode into Tullis. His face was still full of hooded, brooding anger. He said he'd people to speak to, but did not elaborate. Perhaps this was the conversation she was unable to provide. He said he would go to Perth for a number of days, then he'd return. She did not believe him. She knew he was up to no good. She noticed that recently, more often than not, he had his rifle holstered on his saddle. She feared for what might happen.

Keira watched Calum ride out of the yard, his hunched shoulders gently swaying upon the horse, disappearing slowly from sight. She sat on the bench by the front door and looked out over the potato field. She knew that he would follow the track down and if she waited several minutes she would see him turn the corner. She knew that if she did not see him turn in to the left, past the overgrown rowan and the low hawthorn, then he was in all probability not heading for Tullis at all. Or even Perth. In which case it may have been a test, to see if she was going to run away, stay alone at home or take in a visitor, but if that was in his mind then he was more fool than bully: she waited and felt the minutes tick by, and then she saw Marty skitter in the distance, pulling irritably on the bit, twitching round the hedge, and she knew at least he was far enough away to allow her to sit back a little and ease some of the tension from her muscles. The sun squeezed out from between the grey-grit clouds and she felt the warmth against her face.

She closed her eyes and enjoyed the relaxation wash over her, the first time in as many days, like she was starting to breathe all over again. The last thing she expected to hear was my voice.

She didn't answer but she knew it was me and she leapt forward, covered the small distance between us and buried her face against my chest. I stroked her hair with one hand and pulled her close with the other. I felt her legs press against me and felt the warmth.

"Have you been there long?" she asked.

"Since dawn," I said.

"I wondered about you."

"I hadn't heard from you, but I knew he was back, so I stayed away."

"Wise enough," she said.

"I knew things weren't right. I couldn't see my coming over would help too much." I held her in my arms for several minutes. Then, I looked at her face. "I can tell you, it's no' the first time I've been here, waitin' for you."

"It's the first time I've been alone."

I squeezed her and felt her flinch. "Did he hit you again?" I asked.

"Of course," she said.

"He's a bastard."

"I'm at a point where I don't care anymore."

"This has to stop," I said. "You shouldnae stand for it."

"Nothin's that simple, Sean."

"You should leave him. You've got family you could go to."

"As I said, it's no' that simple."

"Oh, but it is simple. For what he's done to you, it's so simple, of course you should leave him."

"But I knew he would beat me. I knew it from the second

day we were married. I should have known before that. It changes nothin'."

"And now?" I asked.

"Not now," she said. "He's moody though. He sits and broods and drinks too much." There was a deep silence, as if the cruelty had choked the talk between us.

"Is he sorry?"

"He says he cannie help himself. He says he's changed."

"Does he know about me?"

"What do you think?" she said, holding my eyes. "He beat me."

"He's a fool."

"I didn't tell him," she said. "He knew already."

"I'll answer for it. I'm happy to."

"More fights? You want that?"

"As long as it's me and no' you," I said.

"He says he's finished with that."

"Till the next time," I replied. "Till the next time he cannie have you."

"You should know: he's no' a man who forgets. He'll come after you. I know him. He's predictable."

"I'm no' running," I said. "Let him come and we'll see where he gets." She said nothing but raised her arms and put them around my neck. "What would you change?" I asked.

"You cannie ask that," she said. She kissed me on the lips.

"Why not?"

"Those are possibilities that don't apply."

"You can change them," I said.

"You spend too much time on books and snails."

"You throw that back at me," I said gently, her eyes close to mine. "Of all the insults."

"The real world has real rules," she said.

"You dinnae have to follow them." I put my hands on her waist, softly because I thought she might hurt. She didn't flinch.

"Take care," she said. "He won't let it rest."

"I know. As I said, let him come."

"There's nothing more he can do to me."

"Well, if he comes, he comes. He'd better make it soon."

"Why?" she said.

"I have plans of my own just now. I've to go away for a while."

"Had enough already?"

"Of course not," I said. "Perhaps it's for the best, it may let him cool down a little."

"But you will be back?"

"I will be."

"And are you saying where you're goin'?"

"Where I'm goin' may be dangerous, I'll say that much."

"Should I be nervous?"

"No, be positive."

"Then, I'll be positive then."

"I'm not knowin' how things will turn out," I said. I looked into her eyes. "Have no doubt about this, when I'm done I will come for you."

"Better you go," she said. "The future can wait. I thought you'd wish to fight him in the yard."

"I'm no' waiting on him," I said. "And I'll no' confront him. Not now anyway."

"And if your house is empty, he may just have to come home and have a go at me instead."

"He may, but as you say, it's me he wants now. Beatin' you will give him little pleasure."

"And you willnae tell me where you're goin'? It seems like you may have had your fun and you're out the door."

"I'm no' abandoning you," I answered. I held her hands in mine. "As I say, the timing may help. And I'm dealin' with things that have already been around too long."

"Ah well," she said.

"What happened between us has changed my life, but it cannie stop my life." I pulled her close to me, kissed her on the lips and held my face against her cheek.

"Will you be gone long?"

"That depends."

"Will you come back for me?"

I looked at her, the green glint of her eyes, the question left hanging. "You know I will," I said, but it was a promise that was never mine to give.

44

MAD BOB AND MRS WEIR

Mad Bob had forgotten now why it was he'd ever landed the name *Mad Bob*. Somehow, he had become *Mad Bob* and everyone knew him as *Mad Bob*. He was not a crazy man, eating cow brains and childrens' fingers. Nobody said they should put him in the mad house although it was true that his grandmother had ended her days there. He was not an angry man, someone who might have thrown his toys out of the pram (if he had had any) when he was a boy or who might later pick stupid fights in a bar. He was none of these things. If you looked at him you might have said: this man is skinny and his hair looks like straw and his nose is too large on a long face, like an oversized knocker in the middle of a plain door. But that was all. He was really quite normal.

Mad Bob had a mirror on the wall just inside the front hall and he could see the reflection from the top of his head to half way down his chest. He wore a grey tunic shirt and a black waistcoat, black buttons too, just the one missing, two eyes from the top. He had a fuzzy stubble on his chin, half pepper grey and the rest black. Time had left him with a permanent scowl. What he lacked was any colour about him, but colour represented joy and there was precious room for that in Mad Bob's life.

As he brushed the hen shit off the porch outside his small wooden house, he heard his wife shout his name from upstairs. She was a woman with a heavy, round face, a mouth like a farthing coin and two eyes like angry stab holes. She was bloated and fat and chewed catmint most of the day, whilst reclining against the Victorian headboard of a sagging bed, swaddled in threadbare sheets and a dusty spread. When the catmint was fully masticated she spat it into a clay bowl. It was three-quarters full already; Mad Bob should have emptied it by now. He heard her shout his name again. He chose to ignore her. He recognized the danger in such a course, but he also calculated that the solution to that problem was in his hands. He brushed the hen shit onto a broken shovel. There was plenty. These hens had a free run over the place but he did his best to keep them out of the house. As he straightened and turned, a Scots grey hen scuttled under his feet and he kicked it hard with his boot, enjoying the flap of wings, the angry squawks, the broken feathers, the panic and the alarm. Life can be precarious, he thought, but it soothed his nerves to see the distress in eyes other than his own. He saw another piece of hen shit under the chair at the corner of the porch. Soft but lumpy, he scooped it onto the shovel. He heard his wife shout his name from upstairs, the volume higher now and he could imagine the rising colour, the beetroot bleed in her swollen face. The eyes would be popping like eggs in hot fat. He went into the house.

Mad Bob stood at the bottom of the stairs, as if deliberating on a very important decision. He was a little breathless and even small exertions such as brushing shit off the porch made him gasp for air. He had a dull pain in his lower gut. He had that pain so often it had become part of his life. If you took the pain away, he felt he would be a different person. She shouted his name again, but he hardly heard her.

"Bob?" Pause. "Bob?" Pause. "Bob?" After a short hiatus it went: "Bob-ay!" Pause. "Bob-ay!" Double pause. "Fuckin' Bob-ay!"

He dug a thumb and finger into his waistcoat and extracted a green pill. He pushed it into his mouth with his nail and crunched it between his teeth. The glucose syrup took away some of the bitterness. His tongue was dry and he swallowed three or four times before it fully went.

When he was shot, he had caught a large part of the fragment in his gut. She'd shot him from about nine feet and it has to be said, it took him by surprise. True, he wasn't in her house for friendly reasons but getting shot by her was the last thing he'd expected; he was less angry about it now.

Hadn't he been the peacemaker? That's what he'd told them at the trial but the truth was something different, he knew that. Maybe if she had been more welcoming, less trigger-happy, things would have turned out differently. The peacemaker: nobody pushed Bob too hard on that explanation. Everyone knew he had his pants down around his ankles. Yet, that was no cause for puttin' a big hole in a man's stomach. Discharging a firearm was an escalation. Once that fuse was lit, God only knew where it was likely to end. In this case, a man had to live his life with only half a stomach, all because some Eastern European got trigger-happy with her husband's rifle. Maybe she did suffer, thought Bob, but he felt that he'd suffered too. He was still suffering.

Mad Bob stood by the closed window. He still had the shit shovel in his hand. He looked out over the rough ground towards the green hill beyond. He thought of Mr Traynor. Traynor had been good to him at first. Traynor had encouraged others to see the facts a little differently. Show a little charity. It was all a matter of perspective. Policemen were not so interested: they had their man. They had him locked in a cell the size of Mad Bob's outside toilet.

For a good while, it has to be said that Traynor looked after him, covered his back and kept him out of trouble. Traynor had the money of course, living in that big place, a good-sized farm, his mother only just alive, succession prospects hopeful. Traynor was a man who'd never left home, had lived with his mother all his life. Mad Bob thought back to his own mother. Where the hell did she go? He could hardly picture her any more. He heard a noise from upstairs. Was it something being thrown at the door? Keep on throwing, my dear. Keep on throwing.

Mad Bob sat down on the chair by the window. He was looking out still but he was seeing nothing. He rested the shovel full of shit against the top of his leg. It was wrong to think he and Traynor had identical interests. That's what he'd tried to tell Traynor the last time they met. He didn't take it too well, seemed to think Bob was showing ingratitude for a man who could have been hung. That was not the way Mad Bob saw it. It was a long time ago, but they had both played their parts in the death of that woman; that was something they had to answer for together. It could no' be brushed under the carpet like so much hen shit. The point was Traynor had to look after him now because it was a reciprocal arrangement they had. After all, he didn't have to keep his mouth shut, he could've blabbed all over Fife. The point was he didnae blab and that meant there had to be a better settlement between him and Mr Traynor. They were in this thing together; they always had been.

Mad Bob thought back again to that night at Salmon Cottage, as he often did even now. He had his regrets alright. Most of all he regretted the hole she put in his gut. He remembered the flash from the rifle's muzzle, how a lot of shot just went straight through the flesh and out the other side, hardly touching anything on its way. There was a medical man in Tullis and that man had saved his life. He was a national hero and deserved a pension. It would be a mistake to call him a doctor because he was not in truth a doctor, but he had practiced surgery on Saddleback pigs and cattle, small children, the odd horse and a cat with a pile prolapse, and that to Mad Bob was a reasonable qualification. Not that there was time to sift through his credentials. Gunshot was a new challenge for him. He dug most of the metal out, even if he did drink a lot of Mad Bob's whisky to give him courage, from the first cut to the last stitch. Mad Bob reflected that his bowel was not too bad, all considered, even today. He could still shit with the best of them. His lungs never got better; always out of breath, it made him think there must have been a piece up there somewhere. It did something to his bladder but he never did find out what; he could pee like a champion, but half a cup at a time. This meant that he had to pass urine three times per hour. That inclined Mrs Weir to joke that he was more Wet Bob than Mad Bob. As he thought of his wife, simultaneously he heard her voice call out his name from the upstairs room. "Bob-ay! Bob-ay!" A minute later she shouted his name again and ten minutes later there was a deeper, angrier tone to her voice. This time it was: "Baw-bay!" Pause. "Fuckin' Baw-baaay!" Impressive, he thought, to hold that note on a second syllable.

Mad Bob rose to his feet and went through to the hall. He stepped towards the front door, turned the handle and pulled it open. He spat a gob onto the porch. He shut the door and turned towards the stair. His eyes followed the treads that slid one upon the other like heavy cards, all the way up to the top. He held the shovel in front of him, gripped the banister with his left hand and began the ascent.

45

SEAN'S DEPARTURE

Farewells made, I was on my way to a destination in Montrose, a place I had never been to, but a good day's ride away, still on the east and not far from the coast. Against my better judgment, I had left the Reicher with Aunt Marion. The Reicher was the strangest kind of four-barrelled gun you were ever likely to see. The product of a Germano-Austrian lunacy, but Aunt Marion had chosen it as her weapon of ultimate defence and I had failed to persuade her that the little old Webley was easier, prettier and more effective to discharge. The fact that it had been used to assassinate an American president counted for nothing with her.

For myself, it was a sad time to leave. I had found a woman who excited and engaged me and yet, as if driven by forces I couldn't properly identify, I was leaving her too – at least for now. I was also aware that I was taking off at the time of her greatest need. I had thought for the briefest of moments that perhaps she was the reason that I should lay down arms and move my life away from its current journey, its unerring pull towards retribution for things past. Keira made me question my purpose in this quest, a pursuit that had consumed my being from the earliest days of my existence. Her arrival at this juncture of my life now forced me to question what was to come of this thirst for atonement. What if I should find that the holy grail of my endeavours turned out to be no more than an empty cup? Instead of quenching that destructive thirst, it might leave me with a salty mouth full of dry, unanswered longings. I thought of these issues and through sheer force of will I cast them to one side. I was far along the road to attain what my life's pursuit had always been. All the gold in Jerusalem would have no power to turn me back.

I was conscious too that I was leaving Lizzie behind in all her clumsiness, her goodness, her soup, her laughter. Not to mention Aunt Marion: woman, eye-roller, mother of mine when there was no other to fulfill that role. I was leaving them all because the time had come to do what I had always intended, to follow the path that would bring me justice or retribution, call it what you will. I was going to settle some accounts and there was no guarantee that I would return to Tullis in one piece. I had my Webley and other useful weaponry, as well as heavy, greasy sticks of brown-papered dynamite retrieved from carefully turned wooden boxes, and a host of incendiary devices designed to bring down hell upon my enemy's head, wherever I might find him. I had my father's very own Snider-Enfield, Kipling's favourite, and nothing was going to stop me.

Aunt Marion stood by the front door as I meandered away that morning, along the hedge-bordered track, between its damp, moss-topped walls, down the road to take me from the farm. Lizzie stood there by her side, her collar open, her skin white against her top. She had hugged me and patted my back with her freckled hands and there were tears in her brown eyes at my departure, no matter how hard she tried to hide them. They both knew well enough where I was going, and for that reason, I presumed, Aunt Marion had kept her questions brief and to the point. Only once, did she ask me to think again about what I was embarked upon and what I intended to do when I got there. She knew it was pointless to seek to dissuade me from something that, like the turning tide, had been a draw against my entire life, a force that had asserted itself for as long as I could remember. We had our discussion earlier about which gun I should leave behind and, her explanation as to why she would have no need for any gun, let alone the Webley. I told her that I had enemies, that I was anxious that they be left alone, that I feared that anything I might do could leave them vulnerable.

"You're being over-protective," she said.

"I am no'. I'm bein' sensible."

"It's sweet of you, I know that, but it's unnecessary."

"We can usually look after ourselves, you know," said Lizzie. "Worrying about us is no' goin' to help."

"But a gun might," I said. "Look, I know how brave you both are..." I began.

"Thankyou," they said.

"But you're alone here."

"So, we're alone. We've nothin' to be frightened of."

"And I hope that's true."

"We'll be careful."

"Okay," I said. "And lock the door at night."

"Of course," said Aunt Marion.

I took my aunt's hand in mine. "Don't take any chances."

"Alright," she said. "Now get out of here, if you're goin'."

I handed her the Reicher. "Shoot rabbits with it if you like."

I left it with her, not because I thought it would be an appropriate protection but because it was the *only* protection she'd accept. She rolled her eyes. "And?"

"And what?"

"And some of those bullet things too?"

I had a feeling that there really was something to be frightened about. I did not know where that sense might have come from. I recognized that I was setting out on a journey in the course of which I would probably upset one or two people, possibly making permanent changes to their life expectancy, depending where the trail led. I would jab a stick in dangerous places and whatever flew out of the dark holes might wish to attack me where I was vulnerable: I knew that home was the logical choice for my enemies, by bringing harm to those I loved. I'd no idea where the attack would come from but I was jittery that it might happen.

Of course, it was no' just the possibility of retribution from those I was intent upon confronting. That was enough to worry about, but I was still on edge about the times I'd sensed that I was being followed or watched. I had identified nobody but that knowledge did not render me any less anxious. It all served to fill me with trepidation, and when I had finished packing the final canvas bag onto Master Henry's back, I was still edgy that something would transpire, not so much to me but to those I left behind. Yet I knew I had to go and I think Aunt Marion and Lizzie knew that too.

46

THE STAIR

The stair creaked under the feeble weight of Mad Bob in his scuffed boots. It was unusual for Bob to wear his footwear upstairs. It was one of her many rules that he did not wear his boots above ground level. She said the cracked soles were a repository for bugs. It seemed to him that she didnae need to go looking at his boots for bugs; if she swept the crumbs, soiled pants, toenail clippings and clumps of head and pubic hair from under the bed, she would see what real bugs looked like. On this occasion he had no intention of abiding by his wife's rules.

He'd married her nineteen years ago because his mother told him that nobody wanted a skinny man with a long head, no money and holes in his gut that made him an incontinence risk. She had married him, so his mother had often told him, because she herself was grossly fat, short of body with very little neck and almost no distance between her shoulders and her waist, with few social skills and very little else for a husband to enjoy beyond the hard-to-locate housing for her genitals. They both therefore came to marriage from a position of deficit. Any hope of maturing a thread of credit from their nuptials was, as it turned out, quite misplaced. It was quickly apparent that Bob's stomach cramps and the eternal passing of small cups of deep, yellow urine were a barrier to romantic love. She made no secret of her belief that he was a useless wretch, less manly than a wilting dandelion, with little useful purpose in life other than to bring her food, empty her pots of masticated catmint and wipe her face with a cloth in the event of any mess during consumption. The boundaries were invisible to both of them as they passed from grudging acceptance, to indifference and, finally, to undisguised contempt.

For two and a half years she had not felt it necessary to spend much time on the ground level of the house because the journey from downstairs to upstairs was an escalating challenge and mounting the stairs was a requirement she approached with diminishing enthusiasm. The trouble with going down was that at some point she would have to go up, and so she attempted neither. She could recline on her Victorian bed and shout for Wet Bob and he would dribble up the stairs with food and other services. She could send him down for more - quite often beer in two-pint jugs was a desirable lubricant for the appalling food - and she liked him to restock the catmint for her to masticate through the flat tedium of daylight hours.

Mad Bob stood at the top of the dusty stair for almost six hundred seconds. On the wall there was a small picture of succulent fruit, a melon, two peaches and a goose feather. It was still light outside, but the grey shadows all around were lengthening. The repeated calling of his name had faded. He imagined she had fallen asleep with exhaustion. A permanent coma would have been too much to wish for. She would awake soon, angrier than ever by his failure to answer her calls. She would expect him to make the usual excuses, curse him for the wastefulness of his imperfect existence, swear at him and shout at him harshly to bring something tasty to kill these fuckin' tummy rumbles.

There was nothing unusual in all this. However, something had happened today inside the brain behind that long face. Mad Bob had decided this time would be different. Today, he had no intention of placating her. He gripped the wooden door handle in his hand and twisted slowly to the left. As he pushed and entered, he smelt the whiff of catmint from the chipped bowl by the bed. The fingers of his right hand were white and bloodless.

47

MONTROSE

Montrose is flat with only the smallest rise from the south to the north, occupying a position on a square basin that sits at the mouth of the River Esk. At that time, it had a population of several thousand, so clearly the town had something going for it. I arrived after dusk the same day as I left Tullis, and followed the multiple houses, terrace after terrace, set gable to gable, along the length of the main street, past the unassuming statue of Joseph Hume, politician, doctor, freethinker, as far as the *Kingfisher*, a public house that bore a sign that offered a room for the night.

The moment I entered the dark, fusty, low-beamed room, I thought to myself that had I been a dog in search of a kennel with quirky eccentricity then this was a worthy candidate. I could smell beer and damp clothing, unwashed bodies, fish, sperm, tobacco and every now and then, the whiff of a small trace of excrement. The floor was caked with grime. There were bound to be types present who would want to know who I was and where I was from and what my business meant to them, so I quickly passed through the shadows of the room, keeping my eyes focused on a skinny man in a faded shirt, marshaling cups and liquids from behind the counter.

"I'm lookin' for a room," I said. He told me the rate.

"How many days?" he said, as if he was concierge at a famous London hotel.

"I'll let you know when I know," I said. "Probably just the one night, maybe two."

He looked at my muddied coat. "Would you mind settling up first please?"

"I'll pay you the first night." I put a handful of coins down on the bar top. "Where do I go?"

He scooped the coins into his hand. "I'll show you," he said and at the same time stepped out from behind the counter.

I followed his curved back along a short passage, up a steep stair, banged my head on the crossbeam and swore under my breath. He smiled and said: "Mind your head, young sir" and threw open the door to my room. It had a window, but for viewing purposes you needed a chair. For sure, it was no' Brown's of Mayfair.

"I have a horse outside," I said.

"My boy will take care of that. I'll tell him." He moved towards the door.

"Don't worry," I said. "I'll be down in a minute, I'll speak to him myself." I didn't want anyone rummaging about in my saddlebags.

"His name's Doug, he'll sort you out," he said. "But we'll need extra for the horse." He smiled for the second time. I chose not to smile back and he closed the door gently behind him.

Later, I spooned up some grey, oily water in the bar - a thin liquid masquerading as soup - and chewed on a stale cut of bread that I dabbed and softened in the soupy mulch. It was surprisingly tasty. I grew used to the smell of my environment. I made a few discreet enquiries of the skinny man in the dirty shirt behind the bar, telling him that I was a cousin of Mr Weir who lived in these parts but that I had not seen him for many years and was not too sure where exactly his home was now. It was a tale as thin as the soup and initially the old man was cautious, wary of speaking to me about Mad Bob or even discussing the weather or time of day in any serious detail.

A short while later, the room was quieter and I hoped to unlock any information by offering the old man a drink. I could tell from the redness of his eyes and the rough, flakiness of his skin that he would find it hard to refuse. I was right. He drank a large whisky in three quick gulps, his hand trembling as he upended the glass. I bought him another that he drank more slowly and I consumed a beer myself and was surprised by the pleasant hopsy taste. By the end of the second drink he'd told me where Mad Bob could be found.

"West side of the town. I can draw you a map."

"I'd appreciate that."

"Mebbe three miles on from the last building. Just keep ridin', you'll find it nae bother."

"Thankyou."

"Course, if you dinnae find it, you'll probably hear it first."

"Why's that?"

"Mrs Weir," he said. "Confined to bed. Too fat to walk."

"That sounds like a terrible hardship."

"For Bob, yes. Hard on him." He paused. "Your cousin, you said?"

"Aye, but distant. Never kept contact, you know."

"Poor fella, Bob. I wouldnae trade places, that's for sure."

I had no' considered Mad Bob's marital status, that he might have a wife. I now considered that rather dull of me because, of course, his situation could have been almost anything. It might not have been just a corpulent wife I had to worry about. He might have had children too. Could I kill a man in front of his own wife and children? I had ma doubts. A seal on the beach was one thing. Would I flinch as I squeezed the trigger? It was no' desirable, I knew that much, but the old man said there were no children, which was a small crumb of comfort. By this time, he was looking at me with more curiosity. My argument was not with her and certainly not with any children there might have been. And nobody wanted relative damage of that sort. I drained the weak froth at the lower end of my beer. I was no' a big drinker, in fact I'd rarely touched the stuff. It gave me an effect I was not altogether used to. I thanked him for the conversation and walked out down the Montrose High Street, thinking about what tomorrow might bring. I would be up early in the morning. I needed to get down to Mad Bob's and survey the target in his lair.

Just after seven the next day, I was over to the stable to look out Master Henry, the sun rising in the cloud-filled sky behind my head. The boy I'd met the night before was called Doug. He was a thick-lipped fellow, who'd been asleep in the next bay to Master Henry. Seemed to live there, curled up on some straw against the wall. When he heard the stable door slam, he stirred and pulled his frayed braces over his shoulders.

"Morning," he said. "I'll get the horse saddled for you."

He pulled the bridle on over the horse's ears, feeding the bit between the teeth. He pushed his knee hard against

Master Henry's gut and pulled the girth tight. I spoke to him about the saddlebags.

"I'll take one and leave the other two with you." I gave him a coin that he shuffled into his pocket.

"Thankyou, sir." He was sufficiently content with his reward to assist me onto my horse and then lead the pair of us out onto the High Street. I thanked him and walked past the front of the pub, but I was conscious that his eyes never left me throughout. I stopped Master Henry in his tracks and then half-walked, half-trotted slowly back.

I flicked him a second coin. "Just about the saddlebags," I said. "I don't want anyone sniffin' around these bags. Would you keep them in a safe place for me?"

He nodded. "Dinnae worry about the bags, sir," he said. "I'll guard them with my life."

"I appreciate that, Doug." He nodded back at me. "If I'm no' back inside a week, of course, the bags are yours anyway. Do with them what you like cos I'll no' be needin' them."

"Very good, sir."

"If on the other hand," I said. "If I'm back, try no' to look too disappointed - we'll sort something out for you anyway." Doug smiled, unveiling a decent set of teeth, a smile that transformed his face. I turned Master Henry around and we set off together at a brisk trot, sweeping through the morning greyness, until Doug could no longer see us.

Leaving the town, it was not long before we came upon the last main building on the right, a solid, stone-built house with a slated roof and a broad, black door. I kept on riding, trotting down between the hedges, breaking into the occasional canter. A mile from Montrose, the air cleared and lightened and the sky seemed to fill with birds, the sound of herring gulls spilling a tuneless honk from the shore. There were a few more houses, sporadically punctuating the land

and set back from the road along which I rode. Then the houses ended abruptly, and I rode along the lane with nothing but trees and hedges around me. Eventually, I came upon the house that matched the old man's description. A bit more than three miles and I came upon a bend in the track between two swathes of silver birch, clumped leafless together, and then down on the right, a scooped out hollow, a stepped up porch and a timber plank construction of some sort built over the top. I saw the hens, strutting stupidly over the earth border in front of the house.

I pulled into the side of a light track leading off the lane, and went in amongst the trees to find a place to secure Master Henry. Once I'd done so, he dropped his head and grazed. I ventured out thirty yards or so to see what more there was. I knelt down on the damp earth, peered out from behind the smooth trunk of an ash tree and looked down upon the house of Mad Bob Weir. The old man behind the bar had said it was a house on its own, well beyond the town, with a porch and a green door – at least once upon a time it had been a green door and it might still be now, but you know, he said. Well, there was the door, closed against the outside elements, the colour of shit but I supposed it might have been green once.

My plan had been to wait, to work out when he came and went, who was there, what were their movements. I would then piece together the information and applying an intellect honed upon Mr Shifner's rosewood library at Tullis School, I would work out how best to respond. Yet, I was there, knees sinking into the damp earth, peering out from behind the heavy branches of the abundant trees, my father's Snider-Enfield laid across my thighs, and I had to ask myself: what did I think I was waiting for? The Plum Fairy? I knelt there for fifty-three minutes but I could not understand why I was holding back. Why was I waiting to concoct a carefully crafted plan when all I needed was to go in there and loose off a few shots from the barrel of the Snider-Enfield? What was justice after all? The attainment of that which is just? Was that complicated? All I knew was that it was one way I could put right the wrong that had been done. Where I could inflict punishment for a wrongdoing. It didnae matter how long ago it was. This man had done evil and it was for me to bring him to account. It made no difference at all that he never did wrong me directly; he had harmed my mother and my father and for that he was going to pay. The thought that Mad Bob was down there in his house going about his business only served to heighten my growing fury, as if the proximity of the man was itself a further incendiary. I thought that I would have been cool and relatively calm when the object of my endeavours was placed in front of me. On the contrary, I was fired up with anger.

In the fifty-fourth minute I made my decision. I took the saddlebag from Master Henry and slung it over my shoulder. My rifle was loaded and ready. Let hostilities begin. I walked down the green slope, my heels sinking into the mud, heading directly towards the house. Fifty yards short of the building, I tossed my rifle on its strap over my shoulder. I reached for one side of the saddlebag, pulled it open and extracted from the inside pocket two sticks of dynamite with beautiful, thread-like fuses hanging off them. I closed the flap and tossed the bag once again over my shoulder. I struck a match against my boot, watched the phosphorous flare brighten and die down, protected it from any breeze and then lit the end of the first fuse. I looked at it as the fuse burnt down, held onto it too long if the truth be known, but then I hurled it overarm straight at the house. It had begun.

The stick bounced on the edge of the porch, aired itself and clattered to a halt by the door. There were hens there strutting around, scratching for a seed or a bug or something worth eating. They noted my arrival and then scattered as the action unfolded. The fuse burnt its way right down and, after a two second silence, it created an explosion bigger and more powerful than I had ever experienced, even on the beach at Tullis. Too heavy on the nitroglycerin and too light on the sawdust. It blew the front door clean off its hinges, the smoke and dust hanging in the air. I saw a hen's leg fly up and crash against the window like a kindling twig. I saw two empty boots by the door, one of which was blown ten yards from the house, the other unmoved, smoking furiously. I could smell the explosive as I crossed the porch and entered Mad Bob's house with all the quiet rage I had nurtured these many years beating like a drum between my ears.

48

MRS WEIR'S RESOLUTION

W hen Mad Bob entered the room, he still hoped that something, some accidental interception, would divert him from his task. Undoubtedly, he'd been treading this water for a long time. He'd put up with her and her bullying, her daily torment, for years. He'd expected one day to reach this point but, if truth be told, his usual course would be to come so far and then scuttle off without achieving anything. No harm done. On this occasion, the current had carried him to the bedroom door and he had the will, like never before, to see it through. As he stared ahead of him he was propelled to a point in time where he could renegotiate all the abuse, the insults, the broken gut, and a hundred other calumnies that he'd suffered. He wanted a new set of cards so that he could play the game of his life again. He wanted to be given a chance to obtain a more equitable result. He just had to see it through. Only then could it all change.

He closed the door behind him without a sound. Outside a dog barked, some Collie from a neighbouring farm he would normally have yelled at or in whose direction he would have loosed off a few wild shots with his rifle. He could hear outside the trees tossing their branches in a sudden breeze that passed as quickly as it had come. Mad Bob stood by the door and looked down the length of the bed.

She was half on the mattress and half off, the grey spread draped against the bed end. She had a leg jutting out awkwardly from beneath the sheet. She had on a camisole that had ridden up against her thigh and he could see the fat that enveloped her protruding limb. He could hear her breathing the stuffy air, in through the nose, steadily, rhythmically, out through the open mouth. Like a fuckin' pig. He heard the sound of her breath as it squeezed out between her lips and the hypnotic rise and fall of her chest beneath the covers. He stepped forward, closer to the dusty, skin-scaled, lumpy bed. Her eyes were shut and her face was turned a little to the right. There was a mark against her cheek made by the indentation of piping on the cushion edge. He took another step towards her. He was almost by her side now and he could smell her sleepy breath. She snorted as she sucked in saliva that caught in her throat. He could see one hand secreted beneath her thigh. Her lips were cracked and there was a brown-orange tinge around her mouth. He stood at the bedside, looked at the window and then back down at his wife. He looked again at the mouth, that speaking thing that uttered such rotten waste. Had it always been that way? Did it ever once whisper sweet things, idle pleasantries or any other kindness? Was he being too harsh? The thought never crossed his mind. To him, her gob was a toilet hole, full of dead sludge; at one time it had been, if not a thing of beauty at least a moderately decorative reception vessel. Here and now, to his mind it was the source of all that rendered his life worthless. Her chest continued to rise and fall, to show that it was still alive. She licked her lips and ran her free hand a glancing blow across her hair then let it slump by her side.

Mad Bob still had the shovel in his left hand, containing a good quantity of hen shit. He raised the shovel above the slack sheets, took hold of the handle with two hands and he rammed it hard against her mouth, splitting the lips at each end. The teeth disappeared into the shovel, her mouth widened and ripped into the comic look of a broad laugh, as if he had said something astoundingly funny. He shoved deep in, his full weight behind the blow, with all the pent up hatred of the many years that had passed. He leaned on the slippery smooth handle and applied his entire body weight. The shovel slid further into her mouth, like he was digging into soft earth that gives under the weight. He saw an open gash that was split now in a tear from ear to ear, like a laughing clown. He threw himself onto the bed, brought his knees down hard against her arms and pinned them to her sides. He pushed harder on the shovel, then pulled it out, and it gulped and oozed a slurp. He thrust it back in again, her mouth flopping wider, gushing blood, and he tilted the shovel handle up the way and watched the hen shit slide down into the tunnel of her throat, into the open bucket that lay beyond her lips. Her eyes were wider now than he had ever seen them, filled with confusion, horror and, at the last gasp, recognition and resignation. She twitched and convulsed for what felt like minutes, but was less than one, and then all movement was gone, her eyes as full now as they ever had been in life, yet vacant, staring, round and wide as thick pebbles in the river. For the first time in her life she had left the room without making a sound. He let go of the wooden shaft and slipped off the bed to the floor, his back to the Victorian spread where his wife lay dead. The shovel stood upright, as if resting between digs.

49

EXCHANGE OF FIRE

As I stood in the narrow hall, the smoking door still hung tenuously on its twisted steel hinge, like a drunk man against a bartop. Mad Bob appeared above me on the landing and squeezed a bullet from his rifle in my direction. Good fortune took the shape of an open door on my left into which I had the quick sense to propel myself head first, moving with sufficient zip to avoid the bullet. From a prostrate position on the grubby bare wood floor, I touched the light wound on my head and examined the small amount of blood. I poked the Snider-Enfield into the hall and pointed the barrel vaguely towards the landing, unleashing several shots of random accuracy. Then there was a lull in the exchange of fire, as each man took stock.

"What the fuck do you want?" shouted the voice from the landing. "Who are you?" I was seeing red. All the anger and frustration, all the patient and considered waiting over many years had come to this. In my fury I remained silent. "Who are you?" he shouted again and fired another shot that ricocheted off the side wall.

"I'm Logan," I said, having recovered some calm. "You know the name."

"Logan?" he shouted back. "I don't know any Logan."

"Think hard," I shouted.

"Where you from?" he yelled.

"Tullis," I said. The place went quiet. "Perhaps you remember now. In any event, it won't matter soon."

"And why's that?"

"You'll be dead."

Mad Bob fired a further shot, the bullet embedding itself in the wall by the front door.

"It's no' me you want!" He fired another and then scurried backwards into one of the rooms behind.

"You'll do for now!"

I heard a door slam. In the ensuing quiet, I pulled my knees up beneath me and hurled myself towards the staircase. There was no movement at the top of the stairs but I was pretty sure he was in the room up there and he'd shut the door. He was too stupid to fake it. I waited a little longer, then pulled myself up and sprang two steps at a time. I could see the closed door he had entered - there was no other. I crouched before it, leaning in from one side, putting an ear close, but I could sense no movement nor hear a sound. I stood back and released a shot from the Snider-Enfield, splintering the wood as it passed straight through the door panel and drilled its way into the room.

I followed the bullet in with a kick box against the door that took the heel off my boot. It was a room with a large bed against the opposite wall. There was paper on the walls, but old, scuffed and dirty. If there was a pattern it had lost its definition and instead presented an overall strain of brown that I had not witnessed before. The floor was bare. To one side there was a dressing table with a chipped mirror above iron feet. The bed had an imposing wooden Victorian bedhead. Slumped against it was a woman with a large head. I looked at the sash window that was wide open, a light breeze blowing in, stirring the dust off the lace curtains. I heard noise and commotion and steered myself towards the window. There I could see a man kicking and beating a horse. Immediately, I thought of Master Henry who I thought would still be tethered where I'd left him. Then there was the thump of hooves clattering along a grass track at breakneck speed. I moved closer to the window and saw the figure of Mad Bob clinging to the neck of an old pit pony, his legs banging hard against its sides, the beast all the while kicking up chunks of mud from the soft earth. I thought I saw him turn his face towards me, but he kept on going and was soon out of sight. I held my rifle at my side and watched him disappear, knowing that I had no hope in hell of shooting a moving target at that kind of distance. He had left his rifle leaned against the wall by the window.

I turned back to the fat woman in the bed. Curiously, her eyes were wide open and she had a large shovel clenched between her teeth and inside a lot of mud and possibly shit bunching up her cheeks. On closer inspection, it looked to me like hen shit. When I put my nose up close to her head, I knew it was hen shit. There was little expression on her face. I looked at her again. I was a little surprised, to be honest, that she had ended her days with a mouth full of hen shit. No doubt, not nearly as surprised as her. She had a large hole in her forehead and I immediately thought well that is sod's own law: the bullet from my rifle could have ended up anywhere and it had to end up buried in this woman's head. I remembered Kipling's *Snider squibbed in the jungle, a big blue mark in his forehead, and the back blown out of his head.* For all the calm acceptance of her condition, the woman's eyes were crossed and between them the bullethole looked like a bindi, that spot they call the mark of Kumkum. She would have plenty of time now for inner meditation and worship. How long had she been dead? Strangely, the back of her head was intact. I figured the velocity of the bullet must have been slowed by its entrance through the door.

Mad Bob was well gone, carried away on a miniature, retired pit pony, grey-white with black splashes, leaving his dead wife behind, his possessions, and whatever shit had been his life. Something even told me I knew where he was going. I looked around the couple's home before I left. I went downstairs first. There was a sink full of dishes, a bag of abattoir meat knives, three cups and a stale loaf of bread. The dishes looked like they had been there for many days and the bread was hard as bullets. There was fat and fungus floating on the oily water. There was a saddlebag in the hall but the pouches were stiff and empty.

I looked inside the room into which I had propelled myself when Mad Bob had loosened off his rifle from the landing. This room was tidy, little cotton-embroidered cushions gathering dust but puffed up, like nobody ever thought to sit upon them. I saw small traces of hen shit on the floor by the window, part flattened by somebody's shoe. In the corner, on the other side of the window, I found a decent sized hardwood desk. I pulled at the top drawer and found it locked. The second drawer flew open because I applied force, thinking it would be secured like the top one. I picked the drawer up off the floor. A small book with a cloth cover showed itself, some kind of log for purchasing timber and screws and the like. The bottom drawer I pulled gently. It had a handgun inside, looked old, the barrel blackened and no sign that it had been fired in recent times. The top drawer was annoying me, so I took the poker from the fireplace, jammed it into the crevice and levered the damned thing wide open like a dog's mouth. It split the wood facing but I was beyond worrying about the integrity of the interiors. There was a letter inside the drawer that I pulled from the recess and took over to the window. I read it in the grey light:

"*Well Bob, I'm no great shakes with the pen but here's a letter anyway. Fucked if you need a personal appearance from me. We shared some business no so very long ago. You may remember. We both played our parts. The consequence of that for me has no been good. You may have holes in your gut but my own father disowned me. I won't see a farthing when he dies, or so he tells me. I recognise you got yourself shot, but I'm told that you live in some comfort and don't appear too stretched for money. I hear old fatboy is doing likewise. All very pleasing I'm sure, but I have nothing, have no prospect of anything and therefore I'm looking to you and fatboy for something. You understand? If you wish to keep the lid on this thing, you could do better than work something out with fatboy and arrange me a money transfer to meet my expenses and keep my mouth shut. Be warned, I am serious about this. It's only fair. I'm desperate and I feel you both owe me.*"

The letter was signed "Turner". Beneath was written an address. I had to read it twice because I was so convinced it could not be right. None of it made any sense. I shook my head. The handwriting was good and surprisingly legible. If it was not for the content you might have thought it had been written by a schoolteacher. I put the letter in my top pocket and buttoned down the flap. Something was not right. It was signed Turner but the man I was after was Traynor. Who the hell was Turner? Traynor came from Buckstone – that was what Fawcett told me. Turner had written part of his address on this letter. It was marked Tullis. Tullis? That made no sense.

As I passed back out the front door, I dropped a small detonator with a black powder wrap. It was an interesting device that I had developed over two months in the old byre that became my office. It lay there on the floor as I stepped away from the house. Between fifteen and twenty seconds later, it exploded into a fireball, the blast carrying up and sideways in a mass of clearly defined orange flame, by which time I was already upon the hill retrieving Master Henry. I looked round to see a long plume of smoke and big tongues of fire licking out the front door. I climbed aboard Master Henry and I rode away from the scene as the sparks crackled through the air behind me. I was not entirely pleased with myself; the cool calculation of what I had planned for Mad Bob had imploded. Mrs Weir got her cremation without asking. Things had a habit of not working out quite the way you planned them. Still, the journey had begun. That job was over and I was on my horse, heading for Buckstone.

50

BUCKSTONE

O n the old Braid Road, by the gated entrance to the Pentland Cemetery and on the east side of Buckstone itself, stands the *Buckstane*, a grey slab built into the existing wall. This is a march stone, about three feet high and one foot wide: a feudal relic, occupying a commanding site on another of General Wade's Hanoverian roads. It marks the spot where the buckhounds were released when the King of Scotland took to hunting the region. It will not surprise anybody to learn that it is from the *Buckstane* that the small town of Buckstone derived its name. I was several miles (four and a half) east of Buckstone when I was almost separated from Master Henry by some mad fool galloping his horse in the opposite direction. He looked at me like a wild man, frowning so hard his eyebrows almost knitted themselves into a woolly bandana; he yelled a profanity and watched me ride away with a look of some curiosity. I did not see why he was so mad at me.

Perhaps an hour later, I reached Buckstone itself. Earlier, I had felt some heat in Master Henry's fetlock, so I walked him as I approached this small conurbation, squeezed by its low, wet-drizzled, black-slated houses, the dry stone dykes, its twisted hawthorn hedges spiking outward, and I sensed a place where hounds might well rip the throats from travellers foolish enough to stray too far off the Pentland Path.

Whatever reason I had for any sense of foreboding, the road transported me through the greyness of Buckstone itself, revealing one and a half storey houses to the left side, ivy-clad, patchy, plastered walls, chimneys smoking and bare ground with occasional shrubs, growth and trees on the other. A stubble-faced man stood in a doorway in a waistcoat, tweed tie and black trousers, drawing on a hand-rolled cigarette in his cupped hand. The chain off his fob watch hung from his waist. He looked at me out of the corner of his eye but there was something about him that made me look twice. I saw a woman through a downstairs window with a child against her bosom. Up a rough track off the main street I caught sight of a boy with a flat cap on his head, as he kicked a dog and I heard it howl. Further on were a number of shops, a man selling buckets and birch tree brushes and a barrow surrounded by more people, maybe just a few, buying bottles of ginger. The road was a broken track full of holes and puddles and I pulled Master Henry up outside a shop with a proud banner above its window: *Domenico Corrolla* it read.

The door in was off a narrow wynd to the side of the shop. I hitched Master Henry to a small metal ring and stepped inside the shop. I sniffed around the shelves and then purchased a cup of beef soup and an oat biscuit off an Italian with a black moustache. I imagined he was part of the immigrant stream that was spreading north, beyond cities like Manchester and Glasgow, into the smaller towns of central Scotland.

I sat on a cushioned chair, a welcome change from the

saddle, and consumed the soup. Some while later, I bought a further biscuit that I secreted in a handkerchief and inserted into my chest pocket. I asked the Italian if he knew where the Traynor house was.

"Gelati?" he said.

"No gelati," I said. "I'm asking if you know a man whose name is Traynor?" He looked dumbfounded, so I repeated the name Traynor.

"Traynor?" he said.

"Yes, Traynor?" I smiled back.

"Corrolla," he said with a heavy smile.

I stepped out of the shop consumed by thoughts of further enquiry, and then, as if struck by a thunderbolt, all the lights went out. My head entered into a deep blackness, punctuated by flashes of a bright, starlike quality, and I felt my chin hit the stone although I felt no pain as it did so. It was an interesting experience. I had in all probability been hit on the head with a fence post, a small tree or a sledge-hammer. As I fell, I was aware that I was falling and I recognized the feel of stone as it brushed against my skin and the resounding thump as it hit the side of my face. I was aware of voices, grunting, rope and the spit off a man's tongue. Then I was inside a basket and it smelt of wet straw. My legs were crumpled beneath me and no matter how much I wished to move them they remained stubbornly unresponsive, as if the link between my brain and my body was uncoupled. I may have lost consciousness, but I was then aware of movement, a rumbling, jostling, vibration, as I was thrown from side to side. I assumed I was in a cart of some sort, moving at some speed, too groggy to know where I was going or even what direction I was headed.

As my brain cleared, I forced myself to raise my hands above my head. I had a sense that there was a lid to my enclosure and if I only pushed I could break out into the light. I pressed with my hands in response to the voice inside my head and the basket top rose an inch or two above the rim. It was clear enough that I was indeed on the back of a horse-drawn cart, moving at speed, houses replaced by open fields, trees and fences and the splash and jolt of wet mud in the pot-holed road. Strangely, I could see Master Henry tethered to the back of the cart, eyes wide, breaking from a fast trot to a canter, his eyes catching mine as if unclear about my intentions. Then the lid rose up out of sight and a hammer or a mallet came down against my skull, just slow enough for me to see the hand that gripped its shaft. The fourth finger was missing. Once again, all was darkness.

51

THE PIT PONY

Once Mad Bob had split his wife's face open with the hen shit shovel, he had slumped to the floor. A great weight had been lifted from his shoulders and he intended to enjoy the moment. Even for a thing like that, you needed to take a second. You needed to bask a little before you faced the reality. Without even articulating the thought, he proposed to sink in the soothing calm of peace and feminine absence, and when he had finished luxuriating he intended to wash down his knives and get to work. Twelve years of his life had been spent doing what he considered to be his dream job, cutting offal at Skene's abattoir. It was a place he could get away to, a place he could escape the whine of Mrs Weir and her incessant complaints, gripes and sporadic swipes of physical violence.

At Skene's abattoir, Mad Bob had been quickly promoted to boning duty and that was when they gave him his own butcher's knives. They were hung on a hook by the back door and he intended to polish and sharpen his knives before a careful dissection and deconstruction of his dead wife's limbs. He had adopted a responsible attitude and had prepared himself for this moment. He had already dug a neat little hole, to a significant depth, beneath the new hen hutch for the purpose of housing Mrs Weir's remains. There they would lie forever and nobody would be any the wiser. It was all prepared.

These thoughts did not progress very much further because minutes later he heard an explosion that broke the calm and dispelled the need for such industry. His moment to luxuriate was over more quickly than he intended. He opened the bedroom door and tentatively stepped out onto the landing, leaning his head towards the stair and straining to see what had occurred. He could observe very quickly that the front door was hanging off its hinges and there was smoke and dust and broken plaster across the hall floor. He was momentarily stunned by what he saw and was unable to make sense of it. Instinctively, Mad Bob reached for the rifle he was in the habit of leaving outside his wife's bedroom door. Some might ask why you would leave a rifle in such a place, but Mad Bob figured that a rifle on the landing was the most easily accessible, from upstairs and downstairs; it was the hub of the house and if he needed his rifle, no matter where he was, he calculated that the nearest point would be on the landing. It was logical and Bob was on the simple side of logical. Besides, it was not unusual for him to take a position at the upstairs window and shoot foxes or rabbits.

At the present time, there were no foxes, rabbits or even dogs to take a shot at because no sooner was the rifle in his hands than he was looking down the barrel and firing at the stranger in the hallway. Whoever the arse was, he'd just entered his line of sight by walking through the broken door like he'd every right to be there. Later he would blame his eyes, his lack of practice, the dirty muzzle, the rusted bullet, the sweat on his fingers, the blocked toilet, for the fact that he missed his target and before he could release further fire, the man had rolled into the room off the hall and was firing back at him with interest and accuracy. Mad Bob cried out to him, who the fuck? What came back was like a long-forgotten tune. At first he could not make sense of it. He thought that name was in the past. He stayed away from Tullis, just for that reason. He'd heard the name Logan. Logan? This man down there was Logan? Mad Bob lurched back into the bedroom, slamming the door behind him. He felt giddy and confused, like he had seen a ghost. He threw the window open. There was no way he was hanging around. He dragged his body out on to the corrugated lean-to beneath the window. Midway through he realized he had left the rifle by the wall inside the window. Too late now, he would have to take his chances. He slid down the iron sheeting and found himself hanging off the guttering just a few feet from the ground. He dropped and ran round to the back of the house. He was panting heavily; the old lung was wasted. That mad bitch, how did he let her do that to him? The old pit pony was tethered there and Bob threw off the halter, jumped on his back and kicked his sides like his life depended on it. There was little time for pleasantries and the stumpy old pit pony reacted with shock, rocketing along the track, away from the back of the house, moving as fast as its stubby legs would allow, hooves beating hard against the earth, propelling the two, man and beast, in a westerly direction. Bob's face formed itself into the shape of a grin. He looked back over his shoulder but could see nothing at the window, no gun, no face, nothing, just a wisp of smoke across the rooftop, dissipating gently in the breezeless air. Mrs Weir dead in her bed but maybe, just a little helpful confusion as to how she died? One thing he knew: this was not a welcome development. Nobody needed another Logan.

52

THE THONET ROCKER

W hen I came to, I was wedged into an early bentwood Thonet rocker. Michael Thonet, a Viennese cabinetmaker, had mastered the art of bending wood under the application of steam and he'd succeeded in producing a lightweight rocking chair with a simple flowing form. The rattan seat of this rocker had been cut from the frame and my rear end had been forced down into the opening. My thighs were pressed hard against my chest in front of me. The wooden strut at the rear of the chair pressed against the small of my back, chaffing the skin and causing it to cut and bleed. My wrists were bound, tied in a greasy knot behind and below me. It was not a comfortable position in which to find oneself. I rocked gently, appropriately, stupidly, in the stillness of the room.

When the rocking motion stopped, or some time afterwards, I opened my eyes and it seemed to me I was in a relatively dark room, full of shadows and unlit corners. My mouth was dry and my lips were cracked. I could make out a window and some white and rose-flowered curtains. I could see the edge of a round, cloth-topped table and three dark wood chairs with red velvet cushions. There was a fire to one end of the room with a white marble mantle and a green insert. The occasional flames puckered out from the cast iron grate and found themselves reflected in the brass coal bucket to the left of the fire. Above the mantle, and supported by it, was a gilt-framed mirror and in the corner, a small upright piano. Seated at the piano I could see the back of a man, and as I gathered my senses, I was able to hear the notes.

I have never professed to be a musician or even to have the ability to fully recognise a crotchet from a semibreve, but in Mr Shifner's rosewood library there was a book of sheet piano music that I had often taken some pleasure in scrutinising. I quickly discovered that it was like learning a new language and I found that with a little application I was able to understand its fundamental vocabulary. It may have been the constant repetition of the main phrase, but it seemed to me I had some understanding of the notes the man was playing. It was a bagatelle – short, pleasant and played in A minor. Set in 3/8 time, the left hand begins with arpeggios alternating between A minor and E major, then C major and G major, before returning to the original theme. Another time I would have shown an interest in such things, but in the circumstances I'd lost my appetite for musical knowledge.

When he stopped playing, I did manage to comment: "Whoever's playing, please stop."

"What's the matter?" came a voice. "Do you no' like Beethoven?"

"It's your pedal technique," I said. "Fuckin' appallin'. You sound like you're workin' a footpump."

There was silence in the room as the pianist took in this

observation, then a second voice snarled from somewhere behind my head: "Turn the fucker round."

I felt myself spinning in the chair, awkwardly wedged, my rear end just inches above the floor. My sight took in the pianist to my left and two other men. When I looked at them and heard them speak from the shadows, swallowed by the gloom, I knew that they were not young men. One of them coughed, clearly weak lungs; they were rough, rasping, middle-aged, one bearded and the other two cleanshaven.

"Not pretty," said the big man, seated on a deep sofa.

"What did you expect?" said the pianist. "Bonnie Prince Charlie?"

Nobody laughed. The third man, leaning heavily against the wall by the door, never raised his head but when he moved towards me he appeared to grow in height. He swayed like a tall tree. "Nothin' bonnie there," he said.

"I'm sorry you dinnae like the music, Mr Logan," said the big man on the sofa, his arms crossed against the top of his large belly, looking like they were too short and would only just reach. "We all love a tune."

"Are you Traynor?" I said.

He looked at me. "Interesting question."

The pianist turned on his chair, away from the keys, and looked into the room. "I thought they said he had a brain."

"Are you Traynor?" I repeated to the fat man on the sofa.

He laughed. "Don't you know?"

"Obviously, I don't."

"You're like a bent, fuckin' compass."

"What d'you mean by that?"

"Like a hunting dog. You set it loose and you tell it, go this way or go that way, and off it goes." He picked some skin off the top of his ear. "Meanwhile the fox has gone back to the hen house and stuffed his face."

"You seem to know *me*," I said.

"I know of you," he said. "I was told you might be comin' to see us."

"Stupid that," said the pianist. "If you dinnae mind me observing."

"Are you surprised?" I said.

"By your stupidity?"

"How long will you be keeping me in this contraption?" I said, indicating the bentwood chair.

"Until we decide what to do with you," said the fat man, unfolding his arms.

"You can't keep me here."

"Can we no'? Just watch us."

"If you get uncomfortable," said the pianist. "I can break your legs?"

"My legs are okay," I said. "But thankyou."

The lanky guy by the wall breezed over, a heavy black beard brushing through his fingers. As he approached, he swung his boot against my rear end. The pain was deep and bruising and brought tears to my eyes.

"Better now?" he said.

For a skinny man he was remarkably strong. He picked up the rocking chair in two hands and then shook me out onto the floor, like a fish from a holding net. Emerging at height, it was a hard landing. My hands remained tied behind me and I hit the floor with the side of my head for the second time that day.

"Why are you here?" said the fat man.

I lifted my head from the floor. "Is your name Traynor?"

"Yes," said the fat man. "My name is fuckin' Traynor and you're gonnie wish you'd never fuckin' heard of me."

53

A MAN CALLED TRAYNOR

By the time Mad Bob was in through the large gate outside Buckstone, his pit pony had nothing left to give. On four short legs, he had galloped the full distance from Montrose without breaking to a trot and the pony's light coat was quickly wet with sweat and foam. His nostrils flared wildly as he drew in all the breath his lungs could take. Bob dismounted by the door, immediately adjacent to a large iron water trough. He crashed through the side door, ran past the kitchen and shouted down the hallway: "Hey? Anyone here?"

"Yeah, we're here," said the big man calmly, emerging from the room to one end of the hall. "What the fuck do you want?"

"We've got a problem, Traynor," he began, but then realised he was panting like his pony and could hardly speak. He pulled a cloth from his pocket, wiped his mouth and then his forehead. "Some idiot," he said. "At my place, he just came in...shooting! No care... nothin'!"

"Whoa! You're makin' me dizzy, you erse. *Who* are you talkin' about?"

"There's a man, Jesus, at my house," he said. "He came to my place, came in there just shootin' his gun at me. Blew the whole bloody door in. May well have killed Mrs Weir!" He stopped to catch his breath. "Total nutcase, I'm tellin' you!"

"And where is he now?"

"He said he was a... you're no' gonnie believe this Traynor!"

"Said he was a what?"

"Said his name was Logan."

"Logan?"

"That's what he said."

"Is that all?" said the fat man.

Mad Bob looked confused. "What d'you mean, *is that all*?"

"You said it was somethin' serious," said Traynor.

"He may've killed ma fuckin' wife!" said Mad Bob. "Are you no' hearing me? He may have burnt ma fuckin' house down! There was smoke. I think that's reasonably fuckin' serious!"

"It is for you."

"It is for *us*, Traynor!"

"Did he mention the business at the farm?"

"In a way. He said he was somebody Logan. Then the mayhem started. I don't know who. But he was serious."

"Is that right?"

"Aye, it bloody well is! He was after me. Make nae mistake, he's after *us*! Christ, he just blew in ma front door. That disnae happen every day of the week!"

"Well, okay. But mebbe you're gettin' over-excited Bob. You been on they pills again?"

"You're no' hearin' me! He's dangerous, Traynor!"

"Fair enough. But why would I be interested in your domestic shite?"

"What?"

"What's all this got to do with me?"

"The clue is in the name," said Mad Bob.

"So, he's a fuckin' Logan. So the fuck what?"

"If he knows about me and feels okay about blowin' in ma door, it stands to reason he knows about you," said Mad Bob. "Let's face it, there's only one thing he's gonnie be interested in. It was no' a social visit."

"I dinnae see the connection," said Traynor. "And he knows nothin' about me. Unless of course you told him?"

"I didnae have time to tell him! He was shootin' bullets up the stair, for god's sake!"

"Mebbe he followed you here? Is that what you've done, you fuckin' maggot? You led him here, have you?"

"He knew where I was."

"So?"

"Seems pretty likely he'll know where to find you too."

"Plenty reasons why he wouldnae," said Traynor. "Unless somebody told him I was there."

"Chances are he's comin'," said Mad Bob. "Don't you see? We're on his list. All of us! We need to be ready for him."

Traynor stood in front of Mad Bob and studied his face. He didn't like what he was looking at, never had done. He'd covered for him, partly to keep the constabulary away. Mad Bob was a bad case, he would spill his own guts if somebody nudged him hard enough. To Traynor, he'd even less backbone than he had stomach. "He's coming after *you*, Bob," Traynor said. "Doesn't mean he's got any beef with me."

"Come on Traynor. We're in this together. It's no' just me."

"You little shite," he said. "Time you started wipin' your own erse."

Mad Bob moved a fraction closer. "Sink or swim: we need to deal with this together," he said, their faces so close that Mad Bob could see each hair growing out of Traynor's bent nose. He wiped his own nostril with his fingers. He smelt hen shit. "Stupid not to," he added more calmly.

"It may be you've led him here. That's the stupid bit."

"What of it?"

"That's what I'm thinking on, Bob. I hope not."

"If I have, then I have," he said. "Tough. But whatever I have or havenae done, he's now your problem as much as mine."

"Is that what you're thinkin', is it? You wee shite. I should've done you ages ago."

"Look, Traynor, we need to deal with this maniac," said Mad Bob. "We can blame each other later, if that's what you want."

"I intend to do just that," said Traynor. "But I dinnae have your patience."

"The thing to know just now is that he's armed, he's got guns and I think he's comin' here. He tried to kill me for Christ's sake! There's every reason to think he wants you too. Just think about that, Traynor."

"And you led him here, didn't you, Bob?" the big man shouted back. "Good old Mr Traynor, is that what you thought? He'll sort this boy Logan out! He'll sort him out for me."

"Mebbe I did. I don't know. I didnae see him follow, but my guess is he was comin' anyway."

"Billy!" A tall, bearded man stepped out of the shadows. "Take Bob out the back, will you? Give him some water. You know what I mean? He looks right fuckin' dry. I bet he's got a thirst on him that would take your breath away." Billy stepped towards Bob and picked him up by the collar. He was light, all air and bone. Nae stomach. "A nice long drink, Bob. That's what you're needin'. Must have been scared oot of your wits."

"I'm sure there's some water in the yard," said Billy.

"Oh come on, Traynor," said Mad Bob, gasping and wrestling to escape. "What's this all about? Where you takin' me?" But Billy already had him out the back door.

A short time later, they climbed up onto the forward seat of the horse cart. The fat man, Traynor, cracked the frayed end of the whip against the horse's rear and the wheels turned with a creak and a jolt, the dust rose from the earth and the short, fat man on the left and the tall, skinny man on the right were away at speed along the track, heading rapidly down the road east, towards Buckstone and Montrose. The cart was unevenly balanced, leaning to the left. The pianist was already some distance ahead of them on a single chestnut horse, ridden at full stretch, with a rising wind pushing at his back, lifting his jacket tails to reveal a scarlet lining.

The town of Buckstone was their first stop but they did not intend to spend any time there. They figured that if this man Logan was coming they might as well get to him first. Not too much time had been wasted and they were already on the outskirts of Buckstone, when they spotted the pianist coming back towards them at a gallop, slapping his hat against his horse's neck. "I've seen him!" he shouted, as he drew up alongside the cart, his horse skittering anxiously. "Move fast, Traynor, he's in Buckstone. We can have him now."

"What are we waitin' for?" said Traynor, wiping his lip, his thin hair wild and wispy across his crown. "Let's get oot there and find him!" he yelled and cracked the leather reins above the horse's back.

54

THE ALBUMBLATT BEATING

I t struck me that something was still not quite right. Whilst it seemed I had come and, to some extent, I had found what I was looking for, there was something missing. Some small piece of the puzzle was a bad fit. If I had it right, all the bits should fit neatly together; there should be harmony, no bumps and no rough edges. The first verse should ease into the second. The string section should fade and make way for the woodwind, the brass or the percussion; they should sound together as if they belonged together. Here, in my mind, the sections were playing the pieces without a conductor, breaking in early, leaving late. I was confused: the overall picture was not making sense.

It seemed to me that I could safely conclude there was a fat, balding man. His name was Traynor and lucky me, I had tracked him down. There was also a bearded, lanky man. And there was a pianist with a missing finger. To what extent they were involved and to what extent they had been involved, I did not know. I had the feeling that they were all involved in some way or another, all covering for each other, and probably had been all these years.

I turned over the pieces in my head. So, the fat man was Traynor. I did not know who the pianist was, but the missing finger on his left hand had not escaped my notice. I did not fancy his chances with a more complicated musical score. I recalled all too well that Aunt Marion had said one had a missing finger and most people, in my experience, had a full complement. My father had said one of them liked to hum too but I had heard little evidence of that. Yet, a pianist might make a good hummer. There was also, it was reported, a tall fellow who played a part. That was what we understood anyway. This man here was lanky as a hangman's noose with an ugly beard to boot. The fat man Traynor had an old lady in the house. Was that Traynor's mother? I didn't get the best look at her from my contorted position in the bentwood Thonet rocker. She came in once they'd started to drag the story out of me, but they were quick to push her out the door and I was not even sure she'd seen me.

"Can I go home now?" I heard her ask. "Can I go home?"

"You're goin' upstairs," said Traynor. The lanky one shuffled her out by the arm. I'm not that sure she knew where she was. "What the fuck is it you're doin' here, Logan?"

"You think you'd just walk in here and shoot us?" said the lanky one, his voice up a pitch. "What were you thinkin'?"

"A stick of dynamite in your pouch and a prehistoric rifle? Is that what you call a plan?" said Traynor. He stepped towards me and knelt down. They had beaten me already, whipped my face with hands, sticks and shoehorns. I think my nose was broken but whatever, there was blood and it was dripping out of my nostril onto the thin rug against the wood floor. They didn't seem overly house-proud because the spillage on the soft furnishings made no discernible impression on them. "Look here, Logan. What're you diggin' up the past for? You're talkin' about things that happened a long time ago."

"Long since done," said the lanky one. "Cannie bring back the dead, man."

"Shut up, Billy!" said Traynor. The lanky one stood back, leaned against the wall and stared at the ceiling. So, his name was Billy.

"Mebbe," I said, my jaw creaking against the words. "My memory's better than yours."

"You weren't even there!" said Billy. Again Traynor looked at him, irritated, but Billy was untroubled this time. "What d'you ken about it?"

"Oh, I was there," I said.

"The fuck you were!"

"I was there," I insisted.

"You weren't even born," he said, moving back from the wall and approaching me. "Think you could come here, did you, take your revenge for a lot of nonsense half a life time since? Get your own back on those bad boys? For something you know nothin' about?" He ran at me and kicked hard at the underside of my legs. "Revenge?" He swung his boot at me. "You piece of shit!" He walked around me. "Look where it's got you."

The pianist sat down at the chair in front of the piano. "What we're gonnie do," he said. "Is play some Schubert. What d'you think, Logan? Maybe you're no' in the mood for Schubert? I always play Schubert when things are tense," he said. "Helps me relax."

"Enough o' your Shubert," said Traynor. "Give me some of your Beethoven."

"Beethoven? Fair dos. Let's play some Beethoven then, shall we?"

He played the notes from the *albumblatt*. It was Beethoven, of course it was. I knew it was Beethoven, even with the fourth finger missing. A minor, E major. C major, G major, and back again. Was this what he hummed when he killed her and I was there, just a heartbeat away?

"Each time I hit this note," he said, helpfully playing a D major with his left hand, "he gets a fucking kick. Okay Billy? Once he's had his kick, he tells us everything we want to know. Everything about this vendetta he's on. If the tune stops or we stop kicking, then that will be it for today. Okay?"

"Aye, seems okay," said Billy.

"Are the rules of the boy's game clear, Logan?" asked Traynor. I said nothing. Billy stepped back towards me. "Fine," said the pianist. "Let's begin. With a one-two-three," he counted, and so it went: with each D major, of which there were many, Billy's boot connected with my shoulder, my back, my legs or wherever looked to be the most desirable fit. It was my first musical beating. The pianist had the skill to reappear seamlessly back at the beginning of the piece, many times over, and the blows rained down in blind musical obedience. Sometimes he got his A minor mixed up with his D major and I got a kick for that too.

55

THE COAL HOLE

A good while later - I cannot say how long it was - I found myself breathing dust in a coal cellar. I thought I was dead, but after careful examination I discovered to my relief that that was no' the case. I worked out it was a coal cellar by meticulous assessment of the available facts. It was a locked room. It was dark. It had a heavy door. There was a huge pile of coal. It smelled dusty. I did not remember how I came to be in there. My throat was dry and grated. My nose was clogged with dry blood. My lips were cut and my face felt puffy and sore. My ribs were layered in heavy bruises and some of those bones may have been broken.

I had sat myself up and I was taking it all in and I was not impressed. I groaned each time I moved. I was grateful that my hands were no longer tied or the circulation would have gone completely. What time was it? What day was it? I tried to think how long I had been in there, but I could reach no conclusion. There were no indicators from which I could get a bearing. I could hear no noise, no sounds, no wind, nothing, and I sat in silence for a long time. On the positive side, it was warm enough in this dusthole: heat, stuffiness and I could smell spermaceti. For those with a limited understanding of liquid fuel development, spermaceti is a wax. Some people believe this wax is coagulated semen, and it may come as a disappointment to learn that spermaceti does in fact come from a whale – and from its head, not its sexual organs. It was also well known at the time as a useful domestic product. I felt along the floor, following my nose, and soon I came across its source: a huge vat of soft spermaceti, no doubt used for fuelling lamps and making candles. Well, spermaceti was about as much use to me now as an invitation to Queen Victoria's garden party.

However, at the exact moment that I concluded my situation was so very desperate, my eye caught something at the top of the room, where the ceiling might be. I thought I had fooled myself but I discovered I could only see it if I looked to one side and used my peripheral vision. The moment I looked directly up, it disappeared. Some things in life you have to come at from the side. I felt my way around the coal. I touched the walls. I felt pipes and what could have been a shovel. I worked out where the coal was and then I set about climbing up onto the pile. The difficulty was as I climbed, either I sank into it or it avalanched down and I made little progress. After a while, the coal pile was flattened out a good bit and I was able to feel the wall and I touched along the stonework to see what else lay there. It seemed important to me to find out what it was that I could see so faintly at the top of the wall to the store, but there was no obvious way to get there. As I moved along the wall, my knuckles clunked against another pipe. It was cast iron and appeared to run vertically from the ceiling down to the floor. It felt rough under my hands, like it had never been painted - it was maybe rusted - but when I pulled on it to see that it was secure it did not move, it was quite solid. The rough surface meant that it was easier to grip. I worked out that if I climbed up the pipe, I'd be able to reach whatever it was up there, close to the top wall of the store. It was dangerous but then what else was there left?

The first two times I failed to get any purchase with my boots and I slipped heavily off the pipe and half way down the coal pile. I cut my hands on the rough surface, drawing blood and making my hands slippery. I cursed myself, my life and all who had ever known me, but the third time, I managed to wedge the toe of my boot into the gap between the pipe and the wall. Eight minutes later, working in short, exhausting stages, I was at the top, where it remained gloomy but I could see that what I had been looking at was a wooden door or a hatch and there was a small amount of light leaking in around its edges. I pulled on the door and then pushed against it, but whilst there was some movement it seemed that it might be bolted or latched from the outside. I needed something with which to prise it open.

I thought for a moment but then realised there was nothing else for it other than to descend back to the bottom and find something that would provide the necessary leverage – and hope that I could get back up again. I descended the pipe, falling the last few feet, and I scrambled over the coal pile. I felt around the room to see if there was anything I might use. There was nothing beyond the coal shovel I'd found earlier. I wedged the shovel beneath my arm and dragged myself again to the top of the coal pile. I then gripped the pipe and one inch at a time, moved on up, the shovel still held by my armpit. I reached the top of the pipe and the weak strip of rectangular light.

I caught my breath whilst pondering how I'd manage to

hold onto the pipe and at the same time apply the shovel to the gap. Despairing of ever getting out of that place, hope deserting me, I ran my hand further up the pipe and to my astonishment, felt it turn at a ninety degree angle into the wall itself. At the underside of the turn, I found a sufficient gap to thread my arm through, beneath the pipe, and in doing so I was able to hook myself to the wall. I used my other arm to insert the shovel into the daylight gap, then wiggled it to and fro, repeatedly, in the hope that this small movement would tease out the securing screws.

Little happened at first but, sensing that this was my last chance, I pressed on. My other arm was taking all the weight and was agonizingly painful and tired. I was terrified that the shovel would break or bend and become of no further use, so I applied the leverage gently at first but soon realized that I was getting nowhere and was tiring fast. I had no choice but to apply further force and leverage and risk catastrophe. And then it began to rock. I could feel the hatch give just a little at first as it creaked under the pressure, and when it did so even more light seeped into the store. As the gap increased, I was able to grab a glimpse of the black hole in which I found myself. I resumed my work, pushed and pulled and as the opening widened I wedged the shovel further into the gap and continued with my effort.

How long this went on for, I do not know, but suddenly it was not the screws that came loose, it was the entire wood panel on the hatch that split with a resounding crack. I stopped all movement, suspended from the pipe, the shovel still in place. Seconds later, I still could hear no sound and I presumed therefore that I'd not been heard by my captors. I edged the shovel in again and pushed upwards, forcing the wood to give way and splinter. I pulled the shovel out and felt for the latch. It was in fact a metal bolt and I was able to lift one side and slide its length away from the hoop that secured it.

The hatch door opened and I could see that outside it was light. It looked to be early morning on a dull day but I could not be sure. What was clear to me was that the hatch I had broken through was the means by which coal could be dropped into the store from outside without the need to enter the house. It was also my escape route, but first I would have to detach myself from the iron pipe and at the same time haul myself, using all the strength I had left in my other arm, through the opening above my head. It was a task I would not have enjoyed contemplating when I was fit and sound, but there is something about fear that feeds motivation, and with little hesitation I made the leap, releasing my right arm and hanging from the lintel by my left. With two hands on the ledge I pulled myself up, squeezing myself through the narrow opening and stretching out, gulping the fresh air, flat on the grass beyond the hatch. I rolled onto my back and sucked in more of the clean air, caught my breath and then rose onto my knees.

I was at the back of the house. The light was coming up but it was still the very early part of the morning. There was a stretch of overgrown grass between where I lay and then there was the beginnings of a small wood, seemingly made up of spruce and birch, good cover for my escape. However, I noticed that to my right there was a small stone building, a kind of outhouse, and I decided to have a look. With my back pressed against the wall of the main house, I moved towards the building. Now I could see the roof was sagging and some of the slates had slipped. The two doors to the building were open and so I went inside.

Head tugging at a bag of hay, there was Master Henry in a makeshift stall. He appeared unconcerned by our predicament. I saw the saddle parked on the side panel of the stall; lying on the floor next to it was the bridle. I patted him on the neck and ruffled his dark mane; he snorted and chomped at the hay. I went back to the open gate and looked over to the house where I was glad to see nothing had stirred. I re-entered the stall and heaved the saddle onto Master Henry's back and then taking the bridle from the floor, slipped the bit between his teeth and the leather strap over his ears and the reins over his neck. I reached under his belly and gripped the loose end of the girth that I pulled and then buckled. I led Master Henry out of the building, along the stretch of grass behind the house, his hooves quiet in the soft earth. There was a small stretch of green scrubland between me and the trees that grew beyond. I knew that this was dangerous since I could be seen or heard from the house, but I had little alternative than to chance my luck. I had nothing to defend myself with – no rifle, no bullets and no weaponry of any sort. It was now or never. I moved at speed towards the wood, leading Master Henry by the reins. I made it across the grassy stretch and, once in amongst the trees, again I stopped to listen, to see if I heard any sound that might indicate the alarm had been raised. There was no movement, no sign of life, no hint that I had been seen and that they were onto me. I put my foot into the iron stirrup and pulled myself up onto Master Henry's back. I rode further into the woods, threading my way between the clusters of silver birch and the ubiquitous spruce and occasional rowan. I ached from head to toe, but the movement seemed to have loosened some of my stiffness and I swayed in the saddle with the rhythm of my horse. I knew that I would not have long before my absence was discovered. I had to move and I had to make quick progress. I kicked him on and Master Henry jolted forward as if he understood my impatience. I had a sense that the sun was positioned forward of my right shoulder, what little I could see of it. That was east by my calculation and east was where I was headed.

56

THE KINGFISHER

I gave Buckstone a wide berth and arrived back at Montrose a little under three hours later. It seemed to be about lunchtime and I was not aware that anyone had followed me. In the distance I could see Joseph Hume, his formidable presence in statue form, appearing strong, resolute, inspirational in the clear late morning light. Before I reached the statue I turned into the opening to my left side, arriving at the *Kingfisher* stable. Doug immediately stepped out and I could not miss the look of surprise upon his face when he saw me.

"Ah, Doug. Were you no' expectin' me?"

"No sir," he answered quietly. "To tell the truth, I was no' sure we'd see you again."

"Has anybody been asking after me?"

"No sir," he said. "Not that I know of."

"Got the saddlebags?"

"Yes sir."

"Looked inside yet?"

"Not my place to," he said.

"Sure about that?" I asked, as I dismounted.

"Yes."

I patted Master Henry on the neck and nuzzled my palm against his nose. His breath was still hot and blowing from the long ride. "Some water, some feed, some hay. Can you take care of that?"

"Of course. I can do that. Are you alright?" Doug asked, studying my face.

"I ran into some trouble in Buckstone."

"You've got blood on you. Is that coal as well?"

"Could be," I said.

"Can I get you something? Maybe you need to get that cut seen to."

"A bath?" I said. I'd forgotten that I must have looked an interesting sight: my face was blackened by coal dust and I was bruised, cut and bloodied by the heavy beatings. I looked down: my clothing was filthy and torn. "I'm going in," I said. "I'll certainly need a bath."

"You're back then," said the old man, eyes yellow and greasy.

"I'll stay a night, if you don't mind," I said.

He sucked his teeth. "Costs gone up a bit," he answered.

"Why's that?" I asked.

"Recent circumstances," he said. "Recent events up the road here. Recent events at Mr Weir's premises."

"Oh dear. Nothing serious I hope."

"Quite serious," he said.

" I still need a room. I want the front this time."

"It's extra for a room with a view," he said.

"A view of Joseph Hume?" I said.

"Take it or leave it," he said. Then he looked at me sympathetically. "I'll throw in a bath for nothing."

I took the deal that was being offered, not because I coveted the expanse of Joseph Hume's backside; rather more because it offered a clear view of the road into Montrose and for obvious reasons I wished to be the first to know of any new arrivals. Still, I told him that for that price I expected to have my clothes washed and pressed. He told me to leave them outside my door and Doug would collect them. "I'll have them fresh," he said. "All inclusive."

I said there would be a tip in it, if discretion was part of the service. "Don't worry," he said. "We dinnae clipe on our customers."

Once in my room, I stripped off and examined my beaten body. Cuts, bruises, maybe a broken rib. Maybe my nose was no' as straight as it was. The bath along the gloomy corridor was filled all of three inches with brown, tepid water that quickly turned black when I immersed myself. Later, Doug delivered a ham sandwich and a glass of warm beer to my room. He came back some time later with a small parcel that he laid on the end of my bed. "Your clothes are here."

"That was quick," I said. "Are they dry?"

"Not totally, but close enough."

I lay back against the bed end, feeling the sharp pain from my ribs as I did so. For once I was in the mood for talking. "Can I ask you something, Doug?"

"Aye."

"What d'you say about revenge?" I asked him. "Is it worthwhile? Do you think you should, take revenge I mean, if you've got cause?"

"I don't know what you mean," he said.

"Well, revenge," I repeated. "You know what I mean. When someone kicks you up the arse and you want to kick him back but twice as hard." There was a moment's silence.

"Doesn't seem much point to it," he answered.

"Why?"

"Cos he'll only kick your arse again and he'll mean it this time."

I laughed. "You might be right," I said. "But imagine the satisfaction of getting' in there first."

"Nobody's done me that much harm," he said. "There's no one I want to kill for it."

"Well, you're lucky," I said. As he was about to close the door, I shouted out to him: "Doug?"

"Aye?"

"Have my horse ready at five, will you?" I shut my eyes. "I'll have to get off early. And if you could pack the saddle-bags, I'd appreciate it. I'm no' sure when, or even if, I'll be back here again."

I heard the door click as he left. My eyes remained closed, but despite my tiredness the old mind was busy and would not lie down. I thought of Keira. That image of her in a white cotton gown would never escape me, belted at the waist just enough to tempt me to discover what lay beneath. Truth be told, things had already moved far beyond that temptation. That skin, so smooth, and those eyes twinkling like green ice in a heavy frost, framed by her long dark hair. I'd forgotten nothing, not a detail, not even the colour of the light as it filtered through the hall and across the tops of her shoulders. I thought we would make a fine pair now, with our blue, beaten faces. With my eyes still closed, I sensed her lips against mine and I breathed in the imaginary fragrance that was Keira. At which point, like a corpse sinking through deep water, I slipped into a heavy sleep.

57

RETURN TO BUCKSTONE

"Mr Logan? Mr Logan?" I was suddenly aware of being shaken violently. "Sir?" the voice said again, more urgently. "Mr Logan, sir! Wake up!" I winced as I became aware of the continuing physical pain brought about by my injuries.

"What is it?" I said groggily, for in my sleep I'd been far away. "Doug?"

"It is."

"What is it? What d'you want?"

"Downstairs!" he whispered. "Men looking for you! Asking questions!"

"Who?" I said.

"Not seen them before," he said. "Not round here."

"You sure they're after me?" I said.

"They're usin' your name."

"Okay."

"You've got to get out!" he said.

"Tall man with a beard?"

"Yes."

"One with a missing finger?"

"I cannae say."

I could see through the window that it was after dark. I must have fallen asleep for maybe five hours. "Master Henry?" I said, then realised I was in my undershorts. "Clothes?"

"In the parcel," he said. "You'd better be quick, they're downstairs now."

"Won't take them long to think of the stable," I said. I put some of the clothes on. They were damp against my skin.

"Horse is ready," he said. "But not in the stable."

Doug led me along the corridor and down by a back stair, passing through the kitchen at the rear and on towards a door that opened out to a small yard. I could see Master Henry was saddled and ready to go. "You did this?" I said.

"Best thing, I decided," Doug answered. "I thought get the horse ready and out of sight."

Doug opened up the large doorway onto the High Street.

"You did well," I said. "I'm in your debt."

"Where will you go?" he asked.

"Backwards," I said.

"Where's that?"

"Buckstone."

"They'll come after you, will they no'?"

"That's what I'm hopin'. Tell them that's where I've gone."

"What? But they'll follow you?"

"Let's hope so."

"Alright," Doug said. "If that's what you want." I swung myself up onto the horse. I heard a door slam and a man shout.

"Before you go," he said. "Can I ask you?"

"Fire away."

"The revenge you were talking about. Revenge for what?"

"Good question. I've asked myself a thousand times. Revenge for what?" Once, I would have had a ready answer: it was what I had built my life upon. It was what Aunt Marion had inspired me to look for. But what was it *for*? Correcting the balance so that life could resume? A means to restore proper functioning? "Revenge for taking life," I said after a long pause. "And it gives me life to think I can do something about it, that I dinnae just accept and move on."

I headed round the front of the building, quietly stepping away, down into the broken earth of the street, keeping close to the side and following the shadows, retracing my earlier route towards Buckstone. I was half naked in damp trousers and shirt, seated on my horse, armed with dynamite and some decent leather saddlebags. I shivered through the cold or because something awful was soon to happen for which I alone would be responsible.

58

MRS TRAYNOR

I rode into Buckstone with my eyes partially shut. Master Henry seemed to know the way. Along the old Braid Road, past the Pentland Cemetery, some yards further I came upon the small town itself. In the darkness, there was little light from the clustered, black-slated houses and there was no movement or sign of people in the street. I passed the shop *Domenico Corrolla* and was reminded of the reason for my raging headache. Closed now, not an Italian soul in sight.

Master Henry walked on through the length of Buckstone and we reached the other side with no acknowledgement of our presence. A while later and we came upon the house that had been the place of my incarceration and earlier beating. I sat there outside the open gate, shifting in my saddle. It was a clear night and, for that reason, a little cold but I could feel the heat from my horse beneath me. I'd travelled in darkness for three hours and twenty-four minutes and my eyes had long since adjusted to the gloom. I could see the house itself, beyond the gate, detached, alone, foreboding.

I eschewed the idea of a front door entry, having had only modest recent success at the Weir house fiasco. I entered quietly through the side door by the kitchen and I was gratified to find on the dresser by the door, four or five oil lamps, ready for use. I could smell the spermaceti oil burn as I lit the nearest of the lamps, and then edged my way into a small kitchen with grey-white plates piled by the window and plain cups hanging off hooks. The place looked tidy enough - almost like it was well looked after. I touched the kettle by the fire: it was still warm and there was hot ash in the grate and a large basket of dry wood close by. In the pale light, I made my way out of the kitchen, through to each of the other rooms on the ground floor. Every one of them was cloaked in darkness as I approached with the lamp, even the larger room where I'd enjoyed a long period in the bentwood Thonet rocker whilst serenaded by the pianist and his boot-happy, lanky friend. Upstairs was all peace too and I was content with the belief that there was nobody there to worry about; I knew the miscreants would be home all too soon. I guessed that I would have an hour over them. I had to get on with it. I had to be ready.

Having turned my back and begun a movement towards the stair, I heard a noise from behind a small door at the end of the corridor. I raised the barrel of my gun, one of two from my arsenal that bore no name but had a deadly pedigree. I felt the cold trigger against my finger as I moved the barrel towards the sound that I had heard. I came to the door and I strained to hear any other indication that someone else was present. I'd been foolish not to check each and every one of the four doors; I had imagined there would be nobody here, but for whatever reason, there was one I'd neglected to investigate. I heard something scrape. I put the two barrels of the gun to within an inch of the wood panel, holding the rosewood stock tight in the crease of my elbow. I gripped the oil lamp a little tighter in my left hand, then looked to either side of me, as if unsure that I was alone, and I listened hard for another sound from inside the door. I could feel, almost hear, my heartbeat thump a little faster. I raised my foot and aimed the heel of my boot hard against the door lock. The door took the force and instantly flew open and as it did so my anxious finger made firm contact on the trigger and before I knew it I had released both barrels.

Imagine my astonishment to find that not for the first time I had discharged my firearm and blown a hole at the headboard of another bed. This procedure had become a force of habit. These coincidences are no' meant to happen. Next to the bed was an old lady, dressed in a white gown, looking as if she had been interrupted whilst preparing herself for bed. She was mid-way drinking from a glass of water.

"Oh dear," was all she said as she looked wide-eyed from the hole in the headboard to the man who filled the door-way. She had a small lace nightcap on her head.

"Oh dear," I said. I moved a step further into the room. "Excuse the interruption, but who are you?" She hesitated and looked at me blankly. I had a suspicion but I continued to press her. "I'm asking, who are you?" I said a little louder. She didn't answer and I formed the view that she may have been very deaf. I knew the loneliness of that place when your senses have deserted you. Then, stranger and stranger: as I held out the light towards her it took a moment or two for it to dawn that I had seen her before. Yes, she was Traynor's mother, but I realised now who she really was, unadorned, unclothed, hatless, even before she opened her mouth.

"Audrey Traynor," she said finally. "At least I think I'm Audrey Traynor. Sometimes I'm not very sure. Who do you think I am?" I remembered an old lady (even then she was an old lady, at least she was to a young boy). "You'll have to forgive me. I don't hear too well." I looked at her again. "Do I know you?" she asked.

Most of all, I remembered the yellow dress and the big, flat, crinoline hat with the goose feathers; not to mention the questions about The *New England Primer* and the challenge to my intelligence when I had failed to answer her questions.

"Why do you stare at me like that?" she said, bringing me back to the present. "Well, come in then. Or are you planning to just gawp in the doorway?" She made me feel just as she had, all those years ago in Mr Fawcett's shop, with my nails clutched in a bag.

"You're gonnie be useful," I said.

"Am I?"

"Of course you are."

59

DOUG'S ORDEAL

Meanwhile, in Montrose, Doug was learning to swim. The visitors from Buckstone held his head in the water trough for longer than good sense permits. When they pulled him from the cold water, he gasped and wheezed. He felt as if he had swallowed a small sea loch.

"I know you dinnae want to answer the question," said Mr Traynor, phlegm smeared at the side of his mouth. "But we've passed that point now, do you no' think?"

Doug was tempted to agree, but still he said nothing. "Time for another dip," said Jesse.

Doug took a deep breath. His stubbornness was made easier by Traynor's wretched fatness. The sight of this man was enough to make you wish your head was still in the trough.

Almost as if he had read Doug's mind, Traynor said wearily, "Let's try again, in your own time, where'd he go?"

"I cannae say," said Doug, still breathing heavily. He knew he would tell them in the end, after all that was what he was meant to do. He had been *told* to do so. It was a matter of picking the right time. They'd found fresh dung in the stable and no horse in sight, so they quickly had him bent over the trough, throwing questions at him. By 'they,' young Doug would have described a lanky bloke with a wild beard and angry eyes; a small man who he now noticed did indeed have a sub-optimal complement of fingers, who carried about him a stink of stale sweat; and a fat man, with thin, wispy hair of an indeterminate colour. The easiest thing would be to speak now. Doug knew that too, but he was stubborn and he had a sense of pride in a job well done.

Just before they ducked him in the water again, Billy threw a punch at Doug's midriff. He gasped before going under and they held him longer this time, long enough for him to feel that if they persisted he'd breathe in the water just for the relief. When they pulled him out again, he wheezed and spluttered and, his pride satisfied, he was ready to speak. The water was streaming down his face. "Buckstone!" he said. He caught his breath again. "Buckstone - what he said! Got on... horse! Took off on road - Buckstone! Buckstone!"

Mr Traynor was unsure. "Buckstone?" he said. "Why did you no' tell us that before?"

"He... he told me not to."

"Why the fuck would he go to Buckstone?" None of it made any sense to Traynor. Why would the man flee from Buckstone and now choose to return there?

"He... didn't... say," said Doug.

"You sure about that? Buckstone?" said the lanky man.

"Yes! Buckstone!"

"If you're lying," he said, his beard close to Doug's ear. "I can kill you now or I can come back later."

"Mama," Traynor muttered. "Fuckin' Mama!"

The three men ran out of the building, but by that time

somebody had loosened the reins on the pianist's horse. Not just his horse but the horse-drawn cart too. They were in the field at the end of the village grazing against the hedgerow. Eventually, the three men had recovered the horse and dragged the cart out of the mud, but by then a lot of time had elapsed. Montrose was fast becoming a nightmare.

Doug was toweling down with a horse blanket in the lobby and the old man was enjoying a small whisky in the bar, when they and a few remaining customers, moved en masse to the window, to witness the departure of the trio. The three men galloped down the road past the pub, in a direction that took them away from Montrose. There was a loud cheer from inside the smoke-filled room as Traynor and the other two pulled past the window, eyes fixed on the road ahead.

60

THE TRAYNOR GANG

I n Traynor's own eyes, not all they said of him was true. Yes, he was cruel, vindictive, took things that did not belong, kicked the dog, broke things, hit things, hurt his mama by being so much less than his father and never read poetry or even Dostoyevsky's *Crime and Punishment*. Yes, he did prostitutes or they did him and he ate more bad food than was good for a man with regular stomach cramps. All that was true, but to Traynor's eyes, there were two sides to everything. We live in a three-dimensional world, he thought, without irony. Not everything comes in flat, uncomplicated shades of black or white.

Yes, he would admit freely to himself that he took liberties with a woman, any woman; it was not pretty, he drank too much, he lost control, he was angry and yes, he had always taken great liberties. Strangely, in that moment he had become someone else and to a degree surely that absolved him of some responsibility? He would admit he ruined another man's life. He hadn't been the first. He'd no hesitation in saying that he'd felt some real shame and it never left him until... well, for some time. Nevertheless, guilt and shame were awkward concepts. He'd killed a man in a fight with an ash-can and a brick and an iron bar and it was true that as a rule he chose to steal rather than work. But shame? Not really. He saw no reason why another man should hold onto his possessions just because he had toiled long and hard to acquire them. Traynor was going to work fast with minimum effort to help him unacquire them. To obey the smooth operation of market forces means to take what you want when you want.

Traynor wiped his nose, his eyes dead ahead. He recognized that he was a fat man with short arms, no cultural preferences, and a lot of grey-black hair on his back and shoulders that did not sit comfortably with the thin, colourless lines on his head. All this was true and unarguable. He was self-aware. He reflected on the clarity of his introspection as he rode back to Buckstone to find this man Logan who was going about being an almighty fuckin' nuisance, all over something that happened a shitload of years ago. Traynor believed that if you put a body in the ground it should stay there. If a dog digs it up, you have to kill the dog too, and that was what he would do to Logan. He would kill the fuckin' dog.

Traynor looked across at the piano man, cantering steadily to his left. Not the first musician to lose a finger and yet Jesse could play most tunes you threw at him. Like Traynor, he had spun a kind of life according to his own moral code, even when it fucked up other peoples' lives. He could've played a different tune, been a proper musician. He killed people instead and never got the chance to enhance his skill on the piano.

To Traynor's right, teeth set against the cold, eyes flashing with his usual anger, the skin stretched tight across the bones, lanky-limbed almost to the ground, Billy Keefe, a man he had known all his life, a rapist, bigamist, sadist, thief, tobacco-smoking killer. Not everything was good about Billy Keefe: his breath would bleed the skin of a creosoted post and his fingernails were grubby as carrots in the field. Yet, at least to Traynor's mind, he was in fine company, the kind of company that demanded respect on pain of death.

Traynor plumped his lips and blinked. He considered their present predicament in the round. He accepted that between them they had cumulatively done bad things. In such circumstances, who could blame a man for seeking retribution? Yet, he considered it a harsh judgment to conclude that they were all bad as human beings. He repeated his own recognition of himself as a man who took liberties, he could not deny the truth of that. Yet, he had refused to take a wife so that he could look after his dear mama. She had always enjoyed his total devotion ever since his father died. Even during that illness that nearly killed her. She had smallpox - blisters everywhere, down her throat, up her throat, choking her to death. But he kept mama alive through that. He had diphtheria himself as a boy, so he knew how to cope with sickness. They had a house together, he made it nice for her, right down to the white and red rose curtains. Her head was with the fairies but he took care of her. She'd had her disappointments. He never married and never had children and she wanted grandchildren. That ship had sailed. He fucked whores if he had the desire. He took serious liberties with his women and with other people's lives.

Jesse was cut from a different cloth. Jesse had a wife and child, and he lived a very different life from Traynor – or so Traynor thought because it was often unwise to enquire. Jesse's wife was from Alloa but you'd never know and again it was best not to ask. She was able to play the piano herself. Jesse was teaching his son, Alex, to play; sometimes he wondered who had the missing finger. Jesse had some sheep and hens, was not averse to honest work, but honest work never kept out the draughts or filled his pockets, so he was always involved in Traynor's capers. Jesse had become his right hand man and he was trusted to kill people for him, should that become necessary. And often it was.

Billy on the other hand did not have a cultured dimple in his body. He had three wives but had lost touch with the first two. Each of them thought they were the first, but they soon learned from Billy that they were just passing through. As for coming first, it was pretty clear in Billy's eyes that only Billy could ever come first. He married Shona because she had an infectious smile that made even he, Billy Keefe, the wild man, feel that he could be a million times better than he was. Shona made the mistake of spreading her smiles too widely and Billy didnae like that. One day she was found bobbing some way below the spring high tide. Strange thing, but her head had been shaved. Other than the alopecia, there was no evidence anything untoward had occurred. The second wife was pretty too, but soon they fought, they drank, she lost her looks, and he beat her with his rifle strap. So hard, she lived three years with 'Made in Great Britain' tattooed on her cheek – or so Billy said.

It was hard to remember now, thought Traynor, but like the first wife, she disappeared and nobody asked Billy where she had gone because questions like that were unlikely to be good for one's health. He was no' scared of Billy but he knew when to look away. There was evidence that Billy's third wife was still alive but then again, would you put your life on it? Traynor knew nothing about her, other than that she had tried to commit suicide after being delivered of her third child in under three years. Her mother and father-in-law had moved into one of the cottages immediately adjacent to Billy's house. The father-in-law appeared to have some personal issues with Billy but was wise enough to keep his grievances private. He drank a lot of grey-sweet cider but he was a drunk who surrendered peacefully rather than fight the world. Still, the local police sergeant had been called in more than once to defuse arguments between Billy's wife and her family. Traynor did not understand Billy to have taken any part in the family disputes and, with the local police sergeant involved, it was just as well. Before long, Mrs Billy Keefe was drinking her husband's beer and some said she went from sobriety to notoriety quicker than a Scottish summer. Traynor had once said that it was to Billy's credit that his three children were never left to starve, they always had a roof over their heads and had a wider than usual network of family support; it was also quite likely that they would grow up to be every bit as cruel, bullying and vindictive as their father.

The one thing Traynor was not too stupid to recognize was that for the three of them their destiny, their lives, their purpose and their survival had all been shaped and forged by that one event at Salmon Cottage, so many years ago. It was their turning point, their life-changer and every step that followed fell in the shadow of that event.

It was well after ten o' clock at night when the three men slowed their horses as they passed through Buckstone. It had been a long, hard hack through the cold, evening darkness. They were tired, sore and aggressively sober. They did not share words as they passed the shopfront of *Domenico Corolla* and they did not discuss what they planned to do when they got to the house. That depended in no small part on what they found there.

"We should be careful when we go in," said Jesse. "We dinnae ken much about this fella."

"We ken he's on his own," said Billy. "Three against one is decent odds."

"Jesse's right, Billy," said Traynor. "We need to take a little care. He slipped away last time, you remember." They did not much wish to remember. Logan was unconscious, nearer dead than living. It never occurred to any of them that he would be able to get out of that coal cellar. They had locked people in there before, days at a time. No trouble. They once had an old fool die in there. No problem, leastways no problem till this time.

Traynor was quiet as they moved through the village and emerged on the other side, following the road, ten minutes from home he guessed, but he was worried about his mama. He left her in the house alone because when they discovered that shit Logan had escaped, they had to get after him and there was no time for tea and Dundee shortbread with mama. He did not like to leave her on her own. She was confused these days. She did not seem to share the same points of reference. She wandered in and out of rooms, stumbling into his business dealings, interrupting orders he had given and generally getting in the way. She didnae seem to know what was going on. Conversations with her were on a two minute loop – things she spoke of at the beginning of the loop were repeated again at the end of the loop. Life did not progress, it just ticked on in endless two minute replays. They say the memory of a goldfish is just ten seconds. Traynor had heard it from a man in a bar and he did not understand how anyone could ever know this. If true, it was a bit like reincarnation six times a minute. Mama had much in common with the goldfish, only her reincarnation was every two minutes.

They arrived at the bend in the road, close to where the track ran in a muddy thread down to the house. You could see the clear outline of it from where they stood, even in the darkness. To the left was a dark copse, full of spruce and birch, ready to cut and lay down for the fires. The wood stretched back over a mile and Traynor expected some of it to provide him with basic necessities over the next twenty years. The more extravagant and unusual expenses, of course, had to be paid for by crime but in the future he planned less crime, more trees. Next to the copse was the house itself and a small spread of green to the side, more grass to the front, trees, shrubs, wild growth nobody ever trimmed back. It was a beautiful house and he had lived here most of his life; he intended to die here. Not today, of course. Then he noticed, with some alarm, that the front door was open and from where they were positioned they could see the light spill out from the hall onto the front step.

"What the hell?" said Traynor. "What is this?" He took off his hat and scratched his scalp through the thin hair. "What's he doing?" To Traynor, a lamp burning in the hall and the door wide open, did not bode well.

"This Logan," said Billy, towering in the darkness. "We finish the job this time?"

"We do," said Traynor.

"Old wounds," said Jesse, thinking aloud.

"He could have licked his wounds, Jesse. Nobody asked him here."

"I never said we did."

"Think he's in there?" said Billy, sounding anxious.

"Does a dog shit? Course he is."

"Are we going?" asked Jesse. "Or are we gonnie have a game of rounders and chat about it all day?"

"Billy?" said Traynor. "Work your way round the back.

Jesse and I'll go in the front door." Billy climbed down from the cart and pulled the handgun from his pocket. "Remember Mama's in there. Be careful what you aim at. I dinnae want bullets flying around the place, her getting hurt and so on." Billy moved off towards the copse. Traynor and Jesse stood side by side; they clicked the firing caps of their guns and then moved forward together towards the house. In a second, all three had melted silently into the darkness.

61

MIRRORS

I n 1856 Karl August von Steinheil and Léon Foucault discovered the process of depositing a thin layer of silver on the front surface of a piece of glass, thereby heralding the first optical quality mirrors. Either Traynor was a very vain man or he was simply a man at the forefront of scientific discovery and development, but he had a number of highly polished mirrors distributed around the house. I took two wood-framed mirrors off the wall in the living room. I upended a Georgian full-length *cheval* dressing mirror from the draped window in the bedroom. I set them up in the front room, the scene of my recent beating. I'd a growing trepidation, a feeling this could all be a mistake but in the end I figured that Traynor was a man who liked to use his own front door; he was no' going to mess around with the side entrance. He would be straight in, all barrels blazing. Well, there was some retribution in just that small victory, even if nothing else came off.

I dragged one chair into the hall and I positioned it adjacent to the door to the living room. I adjusted, sat down, got up, readjusted, and so on. Precision is always important. I steered Mrs Traynor towards the chair in the hall and placed an oil lamp on each of the two tables nearest the chair. I said to her she must sit in it and she must not move.

"Now?" she said.

"If you wouldnae mind."

"Why mustn't I move?" she asked indignantly. "Why shouldn't I move?"

"Your son is coming home tonight," I said. "He wants to see you there in that chair."

"Where's he gone?" she said. "I didn't know he'd gone anywhere."

"Montrose," I said.

"Does he live there?" she asked.

"He lives here."

"Here? Are you sure about that?" She looked away. "My memory is so awful. Where's here?"

"Your home, Mrs Traynor, and he's coming home too. Let's focus on that for now."

"I see," she said.

"He wants to come up the track and find you. It's very important that he finds you here, sittin' in this chair."

"I see," she said again.

"So once you're in the chair, that's it."

"That's it?" she said.

"Yes."

"What do we do?"

"I'll tell you when you're in the chair," I said.

She sat down in the chair and looked as if she was waiting for her photograph to be taken. I laid a blanket across her knees. "Where will you be?"

"I'll be in the living room," I smiled back at her.

"Who are you?"

"I'm Sean Logan."

"I see," she said. "Where are you going now?"

"I've got things to do?"

"I see. And I just sit here?"

"That's the idea," I said.

Before going down to the basement, I stoked up the fire in the kitchen with a steel poker, threw on some dry wood and pulled the big cauldron off the table and hung it over the fire. It had a good draught and it soon caught. I stood there for several minutes, looking into the flames and watching them flicker, build, redden and glow. Before I left the room I put my hand against the metal rim, pleased to find it was already warm to the touch. I went out into the hall and found the door down to the basement. I took the steps quickly and came across the open entrance to a room that was familiar to me. I could smell the spermaceti before I saw it. This time I had light and I could see there was a good quantity of the stuff. What other substance would allow you to light a lamp or a candle or allow itself to be turned into a bar of soap? Just a pity you had to mince a sperm whale's head to get some. I filled a small bucket with spermaceti, took it up to the kitchen and tipped it into the cauldron. I repeated the trip six times and the level in the cauldron was up to within an inch of the top. The heat was rising off the fire as the flames gripped hold of the logs and licked the base of the cauldron. The spermaceti began to melt. My only concern was that it would all happen far too late.

I went out to the back where Master Henry was standing motionless, like he wanted nothing to do with me. He had hay but he needed water. I grabbed a bucket and stepped out to the water trough. I was about to submerge it when I took two quick steps back and almost yelled with shock, like I'd seen a ghost. Something came out of my throat, I cannae say what. I could feel an urge to retch, pushing up inside me. In the water, his nose just proud of the surface, knees bobbing stiffly, lay Mad Bob, dead as stone, offal-cutting days buried forever. At least, I thought it *may* have been Mad Bob. The fact was I'd never seen the man – I'd only seen the back of him as he hared off on a pit pony. Whoever it was, he'd been in the water awhile, and dead too, so his colour was off. If he'd any colour it was blue but it may have been a trick of the light.

My farm existence had perhaps desensitised me to the more gruesome aspects of life and death; very quickly I had recovered my composure and I was able to drag the body out of the water. It sat their stiffly leaning like a thick plank against the trough; rigor mortis had set in and it was difficult to bend the body but it was not impossible. With a little effort I figured I could bend the legs. I knew that rigor mortis was at its peak between twelve and twenty-four hours post-death then it dissipated. That meant this man had probably died less than twelve hours ago or more than twenty-four hours ago. I ripped open his shirt and stared down at his belly. I was in no doubt now that this was Mad Bob, the man who stole a good part of my life. Yet, looking down on his blueness, his face contorted by the desperation of his final moments, I felt nothing for him now, not even anger. I was too late. He was gone.

I recovered my composure and went back to Master Henry who still had no water. This time I filled the bucket from the trough and he gulped at the water without too much concern about its overall quality or provenance and unperturbed by the presence of Mad Bob. I took the saddle-bags off his back, which I had the strong sense was likely to endear me to him, and then dragged them over my shoulder and into the side door of the house. The bags were heavy and by the time I had hauled them upstairs I was sweating; my shirt was damp from perspiration and trough water. My head was pounding like a hammer against stone. I carefully removed the pasted dynamite sticks. I plugged a blasting-cap into the end of the furthest stick and neatly trailed a fuse to the living room. I repeated the process and positioned the dynamite sticks, smoothly wrapped in their waxed paper, in the position I had chosen for maximum effect.

At this stage of my preparations, I no longer questioned what I was doing. I was set upon a designated course: if you followed the trail no doubt it would lead back to a time before I could walk. There was no more likelihood of me letting go now than there was of the moon landing in the front garden here at Buckstone. As I worked, Mrs Traynor sat upon the hall chair and studied my passing movements with an air of expectant curiosity, as if telling me she knew exactly what I was up to, but did not wish to discuss any aspect of it. She eyed the door, clearly remembering that I'd said *something* about her son's imminent return. I was sure she would have no memory of how long she'd sat there or for how long she would sit there. She only knew she had a reason to be there. When I dragged Mad Bob into the house, she turned in her chair towards me.

"Who is that?" she said.

"I thought you would recognise him."

"Now wait a minute," she said. "Is that Bobby Weir? I remember the face. Has he been drinking?

"Mainly water," I said.

"Has he been swimming?"

"You could say that."

Before I'd finished running the fusewire out of the upstairs window, she said that she was feeling the cold and was it absolutely necessary to have the front door open. I gave her a second blanket from the bedroom that she took reluctantly, as if it might host an unpleasant infection, and then spread it neatly across her knees. I smashed the downstairs window and fed the wire through.

I went back to the kitchen to check the cauldron. The heat off the fire was working the spermaceti into a heavy liquid. I took a stick from the fireside and poked it into the mixture. As I stirred, the odour rose off the liquid and clung to the air about me. Five minutes later, the spermaceti was the consistency of clear soup. I had searched the cluttered kitchen, the stable and a storeroom at the back of the house and had managed to find half a dozen buckets or pots of various sizes. I filled each of them and took the individual receptacles to their designated places, the sharp, unpleasant aroma now permeating all corners of the building, upstairs and downstairs. I looked out of the upstairs window. Maybe they were out there, biding their time. Let them come, I thought, but no' just yet. I checked my pocket for the phosphorus matches, a small comb that I scraped with the tips of my fingers, and then made my way downstairs, past Mrs Traynor, still seated on the hall chair.

"What do we do now?" she asked.

"We wait."

"Who are we waiting for?" she said, her eyebrows arched.

"Your son."

"Oh yes."

"When he arrives he'll ask for me."

"Will he?"

"Yes. Tell him I'm upstairs."

"I see," she said. "Is this a game or something?"

"Yes," I said. "It's a game. It's a very serious game. Just tell him Logan is upstairs."

"Is Logan your name?"

"Sean Logan," I said. "I'm very pleased to meet you again."

62

SALMON COTTAGE (3)

T raynor and Jesse moved slowly towards the front of the house while Billy took the covered route through the copse. It was a clear night, stars bright in the sky as far as the eye could see, but it was dark enough to hide them from sight as they approached. They moved slowly, taking care to ensure that Billy had sufficient time to travel the extra distance to the side door. Traynor stood in the grounds of his own house, unseen and unheard.

On the journey back from Montrose he had had time to think some more about all this; time to think over what it was that he was coming back to face. In particular, he was thinking about those events that had coloured his life and led him to this point. In some ways, he considered that everybody was a victim, one way or the other. Every damn one of us. Even the perpetrator can be a victim because when events take hold they dictate the future. The dumb idiot who could not keep his trousers buttoned, he has to be a victim too. This thing happened and it changed every-thing. The conversation he had had in his head earlier kept repeating itself. Yes, he did that thing. Yes, he took that liberty. So what? Move on with it. Then again, he knew there was a word for it and he shied at using that word. Was he scared of a word? It's just a word, he told himself. Yes, he should have known better. Maybe he should have had a father to tell him what was right and wrong, instead of always thinking for himself and always making the wrong choices. He was a victim too, because something changed in him, and for him, that day. They all changed that day. They all became something they had never been. They all did something they had never done. They lost their humanity and they never got it back again, not properly. The whole shit train came off the tracks. Yes, guilty, but there was something that led to all this. Traynor could still smell the gypsy, that perfume permeating so deep into his soul he could remember it today like it was fresh off the petal. Above her on the kitchen table, yes, but did she no' start it? She took the wrong turn when she shot Mad Bob. That was what they call an *escalation*. Still, God knows the little creep deserved it. That was someone who'd be nae trouble to anybody from now on. He'd proved to be a poor swimmer. As for the woman, it was nobody's fault she'd taken the wrong turn. The situation had been inflammatory but she did nothing to take out the heat. Between them, they could have talked the situation down, but she chose to light a match instead and she started a conflagration. She set in train a series of events and they were all stuck with the consequences. Yes, he was on the table and yes, he was on her. Yes, he remembered her skin, a sheet of pale silk, already prophetically corpse-like, a face that had seen too little sun in this northern climate. He had bitten on his lip, bloodless and dry as he moved against her.

He had been a big man, even then, how many years ago? Twenty? Twenty-five? Did anyone care? Clearly this guy did.

Traynor remembered, he had been heavy even then. Heavy on his knees, he could feel the wood off the kitchen table. It was like yesterday. Her skirt was off by then. Somewhere crushed, discarded on the floor. There was a jagged line of sweat off his temples like tiny, liquid jewels, glistening in the yellowing light. It had never been a solitary effort. She had no more strength to kick than say a prayer. Poor girl, you could feel sorry for her. He could see her lips were cut and bruised. They should have stopped. How could they? When she started shouting, one man with a flat, wool hat on his head had stuffed a rag into her mouth. It must have tasted of linseed oil and grit and stale sweat and Mad Bob's blood. She retched. Traynor was annoyed that Billy did that. Her anger told him she was alive. They should have stopped if they knew right from wrong. Traynor pictured himself. He kept on. He did not hear much or see much. He just kept on. Jesse was humming a tune. Traynor knew it was Jesse because he was holding the woman's arm and he could see the missing finger. He wondered if you could actually *see* a missing finger. It didnae make sense.

Jesse nudged him and raised an eyebrow. "Are we movin' or what?" he whispered.

Traynor interrupted his thoughts by glancing at the silver fob hung on a short chain off his waistcoat pocket. It had belonged to his father. He could not clearly see the face of the clock but he was sure it was after nine. He had always worn this fob and chain. He hated his father but always wore the old man's fob and chain. It was another of the contradictions that he lived with. Even that night at Salmon Cottage he had it tucked in his waistcoat pocket. Traynor remembered Jesse still humming. Jesse did not stop humming until Traynor was done. The husband lay out there on the porch, clubbed half to death. He might've been better dead than rotting his life away in a cell. At his side, Mercer lay sliced like a fish. Later, when the dust had settled, Traynor had got Mercer's pigs - they were no use to him dead. The woman never gave up, of course. Eastern blood, thought Traynor. Kept fighting she did. There was real blood by this time, red and sticky. She must have thought she would drown in it as the bright light, the shiny sparks, exploded behind her eyes. To die, drowning in your own blood.

"Give him another second, Jesse. No point in bein' early."

Traynor had not been totally happy when Billy broke her jaw; by doing so, Billy had diminished Traynor's pleasure. Her eyes had flickered and he knew then she would probably die. The strange thing is that the desire left him altogether, so what was the point. What was the point of any of this? He'd climbed off the table and fumbled with his buttons. He knew the other guys knew.

He didn't properly know she was pregnant till it started. It simply did not register she was close to full term. Was that why he lost his desire? He would never know. When it came down to it she'd rendered him impotent. She'd stolen his sexual desire, had embarrassed him and stripped him of self-worth. She'd made him look a fool, weak, impotent. The wind outside the door had risen and the draught had squealed through the house as it died. At that moment, the tall man, Billy Keefe, had climbed onto the woman as Traynor had slipped out the door.

Traynor and Jesse moved forward several paces. They were close enough now to see that the large door to the house was wide open. He could see bright light and he thought he could see his mother, seated with a blanket pulled across her legs. As he approached the door, she looked at him and he looked at her. He launched himself through the door and noticed nothing unusual, other than the stink. The place was rank with spermaceti oil.

"Mama?" he said. "Why the hell are you sitting there?"

"Upstairs," she said. "He wants to see you. I can't quite remember his name."

63

WAITING FOR TRAYNOR

How often do you get caught in rain whilst the sun is still shining? It's not so unusual. How often do the best things happen after you're dead? If you've ever heard the sound of a baby's first cry, it can make a flint wall squeeze out a tear. There's joy at the long awaited delivery and, with it, the blind optimism of what lies ahead. What you hear is the reassuring sound of roots going down and spring buds forming. Plugs in the golden earth. As if someone reset the old Whitelaw clock, with its fish scale frets and cornucopia drop handles, and time was allowed to begin again. A birth confirms that there's a future and even if we're no' there to enjoy it ourselves, we've left something that will survive and resonate with a beating heart as strong as a ticking clock, long after the white orchids on our graves have withered and powdered away. Birth is the nearest we get to immortality.

As I sat there, I knew that the phosphor of conflagration was just a heartbeat away. Out there were the men who would seek to end my life with the same violence with which they witnessed my beginning. I recognized who I was. I was Horatio's son. I was born the son of Tatiana, a chance coupling risen out of a squat called Romania. I thought now of the fact that I came into this world on the same rising sun that saw her depart. I'd shared my first breath with my mother's last. Where was her revenge for the life they'd stolen? Where was the justice for stealing not just her life but mine too? Was this it?

As Traynor and his men drew closer, I sat in the chair to one end of the living room, the pieces osmosing and melting into place. After the men had gone, my father, Horatio, the man who walked from Afghanistan, had lain there on the farm porch, long after creeping darkness had spilled its tendrils across the bloody scene. His head in a kaleidoscopic whirl, his tongue thick with blood and his thoughts groggy, like a boxer drifting in and out of consciousness, feeling blindly for his opponent. He may have met the Iranian Pashtun woman in his galloping dreams. Did he see again the woman who fed him all the healing weeds she had beaten by laying a spoon against his tongue. Did he hear the whine of the Tik-tik fly seconds before it bit his penis? Did he see a horse with no head, just blood spurting through a wound like an open pipe? He had tasted his own blood or somebody's blood and it had zipped on his tongue like metal. Eventually, Horatio was stirred by the scrape of the front door, caught by a breeze, banging, banging, repeatedly against the jamb. He was unsure in the half-light where he was and his sight was still blurred, as if grease had been smeared across his eyes. The door had slipped in and out of focus. How long had he lain there on the ground? It was impossible to know. Maybe he awoke, looked up, and saw Mercer there with his gaping back, stiff in death and the cool of night.

My thoughts shifted. They would be here soon. It would

be settled. But moons past, Mercer lay dead and no doubt my father would wake to see the movement of bugs as they began to hover and dig plots in the wound. Through this curious befuddlement, his recollection would have pieced itself together. He would have called out her name and his voice would have been met by a horrible silence.

Later, my father would have clumsily climbed to his feet and he would have noticed he had no boots. Walking with a sideways, crouching motion towards the house, the door still swinging and snapping in the breeze. Blood down the outside wall where it looked as if a body might have slid like the wipe of a wet sponge. Would he have pictured a man with a hole in his belly? His hand on the door handle, he would have entered the house. My mother, Tatiana, lying broken on the wooden floor, on her side, a shadow behind the kitchen table. Her face swollen, puffy and beaten into shades of darkness. As if looking at her through a cobalt, blue pigment glass. Her front tooth broken, split half way up, blood caked down one side of her face, a dry run from her nose along the side of her mouth. Her gums coated poppy red, I could easily imagine, and her tongue lolling like a sunflower from side to side. I could imagine her jaw, grey and twisted, and the top teeth no longer matching the bottom. Her black, aubergine hair matted and sticky. Was her arm broken? Or her leg? Her left leg would look wrong. Was she still alive? Yes, she was alive and my father, broken-hearted, would have found a cup and trickled water between her lips. Did she cough hard on the first dribble? She would have shivered in his arms as he cradled her; a stiff kind of shaking that would appear to come from the shoulders up. Her eyelids, thick as gorging leeches, would never open, would never see the light again. Did he hold her in his arms? Did she tremble and shake right to the end?

Her breath would have whistled inside her lungs and he would have sensed she and her life were departing.

As I sat close by the window, consumed by the sweep of total blackness, the curtain slightly billowed by the breeze, that much was understood by me. The worst thing was knowing so little. In the hall I heard Traynor speak, an echo of gruff hostility, and then I heard the creak as he placed his boot on the stair.

64

THE INSIDE OF A WHALE'S HEAD

Traynor did not like to leave his mama there in the hall. It seemed wrong; she looked pale and old, like a child lost in the woods. Jesse stood behind him, his gun cocked and his good finger light on the trigger. He looked at Traynor's mother but did not acknowledge her: the woman was a fruitcake. Traynor put his leather boot on the stair and heard it creak beneath his weight. He raised the gun above his head and edged on up to the next step, and then the next. He would shoot holes in the fool. He had every justification. Logan was in his house and he had no recollection of having issued an invitation to the bastard.

Upstairs, the bedroom door was ajar. There was an oil lamp on the corner table that spilled light across the darkened room. Through the gap between the door and the upright jamb, Traynor could see a figure seated in the high chair by the window. He looked at Jesse and moved his head close to the door. They took up positions on either side of each other and Traynor leaned in to take a look. They could see the figure seated by the window. He was smoking a cigarette, probably one of Traynor's, stolen from the desk drawer downstairs, the smoke curling up above his head. He was looking out into the blackness, hoping to see Traynor and his men arrive. Well, they'd arrived alright, thought Traynor, and they were no' in much of a mood for taking prisoners.

"You'd better stop right there, Logan," he said, stepping further into the room with a lightness of foot unusual in such a big man. "Dinnae do anything stupid. I've been using this gun a long time, so I'm pretty good with it." Traynor edged his way deeper across the bare floor of the room, his gun aimed at the back of the chair. He was taking no chances. There was six feet between him and Jesse who stood back and to the side. Both had their eyes trained on the smoking figure in the chair.

"Better raise your arms, Logan," Jesse said. "Nice and slowly, if you would."

The man in the chair continued to smoke. He wore a hat and he stared out of the window, his head set back on his shoulders as if lightly laughing at what he was seeing. He stared out as if all he wanted was to be somewhere out there. Traynor considered that with two guns aimed at your head, you could be forgiven for wishing you were somewhere else. He wanted to wrap up this business now. He'd had a long ride, chasing this Logan bastard all the way to Montrose and back again and he was angry and tired. They'd locked Logan in the coal cellar after Billy had shown him generous hospitality with the boot leather. The bastard had escaped, God only knew how, like some fuckin' bird or wall lizard, out through the top. Well, the bird was home now and he'd made his last flight. Logan had broken into his house, had disturbed mama and no doubt helped himself to food in the kitchen and cigarettes from the desk in the living room. He may have had his hands on the wine too. It was time to close him down and put an end to the past. If it was revenge he was after he would learn that revenge was a very dangerous aspiration.

"Are you deaf? I said, put your arms in the air!" He sat there, motionless, and showed no intention of raising his arms. Traynor waved his gun at him again. "Put your fuckin' hands in the air, like I say, and turn around!"

At that point, Jesse, a man of lesser patience, took the view he had waited long enough already. The middle finger of his right hand squeezed the trigger and the gun released two bullets in voluble quick succession. They struck him in the back of the neck, one bullet passing straight through the chair itself. He rolled to one side as if he was about to be sick down the arm.

"What the fuck are you doin', Jesse? Did I *say* shoot him?"

Jesse lowered the gun to his side. "Quit stressin', will you? He broke into your house for fuck's sake! You're entitled to shoot him!"

"Mebbe," said Traynor, "but I had things to say." He stepped forward and pulled the hat off the dead man's head. He leaned down and looked closely at the figure in the chair. "Holy fuck!" he said, at which point the spark of fuse wire caught his peripheral vision, as it snaked its light through the broken window pane, down the wooden panel and into a treble row of brown-wrapped sticks in grease paper. The dynamite was positioned inside a small box of wood logs taken from the fireplace, on top of which sat a large bucket.

Traynor did not have the time to ascertain what was in the bucket. He did not see the other buckets dotted around the room, filled to the brim with spermaceti. Now that he thought about it, what the fuck was that smell? He did not have time to turn away from the full blast of the dynamite. He did not have time to tell Jesse what he had seen when he took the hat off the dead man, that the face of the guy he'd shot was none other than Mad Bob – which was impossible since Mad Bob had been put out of his misery earlier. In an unfortunate swimming accident. Jesse had just shot a dead man. It made little sense. Although Jesse did not learn this unexpected detail, he was nevertheless quicker on the turn and was halfway to the door when the explosion came. As is sometimes the way with these things, the reverberations from the exploding dynamite and the detonated bucket of spermaceti had different effects on the two men still alive in that room. For Jesse, he was halfway to the door when the force hit him, ripping off his left leg somewhere round about the groove between the groin and the thigh, and in the luminous flash of the explosion he was able to watch the leg as it flew over his head, entirely separated from his body. He watched it land uncannily upright against the painted wall, like a gymnast spinning off the bars. It was strangely like a prosphetic limb waiting for its owner to come and collect. Except he was still conscious and he could see the leg, part of his torn trouser still hanging off the knee, standing there with one small piece of scrotum still attached at the top end. Meanwhile, his blood was running out of him like a river through a sluice.

Arguably, Traynor fared a little better. He was closer to the blast than Jesse had been, but although blown to the floor, spread-eagled like an overturned turtle, he had the good fortune to keep his limbs. He felt as if he had been sledgehammered with a large bat, a blow that had sucked the wind out of him, squeezing the oxygen from his brain and knocking him senseless to the floor, his head bobbing against the wood like a heavy ball. However, there was a

problem for Traynor: he was on fuckin' fire. The explosion
of the dynamite/spermaceti mix had slapped a wet sheet of
fire across the room, and all that it fell upon was quickly
ablaze, including Traynor. In its midst, he recovered
consciousness and felt the heat on his back as the flames
burned through the black coat and came into contact with
his flesh. He saw the flames licking off his head as his thin
hair exploded into a glowing halo of fire. He struggled to
raise himself to his feet, wobbled and crashed against the
doorway, rolled into the hall, beating himself with his hands
in a vain attempt to extinguish the flames. His cuffs and the
sleeves of his coat were now on fire and his only thought
was to escape downstairs, away from the heat and the
flames. He fell from the top landing, rolling in a ball of
flame to the bottom. His mama looked at him then, rigid,
confused, unable to do anything for him. She sat motionless
in the chair that she'd been told she was not to leave.
Traynor regained his feet and ran out into the darkness
beyond, a bright wash of fire moving away from the house,
falling, standing, falling again, a mobile firework entirely
consumed by the flames.

The explosion was well beyond my unholy expectations.
Half the roof was lying in the garden, the black slates scattered like a broken pack of cards. Some of the floor was
spread in smokey pieces across the downstairs room. I was
still seated in my Victorian wing armchair by the window,
where I had lit the fusewire that had sparked its way
through the window to the upper floor, combusting the
dynamite and the raindrop spermaceti to such spectacular
effect. I looked like a ghost, having been showered in plaster
from the devastated ceiling, and there were tiny splashes of
spermaceti on my coat that had failed to ignite. Neverthe-

less, the room was partially illuminated by a number of small fires scattered between myself and the doorway.

I looked up and noticed a man in the doorway. It was the lanky bastard, Billy, the one who had kicked my ribs inside out. He was swaying ever so slightly and the nose of his gun was elevated to a level that would have taken off each of my toes.

B illy didn't have a clue what had happened. One second he was pushing open the side door, edging his way through the house from the kitchen, wondering what the hell the smell was, his gun out and his face looking mean below the swathe of hair and the ragged beard. Then came the explosion that shook the house to its foundations. He'd seen Traynor – at least he thought it was Traynor – roll past and out into the night, the burning man with his hands aloft, his hair crackling, stinking, with a wash of fire. Instead of going up, he stepped beyond the stair and into the room adjacent to the hall, his gun still raised. He looked hard in the gloom, across liquid pools of light released by the small puddles of fire. He saw what he no doubt thought was the wildest spirit he had ever seen, appearing whiter than Banquo's ghost, a pair of mad eyes wide and staring. Billy was no' the type to hesitate so he fired his gun straight at the point he perceived me to be. Not surprisingly, his preference was to shoot the shit out of me first and ask questions later. When the first bullet shattered the image of me, tinkling harshly in the cold darkness, Billy was not too sure what had happened. Which is why he chose to release another bullet in the same place, but this time my face was gone, there was nothing to aim at, just the sound of glass breaking once more.

I once said you needed long sleeves to keep the Colt pocket revolver warm, such was the length of its barrel. Yes, it was the 1849 model so it had been around for a while, but with six chambers, using cap and ball ammunition, loaded from the front with loose black powder and six bullets, with a grip in your hand as warm, comfortable almost maternal as you could wish for. I never even took the barrel from my pocket. It was cocked and I had my hand in there on the trigger. I just squeezed and felt luck afterwards that I still had my feet.

The skull is made up of twenty-two bones of which fourteen form the face. Most of these bones are fused together by joints that lock the bones, like pieces in a puzzle, to form a rigid structure. The bullet from my Colt revolver, missed my feet and hit Billy just to the lower left side of the nose, blowing a clean hole in the maxilla. Its trajectory then took it through the zygoma, deviating the bullet's path into the cranial roof, where it lodged and slowly cooled. One way or another the effect of the bullet had been to break down the facial jigsaw, such that as he lay there on the floor, Billy's face seemed to have collapsed into its constituent parts. The boney joints had dissolved and his face simply fell apart. I was surprised at the outcome because my faith in the mirrors had been rooted more in hope than in confidence.

I'd set up the three mirrors, stretched along the space between the door and my wing chair by the window, with two mirrors on the left side and one on the right. Standing in the doorway and looking at the first mirror on the left, Billy would have seen my face and that was what he was shooting at. The trouble is the image on the first mirror was only a projection from the third mirror. By careful positioning of the first mirror from the chair, I was able to project my image onto the first mirror. This was then reflected onto the second mirror before ending up on the third. My face, on the third mirror, was seen by Billy and, not surprisingly, that was where he aimed his gun, leaving me unscathed.

66

BIRTH

Y ou would think that I might have had a sense of gratitude, as I rode the cart away from Buckstone, Master Henry tied to the back end by a rope and halter collar, trotting hard behind. After all, here was some atonement for the wrongs suffered by those closest to me, the innocent victims you might say. But it was an empty sensation because the proof was that it changed nothing. It brought nothing back. It had wiped the slate but it did not restore the chalky picture that had once existed. It would take a man cleverer than me to realise that perhaps it never could.

I mused to myself, as the cold air cut past me, the wheels thundering down between the hedgerows, that this night had been a long time coming. Since I was born. Since my father delivered me that fateful day, on the cusp of a blood-soaked dawn. Of course, my father had done lambs, calves, piglets, cats, dogs, cows and horse foals in his time. He had a good record when it came to delivering live goods. He had pulled plenty out on the hills and in the hollows on makeshift beds of broken gorse. Many a time it was too late to bring the animals in or the snow was so deep he had no choice than to do it there and do it then. A little human being was no more than a life, a precious life, and you did it just the same as a Blackface or a Galloway or even a Clydesdale foal. As he set about the task, Tatiana was in all likelihood still alive with just the faintest twitch of a pulse. It was easy to tell that he knew what he was doing. He would know he had to be patient: patient but firm. When it was coming, you had to pull and then give it a turn if that was what it needed, just to make the journey a little easier. Sometimes the shoulder might get stuck. The thing was not to panic, take your time, ease and cajole. Don't yank the arm off because the baby won't appreciate your effort. My father would have known that he did not give life; he was a facilitator of life. Facilitating life was what a farmer did - when he wasn't facilitating death. He would have eased the passage between that world inside the mother and this world out here, open to the knocks and throws of life. When I slopped out from the hold, like any lamb he had ever pulled, he must have held me in his arms, pink and mottled, messy, sweet, beautiful and tiny as a gilded toy. Like all babies.

As the night bore on and I edged closer to Fife, I knew I was anything but a sweet, pink, beautiful toy now. The sky lightened, and in the distance I could see the North Sea as it turned down towards the Firth of Forth. My mind went back again to where it had all begun for me. It sounds simple but in fact my father had taken great care. He'd wiped the blood from the kitchen table and then laid two wool blankets, one upon the other. Aunt Marion had told me this; whether she knew from my father himself or from what she put together later, I can't say. He'd lifted Tatiana off the floor and laid her on the wooden table. He wasn't a stupid man, he knew she'd been raped and how she must have suffered. It looked like the table was where it most likely happened. Of course, he had no choice: there was nothing else to put her on. We still have that table today. We all took the view it was illogical to blame the table. The table was not the rapist.

My father had taken the kettle from the stove and filled a pot with water, still warm from the night before. Diluted with a little cold from a large drum by the back door. He would have picked a cloth rag off the floor, not knowing its provenance, and dabbed it deep into the pot of warm water. He would have gently wiped her face from the forehead down. He changed the water more than once and he would have wiped gently at her body, end to end. It was a body he loved and it was a deep tightening anguish that filled his heart as he looked upon the cuts and wounds, the bruises, the broken, twisted bones and the orgy of defilement. Still, I dare lay a bet she said nothing, but her eyes may have opened a sliver and they would have stared up at him like slits in a blacked-out window. Did he know if she saw him? There'd be no focus, searching somewhere beyond him, where she'd go alone. He'd touch the mound of her stomach, bringing his eyes and ears close to her skin, as if to see or hear whether the baby could still be alive. No beating heart, no kicking feet? But he was a farmer and he would recognize how hard life must fight to be given its chance. Touching her again and the sense of something, something small beating inside her. She was as close to dead as anyone could be but could she have been in labour? Would doubt set in? Did he think he might be foolish to harbour such thoughts? Would he have touched her again to reassure himself there was something in there? Something was coming. Would either she or the baby see this through? Would the act of birth be enough to kill her? In his heart, he knew that he and she could only give life by taking life. Just before seven in the morning, on the gored kitchen oak, the premature, blotchy, pink baby was delivered. Tatiana would be barely alive at the delivery. Did she see her son? Did she register the life with her eyes? Did she look, catch her breath and die?

That was how I pictured her, as the cart jolted down the track. Tatiana's skin pale as ivory and the salted sweat dry upon it; the flesh cold to the touch and tighter in death. No hate in her expression; as if being dead had closed her eyes to the horror of what had precipitated death. Horatio, my father, bare-chested, with the baby in his white arms, wrapped warmly in his coarse, cotton shirt. His face softer now, the anger gone. Love, confusion, sorrow and elation all washing back and forth across his features. In his eyes, however, a deep, broken hurt and over time, slowly etched in each line of his face as he slumped in the chair by the stove. Did he sit in that awful silence, bluebottle flies already hovering over the blood inside and outside the house, his body shaking in steady, rhythmic convulsions, and the small baby pressed hungrily against his chest?

He called me Sean, a nod to his Irish roots. Tatiana would have expected that. And two middle names, Andrei and Grigore, after Tatiana's father and grandfather. He would have whispered in my ear and hugged me to him. The father I never had.

Outside, the sun would rise as it always does, bathing Salmon Cottage in its fresh morning light, and he would have heard the gate open and a single voice breaking the stillness.

"Come on oot of there, Logan," is what he would have heard. "Don't try anything funny. Let's see your hands now."

67

JAIL

A s if the rape and murder of my mother was not enough, my father had to suffer the consequences of his own attempt to stop the carnage. For the death of Ben Mercer, he was sentenced to twenty-five years. His entrée was six years at Inveraray prison followed by an uncomfortable departure in a cold, horse-drawn, springless coach to the new Peterhead Prison in Inverness. Each of the six years behind those massive rough hewn, redstone walls at Inveraray was hard to bear. My father was a man used to the open air, the wide, windy spaces. He had crossed many borders, worked his way through the barren desert of northern Iran and skirted the mountains south of the Caspian Sea. He was accustomed to decent air in his lungs. Inveraray prison had no tik-tik flies or Pashtun women but precious little else going for it. At Inveraray he walked the yard just once a day, three small circuits, after which he was jerked back to the cell with the barred but broken window on the third floor. The years that followed at Peterhead brought the pleasurable relief of change, but an eight foot by six foot box was still a box, irrespective of geography.

When you're a prisoner that long, any change is welcome but there comes a point when you've served so much time that all change is like a foreign beast. Better the devil you know or something like that. After six years he'd not yet reached that small crisis but he was perilously close to it.

At Peterhead he was despatched to Stirlinghill Quarry to break granite with a pickaxe. He went from doing very little at Inveraray, confined to his cell for most of the day, to the rough reality of hard physical labour. There were fights, squabbles, deaths and disputes over the slightest trivialities. Life could be extraordinarily dangerous. Still, if they were not breaking granite they were locked up most of the day and it was not always easy to make trouble even if you'd a taste for it. My father, Horatio, sat in a filthy cell with more fleas per square inch than even the Tullis cockerels suffered in the coop, and he thought of that distant place, Salmon Cottage, for much of the day and a fair bit of the night. The mind is a great channel to the wide open spaces.

My father's sister Marion had felt the pain of her brother's torment in every turn of his head, every movement of his eye. She had some serious metal in her water. She was there for the trial and she was there for the sentence. She was someone who could take punches. She had long ago acquired a talent for making what she called *the necessary adjustment*. Any big thing, to her mind, could be taken care of, so long as you made the necessary adjustment. When they took Horatio away, she said simply, "I'll take care of things here." And so she did.

Thus it was that Aunt Marion, and her fifteen year old daughter Lizzie moved from their cottage in Glenfarg to Tullis and their new home at Salmon Cottage. "I'll give you a better life than you might've been expecting," she'd said to me.

"I'll give you milk," said Lizzie, holding a bottle up to my face. "A sight more useful."

My mind was full of such thoughts as we entered Tullis in a dead man's cart. The events of the night had made me tired. I longed for home, for Aunt Marion and Lizzie, for the arms of Keira. The revenge I had sought had left four men and a fat woman dead and a deep hollow inside me.

68

THE STAND OFF

A s I stood there by the gate to Salmon Cottage, I knew all that spermaceti must have shrunk my brain in the night. I recognized now what a mistake it was to leave the Enfield holstered on the other side of grass-munching Master Henry. I stood there, my fingers brushing the splintery surface of the gate, and I could see Lizzie and behind her Aunt Marion standing just proud of the door, frozen on the step, like ghosts from the past, faces skewed by the sight of three men holding Colt army handguns aimed at the back of my head. Even at that distance, they looked pale. I had heard the three clicks as they cocked their guns and what colour still remained had quickly left my face.

"I was hopin' you'd drop by," said Calum Wilson.

"Oh, aye?"

"You disappearing off like that had me worried that we wouldnae get to meet up."

Even though I hadn't heard it that often, there was no mistake about the voice, the sneer that threaded right through, then filled my ears. "You only needed to make an appointment," I said.

"Humour. I'm very impressed. Did you hear that?"

"But very unwise," said a voice I recognized. "To be makin' jokes at a time like this."

"What do you want?" I said. I could hear irritation and tiredness in my own voice. "It's no' the time for this."

Calum moved closer in behind me and the other boys followed suit. "Oh, there's plenty of time," he said.

I turned round, holding in my mind the thought that I would tell him where to go, but I had revolved only ninety-seven degrees when he whacked me in the face with his fist, still clenching the gun. It was a miracle he didnae blow my nose off or take my eye out. I got back off the ground, aware of the pain in my neck and the throb up one side of my face, but I said nothing this time.

"Who's she?" He was pointing at the old lady in the cart.

"Mrs Traynor."

"Who is she?"

"Mrs Traynor."

"What's she doin' here?"

"I'm lookin' after her."

"You're lookin' after her?" he said.

"Aye," I said. "She's touring Fife."

"I don't find you funny, Logan."

"Then feel free to leave."

He looked me in the eyes. "Want me to hit you again?" He turned his mouth downwards, as if he'd eaten something that didn't taste right. "The problem with you, Logan, is you take things."

"Mebbe I take, but I don't steal. There is a distinction."

"I cannae see your distinction," he said.

"I take. Men like you steal."

"Where did you *take* the old woman from?"

"For your information, I didn't take Mrs Traynor," I said. "She's here because she wants to be here."

"You're always taking things that don't belong, Logan."

"I don't think so."

"I don't like what you do."

"What is it that bothers you?"

"People like you."

"People like me?"

"People like you who think they can mess around with a man's wife and just move on, like it never happened."

"Ah," I said. "Now we're getting' there." I lifted my head and decided I might as well be brave. "If she's your wife," I said. "Mebbe, you should've treated her like a wife." I looked at him wearily. I had had a long week.

"Is that so?" he said. "Do you no' think if it's my wife, I can treat her the way I fuckin' well want to?"

"No I don't, as a matter of fact. She doesn't belong to you," I said.

"Well, that's your perspective, and we're all right grateful."

"People don't belong to anybody," I said.

He looked concerned. "What are you saying? The wedding vows, Logan? That's all just bullshit, is it?"

I looked back at him and studied his face. A man with whiskers bushing in every direction, little clumps of pale hair in his ears. Of a height shorter than you might expect, eyes bagged and something yellow and liverish in the whites. "Where did it say in your vows you could beat her with a paddle?"

"My wife," he said. "is my business."

"I've made it *my* business."

"Where did you get the right to do that?"

"We all have that right," I said. "It's a *human* right."

"To mess in my marriage? That's curious."

"You wrote the invitation when you beat her."

"I don't care to discuss it," he said, and just as quickly changed his mind. "D'you know *any*thing about women, Logan?" His eyes were sparkling now with renewed anger. I stared back at him.

"I know they turn blue when you hit them."

"Keira likes to be hit with the paddle," he said. "You find that so hard to believe?"

"She likes to be hit?" I said, scratching my head. "You think she *likes* to be hit?"

"Have you not learnt anythin' at school?"

"No," I said. "There was nothing about that. I'm sure I would've remembered."

"Don't you understand?" he said, like I was very, very stupid. "The paddle tells her when she's out of line."

"Oh," I said, tapping the side of my head with a finger. "I see now. Keeps her on the straight and narrow."

"Yes it does."

"Like a field full of traps? You stand on a trap and that's you. You know not to do it next time?"

"Exactly."

"But at least next time you know how far you can go."

"That's right," he said. "It's a route map."

"Well," I answered. "Thanks for the philosophy. Now put your guns away and get out of here, will you please?"

There was the shortest silence and I wondered if I had pushed him too far and all this was going to end badly. Yet I hoped that having allowed him the opportunity to discuss – and perhaps justify – his violence, he might now leave us in peace.

"We'll go when we're good and ready," said Joe, speaking

for only the second time. Tom stood by him, holding the other gun, casting a wide eye over at Joe, whilst smiling like a puppy. Calum's hooded eyes moved away from me only briefly, as if Joe was intruding on personal grief. Joe failed to register or simply ignored that look from Calum. "In the meantime," he said. "Do you no' think it would be nice to take advantage of the facilities you've got here."

"What are you on about?" said Calum, finally showing his irritation.

Joe licked his thin moustache, looking with slitted eyes at Lizzie by the step to the house. Tom laughed and his gun wobbled in his hand. "Hello, Lizzie," he shouted over and raised a wave with his left hand.

Calum smiled. "You can't blame him, Sean. Like yourself, he's got needs."

"I've got to admit I'm interested," said Joe.

"It's only natural," said Calum.

"Natural?" I said.

"People go around taking things that don't belong to them. That's what people do. You said so yourself," said Calum.

"I'm bored," said Joe. "There have got to be better things to get on with round here." He looked at Lizzie again.

I followed his line of sight. "That would no' be your best idea," I warned.

"That's what we all want," said Calum, nodding his head. "We all want some kind of retribution. We all want to avenge something."

"Some have cause."

"I agree," he said. "I feel the same about my wife."

"Maybe you earn vengeance," I said. "There has to be something that deserves to be avenged."

"You make my point for me," he said.

"You're missin' the point, you dimwit."

We were facing each other straight on but I assumed a look of calm even if there was none beneath my skin, one arm raised and resting casually on the cross bar of the gate. "You have to earn vengeance," I said. "You can't just do what you like and dress it up as vengeance."

"Well?" he said. "Haven't I paid enough already? Haven't I paid with my wife? Don't I get your blood for that?"

"Keira is her own person. She answers for herself."

"You fucked her," he said, pulling closer, his gun pressing in against me. "That means you've made me very angry."

"It doesnae work like that," I said.

"It does."

"Who says I wronged her?"

"I do."

"If you were right to be aggrieved, you lost it when you beat her."

"That's no' how I see it," he said.

"You're a man with no eyes."

"The way I see it, you took something."

"I took nothing."

"You took it and it was mine." He pushed his face closer. "My right," he said, "is to come after you."

Who knows where this strange dialogue was going to lead – nowhere good, that was for sure. However, Aunt Marion, who had never fully emerged from the house, had slipped back inside, shielded by Lizzie, and at that moment she reappeared. She gave no warning or necessary introduction, but was holding the Reicher in her hands and we discovered very quickly that this time it was fully loaded. Oh my God, I had wanted to see that gun fired! But here? Now? She pulled the trigger and four bullets released simultaneously from four barrels of the same gun. What madness was this? What deafening noise it created! Almost each and every man present hit the ground with the pointed part of their faces whilst the bullets whizzed and ricocheted around our ears.

The trajectory of each bullet was an issue of subsequent debate. One hit the world's most unlucky hen and removed its head but the message was slow to reach its brain, its thin legs pumping around the yard, oblivious to its changed circumstances. The second bullet went straight up in the air over our heads; just God and a few startled Blackface sheep would know where it landed. The third hit the wooden gatepost and, if it had not deflected, I fear I might have ended up in the same headless territory as the hen. The fourth hit the side of Traynor's cart, off which it pinged, slowed and distorted by the impact, and thereafter whirred in the direction of Tom and Joe, before choosing the bigger target - Tom's fleshy arse - in which to sink its nickel neck. As it impacted, the smile escaped his face quicker than bacon off a pig. Meanwhile, in my singularity, I did not fall on my face, but for a tired, bruised, out-of-sorts lowland farmer, I did well enough to throw myself to the back of dead Traynor's cart, roll under Master Henry and whip the Enfield from the holster before anyone fully registered my acrobatics.

"What the fuck?" said Calum, getting off the ground, his sight still trained on the retreat of Lizzie and Aunt Marion who had hurled themselves back into the house, followed by three slugs from Calum's gun, embedded in the post by the door. Tom was still lying on the ground, on his side, his rear end hoisted, screaming and moaning, and full of objection at having an extra hole drilled into his buttocks. Joe was off the floor now and pointing his gun at me. I had my Enfield pointed at Calum.

"Shall we shoot the women too?" shouted Calum. "Mebbe Joe and I should enjoy them first?"

"Good plan, Mr Wilson," said Joe, looking straight down his gun at me.

"Ahm in fer a f-f-feck an' all!" shouted Tom, his hand slapped against the hole in his buttock.

"You're injured, you fool!" shouted Calum.

"I'm still up for it!"

"D'you want me to shoot *you* Calum?" I said. "I've got you in my sights and it's no' the most difficult shot." Calum looked at me out of the corner of his eye, a sneaky fox-like glance that told you more about him than any words could. "Not so easy for you, Joe," I said. "You might shoot my horse first." I took my left hand off the barrel of the rifle and stroked Master Henry's withers.

"I might," he said.

"You got somethin' against horses?"

"Take it easy," said Calum, to me or more likely to Joe. "Nobody needs to get shot here. Least of all, me."

At that point came the sound of a thunderous commotion on the track behind us, mud thrown up behind the wheels of a small, black, one-pony hansom cab. We all turned in its direction, as much as we dared without taking aim away from our intended targets. The cab was heading towards the house and gave the impression it was going to crash into the lot of us as we stood there transfixed in a coagulative impasse by the gate: Joe's gun pointing at me; my gun at Calum; and Calum's Colt army hand gun .44 caliber cap and ball pointing towards the house, where Aunt Marion and Lizzie had retreated, clutching the Reicher. Tom was still on the ground, whimpering, with a hand fixed to his buttock.

It took me a second or two to realise who the velvet-coated figure was driving the cart straight at us, but during that time Joe had moved his gun marginally away from me and now fully released a shot directly towards the oncoming cab. The horsecart did not deviate initially and it appeared that the driver was unharmed, largely because a skill-free idiot like Joe was hardly likely to hit a moving target with a handgun. However, in a sense I was very wrong about that. The shot came nowhere near the man in the driver's seat but instead spooked the horse pulling the cart. Suddenly, the thundering beast deviated to the left, looked as if he might jump the wall, but in fact galloped along the rough verge of the track. The cart bounced on its thin wheels behind the horse, crashing from side to side, forward and back, cuffing hard against the rocks, the earth and everything else that stood in its path. I had the impression it was going to gallop on past, some distance to our left, and in all probability pull up at the corner of the field. If it tried to jump the wall, God knows what would have happened. In the event, the horse, still spooked out of its mind by Joe's gunshot, bailed out of turning left and, knowing its limitations, refused to take on the wall. Its only course was to whip round to the right and swing the cab in our general direction. The trouble was that, by this time, the far wheel had buckled, its spokes twisting and cracking, and the cart was half way to toppling over. It came ever closer towards us and we were scattering to avoid the impact, other than Tom who was still on the ground, clutching his wounded arse and not really knowing what sort of further danger he might be facing. At that moment, the broken wheel caught itself against a large rock, stopped

in its tracks and the whole cart went over on its side, dragging the horse with it, tethered like a chicken on a spit. The
driver was thrown from his seat, his velvet tail floating high
in the air, impacting with his full weight against the overturned cart.

Like the rest of them, I was reacting to events. I was
down on the ground but I pulled myself up with the intention of getting across to help him, when Calum fired a shot
from his handgun that popped near my left ear and deaf-
ened me as the bullet shrieked close to the crown of my
head. I crawled round to the back of the cart and from there
I could see Mr Hamilton, his florid face looking out at me,
defeated, from the broken lean of the stone wall. Nearby, the
harnessed horse was still kicking its hooves to free itself
from the twisted wreckage, yet unable to escape. It was
almost dead. I ran across the gap between myself and
Hamilton, expecting to be picked off by a shot at any
moment. I was halfway when a bullet pounded off the
ground just an arm's length from my boot. Incentivised, I
kept moving. Then, I heard a repeat of the extraordinary
explosive noise created by the Reicher. Aunt Marion must
have reloaded, for the bullets were crashing around the
yard, albeit nobody's life was seriously threatened by a
direct hit.

I threw myself down at Hamilton's side and I knew
straightaway that his situation was far from reassuring. He
was already drifting in and out of consciousness.

"Mr Hamilton?" I said his name a number of times
before he opened his eyes and looked at me. He looked
puzzled and then appeared to recognise who I was.

"Sean? Thought you might need some support," he
wheezed and then coughed, light droplets of blood spraying
thinly against his chest. He wore a waistcoat and a bottle

green velvet jacket – not blue as I had thought. He was sweating and I loosened the collar on his shirt.

"How did you know I was here?" I said. There was then a blast of three or four shots, causing us instinctively to duck. However, the shots were not aimed at us and they hit the ground in front of Calum and Joe.

"I'll shoot you if I have to." He was stood on the roof of my old barn and he had one of those American Winchester rifles pointed down at us. These rifles I had read about: they had a lever action which meant you could load a magazine full of bullets and fire up to fifteen shots before you had to reload. He spat a large gob from the side of his mouth that ricocheted off the lower part of the roof. It was hard for those on the ground to see him, because there was strong light coming from behind that gave him a holy messianistic appearance, but when it dawned on Joe that the man on the roof was Rory, you could see the smile creep across his face like a new dawn. Joe began a slow, triumphant walk towards the gate, basking in his mastery of the moment.

"Nice to see you, Rory," said Joe. "I didnae know you were comin' but I commend your punctuality."

"Glad to be here," said Rory. "Put your gun on the ground."

Joe stopped in his tracks. "What d'you say?"

"I said put your gun on the ground. You too, Wilson. Put the fuckin' guns down on the ground in front of you." They did not appear to move fast enough for Rory and that compelled him to fire another two shots into the grass in front of them. "Do it!" he shouted. The effect was to galvanise Joe and Calum to drop their guns right where they stood.

"Come on, Rory. Don't be an ass! You're one of us," shouted Joe.

"Really? I got bored with your bullshit a long time ago," he shouted back, the blond hair falling off his ear and hanging across his brow.

"You better be careful what you say," said Joe.

"I'm holdin' a gun," said Rory. "Did you no' see that? I don't need to be careful."

"Why are you with him? We were always against him."

"I don 't know what good it did."

"We faced things together. That's what we did."

"I don't know much about that," said Rory. "Mebbe time to grow up, Joe."

"You're makin' an enemy of me, that's the point I'm makin'."

"I can live with that," said Rory.

"Don't count on it."

"Besides, he saved my life."

"Hurrah."

"Logan saved my life and I appreciate that."

"Hurrah again."

"You never would have done that, Joe. You would let your own mother drown if it meant you kept your feet dry."

"This is a mistake, Rory."

"We'll see."

"I'll fuckin' kill you."

"That's nice."

"Think on it."

"I have," said Rory. "I'm gonnie give you all thirty seconds. If I can still see you by then, I'll shoot you." He paused to let them take this in. "Okay?"

"Come on," said Joe.

"Sorry, but those are the rules. As an old friend, trust me."

"This is dumb."

"Clock starts now," said Rory. "Thirty seconds."

Tom had heard enough to get to his feet. It was not easy but he was well motivated. He did not fancy a second bullet. Once up, clutching his rear with both hands, he was the first to turn and stagger off down the track, pulling as fast as his legs would carry him, away from the rooftop firearm. Joe stepped back a few nervous paces, waved a grubby finger at Rory and then he too turned and ran.

"Don't feel you have to stay, Mr Wilson," said Rory. Calum needed no reminder and moved away from Salmon Cottage, just intermittently glancing back over his shoulder to see how serious the situation was. At the end of thirty seconds, true to his word, Rory fired over their heads and enjoyed the reward of three men moving at quick pace.

I turned back to speak to Mr Hamilton. He was still conscious. "What do you think of the rifle?" he said. I didn't answer. "Winchester '73. Repeat action. Fifteen -"

"Shots to every magazine," I finished. "A repeater rifle with a single barrel."

"You had a good teacher," he said weakly.

"You okay?" I asked. "The fun seems to be over now. We can get you inside. Aunt Marion will help you with the gunshot."

"Sorry to disappoint you."

"What d'you mean?"

"It's no'… It's no' a… gunshot wound," he said.

"Is it no'?" I said.

"No."

"What is it then?" I looked down at him and noticed from the way he was lying that his front seemed to be bowed out. I twisted my head to look beneath him and because he was slightly turned to the side, I could see the wooden spoke from the wheel sticking up from the ground, deep into his back. There was a lot of blood pooling under him. I looked back at him and it was easy for him to register my alarm.

"See what I mean?" he said.

"We'll get you to the house."

"I'm no' goin' anywhere," he said. "Oh God, I feel cold."

I took off the coat I'd taken from Traynor's hallway. I laid it over him. "Is that better?"

"Thankyou," he said.

"We'll get you a doctor."

He ignored me. "Where've you been then?"

"Why?"

"You dinnae look good."

"*I* dinnae look good?"

"I'm older than you. I'm entitled to look like this," he said. He winced as he twisted his body on the spoke embedded in his back. He was like a butterfly pinned to a silk board. I did not say anything. I was thinking whether I should tell him where I'd been. "Are they dead?" he asked suddenly, as if reading my mind.

"Are who dead?"

"Look," he said. "You know I'm dyin' here. I know it too. So, we could sit and chat about the weather or crop varieties or hat pins but I've no' got time for that." He swallowed. "I'm moving on. You understand that?"

"Yes, I do."

"Did you kill them?"

I looked straight at him. "Tell me, by 'them' who do you mean?"

"Christ, Sean, I know you went there." He was wheezing. He sounded like he was speaking in a funnel. "And I know people in Montrose. I want to know if you killed them."

"There were some casualties," I said.

He coughed and caught his breath. "Is that the same as

dead people?" he asked and winced again. His face was yellow-pale as old milk and a damp mist floated over him. He was in a cold sweat.

"How much do you know?"

"Oh," he said. "Some. Quite a lot actually."

"How?"

"Because," he paused, catching his breath. "Put it this way. I was there." I did not quite understand what he was saying. He was there?

"You were where?"

"Up here, just where I am now. Salmon Cottage. Except it's worse than that." There was a clear film of sweat on his forehead now but he was cold and he was beginning to shiver. He had blood on his teeth, like he had just eaten a raw piece of meat.

"You dinnae have to talk," I said. "You need a doctor."

"I need an undertaker," he answered.

"Dinnae speak."

"I need to speak," he said. "I was there. The night."

Aunt Marion and Lizzie had come out from the house and were standing behind me. Aunt Marion overheard. "That's no' true," she said. "How could y'have been? You'd have been recognised."

"Is that a woman's voice?" he asked. "You know things are bad when you can't tell the men from the women."

"It's Aunt Marion," I said.

"Ah, well. My eyes are going." He brightened suddenly. "Anyway," he continued. "I was here, in a sense I was here. That's why," he said, catching his breath. "That's why, it's worse. That's why you should hate me. There's no other reason."

"I'm no' hatin' you," I said.

He paused. "Well maybe you should." He closed his eyes. "I wasn't here, myself, no. But my son was."

I said nothing at first. Eventually, I said, "You have a son?"

"I did." He broke into a fit of coughing that saw a heavier stream of blood drip from his mouth and down his chin. "He's dead now."

"I didn't know that," I said. "You never mentioned it."

"No, it's true. I did not. And for good reason."

"What was his name?" I said, not thinking too carefully why I'd asked.

"His name was Turner," he said. I heard him say the name and a series of sliding doors opened before me. "He was a young boy, stupid with it." He coughed again. "Fell in with those bastards. A bad crowd. He was always in trouble. I could never seem to get him out from under them."

"He was here that night?"

"He was." Hamilton kept on talking, his eyes barely open and his voice weakening. "I tried to stop him, but he was a big lad, bigger than me. He did what he wanted. He didn't need to ask me. I couldnae have stopped him. I couldn't have stopped any of them from comin' up here that night."

"If that's true, you could have spoken at the trial," I said.

"What for?" he said. "What for?"

"You might have kept my father out of jail."

"Don't think so," he said. "He was always going to jail. They fixed it that way."

"Who fixed it that way?" I asked. "How could anyone fix it?"

"Traynor was well connected. He had money behind him. You've seen his house. Nice house, is it no'? Always had plenty of money." It *was* a nice house. Not now. Not with no roof. "He knew a lot of lawyers. They were all on his payroll. All getting' a bribe here, a hand-up there."

"They fixed the trial?"

"Not exactly, but they moved it in the direction they wanted. They knew enough people to do that."

"Which was what?"

"Only your father would see jail."

"Couldn't you have stopped them, if you knew all this?"

"What did I know? I'd seen nothing. I wasn't even there. Physically. I just knew, that's all." He breathed quickly through his nose. "He was my son."

"I already knew of him," I said. "I came across his name. I just couldn't work out how he fitted in."

"He fitted in alright."

"But you knew all this and you did nothing?"

"There was nothing..." He paused. "Well, who knows? Maybe I was a coward too," he said. "I realised there was no stoppin' them. My boy, Turner, was tied up in all that." He took a deep breath and continued. "He was in on it and I couldn't stop him or any of them. I just hoped it would come to nothing."

"What happened?" I asked.

"I drank," he said. "Makes it easier to deal with. Everything begins to look the same colour when you drink."

"What happened that night?"

"They came up here, you know that already. Never occurred to me they would rape your mother. I never thought they would attack any one." He swallowed hard. "Never thought that, not once. Rough words, yes. Waving sticks at your old father, maybe. But that kind of violence, no. Don't ask me why it happened. There was a madness around. I don't know why. It made no sense."

"And Turner, dead now you say?"

"Oh, well dead," he answered absently. "Long gone." He paused, blinked, and then he said: "I shot him with the last gun I gave you, the Devisme revolver." He registered the look on my face. "Nice gun," he said. "That gallic curve to it. Could only be French. You know what I mean." He shifted against the spoke and winced at the spasm of pain that shot through him. "Anyway," he said. "What else could I do?"

"He wrote to Mad Bob," I said. "I found his letter. I think he felt they'd been unsupportive."

"He stayed out of jail, that should have been enough."

"Why did you shoot him? He was your son, no matter what he'd done."

"I killed him because he was an animal, even if he was my son. I had to kill him and I didn't want to kill him. But I knew I had to. I knew I had to."

"How did it happen?"

"I drank. I drank a lot. I got myself so I could hardly walk let alone fire a shot at him. But he tried to take the gun off me, the Devisme of all guns, you know?" I nodded. "Well, the gun just went off and there he was, room spinning around my head, and him on the floor. Died very quickly as a matter of fact." His eyes were full of tears. "Anyway, there was no road back from there. Sat with him all night. Just staring at his dead body on the floor."

"Where is he now?"

"I found a place," he said. "I said goodbye."

"Is that why you gave me the guns?"

"I had to do somethin'."

"You knew I would come to you sometime?"

"I thought you would," he said. "Everything told me you'd come. That old schoolteacher of yours, Shifner, he always told me you had the curiosity that would never leave this thing alone."

"He never spoke to me about it," I said.

"He would never want to know about it. Schoolteacher for God's sake! But I knew you'd have to find these men and deal with them." He clenched his teeth and waited for the pain to pass. "He died," he said. "My son died and so they had to die. These men had to die. It was only right that they should die. They should have died long ago for what they did."

"So, you used me to get to them?"

"Yes," he said, placing his hand on my arm. "If you want to look at it that way."

"You used me?"

"I did, but don't tell me our paths were no' headin' in the same direction?" I looked away. "I had to do somethin'," he said. "The worst thing is doin' nothin'."

"But, you killed him? You killed your own son?"

"I did. But he was ruined. They ruined your life too. Call it revenge if you like," he said. "For both of us. For all three of us."

"For my father and mother too. Revenge for all that too."

"It was revenge. That's what it was and there isn't much point in dressing it up as something pretty. A pig's still a pig, even when it smiles," he said. He coughed blood against the back of his hand. "Bad as it was," he said. "Your parents were not the only ones to suffer. We suffered too."

"You taught me all about the guns, you encouraged me." I looked at him. "My God, you played me very well, did you no'?"

"You didn't need much encouragement, Sean. If you remember, you came lookin' for me, by the graveyard. No' the other way round."

"You knew I was comin'. You knew where I was goin'. You knew why. You'd thought it all through."

"Well…"

"You knew what to say to me. So when the time came I'd do it."

"I knew you would kill them," he said. "I knew you wanted that as much as me."

I pointed up at Mrs Traynor, still seated in the cart, looking ahead blankly, her hands crossed in her lap. "What about her?"

MR HAMILTON

F ollowing the spermaceti fire bomb in Buckstone, I had taken the dead Traynor's cart, sat his mother up there on the bench with me, put a hat on her head and a blanket across her legs, and I brought her back to Tullis. She did not say much on the journey and I had not been in the mood for talking. I knew I had to bring her with me. There'd been nothing else I could do. How could I leave her in the wreckage of that house in Buckstone, amongst the smoke, the roof all over the garden and the fires and all that stinking spermaceti? Not to mention her son quietly carbonized, smoking dead like the tail end of a campfire. She was half-demented already. She had little real idea of what was going on. I had to bring her back with me, but the miracle was she'd sat up there in the cart, looking down at us, and not once had she said anything. All these bullets buzzing around like a plague of lochside midges, carts tipping over and more shots being fired than she ever knew, and she just sat there watching it all, like this was all just so much noise.

"Who is she?" he asked. "I'm no' seein' too good."

"Traynor's mother, " I said. "I think he was at the front when they attacked the farm."

"The mother?" he said. "You'll no' need her. Any event, there was only one leader." He coughed heavily. "My son. He was the front man, the fool. And he's dead, he's dead for his trouble."

"He's dead, that's true. What I mean is, she's lost a son too."

"Her son wasn't the main trouble."

"You cannae say that."

"Whatever," he said. "We disagree."

"I heard one of them crept away. Slipped out the back."

"Not Turner," he said. "Turner wasnae like that. Turner was a beast. He would have just taken what he wanted. Just like the rest." He opened his eyes again and stared up at the sky. "They were just six idiots who lost control."

"Aye, but just the one who took off, who didn't rape or kill anybody. We don't know who that was."

He sighed and swallowed. "We'll never know, but someone is carrying a heavy secret out there," he said. "But in the end, you got your revenge." He coughed up more blood across the back of my coat. "And in the end,' he spluttered. "I got mine."

"In the end, it tastes of shit. It tastes of nothing," I said.

"Maybe now it does, but it may be a taste that gets better with time," he said. "Like a fine wine," he added. "Good Burgundy always gets better."

"I'm not sure about that. Today it tastes worse than shit."

"True it never brings people back."

"You should've told me."

"I'm tellin' you now," he said. "Before I die."

Hamilton lay there for a little longer, cold but covered by my coat. Gradually, he stopped talking. He drifted into hallucination, spoke of Dutch windmills, apples, open windows, an old Spanish horse, one white sock, called George. The words petered out, becoming monosyllabic, punctuated by grunts and occasional light curses. Finally, he grew quiet again, looked straight ahead of him and then he half closed his eyes and let go of the rope. He died, as if he'd said all he wished to say and was ready to leave.

On my knees, I pulled the coat up across his face. I stood and hugged Aunt Marion and Lizzie to me. We had reached a milestone. Rory had squatted on the roof through all this time. Eventually, satisfied that Tom, Jo and Calum were indeed gone, he delivered a final spit and then climbed down off the roof where he had been patiently waiting. He lifted the coat from Hamilton's face, looked at him hard for a moment and then put the cloth back. I shook his hand.

"Did he give you the Winchester?" I asked.

"He insisted," said Rory. "He hardly knew me."

"He knew you well enough," I said.

I helped Mrs Tray-nor down off the cart. "Are we there yet?" she asked.

"Yes," I answered.

"Where are we?"

"This is my home."

"I don't think I've been here before, have I?" she asked.

"Let's go inside."

"Am I staying?" she asked. There was something sad in her look. "I can't really remember anything. I am a fool, aren't I?"

"Sometimes it's better not rememberin'," I said. "And you can stay here, sure you can." I took her hand and helped her off the box seat.

Aunt Marion put her arm around my waist. Lizzie touched my shoulder. I held Mrs Trainer's hand, her looking left and right and utterly confused. We walked through the open gate, towards the door of the house. All was quiet now at Salmon Cottage. The voices in my head that had so long cried out for answers were still or at least temporarily muted. The choir of the Tik-tik fly had put away its chorus and finally I could rest in the silence that swallowed me. I could not help noticing a Reicher bullet wedged in the upright by the door. I smiled at Aunt Marion. How did she make that bullet go backwards?

Printed in Great Britain
by Amazon